I drew her close to me again, breathing in the sweetness of Nicoletta's garden and the far more intoxicating sweetness of her skin. I felt her heart beating against mine—the slow, powerful strokes of an immortal with power amassed over the centuries. I felt my own heart slow. Nicoletta's lips again found mine. My fear vanished. I knew my heart would not stop. A moment longer and our hearts beat as if one.

I do not know how, but Nicoletta had imparted some of her ancient *Vampiri* power to me, a trick not even Wolf could perform. Nicoletta had made me as strong as she—or nearly so. A peculiar energy set my nerves to tingling. Such tremendous strength! If I'd commanded the ruined Roman temple to reassemble itself, I do not doubt the fallen columns and buried pilasters would have risen into the air and fit themselves back together like a titanic puzzle.

Yet the best part of the dream was the wonderful sense of freedom it imparted. For the first time since I'd joined the *Illuminati*, I felt the heavy sense of responsibility lifted from my shoulders. I even forgot that I was no happier as one of the *Vampiri* than I'd been as a mortal.

"Until Jerusalem, my love. Until Jerusalem . . ."

And then, as suddenly as it had taken shape within my mind, the dream ended.

Also by Michael Romkey
Published by Fawcett Books:

I, VAMPIRE
FEARS POINT

THE VAMPIRE PAPERS

Michael Romkey

FAWCETT GOLD MEDAL • NEW YORK

A Fawcett Gold Medal Book
Published by Ballantine Books

Library of Congress Catalog Card Number: 94-94200

ISBN 0-449-14804-1

Printed in Canada

First Edition: August 1994

10 9 8 7 6 5 4 3 2 1

For Carol, Ryan, and Matthew

So we beat on, boats against the current, borne back ceaselessly into the past.

—*F. Scott Fitzgerald*

Contents

Exordium

VENICE—IT IS early evening, the day barely holding off the dusk, shadows lengthening as the sun's rays slant across the rooftops at sharpening angles. Soon darkness will fall across the canals and Renaissance palazzi in this water-bound city.

The peculiar quality of the light in Venice is especially striking at the end of day. The air glows as if suffused with an inner brightness. This muted incandescence is seen everywhere—in faces, in the stone casements of ancient buildings, in the waves that scallop the Grand Canal, where the sun has scattered a million diamonds to skip and glide across the water.

Venice is the perfect city for contemplating the *Vampiri*. It is the beauty one notices in Venice, not the decay.

The sun has nearly departed. A single spear of platinum light cuts diagonally across the picture framed by my window, the beam focused on the gondola pausing against the canal's opposite shore. The boatman stands at attention, the pole idle against his right shoulder, his eyes focused on some distant object, perhaps some distant thought. His chest rises and falls. Even from my balcony window, I see him sigh.

"Life," Le Corbusier said, "always has the last word."

A few lines of explication are in order from the editor entrusted with the task of compiling this chronicle. These collected papers are drawn from police records, interviews, diary excerpts, letters, and personal notes and remembrances collected in New York City during the early months of 1991, and in Jerusalem, Mississippi, during the spring and summer of the same year. In the main these papers speak for themselves. I have made no effort to recast the material into a narrative of my own making, with several noteworthy exceptions.

Documents relating to the final confrontation between antagonists in Mississippi are scarce for reasons the reader may well imagine. The principals were, in many instances, either dead, missing, or emotionally indisposed to providing closing testimony to researchers. It was, therefore, necessary for me to relate the dénouement in my own words. I believe my work represents an accurate and complete picture of what ultimately occurred at Arlington Plantation.

My only other intrusions into the narrative are the brief *explications de texte* that precede each of the collected papers, identifying the document's nature and telling, when relevant, how it was collected.

With these unavoidable exceptions, I have obeyed the precepts of a responsible editor and endeavored to keep myself as much out of the story as possible.

I would be remiss in failing to thank my friends in the *Illuminati*, especially those in Research and Archives, for the support and material they provided. Without their help, the assembly of these papers into a coherent whole would have been impossible.

Respectfully submitted,

Michael Romkey

Palazzo Bellini
Venice, Italy
December 1, 1992

PART I

✧

New York City

I

Kewpie Doll

CHRONICLE NOTES: He called himself "Becker Thorne" in New York City. His real name would have attracted attention even from those who did not know about the *Vampiri.* The following excerpts are from "Thorne's" diary.

—Editor

This city has *magnificent* Neon.

I read tonight about a gallery near the Plaza Hotel where an entire showing has been devoted to Neon sculpture. I have not been there yet, but my soul quivers with the anticipation of visiting such a Holy of Holies. Imagine the epiphany of being surrounded by the divine hum and glow of creation, like a butchered martyr borne Heavenward upon the snowy doves' wings of angels!

I must wait until the proper hour has come around before I put off my shoes to worship in the presence of my angry god. I will visit the sacred place after midnight, when the others have gone. I dare not go with others present, for I might find it impossible to control myself amid the bliss of such Revelation. Afterward, filled with inspiration, I will give myself completely up to bliss and joy. I shall stroll through Central Park. There is a new pastime in America called "wilding." I am keen to try it! After drinking from the Neon fount of inspiration divine, I shall be in precisely the right frame of mind to establish a new standard of *wilding* savagery. These children know nothing of Neon, of the abandon and power it brings.

I will always remember the Grace I experienced the first time I *saw* Neon and *knew* it. It was in 1928. I'd returned from our first long stay in Europe. I bought a bloodred Auburn and set off for the drive to Mississippi. I'd just come around a curve. There it was: the shivering electric vision! Oh, hallowed moment! I knew then how Moses must have felt when he went up on the mountain and beheld the burning bush.

The Neon flamingo sat atop a roadhouse on a deserted stretch of highway. It was a magnificent electric creature, wondrous and terrible. And I knew deep in my soul, in a place beyond words, that I was in the presence of a seraph—or some similar angelic being, for the heavenly apparition was unlike any of the ten families of angels I'd learned about when I was but a sweet and innocent babe, sitting on dear Mother's lap, learning to read the Bible. No, this was a new kind of angel, an angel of the Neon, come to Earth to give me God's sign.

And I knew that only I could *see* the messenger. Only I could understand what it signified.

Trembling, I pulled the car to the shoulder and turned off the motor.

God's messenger stared down at me with its chilling gimlet eye—an eye the incandescent red of Hellfire. And the Neon spoke:

Bold hunter, brave warrior,
You have been chosen as My Fury.

I *heard* the words not with my ears but with my heart. I fell down across the seat of the automobile and hid my face, prostrating myself before the messenger of the Lord. I was unworthy—yet, I, who had suffered so much, who had wandered more than sixty years in the wilderness, struggling to develop my hunter's spirit, had been *chosen*! Miraculous be the ways of Neon!

I cried with disbelief, not daring to raise my face, fearing some terrible mistake. I wanted to ask why, yet I didn't have the courage to question God. But knowing all, the Neon saw the doubt in my heart and answered.

Your vengeance knows no mercy.

Which I knew was true.

Go to Jerusalem, My Fury.
The daughters and sons of the wicked must be punished.

And then I *understood*! I was the Neon's Fury. My work

was filled with wrath, and because it was righteous, it found favor in the eyes of Neon.

I stayed in that car late into the night, crying and singing hymns of praise, humbling myself before the Neon's mighty power.

The roadhouse closed.

The electricity that connected the Neon messenger with the Beyond was shut off.

A man—I remember he was fat and balding, with greasy eyes and a bartender's apron still tied around his tremendous waist—came out the front door. He turned and locked the door, eyeing me suspiciously as he waddled toward his battered Ford. I looked into his porcine mind and knew that he carried the evening's cash register receipts in one back pocket and a revolver in the other. I could see the gun jutting out from his hip, looking in silhouette like the tail on the rump of a hog.

I looked up again at the sign. The Neon was invisible without electricity to make it glow, but it wasn't gone. It was hiding—inside of *me*! I could feel the Neon's icy hot fingers probing my bowels, lacing up through my organs and veins until it touched my heart and made me think it would freeze in midbeat.

I knew at that moment that I was forever at one with the Neon.

"Hallelujah!" I screamed.

The fat man, alarm evident in his eyes as he glanced at me over his shoulder, threw the Ford into gear, throwing gravel as he sped away.

Neon, the blood of Creation, was in me and with me. Blood and Neon intermingled as one in my veins, for I was the Fury of the Lord. I had been called to smite the wicked and punish the transgressors—and their children, and their children's children, and their children's children, down through seven generations. For so it has been written, for so it shall be done.

I had become the instrument of a divine and terrible justice. I knew exactly what I had to do.

If it hadn't been for the pyromaniac Isaiah Buchanan—and *her* meddling interference—I would have killed them all in 1928 and been done with it. As it turned out, another six decades passed without Jerusalem's punishment. But now I have returned again to America. My work in New York City is almost done. Then I will return to Mississippi and make the sinners pay. I will bring down the temple and all of them with it, so that no one will ever utter the name of that accursed place without remembering the price its people paid for their transgressions.

I hear mortals talk about the night.

"A beautiful summer evening."

"It's lovely, if a bit humid."

But the fools know nothing about the night. I *know*. I can *see* perfectly into their minds, although "mind" is a generous word to describe the receptacles that hold their muddy, petty concerns and fears. Their feeble brains can barely comprehend the stars and the moon and the darkened woods where the whippoorwills cry lonely over the lost, unmarked graves of Confederate soldiers. They do not understand the holy hours between sunset and sunrise that are most truly lighted by Neon's glow—that Neon and blood, two manifestations of the same Universal energy, bind the world together in the darkness.

When I set out on my long nightly rambles, I navigate by Neon reflected on the rain-slick streets where I hunt alone. Old signs are the truest—Hamms, Rolling Rock, Schlitz. These harbingers shine out in the darkness like beacons to the solitary traveler, never failing to bring me good sport. A blinking script advertising "Maid Rite Eats" must, of course, be obeyed, even when the quarry is unattractive.

Yet the most sacred of Neon's messengers (so much so that I have adopted it as my personal emblem) is the winged horse Pegasus. The burning winged horse—its outline glowing red in the darkness, a magnificent messenger flying out of Hell to carry its avenger on his mission of divine retribution against the damned—is a sign that promises me especially exquisite pleasures somewhere ahead in the night. Whenever I find Pegasus, or the bloody seraph finds me, I forget caution and abandon myself to a Bacchanalian orgy in worship of the great and glorious Neon.

The high brittle buzz; the mysterious, twisting hollow glass tubing that would be utterly transparent were it not for the pulsing, glowing opalescence of the magical gas held within. Neon communicates directly with my blood. It is *my* blood. When I take a life now, it is not merely for pleasure, as it is with *her*. It is a sacrament.

I have been born again as the Neon's Fury. I have baptized myself in the blood. I have been chosen to mete out divine justice for timeless sins. It is as it was told to me by the Neon, as it was prophesied in the holy Book of Revelation:

Clad in a robe dipped in blood . . .
Behold, I am coming soon, bringing my recompense, to repay every one for what he has done.

Guided by Neon, I have punished many strangers for their secret wickedness. But I will also punish those sins I have sworn to never forget—my oath for revenge burned into my soul with a white-hot iron heated in the fires of Hell.

As if I could ever forget . . .

Events have the power to melt down your life and recast it in a form of their own making; once the cast is removed, the shape remains forever.

I could *never* forget.

If I forget thee, O Jerusalem, let my right hand forget her cunning.

I will never forget you, Jerusalem, Mississippi, or what your sons and daughters did to me. So prepare yourselves, children of Jerusalem. The Fury will return to Jerusalem, and justice *will* be done.

You know, dear diary, that I did not want to come to New York, but the past few years have led me to revise my opinion of this place. Perhaps *she* was right. The Golden Age is ended in Europe. *She* saw it coming, of course. The tedious, confused people now running like wild dogs in the streets of Bucharest and Tbilisi, howling for democracy.

The so-called reformers in my former home in the Caucasus will not be satisfied until they have ruined everything. They talk of freedom, these Eastern European peasants, but they will never know the freedom I had there. The Iron Curtain countries used to be such wonderfully backward places. You could do whatever you wanted, as long as you had power and ruthless courage. But that's all ending or ended. Before long, Budapest will be no more exciting than Cleveland.

New York is a hospitable place to someone of my kind. This part of the Union is no longer populated by the busybodies and stiff-necked Yankee Puritans I remember. The social order is breaking down, as we predicted. John Brown's true legacy. This is a lawless city of towering buildings and vast slums. I find it wonderful. The Yankees won, and in winning, lost. The social chaos here provides me with a perfect camouflage. It is almost like being back in Bulgaria. And in New York City, it is possible to be perfectly anonymous among the city's millions. No one is his brother's keeper, and I am able to be shockingly indiscreet, when the Neon moves me.

I am most disappointed with the current state of the theater. Tonight I attended what they call a Broadway hit. I found the acting to be extremely understated. It rather reminded me of my brother's bloodless style in front of the gas lamps. I can't say I was impressed by anything beyond the production's technical aspects; the lighting especially is far superior to anything in my day.

I went prowling after the theater. This sole pleasure never stales.

I wandered into a seedy section off of Times Square, looking for interesting things to see and do. I visited an unusual men's club. It was a congregating place for sodomites—a type of person I know very well from my own time in the theater, so long ago. The African-sounding music was loud, with a pumping, animal rhythm. The air was thick with the smell of sweat, beer, and sex. I stayed long enough to have one drink and turn down a half-dozen invitations to dance and participate in abominations. Not at all my métier, yet I found it oddly stimulating.

I left the club seeking companionship more to my tastes. Outside a disreputable hotel, I met a lovely Kewpie Doll. She told me her name was Jeanie. A lie, of course. Kewpie wore flat canvas shoes and a one-piece knit minidress without underwear. Her black hair was cut short, like a man's, making her look even younger than she really was—a little like one of the prettier young sodomites I'd seen earlier. There were dark circles under Kewpie Doll's eyes from a lack of sleep. Her body was thin to the point of gauntness and her blood gave off the stale smell of nicotine and oxidized cocaine. A drug addict. There are a great many of them in New York City these days. Her cheapness and bodily filth did not repel me. You know how I adore sluts, dearest diary. The more whorish they are, the more it excites me.

We stood talking beneath a flashing Neon sign that was urging me to eat and drink. Each time the sign blinked, it made a harsh crackling noise. An unworthy tabernacle for the godhead. Everything is shoddy and corrupt in this city now, even these holy things.

Kewpie Doll's soul reeked of sin. The Neon whispered to me that her mother had been a whore, and her mother's mother before her, whores begetting whores.

> *They and the Beast hate the harlot; they will make her desolate and naked, and devour her flesh and burn her up with fire.*

Kewpie Doll said I could do whatever I wanted to her for fifty dollars.

"You can even fuck me up the ass," she said.

I asked why she would sell her body. She answered that she needed the money for this new drug they call "crack." I'd heard about it before. As a former connoisseur of opium, the idea of sampling this powerful new type of cocaine intrigued me. I arranged to purchase a quantity of the narcotic from a nearby vendor Kewpie Doll knew. I followed him alone into an alley and took his entire night's inventory off his hands, as well as his money and his life. No point in leaving loose ends.

Alas, this new drug, so dangerously potent according to the accounts I've read in the newspapers, proved disappointingly weak. It only mildly stimulated my system—which is, admittedly, resistant to such pleasures.

Kewpie Doll was plainly a slave to the drug. I found it rather pathetic. I plied her with so much of it that she scarcely whimpered when I used my penknife to open a vein and draw off enough blood for the ceremonial first drink from my favorite silver hunting cup. As long as my supply of the drug remained, she was mine body and soul.

Invigorated by my first taste of blood, I took her. I had her first the usual way. Then I rolled her over and, reminding her of her earlier offer, did indeed fuck her up the ass. She sucked the glass pipe while I did her this way, then grabbed the damp sheets in her fists and threw herself into the act with renewed enthusiasm, enjoying our perverse copulation with the mute abandon of a dumb beast.

Ah, but I liked this girl!

I had been without a woman for several nights, and so I was in no hurry to conclude our fun and games. Kewpie Doll was a strong and willing partner, as long as she could continue stoking the glass pipe. When the drug ran out, she became shrill and difficult. She demanded more. She complained about the small injury I'd caused her wrist, and threatened to go to the police if I failed to obtain more of the drug for her. Such threats, indicative of her poor Yankee breeding, excited my rage. I tore up her cheap dress—*make her desolate and naked*—and threw the scraps and her cheap purse out the window.

She brought a chair slamming down on my head with all her strength. I paused and slowly smiled, feeling the dull pain in my upper jaw as my blood teeth slipped down from their recesses.

Kewpie Doll began to scream. I doubted the hotel was the sort of establishment where screams attracted much attention, but for the sake of prudence I stuffed a towel in her mouth and bound her hands with a strip torn from the bed sheets. She began to gag as I took her again from behind, thinking that sodomy had certain unsuspected virtues. I didn't pull the towel out of her mouth until I was finished. Her face had already turned blue. I had to slap the breath back into her. I decided to be more careful. My carelessness had almost ended my fun before it had begun in earnest.

"I know you want more cocaine to smoke," I whispered in her ear, tenderly stroking her hair. "The truth is that you're addicted. But don't worry. I'm going to take care of you so that you'll never need to take drugs again."

I made good on my promise. And when I finished with her rehabilitation two hours later, I cut off her ring finger for my collection.

I threw Kewpie Doll's body onto the subway tracks and watched the train hit it. It was a perfect moment: the blackness of the tunnel; the blinding flash of the subway's Cyclops eye; the tremendous roar; the sparks—*burn her up with fire*—streaking up from the iron wheels; the explosion of blood and flesh.

New York isn't the Balkans, but it will do.

II

Dinner with Mozart

CHRONICLE NOTES: The following excerpt is from David Parker's journal.

—*Editor*

Wolf and I had dinner in Greenwich Village at The Gita—again. I've eaten so much Indian food in the past month that I'm beginning to share Wolf's passion for curry, one of his current obsessions. Wolf says The Gita has the best curry in New York, and if he says it is, it must be true. Wolf quickly becomes, in all things that attract his interest, a studied authority whose judgment can be trusted implicitly.

The Gita is on a side street barely wide enough for automobile traffic. When we came outside, there was a single cab parked in front of the restaurant. The sullen Rastafarian driver glared at us from behind the wheel of the yellow Caprice, as if his stare could stop us from disturbing his ganja-induced meditation.

Maybe it did.

I had thought we would get into the taxi and ride uptown, but Wolf, pausing long enough to nod to the cab driver, wandered across the street. I followed, of course. That's the way our friendship works: Wolf leads and seldom explains; I follow and usually end up learning something.

Across the street from The Gita was a chess shop wedged between a bookstore and a store selling dubious antiques. The chess shop's name was painted in peeling golden letters on a horizontal sign that ran the width of the business: THE BLIND KING. And, in smaller letters along the bottom: CHESS BOOKS, CHESS MAGAZINES, CHESS SETS, AN EMPORIUM DEDICATED TO THE

ARCANE SUBTLE GAME OF CHESS—a game more subtle than the sign maker's sloganeering.

The Blind King was the only busy place on the quiet street. Chess contests spilled out of the store and onto the sidewalk, where several card tables had been set up to accommodate the evening tournament's players despite the chill. Looking through the window panes, I saw game boards spread out on every horizontal space, even on the floor. The faces of the players and onlookers, each equally intent, were turned downward, concentrating on the pieces arranged on the boards.

The chess shop was larger than it appeared from the street. The building was narrow and deep, then split apart into two wings like the letter T, the wings occupying space behind the establishments to either side.

The Blind King was dimly lighted, the aisles serpentine, laid out according to a logic discernible only to the proprietor. The shop reminded me of an English topiary garden, but instead of benches or statues spaced at intervals within the impenetrable maze, there were tables and chairs and old, broken-down couches where players sat on worn velvet cushions, deep in concentration, a small crowd of observers looking on at the quiet struggle over the chessboard balanced on the cushion between the players.

I'd passed up two invitations to play by the time I located Wolf, already deep in a match. His opponent moved a knight and muttered something in Polish. Wolf replied in the same tongue. I've gotten beyond being surprised at the things Wolf knows.

I asked, a little tersely, if he was planning to stay.

Wolf nodded without looking up from the board, his red ponytail bobbing up and down.

"Just for a game or two. You should return home."

"As long as it doesn't inconvenience you, Wolfgang," I said a little sarcastically. "My head is pounding."

"I know."

Of course. Wolf always knew.

I watched him move a knight. His eyes flickered up to me a moment, then returned to the chessboard. "You're going to get a telephone call."

"From Tatiana?"

The other player gave me a disapproving look. He considered me rude for my role in disturbing the sacred silence of the chess trance. I felt my face color—and it had nothing to do with chess. I'd just reminded Wolf—and myself—that I continued to think about Tatiana constantly.

Wolf moved a chess piece. Heads in the circle around him nodded in appreciation. His opponent leaned back to stroke his beard, contemplating an escape from the inescapable trap Wolf had constructed in a few opening moves.

Wolf looked up at me through his eyebrows and shook his head slightly, knowing, no doubt, the unhappy thoughts that were going through my mind.

"*He* is back with us tonight," he said in a quiet voice.

My heart sank. Not again. Not so soon.

"You expect me to continue dealing with this alone?"

Wolf nodded.

I could not work out why Wolf, who knew so much, refused to help me. His powers were infinitely greater than my own. He usually knew when, though apparently not where, the killer was about to strike. I'd already admitted to Wolf that I'd failed miserably and needed his help. Although it was hardly *my* fault. It was too easy for the killer to hide in New York. In a smaller city, I might have been able to track him. He was obviously an old and cunning killer. But New York was too large. There were too many people for me to be able to *feel* him—and he was too clever to leave signs I could have used to track him.

"Can't you help me just tonight?"

"I am sorry," he said, not looking up from the game, his detachment undisturbed. "I have other problems."

"What could be more important than this?"

"Do you mind?" Wolf's opponent snapped. He snatched his queen and moved her forward three squares, banging the piece down on the chessboard.

"Checkmate," Wolf said, smiling faintly as he captured the black queen with his knight, pinning the black king.

The man looked from Wolf to the board and back with a stare that showed his amazement. A perfect kill; he hadn't even seen it coming.

"Care for another game?" the player asked, unable to believe he'd been so easily bested. A fluke, he thought. Then, looking at me, he added, "*If* we could have it a little more quiet so that I could concentrate."

"Of course," Wolf said soothingly. "I apologize. If you would be so kind." He nodded for his opponent to set up the pieces again. "A few more moments' indulgence." Then, to me, "All I can tell you, David, is that I have problems of my own to deal with that are just as complicated. Learn what you can. We will talk tomorrow. Then I must leave New York for a time."

"Leave New York?" It was humiliating to hear the desperation in my voice.

"I must go abroad. A special trip."

A special trip. The *Illuminati*, in other words.

"Great," I muttered and turned away.

The killer was on the prowl. I hadn't the least clue who he was or how to stop him, and Wolf wouldn't help me. I continue to feel a responsibility for each murder. I was ordered to kill the killer—as if it were that simple. I've failed, and now it is partly my fault each time the police find a corpse drained of blood, mutilated, each missing a finger, trophies the killer takes away with him for God-only-knows-what twisted purpose.

And still, as embarrassed as I am to confess it, the killer was not foremost on my mind.

I turned back and knelt beside Wolf. "Listen," I said softly, "since it's come up, if you *do* happen to talk to Tatiana . . ."

Wolf didn't look at me as he straightened his pawns. It was embarrassing for me to ask him to intercede. Especially considering that he had been her friend longer than he'd been mine—a *lot* longer.

"I may speak with her," he said finally.

"When you do, tell her . . ."

My voice trailed off.

Wolf looked at me, his face an impenetrable mask.

I didn't know what to say. What did I want Wolf to tell Tatiana? That I loved her? That I could not stand for us to be apart? That the despair and guilt of not being able to stop the killer was driving me mad with frustration and grief? That I was ready to snap over the trouble I was having with my opera—my masterwork—yet that it had become an inconsequential annoyance compared to the other things I had to deal with? That I could not stand to continue living without her? That I needed her, truly *needed* her, to keep from losing my mind?

"Go home and wait for the call, David," Wolf instructed me with a sad smile. He respects the privacy of my mind, but I know that he could see my despairing thoughts reflected plainly in my face. If anyone could tell Tatiana about what was going on inside my wounded heart, it would be Wolf.

I stood without another word and found my way through the

crowded, twisted aisles and out of The Blind King. I had to get back and await the call. I had another date with death.

III

Making Movies

CHRONICLE NOTES: The following audio transcript was made from a videotape "Becker Thorne" recorded in March of 1991, using a camera hidden in the bedroom of his Manhattan penthouse. The tape was recovered from a safe in Arlington Plantation. There are two people on the video, "Thorne" and a girl whose identity is unknown. The girl is in her middle to late teens, judging from appearances, attractive but coarse, with a tangle of red hair and a unicorn tattooed on her left breast. The transcript begins twenty minutes into the tape, following a section showing them engaged in various sexual acts.

—*Editor*

GIRL: So you're an actor.

THORNE: I used to be. You might say I'm retired.

GIRL: Is that where you got the money to pay for this place? It's fantastic, you know.

THORNE: Thank you. I made my fortune on Wall Street, Kewpie Doll.

GIRL: Were you in any movies I've seen?

THORNE: No. I've never even been to Hollywood, absurd as that seems.

GIRL: You were on TV? You kind of remind me of a dude that used to be in *Santa Barbara.*

THORNE: No, I've never been on television.

GIRL: What kind of actor were you if you weren't in the movies or on TV?

THORNE: I was on the stage, my dear girl, in the legitimate theater.

GIRL: Oh.

THORNE: It merits rather more than "oh." I was highly regarded, if I do say so myself. My interpretations of Macbeth and Hamlet defined the roles for my generation. The critics said my Brutus was sublime, but my Richard the Third was my crowning glory. Not even Olivier's Richard was as good as mine.

GIRL: Richard *who*?

THORNE (reciting Shakespeare, his voice melodramatic, as befitted nineteenth-century tastes):

> *I, in this weak piping time of peace,*
> *Have no delight to pass away the time,*
> *Unless to see my shadow in the sun*
> *And descant on mine own deformity.*

GIRL: What?

THORNE: Shakespeare, Kewpie Doll.

GIRL: I didn't understand a word of it.

THORNE: The language is very old, like myself.

GIRL: Oh, you're not so old. I like older men.

THORNE: I am glad of it.

GIRL (wistfully): It is too bad you weren't in the movies.

THORNE: But no, my dear child, the real acting is on the stage. Motion pictures are mere spectacles contrived to dazzle the unwashed masses. Acting and movies have nothing to do with one another.

GIRL: Oh, I don't know. I think Tom Cruise is a pretty good actor.

THORNE: Dear child, there are no more than three or four real actors working in motion pictures, and Mr. Cruise is most definitely not to be included among them.

GIRL: Well, I like Tom Cruise.

THORNE: I'm sure you do.

GIRL: I'm going to Hollywood. I don't know how, but I'm going to get into the movies. I just know it.

THORNE: I have no doubt that a young lady like you will be in a movie sooner than you think.

GIRL (fervently): Do you think so?

THORNE: I'm quite positive.

GIRL: *Really?*

THORNE: Really.

GIRL: God! That would be, like, the best.

THORNE: What is it about motion pictures that attracts you most?

GIRL: Oh, everything. Movie stars are beautiful. And rich. And famous. (A thoughtful pause.) And the other thing about movie stars is that they—no, never mind. You'll think it's silly.

THORNE: No, please.

GIRL: You'll laugh at me.

THORNE: I promise not to. Tell me.

GIRL: Well, I don't know exactly how to say it, but I'll try. I love Marilyn Monroe movies. You might say that she's my idol, though I'm not, you know, a blonde. The last time I saw a Marilyn movie, I thought, like, she's *dead.* And even if she wasn't dead, she'd be an old woman now. But she's young and beautiful in the movies. And the thing is, she'll be young forever in the movies.

THORNE: Movies make you immortal.

GIRL: Yes, that's it. They make you rich and loved and it lasts forever.

THORNE: Movies do make you immortal, but only after a fashion.

GIRL: What do you mean?

THORNE: It is not true immortality. The celluloid Marilyn continues to live on as a beautiful woman on the movie screen, but the real Marilyn is a rotting corpse in some crypt.

GIRL: Oh, gross.

THORNE (picking up a letter opener from the table beside the bed): Movies, you see, are an illusion. Allow me to demonstrate. As it says in the Bible, if thy right eye offendeth thee, pluck it out!

(Without warning, Thorne plunges the letter opener into his eye.)

GIRL (becoming hysterical): Oh, my God! Your eye!

THORNE (grabbing the girl by her hair and forcing her to look into his gory wound): Do you think it's serious?

GIRL: Oh, God, God, God, it's your eye. It's terrible.

(Thorne buries his face in the sheets. The girl, not sure what to do, tries to comfort him and call 911 at the same time. She isn't able to get through, either because she is too hysterical to dial, or because the telephone has been disconnected.)

THORNE: My eye feels better now.

(Thorne begins to laugh as he lifts his face from the sheets.

His eye has healed itself, thanks to the Vampiri *regenerative powers, although his face is streaked with blood and vitreous humor, the colorless jelly that fills the eye's interior.)*

GIRL (completely confused): What—your eye . . .

THORNE: A simple illusion.

GIRL (in a rage): You bastard!

(The girl strikes Thorne with all her strength, but the blow glances off his cheek without effect.)

GIRL: I'm out of here. You're one sick fuck.

THORNE (grabbing the girl with one hand while finding the bloodied letter opener in the sheets with the other): But I can't let you leave yet, Kewpie Doll. Not until I've taught you my little trick.

(The girl screams hysterically, but Thorne ignores her, using his superior strength to pin her to the bed.)

THORNE: This illusion will serve you well if you ever do get into the movies. In fact, dear girl, you're in the movies now, and you don't even know it!

(Thorne straddles the girl, his knees on her arms, holding her face with his left hand as he lowers the letter opener. The girl continues to shriek.)

THORNE: Now you must hold *very still* and open your eye as wide as possible. . . .

IV

At the Scene of a Murder

CHRONICLE NOTES: David Parker's journal, continued.

—*Editor*

The telephone was ringing when I arrived home from dinner with Wolf and our visit to The Blind King. I hurried to unlock the door and then snatched up the receiver, hoping it would be—well, of course, *Tatiana.*

It wasn't.

It was a secretary in the police department's central dispatching office, a civilian retained to make sure I was notified whenever there was another serial killing. I hired her early on as insurance against the possibility that Lieutenant Mowbray might one night "forget" to phone me—as he had now for three consecutive killings.

I made a mental note of the address, promised my source I'd put the usual fifty-dollar bill in the mail to her the next morning, and hung up.

It was another "Dracula" killing. That's what the tabloids had started calling the killer—"Dracula"—because his victims were always found drained of their blood.

The map of Manhattan in my study is studded with red pushpins, one for each killing—twenty since I've been following the trail, a new pin coming, on average, once a week. Pushpins have been added at a quicker pace recently. Two this week, counting tonight's.

The usual Hunger cycle is once every two weeks. The older the vampire, the less the need for blood. Tatiana feels the Hunger only once a month. Wolf hardly ever feeds. The killer is, I'm certain, closer to Wolf in age than he is to Tatiana or me, meaning he is feeding far, far more often than he needs. But then, it is obvious that he does not kill to satisfy the Hunger. He kills because he likes killing.

Fresh blood—a powerful intoxicant to the *Vampiri*.

It is impossible to describe the rush of power and strength we get from taking even the small amount of blood we need to stay strong. The sensation is somewhere between electrocution and orgasm, an explosion of unimaginable bliss that makes you feel as if the molecules of your body are rocketing away from you faster than the speed of light and mingling with all of creation, for a moment controlling it, and being controlled by it, a moment of complete, all-encompassing harmony, a moment of perfect knowledge.

When I was mortal, the high I got from cocaine didn't begin to approach the powerful high fresh blood gives me. . . .

But these are unhealthy thoughts.

Thinking about a sip of that most sublime of all wines makes my nerves tingle and my upper gums ache.

It is not time for *that*.

I must set down what happened tonight.

* * *

The map in my study occupies half the north wall. When I stand in the middle of the room and look at it, I see the push-pins form a semicircle that begins on Central Park West, arcs toward the East River, loops around the north end of the park, and ends in the vicinity of the Metropolitan Museum. A perfectly angled crescent of death.

The murders radiate from a central point in the middle of the crescent. (Except the prostitute, whose mutilated body was thrown in front of a subway south of Times Square.) Unfortunately, the scale is too large for me to be able to narrow the critical central point to an area any smaller than a general neighborhood involving a dozen blocks in Manhattan.

My aim, as I've described in earlier journal entries, is to chart the killer's territory and activity patterns in order to predict where he will strike next. Or, alternately, to help discover where he hides during the day. He is a nocturnal hunter, and, as I have theorized, may not have developed sufficient powers to withstand the sunlight.

I've spent the evenings walking the area at the epicenter of my pushpins, straining to feel the slightest psychic twinge that would alert me to the outlaw's presence, or the fact that he has come that way, but thus far my efforts have been as fruitless as Lieutenant Mowbray's.

Then, tonight, a startling difference.

As I stood in front of the map before heading out to the crime scene, scanning for the streets to insert the latest push-pin, the significance of the new address struck me. This newest killing had not been with the others along the pushpin crescent in the outlaw's usual hunting territory. This time, he'd killed in almost the exact *center* of his hunting ground.

I jabbed the pushpin into the map, grabbed my notebook, and ran out the door.

"You can't come in here."

I'd gotten past the cops downstairs and ignored the yellow tape across the hall by the elevator with the words POLICE LINE DO NOT CROSS printed in boxy black letters. Now a uniform blocked my way into the apartment.

"It's all right, Ingersoll," Mowbray said, glancing up at me. He was on his hands and knees next to the coffee table, putting fibers into a plastic bag with a pair of tweezers.

I stepped around the uniform.

Mowbray gave me a sour look. He was wearing a rumpled blue blazer that was shiny at the elbows and had white spots at the edge of each sleeve where the material had worn. I'd never seen him without that sports coat. It was either the only one he owned or his good luck charm. Except Mowbray hadn't been having any luck.

"Gee, I'm beginning to think you don't like me," I said, and grinned. "My feelings are hurt."

"What are you talking about, Parker?"

"You didn't call me tonight. Or the last two times before tonight, if I remember right."

"So now we're going to have a lovers' quarrel?" Mowbray made kissing noises at me. The other cops snickered.

"I thought we had an agreement," I said, still smiling.

"You talking about the cooperation I was ordered to extend to you?"

I shrugged. "Whatever, Lieutenant."

"I shouldn't have to tell you the investigation comes first, *Mr.* Parker. Official cooperation with pencil-necks who get their rocks off writing books about sick fucks like 'Dracula' is somewhere farther down the list priority-wise, along with filling out paperwork, stopping to buy lottery tickets, and putting gas in the car. Okay?"

I kept grinning, and Mowbray kept up his harangue, which I took as another indication that he was upset and frustrated, that there wasn't any more evidence at this crime scene than the others. He was just taking it out on me because I was handy. He was under terrific pressure, both from the newspapers and from his superiors, to make an arrest, yet he was no closer to apprehending the killer than I was.

"In case you hadn't noticed, we got us an investigation going here, Mr. Parker. But I'm sorry if I got too busy and hurt your feelings by forgetting to ask you to tonight's dance. I wouldn't want the captain to think I treated you rudely."

"Forget it, Mowbray. I'm here."

He gave me a cold, appraising look. Policemen have a way of looking at you as if you're naked. They want to see your flaws and weaknesses, and if they don't, it only makes them more suspicious than they are to begin with.

"So who's been tipping you off?" he said finally. "Who's your pal with a telephone?"

"Maybe I heard it on the scanner." The fact that there were no reporters outside told me that the police had kept away from their radios. It didn't matter. I was just politely telling Mowbray to go to hell, and we both knew it.

"Yeah, right, and I've just been named the first Jewish pope."

"Congratulations, Your Holy Eminence."

"Okay, smart guy. I'll give you five minutes. But if I find out who is spoon-feeding you, I'll have his balls. Okay?"

"Yes, Your Holy Eminence." I thought Delores was safe in that respect. I peered over his shoulder. "This one just like the others?"

"Something new this time. You wanna look?"

"Not really, but that's why I'm here."

Mowbray put his fist in front of his face and began to hack. He was overweight, smoked, and had the wan complexion of someone who was going to end up with a quadruple heart bypass, if he made it that far. His face turned purple as he continued to cough, chin pulled in to his chest, shoulders squeezed high. I wondered if it was the Big One, but Mowbray stopped hacking and straightened up.

"Okay, but don't say I didn't warn you."

I nodded. I didn't have to pretend that the killer's handiwork sickened me. I think it must have turned Mowbray green a time or two, although he never would have admitted it.

"Every courtesy. Every fuckin' courtesy."

I followed him into the bedroom. Mowbray was right to have warned me. It was bad, the worst yet. The killer had elevated his savagery to a new extreme.

The victim was a woman somewhere in her middle thirties. She must have been attractive before the killer got hold of her. She was naked, on her back, arms and legs restrained with what looked like curtain tie-backs. There were candles on either side of her head; they'd burned down halfway before someone had blown them out. The bottles and jars that once sat upon the dresser had been swept onto the floor with an angry gesture that left some of them lying broken against the wall on the far side of the room. The characteristic neck wound—the jugular savagely torn out—was present. The killer also left his other signature: the ring finger on the woman's left hand had been severed and taken away as a trophy.

The woman's chest had been cut open. There was a purplish hole where the heart should have been. Blood was sprayed everywhere. It had soaked into the carpet, over which evidence technicians had laid paths of clear plastic to keep from getting it on their shoes and clothes, and to preserve possible evidence. I'd never seen so much blood. It looked like five people had been killed in the bedroom instead of just one. He couldn't have gotten much blood out of her neck.

Mowbray pointed at the hole in the woman's chest with a yellow No. 2 pencil.

"This is the first time he's cut out the heart, but I don't have to tell that to a smart guy like you. And look at this." He pointed to the ceiling with his pencil. "See how much blood is sprayed up there? It was fuckin' dripping on us when we got here. Forensic's guess is that he cut it out while she was still alive."

"Jesus," I whispered.

"Note the ritualistic elements. That's new. The bound hands and feet. The candles. The drawing on the wall. It looks like our freak is some kind of fuckin' satanist on top of everything else."

The mirrors behind the dresser had been taken down and lay smashed on the bed. Painted on the wall above the victim was a crude representation of a horse or cow—I couldn't tell which—with wings coming out of its back. It reminded me of the Babylonian idols of the winged men-bull gods at the Metropolitan Museum. The killer had used the victim's blood for paint.

"What about these circles?"

"These rings on the dresser? They're blood. Evidently from some kind of glass or cup. He was either drinking while he butchered her, or else he used the cup to drink some of the blood. Charley?"

"Nope. Haven't found it, Lieutenant," one of the cops said.

"Figures," Mowbray said with disgust. "Son of a bitch couldn't leave me a glass with some lovely fingerprints. Say, Parker, you're looking even paler than usual. I been telling you that you need to get out in the sun more. Or is all this making you feel a little queasy?"

I heard laughter behind me.

"Tell me you're not, Lieutenant."

"I got to agree that this one is a real piece of work."

"Are you sure it was him? There are enough differences for it to have been a copycat."

I should have *known* myself, of course, but no trace of the killer's presence remained behind. The room was completely blank. I felt every bit as frustrated as Mowbray, although I couldn't admit it.

The detective made a face, pushing his lips into a pout to think it over. "Yeah, I'd say it was him. The neck—everybody knows about that, thanks to the fuckin' newspapers. But only a few know about the fingers. You haven't been flapping your lips, have you?"

I shook my head.

"No, of course not. And you haven't been doing any of your own detective work? Haven't been chatting up any suspects you've neglected to tell your old Uncle Bob about? No? Then I think we have to assume it was him. It's got all his trademarks."

"But why these improvisations? He's been at this a while. Always nearly the same details. Why change now and start drawing weird pictures of idols on the wall and cutting out hearts?"

"What was that about idols?"

"That drawing of a horse or cow with wings. It looks either like Pegasus, the flying horse from Greek mythology, or one of the winged bulls the Babylonians worshiped."

Mowbray looked at me suspiciously.

"They've got one over at the Met. A statue of a winged bull. I saw it. The ancient Babylonians worshiped them."

Mowbray blew out a long breath. "Shit keeps getting weirder and weirder. You write that down, Charley?"

"Sure, boss."

"I'll check that out," Mowbray said, his eyes narrowed.

"Do that."

"I suppose it might mean something." He blinked and looked at me with renewed distaste. "But I doubt it."

"You didn't answer my question. Why do you think he's changing his methods now?"

"Who knows how this freak's mind works?" the detective said impatiently. "Maybe he thinks Satan is telling him to off women. Son of Sam thought his dog was telling him to kill, for Christ's sake. Or maybe he's getting more desperate for attention, which is definitely what he'll get if the press gets wind of this. And the papers better not hear about it, okay? These new twists are the confidential details of a police investigation. I can throw your ass in jail if you talk to any reporters."

"Maybe he's entering a new phase, becoming more violent, more dramatic."

"Yeah."

"He couldn't have gotten much blood out of her. That means he may kill sooner next time."

Mowbray regarded me closely.

"Considering the fact that he's always taken the blood away with him before, he must have some use for it. He didn't get much this time. If he really thinks he needs blood, he'll have to get it somewhere else."

"Hmm. Could be," Mowbray said. "Tell me something, Parker. What the hell do you suppose he does with that blood? You must have a theory."

"I think he drinks it."

"You really believe that?"

"All I know is what I read in the papers."

"Don't kid me. What do you *really* think?" Mowbray asked in a low voice, stepping nearer so the others wouldn't hear. "Do you think this guy is a fuckin' vampire, like every rag in this town says?"

I looked at the detective for a long moment before answering. This was the first time Mowbray had asked my opinion about the case. His question seemed genuine.

"Yes. I have no doubt that the killer is a vampire."

"Shit." Mowbray looked at me as if I'd just said something embarrassingly, even pathetically, stupid. "I knew it! I knew you were off the fuckin' wall."

"By definition, a vampire is anyone who feels compelled to drink blood."

"Yeah, right."

"I don't believe the killer flies in and out windows in the form of a bat, leaving behind no physical evidence. I don't think he spends the daylight hours sleeping in a coffin sprinkled with the soil of his native Transylvania. There are no vampires in the Hollywood sense. But I do believe there are individuals who, for whatever reason, find themselves irresistibly compelled to drink blood. People who are, for all intents and purposes, vampires."

"A fuckin' vampire," Mowbray said, looking at the ceiling.

"There have been studies of clinical cases. I could send you copies of the reports. I have them in my research."

"Save your stamps, pal," Mowbray said, and turned away.

* * *

I looked slowly around the room once more, reaching out with my senses, feeling for traces of the vibrations the killer might have left behind in the air.

Nothing. The killer had been careful, as always.

I tried harder. I knew he'd been there. He had to leave some trace of himself behind. I strained to feel something, anything in the air. . . .

Nothing.

I realized too late that Mowbray was studying me closely. The whites of his eyes had a yellowish tinge and were discolored in several areas from broken blood vessels. One of the evidence technicians interrupted as he was about to speak.

"We're ready to remove the organ."

"Oh, you'll want to see this, Parker." Mowbray jerked his head in the direction of the love seat in the living room. "It's the best part."

Two technicians in blood-spattered white lab coats were getting to their feet, one filing various packets of evidence in a case that looked like a big fishing tackle box, the other taking film out of a camera and replacing it with a new roll. Behind the love seat, like a discarded towel on the floor against the baseboard, was a piece of bleeding flesh.

The heart.

"You're interested in all the vampire details. Check this. It'll make good copy."

Mowbray got down on one knee, grunting, poking at the heart with his wooden pencil. There was a laceration in the organ, a pinched depression in the purple muscle.

"See that?"

I nodded.

"Fucker took a bite out of it."

I had to look away.

Mowbray pushed against his bent knee, grunting again as he levered himself upright, bumping his shoulder into the wall.

"Okay, guys, get it the fuck out of here. And I think you've wasted enough of my time, Parker."

"Sure. Thanks."

Mowbray tried to take my elbow, but I moved out of his range, heading for the door. He followed me into the hall, indicating that Ingersoll should go into the apartment so he could talk to me in private.

"You know, this vampire shit is about the last fuckin' straw."

"You ought to consider it."

"Enough with vampires, okay? I want to know what you're really up to, Parker. I've seen you sniffing the air, acting as if you can see things nobody else can. What gives?"

"I don't know what you're talking about."

"You don't think you're some kind of goddamned psychic, do you?"

I laughed. "Come on, Lieutenant. I'm writing a book about serial killers. You've seen my book contract. I'm interested in evidence, not ESP."

"Good, 'cause I told you I don't work with psychics. Bob Mowbray is not calling in Madame Sosostris to consult in any of his cases. Understand me? And I don't work with writers, either, but I've been volunteered to make an exception this time. How many books you written, smart guy?"

I studied my shoes carefully. There was a splotch of brown on one of the black loafers. At first I thought it was blood, but then I realized it wasn't. "None," I answered, "but you have to start somewhere."

"Was that you I read about who went to Philadelphia to play piano with the orchestra, or just somebody else named David Parker whose picture in the paper looks like you?"

"You've been checking up on me, Lieutenant."

"You going to answer the question?"

"It was me. What of it?"

"You've got pretty wide interests. Music, books about serial killers."

"I'm a musician *and* a writer, Lieutenant. There's no law saying you can't be both."

"That's messy, Parker, very messy. I've had a funny feeling about you ever since we met. I want to know why you're poking your face in my business, Parker."

"You know why. I'm researching a book on serial killers."

"You're not leveling with me."

I was beginning to understand why Mowbray was such a good detective. It was his intuition. He could sniff out things that aren't really there—but are.

"Look, Lieutenant, why else would I be following you around Manhattan, looking at things I otherwise would do everything in my power *not* to see?"

"That's what I want to know. I was asked to show you every courtesy by the commissioner. Ordered, in fact. Only now

I find out that you don't know the commissioner. Not personally, like you so cleverly made it sound."

"I did not intend to mislead you. He did sign off on me having access to this investigation for the purposes of researching my book."

"Your juice comes from higher up. And that makes me wonder even more. You won't level with me, but I'm going to level with you. I think you're a fuckin' psychic. Or at least you think you are, because I don't believe in psychics. But as we both know, the mayor does. Gets his horoscope done every month, just like Ronnie fuckin' Reagan. The second victim was, as you know, the sister of a woman who's married to a senator. The senator's wife has suggested not once but twice that we bring a clairvoyant in on the case. All before you came sniffing around. And you know what? Since then, I ain't heard boo out of her."

"Your imagination is running away with you, Lieutenant."

"I'm a cop. I don't have any fuckin' imagination. But you're worse than a nut who thinks he has ESP. You're a nut who thinks he has ESP and believes in vampires. I know what you are, Parker. Beneath all the other bullshit, I know what you are."

I stared at him with something between horror and fascination. Did he really know what I was? The answer was yes, in part.

"You think you're a vampire hunter, don't you? The last of the great fuckin' vampire hunters! See, Parker, for a long time I wondered, Why me? Why this case? Then it dawned on me." He snapped his fingers. "The little light turned on. You're not interested in serial killers, you're interested in vampires. And it's got you spooked! I see the way you look around at things, like you expect some fuckin' ghost—some fuckin' vampire—to jump out from behind the curtain and try to get you."

I didn't know what to say. He was damned close to the truth.

"You've been working too hard, Mowbray," I said with a laugh. "You need to take a couple of days off, give your nerves a nice rest."

"You shut the fuck up and listen. If you think I'm going to help you make a monkey out of me and my investigation, you're even crazier than I think you are. If you know what's good for you, you'll sit back, read the newspapers, and write your fuckin' book from the clips and whoever you can get to talk to you. You can even show up at the crime scenes and look around a little. But you keep the fuck away from me. You got that? I don't care if George fuckin' Bush wants me to talk to you about this case, I ain't doing it. Our little partnership is finished."

"Come on, Lieutenant, be reasonable."

Mowbray had already turned on his heel.

"Don't fuck with me, Parker," he said over his shoulder.

"Yes, Your Holy Eminence."

Mowbray stopped, turned, and repeated himself with emphasis, punctuating each word with a jab of his forefinger. *"Don't fuck with me!"*

Then he turned and went back into the apartment.

I stared at the fleur-de-lis wallpaper and wondered if it mattered that Mowbray had refused to help me further. His assistance, such as it was, had been useless up to that point. And now, I thought, things had changed.

I looked up and down the hall and thought about how I was standing on the spot marked by the latest and most significant pushpin in my map at home. I knew that the outlaw had killed very close to home this time. With luck, it would lead me to him.

God, I thought with a creeping dread, he might even be behind one of the doors along the hallway, *feeling* my presence, masking his own. . . .

My heart filled with equal measures of elation and fear, I stepped into the elevator and pushed the down button.

V

Lunch with Gianni

CHRONICLE NOTES: David Parker's journal, continued.
—*Editor*

I met Gianni Rourke today for lunch[1] at Bethsabee's, his favorite French restaurant.

I came in through the street entrance at the same time he entered from the hotel, his arms jutting from his sides like a pair of overstuffed sausages. He greeted me with an air kiss and an extended left hand to save his right elbow, which is afflicted with gout. He was carrying his two trademarks, a cape lined with red satin and a gold-headed cane. He's also taken recently to wearing a black fedora to hide his thinning hair. His beard hides nearly all of his face but his nose and eyes—sleek, porcine eyes through which he peers out at the world like a well-fattened hog on the lookout for truffles.

He asked straightaway about Tatiana. He said she is this season's best prima ballerina. Although he flatters everyone, he sounded as if he meant it.

Rourke has a regular table—two tables drawn together, actually—at Bethsabee's. We were shown to it with the fanfare usually accorded visiting royalty. A well-trained waiter brought Rourke his escargot before I had time to spread the linen napkin across my lap. Rourke tore into the snails, making some off-handed reference to Bernstein. Tatiana was right about him being pathologically incapable of failing to remind people he

[1]Like all members of the *Illuminati*, Mr. Parker's control over his metabolism was such that he could go outside during the daylight without fear of being harmed by exposure to solar radiation. Less-skilled *Vampiri*—primarily criminals who choose to exist outside the benevolent sphere of *Illuminati* law—risk death by exposing themselves to the sun's rays.

was once Bernstein's protégé. It is amazing someone with so much pretension and so little talent could wind up heir apparent to Goddard Cosima. But then Cosima is a very old man and in ill health and apparently not as discriminating as he used to be.

I remained patient while Rourke conducted his usual arrogant monologue through most of lunch. Finally, as he was loading an enormous bite of chocolate torte into his mouth, I brought the conversation around to the matter we'd come to lunch to discuss, not knowing whether he'd been avoiding the subject to tease me or to delay delivering bad news. I reminded him he'd been courting me over *Vanity Fair* for six months. It was time for him to make a commitment. Would he, or would he not, stage my opera?

"Gianni, darling."

It was Pauline Bettendorf, president of the Metropolitan City Opera Guild, the opera's most powerful patron. She tells people she runs the Guild wearing a velvet glove over a chain-mail fist, but from what I hear, she seldom bothers with the velvet glove.

The fat man rose with amazing agility, took the woman's wrinkled hand between his two massive paws, and kissed it.

"Do sit back down, Gianni," Pauline said, her voice husky from years of cigarette smoke.

"Mrs. Bettendorf, may I present Mr. David Parker?"

"How do you do, Mr. Parker. I was at your Carnegie debut. I enjoyed it immensely. Your interpretation of Mozart is the finest I have heard."

I thanked her and wondered how she'd react if I told her Wolfgang Amadeus Mozart had personally rehearsed me for the concert.

"You always have such elegant young men around you, Gianni. You will be at my dinner party?"

"But of course, Pauline. I instructed Basil to RSVP your secretary this morning the moment the invitation arrived."

"And Luciano?"

"Could there be any question, darling? You know he'll love to perform. He adores you, Pauline. As do we all."

"I'm so pleased. Well, I must get back to my luncheon party."

"Lovely to see you, Pauline. Thank you for stopping."

"It was a pleasure meeting you," I said.

Pauline Bettendorf looked back at me over her shoulder, a knowing smile on her lips. I could see the wheels were turning in her head. She raised one eyebrow and moved away.

"Now," I said, "about *Vanity Fair.*"

"Ah, yes," he said, removing a crumb from the lapel of his suit with a flick of his right middle finger. "There is that to discuss."

I felt a dull twinge of pain behind my eyes as if they were swelling.

"David," Rourke said, followed by a lengthy pause as his eyes roamed the table vainly searching for more food before they settled again on me, where they switched from hungry to cunning. He rearranged his facial hair to approximate a patronizing smile, brushing the gleaming mustaches to either side of his upper lip as if to clear the way for action.

I felt a tightening in the muscles of my shoulders and neck. I didn't need to look into his mind—where God-only-knows-what appalling things lurked—to know what was coming.

"You know how much I admire your first effort at opera." His hands opened in front of him as if to reveal a present within. They were empty. "And you know how much I admire your talents as a pianist."

I looked at him sourly and wondered if Pauline Bettendorf knew Rourke's real name was Eugene O'Rourke; that he was from Lincoln, Nebraska, not Boston; that he learned his accent through elocution lessons from a well-bred gentleman living in New York in reduced circumstances.

"We have decided," Rourke said finally, "that you're not ready."

I patted my mouth with my napkin, put it back in my lap, picked up a glass, took a sip of water, put it back down. My father tried to teach me to accept rejection like a gentleman; I'm not sure the lessons were entirely successful.

Rourke, for his part, made no move to speak. He enjoyed seeing me squirm. This was fun for him. Dangle the big prize in front of my nose for months, then snatch it away and watch my reaction.

The invisible vise tightening on the back of my neck screwed tighter.

"When the work was presented to you," I said quietly, measuring my words, "you were enthusiastic. More than enthusiastic. As I recall, you gushed."

"I? Gushed?"

"Gianni, you promised me a production."

"No," he said with great finality, and looked at me sharply with his shrewd pig eyes, "nothing was promised. Nothing is promised until a contract is signed."

The blood vessels in my temples constricted. It had been a long time since I'd suffered a migraine. In fact, I'd imagined it was impossible for a vampire to get migraines.

"I don't understand any of this. I specifically asked you for your opinion before submitting, whether you thought it was ready for production. You know how much I respect your opinion," I lied shamelessly, knowing flattering Rourke could not hurt. "You told me yourself, sitting at this same table, my opera was ready."

"You misunderstand. I didn't say your *opera* wasn't ready. I said *you're* not ready. An important distinction."

I looked around for our waiter to ask for aspirin. He'd hovered at our elbows through lunch, but now, probably on some signal from Gianni that he didn't wish to be disturbed, the waiter was nowhere to be seen. Not that I thought aspirin would help, but the spike of pain stabbing at the base of my skull was enough to make me desperate to try anything. What medicine is strong enough to help a vampire?

"Then I do misunderstand," I snapped. "The opera is ready, but I'm not—what the fuck is that supposed to mean?"

"I refuse to discuss this if you're going to take that tone."

Through the frustration and the pain, the absurdity suddenly struck me.

Hiding during the daylight hours in his lair near the last pushpin added to my map of Manhattan, the killer was planning his next act of bestiality while I lunched with a buffoon. Lieutenant Mowbray was probably eating a sidewalk vendor's hot dog between interviews with possible witnesses. I had an even greater responsibility than Mowbray to stop the killing, yet there I sat, allowing an obnoxious phony whom I neither respected nor liked to waste my time over an opera that, no matter how brilliant I happened to think my work was, was not worth the loss of a single human life.

"Please explain why my opera is ready but I'm not," I said. "I'm afraid that I can't follow the logic."

"The program board was extremely impressed with *Vanity Fair*, as you know. Good story, good characterization, thoroughly modern and yet very—what is the proper word?—musical. Contemporary music tends to be unlistenable, and so few are willing to pay to have their ears assaulted. But your opera was extremely, dare I say even *consummately*, listenable."

"So why won't you produce it?"

"As Cosima says, 'People don't know what they like, but they like what they know.' Our patrons like to hear their favorites: Mozart, Verdi, Puccini. We could produce Rossini's *Barber of Seville* every season and be able to rely on selling out the house. What do you think would happen if we put Parker's *Vanity Fair* on stage?"

"Yes, I can see the problem, but you said you were ready to try something *new*."

"New, David, but not necessarily unknown."

Rourke's eyes began to glitter. I could see he was bearing down upon a truffle.

"We are looking for a new opera, David, but we also need a *name*."

"And my name is insufficiently well known to sell tickets?"

"That is it exactly. You are so very perceptive. You are known to the cognoscenti, but you've yet to make your mark with our more casual aficionados."

"With all due modesty, Gianni, I submitted an excellent piece of work. Won't good reviews and promotion—of which you are an undisputed master—sell tickets?"

"Perhaps, but the risk is too great. We could not sustain an outright flop. Which is why I decided it would be more prudent on this first outing into the twentieth century to go with a name that could be easily marketed to our audience."

"And did you manage to find such a name?"

Rourke, grinning, nodded.

"Am I going to have to pry it out of you a syllable at a time, or are you going to tell me whose opera you're producing?"

"Mine," Rourke said.

I squeezed my eyes closed against the fire in my brain.

"I don't know why I didn't think of it sooner. It's perfect. Everybody in opera knows Gianni Rourke. I was in both *Time* and *Newsweek* this year, you know. *USA Today* is doing a story on me next month. The name Gianni Rourke is, if I do say so myself, synonymous with opera. Perhaps after I pave the way, you may follow me the next season."

I was barely listening. My head hurt so badly that I wanted

to scream. Rourke, oblivious, rejoiced about how the world would celebrate his future triumph.

"I call it *Warhol in Hell.* It will be *the* sensation of the next season. You're going to hear the same thing again and again from smart people after my opera debuts, but remember you heard it here first: *Warhol in Hell* will revolutionize opera. I'll sell more tickets than *Phantom* and *Les Mis* combined. Properly produced, with the right staging and special effects, *Warhol* could be the first opera to kick the shit out of Broadway, box office–wise. Some will say opera is not ready for nudity, but that is what they said when *Oh, Calcutta* was preparing to open on Broadway. If it will work for theater, it will work for opera. I'm going to bring my opera company into the twenty-first century, bypassing the twentieth century altogether, if I have to drag it kicking and screaming. Cosima disagrees on all points, of course, but this time I have him outmanned and outgunned."

Rourke rubbed his hands together gleefully.

"Now that I have my people on the program committee, I shall do as I please. I don't need to tell you Pauline Bettendorf is a powerful ally. Cosima will just have to lump it. Are you all right, David? You're looking a bit peaked."

I shook my head, but Rourke paid no attention; his inquiry was merely *pro forma.*

"I'll open with a tribe of naked devils dancing to a primitive tattoo." He beat the rhythm on the table with his left hand. "Warhol—"

Bursts of light were shooting before my closed eyes. I pushed my fingers against my temples as if I could force the fire from my skull.

"—descending in a neon cloud, with laser lights—"

The plate glass window behind us exploded.

Thousands of tiny bits of green-hued double-pane glass rained down on the room, while dozens of small bursts popped as water goblets and wine glasses shattered throughout the restaurant. Women screamed. Waiters dropped trays and ran. People threw themselves to the floor and scrambled for cover. The maitre d', running for the door at full speed, slammed into a bus cart, sending a stack of dirty dishes flying.

"Get down, you fool!" Rourke shouted, trying to hide his massive girth beneath the table. "They're trying to shoot me!"

"There isn't any shooting," I said, my voice oddly calm.

I was a little unsteady when I got to my feet. A crowd was

gathering on the sidewalk, looking at all the shattered glass in mute amazement. Inside the restaurant, people were picking themselves up and gingerly removing glass from their clothing.

"My God," I muttered. Realizing my hands were trembling, I surveyed the damage I'd unintentionally caused. It was a miracle no one had been hurt.

"Is the shooting over?" Rourke asked from beneath the table.

"I said there wasn't any shooting," I snapped.

"What was it? A sonic boom?"

"It must have been something like that." I rolled my head a little to the left, a little to the right.

My migraine was gone.

"Give me a hand, would you?" Rourke asked, reaching up with a grunt.

I turned away from Rourke's hand and walked out.

VI

Another Murder

CHRONICLE NOTES: David Parker's journal, continued.

—Editor

Another horror—this one so close that I wonder if the killer knows about *me* . . .

I must not let that possibility, or my emotions, cloud my mind. I must bend myself to the task at hand, setting down the details as precisely as possible, as the *Illuminati* demand.

It started tonight when I decided to revisit the building where Sharon Patter had died. As I turned onto her block, I decided to open myself completely to see what my *Vampiri* senses might discover. I let down my shield and reached out for even the faintest trace of the killer's presence. If I could only get some weak hint of the monster, I thought . . .

A terrible mistake.

Voices came roaring into my head so fast that I nearly fainted. I closed my eyes, stumbled, felt myself bump against the exterior wall of a building. There seemed to be a thousand voices inside my head, all speaking at once, muttering, muttering, muttering in the most maddening way. But then a single emotion began to emerge from the dissonant tangle, building until it overpowered the others warring for preeminence within my reeling mind. The next thing I knew raw fear was pumping into my body like a lethal jolt of electricity. A thousand frightened souls were crying out in the night, their horror striking me with such force that I nearly screamed.

It was more than I could stand.

I closed my mind to everything.

The night became quiet. Not quiet, of course, but relatively so, for it is never truly quiet in New York. Still, the hum of traffic and buzzing arc lamps was soothing after the relentless roar of so many terrified minds.

More careful the next time, I opened my mind by the merest fraction of a degree, reaching out to probe for a single mind.

The horror grabbed more strongly the second time, as if its initial probe had found my weaknesses and now sought to exploit them to the fullest. The fear—so inadequate a word for what I felt!—pulled me off balance, spinning me around to the left. I felt a flash of pain as elbow and then cheek scraped against the rough brick wall. I pulled my hands up to protect my face, as helpless as a blind man attacked by dogs. I was dimly aware of people stepping widely around me, no doubt thinking I was a dangerous psychotic having a fit.

I was falling forward into a vortex of fear, spinning downward in a sickeningly quick spiral.

The spinning abruptly stopped.

No longer on the street, I gradually perceived that I was within the nightmare of a woman who imagined herself the fiend's next victim. She clawed against the killer's laughing face—I clawed against it, too, feeling pain as my knuckles blindly struck brick.

A street person—a ragged old man conversing with the shoe he cradled in his hands like an infant—watched me with interest. Battling imaginary devils was an activity he seemed to understand.

I shook off the horror and stood there on the sidewalk for a long minute, taking deep breaths, fighting to regain control of my mind.

I dared not open myself up like that again. Terror hung too heavy in the air that night.

And then, like someone slowly understanding that the person beside him in bed won't wake up because she is dead, a terrible realization began to coalesce. The fear was too intense, too focused, too immediate, to be merely ambient anxiety the night after a savage killing in the neighborhood. It was more than that. Mortals are, after all, as capable as the *Vampiri* of receiving psychic impressions of things they might not yet "know" via the ordinary five senses. What I was picking up was not the fear radiating from the previous night's murder. The sensation was far too strong, far too *fresh*, for it to be just that.

The killer had struck again.

I began to run toward Sharon Patter's building, sensing that was the dark vibration's nexus. The reflections of flashing red lights were thrown against the buildings on the opposite side of the street when I turned onto the block.

The same neighborhood.

The same building.

"Dracula" had returned.

I pulled my coat around me against the evening chill, even though the night was, in fact, rather warm.

I psychically misdirected the uniforms so that they looked the other way when I slipped through the yellow plastic cordon and into the lobby. The homicide detectives were gathered in one corner by the concierge's desk. They didn't see me. I made sure of that. I was invisible to their minds.

A man's shoe lay discarded in the middle of the lobby floor. There was a black sock in the shoe. I looked closer. There was a part of the foot in the sock, bone snapped off at the ankle.

This was where it had happened. Not upstairs, behind the safety of a locked door, but in a public space visible from the street or by anybody using the elevators. It was impossible to fathom such carelessness, or to imagine a vampire so oblivious to the danger of being seen by people passing by on the street outside the window-lined lobby.

I looked around slowly, *seeing* everything. It had been *him*, of course—my murderous nemesis. A faint trace of his poisoned vibration remained in the air, fading quickly. I looked left, then right. There was no directionality to his trace. He was as careful as always. I wouldn't be able to track him more than half a block.

"Hey! What are you doing in here?"

I'd allowed the blocks I'd placed in the policemen's minds to dissolve. I needed to speak with them.

"My name is David Parker."

"So?"

"I don't see Lieutenant Mowbray."

"He's not here. Beat it." The short detective whistled through his teeth and pointed toward the uniforms. "Who let this guy in?"

"What do you mean Mowbray's not here?"

"Your vision's good but your hearing is a problem. I just said that Mowbray's not here. So unless you want me to run you in for obstructing police business, get the hell out of here. Now."

The detective was shorter than the others, barely tall enough to meet the departmental height requirement. Short cops were always trouble.

"I'm writing a . . ."

"I know exactly who you are and what you're writing. Mowbray can talk to whoever he wants, but I ain't working with any ghouls."

I held up my hands to placate the cop and began walking backward, meeting the little policeman's glare with my eyes.

"Okay, I'm going, but where's Mowbray tonight?"

"Do I look like his mother?"

"Give me a break. Where's the lieutenant?"

I sent out a gentle suggestion, nothing to provoke resistance in the detective's stubborn mind, just a gentle nudge: *It's all right. Tell me where he is.*

The cop blew out his breath through his teeth. "He didn't come in to work. Must have the flu or something."

"And nobody called him about this? Come on. This is another 'Dracula' number, isn't it? Isn't he coming down? Somebody must have called him."

"Judas priest," the detective exclaimed. "He wasn't home and didn't answer his pager, if it's any business of yours, which it isn't."

Strange, I thought.

"Not a female this time?" I nodded toward the severed foot.

I'd backed most of the way to the yellow cordon. I didn't expect the cop to answer, but he surprised me.

"The doorman."

"The doorman?" I repeated.

"Is there some kind of echo in here?" the cop said, taking a step toward me that was intended to make me beat a faster retreat. Instead, I stopped.

"But that doesn't fit. Not the doorman."

It didn't fit. Not at all. The others had all been women.

"Tell me something I don't know, Parker."

The little cop continued to surprise me by offering a few details. He hadn't wanted to talk at first, but now that he'd started, he didn't seem able to stop.

"He ripped out his throat and tore the body in pieces. And I mean fucking pieces. Fifteen years and I ain't never seen anything like this. Not ever. Guy must have the strength of a gorilla. And a slimeball like that doorman after so many good-looking women. How do you explain that?"

I shrugged. That made two of us who didn't know.

"And not clue one. I really hate this guy. He's making us all look like incompetent assholes."

I looked down at the white floor tile, trying to bring the information into focus. A pool of blood had formed beneath the severed foot. The blood looked purple rather than red beneath the lobby's fluorescent ceiling lights.

Where *was* Detective Mowbray? His absence made my stomach feel uneasy.

I looked up to ask the little cop another question and realized he'd already walked away.

There was a pay phone outside the Korean grocery store around the corner. I dialed Mowbray's apartment. The phone rang. I stared at the neat rows of oranges, apples, and plums arranged on the slanting outdoor display shelves. One plastic five-gallon bucket held bundles of carnations, another individual roses.

No answer. I didn't know his pager number. I could have lifted it out of the little cop's mind, if I'd thought it would have done any good.

I got into a taxi and gave the driver Mowbray's address. I didn't say to hurry. My sense of foreboding told me that there was no reason to hurry.

Mowbray lived in an Italian neighborhood, upstairs over a

dry cleaner. I paid the driver and got out. I could feel it immediately. The presence hung in the air like the smell of ozone and burned hair. I followed it straight to the street door that led up to Mowbray's apartment.

I paused, reaching out carefully with my senses, tentative after my earlier shocks in Patter's neighborhood. The killer was not there, unless he was masking his presence, watching me from a darkened doorway. I looked up and down the street. There was no reason to believe the killer was still there.

A Eurasian girl walked past me, her long black hair luxuriously fine. I felt the Hunger tug at me. I did not need to answer it, yet the urge was powerful—almost too powerful to resist.

I told myself to get a grip. Otherwise, I'd end up like the doomed monster I was hunting.

The girl looked back at me over her shoulder. She saw me watching. She smiled.

I turned away.

I had to maintain control.

The door was unlocked. I went through it and up the stairs without bothering to ring Mowbray's bell. I tried his door. It was unlocked, too. I didn't open it at first, but stood with the knob in my hand. I closed my eyes and made a conscious effort to focus. I could not allow what I saw—or *felt*—to prevent me from observing everything. The devil is in the details, Wolf likes to say—and in this instance, almost literally.

I opened the door to Mowbray's apartment.

A reservoir of the killer's presence rolled over me like smoke from a closed room, flooding my mind with the disorienting fog of lunatic frenzy.

For the first time in the months I had been stalking the killer, I had a sense of what he was really like. The vampire was old—not as old as Wolf, perhaps, but nearly so. He'd killed countless times. He was mad, of course, but not in a way that prevented him from passing in the mortal world. He was brilliantly calculating, a wolf among sheep.

I sensed a strong determination in his seemingly random violence. There was a purpose behind his actions. I detected no weariness, no desire to be stopped. He enjoyed killing, and intended to go on killing, and would make no unconscious mistakes to help those who wanted him stopped.

I had a strong sense that it would be difficult to stop him. Maybe impossible—at least for me.

The dim remanant of the killer's trace was fast ebbing out of the room. A dozen small impressions came to me in a rush as I plugged myself into his vibration:

—A woman named Anna Lee, whose long, blonde hair was tied up in satin ribbons.

—Three words of Latin: "Sic semper tyrannis!"

—Terrible pain and the sensation of drowning.

—A shadowy Vampiri *woman so powerful that even the savage I was hunting feared her.*

—A frail young woman, unclothed, her hair cut short, shivering with fear in the corner of a dingy room. (Unlike the others, this memory was recent.)

—And, beneath all else, a hunger for revenge and a consuming hatred—of whom or what, I could not say as I set out to search Mowbray's silent apartment.

Before me was a short hallway leading into a living room. The furnishings were sparse and masculine to the point of severity. The home of a middle-aged man with simple tastes who lived alone. Mowbray was divorced. He had grown children somewhere, he'd told me without offering details.

The apartment was dark except for the kitchen, I walked toward the light, moving my feet as if they had weights attached to them.

Mowbray was on the kitchen floor on his back. His neck was twisted to the left at an unnatural angle. It was broken.

"You'll never know how hard I tried to help you," I said quietly to Mowbray's corpse. Send a thief to catch a thief—wasn't that the saying?

A chair from the dinette set was tipped on its side in the middle of the room near Mowbray's feet. The glass cover from the ceiling light had been removed and placed on top of the refrigerator, along with a lightbulb from the fixture. A second lightbulb was shattered on the floor in front of the sink.

I knelt beside the body.

Mowbray's eyes were frozen open in an expression that was more surprised than horrified. He must have known the truth at the end. By then it was, of course, too late.

There were too small, pink marks on Mowbray's neck over the jugular vein. The enzymes in the vampire's saliva had nearly healed the twin punctures, even in the tissue of a clinically dead man. The coroner would take no notice of the bite marks during the autopsy. The cause of death would be officially recorded as an accident, a broken neck resulting from a fall while changing a lightbulb in a ceiling light fixture. Death by misadventure. His family and friends would shake their heads and try to forget.

The killer didn't typically bother to disguise his handiwork, but he was too smart to link himself to a policeman's death. That would be risking too much. The killer had even left Mowbray's ring finger attached to his hand. It must have been hard for the criminal to depart without his usual trophy.

As I stood looking at the dead detective, I realized the doorman had been killed because he'd seen on to something. Whatever it was, Mowbray must have found out about it, and now he was dead, too.

I quickly went through the darkened apartment. There were a few faint, fading signs of the murderer's presence glowing in the darkness, a hint of green phosphorescence. The killer had searched the apartment well. If Mowbray had anything that revealed what the murdered doorman had told him about the killer, the killer had found it and taken it with him.

I locked the door behind myself when I left.

VII
Dreaming

CHRONICLE NOTES: David Parker's journal, continued.

—Editor

I had the most peculiar and vivid dream. It started with the woman's voice. . . .

It was late at night. The streets were deserted. I did not recognize the town. It was certainly not New York, and it didn't look like London. The streets were narrow alleys hemmed in by ancient buildings four or five stories tall built all the way to the curbstone. The architecture was Mediterranean—Italian, or perhaps Greek.

There was a woman in my dream. Her name was Princess Nicoletta Vittorini di Medusa. I do not know how I knew her name, but I did. Dreams have their own peculiar logic.

Nicoletta led me to a park in the middle of a roundabout where four streets intersected. The park was in the middle circle, just iron benches around a fountain. Lily pads grew in the water, and the free stretches reflected in moonlight the statue of the woman on horseback that the fountain commemorated. We were in the Mediterranean somewhere.

Nicoletta sat down on a bench, and she touched my hand, inviting me to sit beside her.

"I must tell you something, David Parker."

There was only a trace of Italian accent in Nicoletta's voice. A woman of culture, widely traveled and widely read. It must have been her classic beauty that made her face seem familiar. Renaissance artists like Botticelli had picked women who resembled Nicoletta as models for their paintings. Her face was heart-shaped, with almond-shaped Tyrrhenian eyes that glowed with their own inner light. Her flawless skin was milky white, and the creaminess of her complexion was set off by the long, obsidian hair that she parted in the middle and wore free so that it fell in gracefully turning curls past her shoulders. She was no more than five feet tall and delicately made, as perfectly formed as a Michelangelo statue. Yet there was something almost frail about Nicoletta's appearance, as if her bones were made of porcelain, not marble. I felt an instinctive protectiveness toward her.

"I know why you've come here." Her voice was soft, the whisper of two pieces of velvet brushed against one another.

"You do?"

I did not try to resist the impulse to touch her luxurious hair. She smiled when I touched it lightly, and I felt the tingle of electricity arcing between us. We were sitting very close, her face upturned toward mine, her cheeks as perfect as newly fallen snow, her lips the color of wet cherries. The cleft between her breasts was just visible beyond the final button of the black silk blouse. I wanted to kiss her forehead, her lips, to bury my face in her breasts and die a thousand agonizingly sweet deaths in her arms.

"You have come to kill Scorpio's master."

No, I thought. This is not how I want my dream to go.

"You must, for that is your fate. Only then can I be yours."

I stared at Nicoletta.

"Scorpio is his secret name. He's known by other names in other places, but surely you must know that. The same is true of his new master."

"Scorpio—is he the killer I've been seeking?"

"He is very dangerous," she said obliquely. "But not as dangerous as his master."

"Where is he—where are they?" I asked, trying to keep my voice from betraying my agitation.

"He's no longer in New York City."

I nodded. She was talking about the outlaw. He hadn't killed for two weeks—at least not in New York. I already suspected he'd fled the city.

"Where is he now?"

"In a small town."

"Where?"

"You will find out soon enough. He is completely insane. He is an animal that does nothing but kill. Many have tried to stop him and many have failed. But you, *mio*, will stop his madness forever."

I felt her small hand on my arm, another alighting like a sparrow behind my neck. She pulled me toward her and sealed my smile with her kiss.

"I know a great many things, David Parker," Nicoletta whispered into my ear as I held her, "more than you imagine. I know all about the killer, about you, your friend Wolfgang, the *Illuminati*, and Scorpio. Only I can bring you real peace, my love. I am wiser than them all because I have lived an eternity. You must learn to trust me as you trust no one else, David Parker. And you must do as I say."

I looked into her Tyrrhenian eyes and saw such knowledge, such *understanding*, for me, of me.

"You must not upset yourself over these absurd errands the *Illuminati* command you to perform. They are like children with the games they play. You do not need the *Illuminati*. You do not need Mozart. They cannot help you."

She put one hand—small and delicate as a bird's wing—against my cheek.

"I have been waiting for you for a long, long time, David Parker. I can give you what you need. Soon, you will come to me. And we will be together. Forever."

I could not take my eyes away from hers. Her words were like fire poured into my heart.

"We will fly away to my villa in Sicily when we are finished with them all, *amore mio*, and spend the centuries making love."

Nicoletta's kiss transported me to a summer garden beside the Ionian Sea. Moonlight splashed across Roman ruins, which a master gardener had skillfully incorporated into the living landscape. The air was sweet with the aroma of herbs, cedar, and sleeping flowers. Somewhere beyond a sentry line of trees, water splashed in a fountain, the sound a lighter counterpoint to the deeper rhythm of waves washing up on the rocky shoreline.

In her magical garden, Nicoletta Vittorini di Medusa looked like something infinitely more wonderful than a mere princess. Standing there, with silvery moonlight washing over her raven-black hair and flawless skin, she seemed to me to be a goddess. The Goddess of the Moon. Or the Goddess of the Night. Or someone out of mythology, like Diana, whose sign was the moon and who ruled over the hunt.

I drew her close to me again, breathing in the sweetness of Nicoletta's garden and the far more intoxicating sweetness of her skin. I felt her heart beating against mine—the slow, powerful strokes of an immortal with power amassed over many centuries. I felt my own heart slow. Nicoletta's lips again found mine. My fear vanished. I knew my heart would not stop. A moment longer and our hearts beat as if one.

I do not know how, but Nicoletta had imparted some of her ancient *Vampiri* power to me, a trick not even Wolf could perform. Nicoletta had made me as strong as she—or nearly so. A peculiar energy set my nerves to tingling. Such tremendous strength! If I'd commanded the ruined Roman temple to reassemble itself, I do not doubt the fallen columns and buried pilasters would have risen into the air and fit themselves back together like a titanic puzzle.

Yet the best part of the dream was the wonderful sense of freedom it imparted. For the first time since I'd joined the *Illuminati*, I felt the heavy sense of responsibility lifted from my shoulders. I even forgot that I was no happier as one of the *Vampiri* than I'd been as a mortal.

"Until Jerusalem, my love. Until Jerusalem . . ."

And then, as suddenly as it had taken shape within my mind, the dream ended.

* * *

Our table at The Gita was beside the front window. I could look out through the diagonal latticework at the street and be reminded that I was not in a maharaja's palace in the shadow of the Himalayas, but in New York City, where the murderer I was hunting had stopped murdering—a development that did little to ease my apprehensions. I could see The Blind King across the street, the usual assortment of oddballs loitering around the chess shop's door.

"Rourke has decided not to produce your opera."

"As if that matters."

"Staging that farce of his instead," Wolf continued with an expression of great disgust. "I suppose there is no reason you cannot be expected to fulfill the commission the *Illuminati* have given you."

I glared across the table. Our relationship had been strained by Lieutenant Mowbray's death.

"Ach, you are so irritable these days, *mein Herr.*" Wolf smiled blandly. "Be all of that as it may, it is fortunate that you are free to accept a position with the Morningside College Visiting Artist Program. I arranged for your agent to say as much. You are to visit his office in the morning to sign the necessary contracts. You'll need to get packing. You should be off to Jerusalem within the week."

I felt something tighten around my heart. "Where?"

"Not in the Middle East," Wolf said with an enormous smile. "Your destination is somewhat less exotic. You are going to Jerusalem, Mississippi. What is wrong? You look quite pale."

"It's nothing," I lied. The memory of my peculiar dream—and Princess Nicoletta Vittorini di Medusa—came back to me with unusual strength. She had hinted that we'd meet again in Jerusalem. Her voice returned to me from the dream: "*Until Jerusalem, my love. Until Jerusalem . . .*"

"You have been to this place before, perhaps?"

I shook my head.

"Yet you are no stranger to Jerusalem."

There were things that could not be hidden from Wolf. "I had a dream about a town called Jerusalem, that's all. I thought it was the Jerusalem in Israel."

Wolf looked at me with great interest. "You did not tell me you had been dreaming."

I shrugged. Dreams contain coded messages about the future, Wolf said, and he'd often encouraged me to discuss my dreams as a way of teaching me to translate their meaning. However, I disliked the exercise so much that he finally quit asking. Dreams are mostly made up of meaningless imagery; I found talking about them embarrassing.

"Tell me about this dream."

"You sound like a Freudian analyst."

"I knew Freud in Vienna, and I can tell you that I most certainly do not. Tell me about this most interesting prophetic dream. When did you have it?"

"A few nights ago. I thought it was just a dream."

"But this has been my point precisely. There is no such thing as 'just' a dream, and you have again proved it. Tell me in detail. Leave nothing out."

"There's nothing to tell."

I didn't want to tell Wolf about Princess Nicoletta; I suspected she was no more than an idealized version of the real princess in my life.[1] I wondered how Wolf would react if I told him my dream princess had said that the *Illuminati* would not be able to help me find happiness—something I'd started to suspect long before she suggested it.

"The outlaw has gone to Jerusalem?" I asked to change the subject.

"Ja."

"How do you know?"

"I have been doing my own dreaming."

"Do you know who he is—the killer?"

Wolf's expression became dark. He shook his head. There were limits even to his powers.

"We digress. You must try to remember the details of your dream, David. The smallest remembrance could prove significant."

I sighed, realizing it would be easier to concede. "I think I dreamed that the killer has an accomplice, a mortal named Scorpio."

"I find it difficult to imagine him hunting with a mortal. Outlaws are not like we of the *Illuminati*, David. The only relationship they have with mortals is that which exists between predator and prey. A servant, perhaps—I should more properly say 'slave'—but never an accomplice."

[1]David Parker was estranged from his *Vampiri* wife, Princess Tatiana Nicolaievna Romanov.

"Then maybe my dream about Scorpio simply means that he is a Scorpio, that the outlaw was born in whatever month Scorpios are born." I blushed to hear myself assign such a preposterous meaning to something I was certain was essentially meaningless.

"That is a possibility," Wolf said, pleased with the thought. "It may help. A bit at a time, the pieces make the whole."

The waiter brought us two more bottles of St. Pauli Girl.

"When do I leave?"

Wolf looked at me sharply, then began to smile. He'd doubted I would agree to follow the criminal to Jerusalem.

"You must leave just as soon as you can, *mein Herr*. I have arranged the summer residency for you at the local college in Jerusalem. How does one put it? Ah, yes, the residency will be your 'cover.' And I have a treat I know you will enjoy. The school wants to mount a production of your opera in August at the Morningside Summer Festival. You may not have heard of it, but it is a rather respected August workshop for university-level musicians, a Southern Spoletto. Gianni Rourke's loss will be the festival's gain."

"Of course I've heard of the Morningside Festival."

"You do not sound excited."

"How can I worry about music while the outlaw continues to kill?"

"You must, *mein Herr.* Do not let this shadow touch your heart, David, or it will pollute your soul. Go to Jerusalem. Produce your opera. Stop the outlaw. A good summer's work."

"At least Jerusalem is smaller than New York. That will make it easier to find him."

"Just remember that it can work the other way 'round. Be careful that he does not find you first."

"I'll take all the usual precautions. I'll mask my presence."

"He knows a trick or two himself. Be careful, *mein Herr.*"

"Why don't you come with me to Mississippi? For the hundredth time, please help me with this. I don't think I have what it takes to stop the son of a bitch."

"I am helping you, David. I've told you where the outlaw has gone. He should be no match for you, if you keep your head about you. Like most killers, I'm sure he is a barbarian who knows nothing of the higher powers."

"*Please* go with me," I asked with heavy emphasis.

"I am sorry, but I cannot. This *Illuminati* assignment is yours, my friend. How will your powers develop if you do not exercise them? Besides," Wolf added darkly, "I have my own affairs to attend to."

"Yes, and you won't let me help you with your problems, either."

"Your concerns are yours, David, and mine are mine. We must each do what we must do."

Wolf sat looking at me, his expression implacable. I saw that he could not be moved.

"Then it seems I'm going to Mississippi." I paused. "Alone."

Wolf studied me closely. "You are still feeling pain about Tatiana."

I must have looked as if ice water had been thrown in my face. Wolf reached across the table and lightly patted my arm.

"Give it time, my young friend," he said kindly. "There will be other loves and other dreams. Trust my experience when I assure you that it will be so."

I told myself that Wolf had to be right, for otherwise he wouldn't have had the will to have lived so long. Perhaps the proof of what he said was the tenderness I felt for the imaginary princess who'd come to me as I drifted in the twilight space between sleep and wakefulness.

But still I did not tell Wolf about Nicoletta.

She was *my* dream.

PART II

Letters and Documents

I

Lab Report

CHRONICLE NOTES: "Becker Thorne" was bending over the dying doorman when police arrived. The killer ran to the second floor, smashed through a window in the back of the building, and leaped to the alley. Broken glass slashed one of "Thorne's" arteries, enabling police technicians to gather blood specimens for testing.

—Editor

To: New York Police Department, Homicide Division
From: Dr. Richard Thompson,[1] Chief of Hematology, Benson Labs
Subject: Blood sample SA-10056-B

Part I: Introduction

New York Police Department evidence technicians collected specimen tagged with NYPD Identification Number SA-10056-B. Said specimen was drawn from a pool of fresh blood on the sidewalk beneath a broken window. The investigator's initial hypothesis was that the blood was from person or persons unknown involved in the Nick Reilly homicide. The

[1]Dr. Richard Thompson was killed the night after the doorman and Lieutenant Robert Mowbray were slain, when his Porsche struck a bridge abutment in New Jersey. The blue paint from another vehicle was found on the driver's side of the red Porsche, leading police to conclude an unknown second vehicle had been involved in the fatal crash. Dr. Thompson's lab was ransacked the same night and an arson fire set, destroying the blood specimens as well as the pathologist's notes and records. A syringe containing traces of Demerol was found near the emptied drug cabinet, making it appear that an addict had been responsible for the damage. David Parker searched Dr. Thompson's Long Island home and recovered the pathologist's handheld Sony tape recorder. The microcassette in the recorder contained the only version of Dr. Thompson's report on the *Vampiri* blood specimen to survive him.

secondary hypothesis was that the blood belonged to the victim of the aforementioned homicide, to wit, Nick Reilly, a white male, age 32.

The specimen was immediately noteworthy in its failure to coagulate. Blood exposed to air typically begins to lose its viscosity within eight to ten minutes. The blood was on the sidewalk approximately one hour before a sample was drawn, yet it showed none of the usual signs of coagulation. Initial testing indicated the specimen was chemically similar to blood serum, which lacks fibrinogen, the chief clotting agent in whole blood.

Approximately six hours after arriving at the lab, the specimen—by then divided into a number of subsamples for analysis—underwent a dramatic and unexplained morphological modification, transforming itself from a free-flowing liquid to a tough, non-water-soluble compound resembling Teflon.

The possibility exists that the specimen was contaminated prior to arriving at the lab with an unknown substance that led to the reaction. Further analysis is required to identify the change agent.

Unfortunately, the specimen's sudden desiccation rendered it questionable whether enough DNA could be extracted for genetic matching to a suspect. Further attempts to extract DNA from the specimen are continuing at this time.

Part II: Testing

The complete battery of hematological tests were underway on the sample at the time of desiccation. Full or partial tests were run in the following areas:

1. Blood typing (red-blood-cell antigen analysis)
2. Red and white blood cell counts
3. Hemoglobin concentration
4. Sedimentation rate
5. Blood cell structure
6. Characteristics relating to hemoglobin and other plasma proteins
7. Blood chemistry
8. Enzyme activity

The technical report, including copies of the autoanalyzer printouts, complete where available, accompanies this report.

Part III: Anomalies present in specimen

A number of abnormalities and irregularities were observed in the specimen.

A: Clotting factors

As previously mentioned, until the moment of dramatic desiccation the specimen exhibited characteristics similar to blood serum, from which the fibrinogen has been removed to prevent clotting during storage and transfusion. Indeed, no fibrinogen appeared present in the initial battery of tests. There are two possible explanations for the absence of fibrinogen in the sample:

1. The first possibility is that the fibrinogen had been removed in a blood lab. This seems unlikely, since it would mean the blood found on the sidewalk did not come from a cut but was spilled from a plasma bag. Or, an even more unlikely scenario, perhaps the subject cut on the broken glass recently underwent a massive plasma transfusion. Both possibilities seem remote.

2. Another, more likely, explanation is that the absence of fibrinogen resulted from unknown biological actions in the donors whose blood was commingled in the specimen. (See below.)

A pronounced absence of thrombocytes was observed in the specimen. A typical adult has between 150,000 and 400,000 platelets per cubic millimeter of blood. Fewer than 10,000 platelets per cubic millimeter were present in the specimen. A platelet count of this level is typically indicative of a number of serious pathologies, including leukemia, thrombocytopenia, hemophilia, and von Willebrand's disease.

Data and analysis time were insufficient to identify the exact nature of the pathology responsible for the platelet count and other anomalies.

In summary, it appears likely that the individual whose blood was recovered on the sidewalk suffered from a pathology that depleted his blood's fibrinogen and thrombocyte levels. Further implications of such a condition are discussed in more detail below in this report.

B: Red cell malformations

Three types of erythrocytes, or red blood cells, were identified in the specimen:

1. Healthy adult red cells: Biconcave in shape, with no visible structures within the cell membrane, each lacking a nu-

cleus, as is normal in mature erythrocyte cells. These cells measured approximately 7.8 micrometers. Hemoglobin—which transports oxygen in the blood—constituted about a third of each cell, as is typical in a healthy adult.

2. Diseased red cells: These erythrocytes were approximately the size of the healthy cells, but exhibited an abnormal elongating similar to that present in sickle-cell anemia. The abnormal cells resembled the "ghost" cells that dying red cells become after they lose their hemoglobin. Each of these cells contained a nucleus that appeared to be densely packed with genetic information. Since healthy red cells lose their nuclei as they mature, the presence of DNA in the nuclei of the diseased erythrocytes indicates an unexplained abnormality in the donor's capability to produce healthy red blood cells. Additionally, these abnormal cells displayed an anomaly that is unmentioned in the medical literature. These DNA-rich "ghost" cells displayed a faint bluish tint, due, preliminary test results indicated, to the unexplained presence of *hemocyanin.* (See further discussion of hemocyanin below.)

3. Hybrid cells: These cells appear to be the result of an unknown biological action—potentially resulting from action of a retrovirus—in which abnormal erythrocytes inject the healthy red blood cells with foreign genetic information, resulting in the formation of a "super" erythrocyte. These mutant cells were larger than the typical normal red blood cell, measuring approximately 10 micrometers in diameter. Preliminary evidence indicated that the hemoglobin in the hybrid cells had superior oxygen-transport capabilities. A hemoglobin molecule contains four iron atoms, each binding with one oxygen molecule as the blood passes through the lungs. Subsequent tests—incomplete at the time the blood desiccated—indicated the hemoglobin in the hybrid red blood cells had a much higher affinity for oxygen than the normal cells, each molecule of hybrid hemoglobin capable of bonding with *eight* oxygen molecules. These "super" erythrocytes, however, appeared to be extremely short-lived. The cell membrane in the hybrids was abnormally thin, perhaps due to the stretching required to contain the greater cell volume. This additional stress to the cell membrane seemed to make the hybrid cells especially prone to hemolysis—the rupture of cells, resulting in the hemoglobin dissolving into the plasma medium. A high percentage of the hybrid cells observed in the specimen evidenced premature

coagulate necrosis and other morphological characteristics associated with cell death.

C: Blood typing

A portion of the specimen was put in a centrifuge to separate the red blood cells from the plasma. Additionally, this action separated the healthy cells from the diseased and the hybrid cells. The division of red blood cells made it possible to identify the blood group among three distinct sets of cells. This, in turn, led to the discovery that the sample of blood was not from one but *two* distinct donors. Furthermore, blood grouping tests indicated that the hybrid cells were apparently formed from the healthy cells of Donor A after undergoing a retrovirus-like action instigated by the diseased cells of Donor B.

Blood cells are broken into four major groups according to the antigen molecules attached to the cells. These common types are A, B, AB, and O. The healthy cells tested to be type A. The damaged cells possessed the antigen properties of group B. The hybrid cells proved to be type AB.

Although the blood group of the hybrid cells could indicate the presence of a third donor, it is my opinion, based upon the other available test data indicating the action of the B-type cells against the A-type cells, that the AB hybrid cells are a result of the reaction, heretofore unobserved in the medical literature, of the B cells against the A cells.

This hypothesis is strengthened by the consideration that the homicide victim had type A blood. Further evidence supporting this hypothesis is found in the fact that the AB cells had a very weak antigen reaction—so weak that the blood group was only able to be identified using the lab's most sensitive equipment. Although confirmation requires further testing, it appears that the antigens in the AB cells are so mild that the specimen could be transfused into virtually any recipient without provoking the adverse reactions common to mismatched transfusions.

D: Other anomalies observed in the specimen

Other unusual pathologies among the diseased cells in the specimen were observed:

1. The low density of red cells in the B donor was indicative of severe polycythemia.

2. A blue pigment known as hemocyanin, noted above, was isolated in the damaged cells. This pigment, which is blue because of its copper content, has not been observed before in

the hemoglobin of human specimens. (Human blood gets its distinctive red coloration from its iron content.) Hemocyanin is typically found in crustaceans and other invertebrates with "open" blood systems, and is not especially efficient at transporting oxygen. The presence of hemocyanin in the unhealthy cells remains unexplained, and has never before been noted in medical literature.

3. High protein count. The plasma in the sample was remarkable for its protein content. Instead of the usual 6% to 8% protein found in mammalian blood, the aggregate sample was 80% water and 20% protein.

4. Abnormal pH. The pH of healthy blood is acidic. The sample, however, was a flat neutral balance between acidic and alkaline.

5. Elevated globulin. Globulins are plasma proteins that fight disease and toxins. Globulins were present in radically elevated levels in the specimen, indicating either the presence of a massive, potentially lethal infection or a pathology such as leukemia. It is also possible that, given the unique structure of the hybrid red cells, Donor B possesses other undescribed physiological advantages, including an extraordinary immune system, as evidenced by the globulin level.

Part IV: Preliminary conclusion

The aforementioned abnormalities lead me to believe the specimen may have come from an individual suffering from an extreme and inadequately explained condition known, albeit more in popular culture than medical literature, as *vampirism.*

In summary, the person lacerated during the most recent homicide—and whose blood was recovered from the sidewalk outside the crime scene—likely suffers from a rare blood disorder that compels him to seek transfusions of fresh blood to compensate for inadequacies in his own erythrocytes. As the "donor's" blood enters his system, genetic information from his own diseased red blood cells enters and transforms the donor's blood, resulting in a hybrid cell that has superior oxygenating characteristics—but is short-lived.

Cases of genuine vampirism are extremely rare but have been recorded in medical literature, though not in great detail. (Pathological vampirism differs quite distinctly from the somewhat more common psychological version, wherein the craving for blood has no biological basis.) Vampirism is often linked to porphyria, a state that renders individuals extremely sensitive to light and is characterized by the abnormal presence of porphyrins in the urine, which in turn stem from the breakdown of hemoglobin in the subject's own blood—and the consequential craving for blood to replace the lost hemoglobin.

I emphasize, however, that none of the recorded cases of porphyria discuss the remarkable ability to synthesize hybrid red blood cells from a reaction between the subject's diseased cells and the donor's healthy cells. Nor does the literature mention the extraordinary immunological properties present in the specimen in question.

My overall conclusion is that the person the specimen was drawn from suffers from a condition that is unreported in the literature, with far-reaching implications that present dramatic possibilities for unlocking hematological secrets that might even lead to new treatments for leukemia and other diseases of the blood and immune systems.

It is *imperative*—from a medical as well as a police standpoint—that the subject from whom this specimen was collected be taken into custody and held for further testing and study.

II

Vampires in Literature

CHRONICLE NOTES: The October 1990 edition of the *North American Literary Review* published a paper titled "The Female Destroyer: The Archetypal Vampire in Romantic English Poetry," by Victoria Buchanan, Ph.D., professor of English and Romantic Poetry, Morningside College, Jerusalem, Mississippi, from which the following is excerpted.

—*Editor*

. . . The English Romantic poets tended to present malignant supernatural beings as female. In doing so, the Romantics hardly broke new ground. One need look no further than the seminal works of literature to encounter this phenomenon. In the *Odyssey*, for example, Homer's most memorable monsters are female. Circe, the witch who turned Odysseus's men into pigs; Calypso, the nymph who detained the Greek hero as her lover for seven years; the Sirens, whose beautiful voices lured ships and their crews to destruction on the rocks—all female. Only Polyphemus, the Cyclops, was male.

The Romantics' tendency to portray monsters as women—usually sexually desirable women—seems rooted in no particular antipathy toward women. (Some feminists might argue that nineteenth-century Europe was inherently sexist, and therefore its literature was also, but that is not my view.) There is no overt evidence of misogyny in the text—or indeed the lives—of the English Romantics. On the contrary, the evidence in their art as well as their letters suggests that Byron, Keats, and Shelley greatly depended upon women as sources of inspiration. . . .

These poets were themselves attracted to their seductive female monsters, further blurring the line between the natural fear of death and a peculiar longing for death's release—an attitude typical of the writing of this period.

The Romantics were, in short, in love with the idea of death, a further turning of the earlier Elizabethan use of "sweet death" as a metaphor for sexual release. For Keats, wasting slowly away from consumption as he approached the apotheosis of his creative life, death became the object of the highest kind of romance:

Darkling I listen; and, for many a time
I have been half in love with easeful Death,
Call'd him soft names in many a mused rhyme
To take into the air my quiet breath;
Now more than ever seems it rich to die,
To cease upon the midnight with no pain. . . .

The English Romantics who followed Wordsworth and Coleridge all died young—and Coleridge's long addiction to opium must have seemed like a living death. Keats succumbed to tuberculosis; Shelley drowned while sailing; Lord Byron contracted a fatal fever while fighting in the Greek revolution.

There was nothing especially startling about the brevity of these poets' lives. The life expectancy in the nineteenth century's first half was abysmally low. Children died, as often as not, in infancy. Medical practices were primitive, with doctors likely to "treat" most conditions by bleeding the patient. For the creative mind in the nineteenth century, death was ever a constant companion. Today, most of us are able to devise strategies for denying death; the Romantics enjoyed no such luxury. Indeed, they could not escape the specter of Death; it walked with them always. . . .

Thus it is easy to understand why the Romantics carried on these passionate flirtations with seductive female monsters in their literature. It is hardly surprising that the Romantics chose to represent Death, not as a mute skeleton enveloped in a hooded black cloak, but as a beautiful woman, whose whispers and caresses were, ultimately, too sweet to resist. . . .

The Romantics' supernatural entities were frequently reinterpretations of the vampire myth.

The vampire as it is known today retains the form given to it by writers in Victorian England; they, in turn, borrowed heavily from Eastern European folklore. It was only Bram Stoker's lurid *Dracula*, published in 1897 at the close of the sexually repressive Victorian era, that recast the vampire as a male monster. Before the Victorians, vampires were nearly *always* female.

The vampire myth is, however, much older than Transylvania's Dracula (in translation, "Little Dragon"). Vampires are as old as writing and probably older, the product of the ancient oral traditions predating written culture. The vampire, much cheapened by our popular culture, is, in fact, one of the world's most enduring literary archetypes.[1] Scholars have traced the vampire back to the earliest cuneiform tablets found at Sumer and Ur. It is noteworthy that, aside from Eastern European folk traditions, the vampire archetype in literature has been almost exclusively female.

The first identifiable vampire in literature was Lilith, an As-

[1]Dr. Winthrop Malvakian's groundbreaking work, *Literary Archetypes: The Mythical Foundation of Western Fiction and Drama*, provides the framework for discussing the reoccurrence of certain common features in literature in different cultures across the ages. Dr. Malvakian's system borrows from Jung's concept that we all share a collective unconscious that reflects the experiences of primitive society. Dr. Malvakian does not specifically recognize the vampire in his system of classifying myths, although Dr. Buchanan appears to demonstrate that such an archetype does exist.

syrian demoness of the night who sucked the souls from her victims along with their blood. Rabbinical commentaries identify Lilith as Adam's first wife. Dispossessed by Eve, Lilith served as the mother of a darker race—the vampire race. According to Coptic legends about man's fall from God's grace, the serpent in the Garden of Eden was not Satan but Lilith, who used her supernatural power to transform herself into a talking snake. The vampire Lilith appears briefly in the Old Testament, although the broader significance is obscured in contemporary translations. The Revised Standard Version of Isaiah XXXIV 14 uses the phrase "night hag" in place of the more specific language found in the original Hebrew:

Yea, there shall the night hag alight,
and find for herself a resting place.

The night hag is Lilith, mother of the vampire race.

The Lilith tale is echoed in certain medieval legends that cast Cain as progenitor of the vampire race. According to these later stories, Cain, whose hands were stained with his brother's blood, was banished not just from the Garden of Eden, but from mankind. As punishment for murdering Abel, God transformed Cain into a being doomed to the immortal horror of death-in-life, shunned and feared by mortal society, forced to draw sustenance by feeding upon human blood.

Another adaptation of Lilith's tale involves the lamiae, a race of shapeshifting vampire-witches who can take the form of a beautiful woman or a serpent. The lamiae sucked children's blood. . . .

The Romantic poets, in their own interpretations of this ancient myth, were in step with a rich tradition when they cast their vampires as beautiful women. Although the female vampire might seem an unlikely theme for Romantic poetry, closer study indicates that these seductive creatures are an extremely apt symbol for a generation of poets "half in love with easeful Death." The vampire is—or was, before Bram Stoker debased the myth—the most alluring member of the world's pantheon of demons and hobgoblins. One hardly needs be a Freudian to recognize the sexual component in the way the victim surrenders completely to the monster, body and soul. Popular author Anne Rice was quoted in the *Chicago Tribune* as saying, "Vampires are the aristocrats of monsterdom." . . .

Keats dives headlong into the vampire archetype in his

Lamia. Written in 1819, *Lamia* is a continuation of the ancient Greek myth of the lamiae, in which Hermes transforms Lamia, a vampire-witch, from a serpent into a beautiful maiden who lusts for the handsome Lycius. Lycius's teacher, Apollonius, has the wisdom to recognize Lamia for what she truly is. Apollonius banishes Lamia with the power of his philosophy—a more elegant weapon than the Transylvanian's wooden stake through the heart! Alas, it is not enough to save Lycius, who, like most mortals who become romantically involved with a vampire, dies.

Keats' shapeshifting, polymorphic vampire *Lamia* contains images much more disturbing—and poetic—than anything Bram Stoker imagined:

> *Left to herself, the serpent now began*
> *To change; her elfin blood in madness ran,*
> *Her mouth foamed, and the grass, therewith besprent,*
> *Wither'd at dew so sweet and virulent;*
> *Her eyes in torture fix'd, and anguish drear,*
> *Hot, glaz'd, and wide, with lid-lashes all sear,*
> *Flash'd phosphor and sharp sparks, without one cooling tear.*

As with all vampires fitting the classical archetype, Lamia possesses telepathic powers that allow her to leave her body and travel abroad in the night.

> *. . . Where she willed, her spirit went . . .*
> *And sometimes into cities she would send*
> *Her dream, with feast and rioting to blend;*
> *And once, while among mortals dreaming thus,*
> *She saw the young Corinthian Lycius . . .*

Almost all vampires, no matter what the culture or era giving birth to them in literature, possess the power to deceive mortals, to disguise their true selves and trick their victims into letting down their guards. Lamia's deceptive powers of mind help maintain the illusion she is a mortal woman, and not a monster:

> *. . . And clear his soul of doubt,*
> *For that she was a woman, and without*

Any more subtle fluid in her veins
Than throbbing blood . . .

Yet Lamia's powers are insufficient weaponry to oppose Apollonius's philosophy. Like a Count Dracula trapped by the sun's rays, the light of Apollonius's purifying reason burns through Lamia's artifice. Once the monster is discovered, she proves vulnerable to the superior power of goodness, and soon everyone can see the vampire for the abomination she is:

A deadly silence step by step increased,
Until it seem'd a horrid presence there,
And not a man but felt the terror in his hair.
"Lamia!" he shriek'd; and nothing but the shriek
With its sad echo did the silence break.
"Begone, foul dream!" he cried, gazing again
In the bride's face, where now no azure vein
Wandered on fair-spaced temples; no soft bloom
Misted the cheek; no passion to illume
The deep-recessed vision:—all was blight;
Lamia, no longer fair, there sat a deadly white.

Yet despite Lamia's imminent demise, there is, of course, no escape for the mortal who has had the poor judgment to have a dalliance with a creature of darkness. Lamia is vanquished, but poor Lycius, too, must die:

. . . With a frightful scream she vanished:
And Lycius' arms were empty of delight,
As were his limbs of life, from that same night.

III

Pentimento

CHRONICLE NOTES: The following is excerpted from an article[1] Dr. Joan Oppenheim published in the *Language and Culture Quarterly*, Spring 1991 edition.

—*Editor*

The graceful *Adagio molto e cantabile* movement of Beethoven's Ninth Symphony inspires listeners' awe. Transcendent melody; sublime harmony; meticulously structured counterpoint—all these combine to create a blissful atmosphere of peace.

It is deceptively easy to imagine that such a perfectly achieved work must have sprung completed from the composer's mind, like Athena from the head of Zeus. The last thing we think of when listening to the Ninth is the labor and frustration inevitably involved in framing such an immortal work of genius. And yet how wrong we are to overlook the struggle that is part of the birth of any great work of art.

The close textual analysis of numerous original scores has given me a belated appreciation for the amount of trial and error involved in creating the world's musical masterworks. I have noted themes written and revised; entire movements interpolated, transposed, rewritten—and thrown out entirely. Manuscripts-in-progress and original scores are indeed rich

[1] *"The Amanuensis's Hand: Tchaikovsky Copyist's Handwriting Shows Up in Surprising Places; A Key to Deeper Patterns in Composer's Work?"* by Dr. Joan Oppenheim. According to the editor's note, Dr. Joan Oppenheim was a music professor at the University of Southern California and author of two books on the history of European music. She was educated at the University of North Carolina and Yale, where she earned her doctorate in 1980. She was also listed as vice president of the Society of American Music Scholars and editor of its bimonthly journal, *Epoch*.

sources of information about the false starts and dead ends our most-loved composers pursued in shaping their works. Passages scratched out in frustration give evidence to the struggle that is integral to the artistic process.

Conversely, working manuscripts also reveal which sections came easiest to the composer—sections in which the creator seemed to have been taking dictation directly from the Muse, the penmanship rushed as the artist hurried to finish before the inspiration left him.

Other kinds of clues can also be found in great composers' original scores.

Recent studies into individual composers' patterns and practices of employing amanuenses have started to provide musicologists with important new critical insights into the problems and work patterns of preeminent musical geniuses.

Composers have employed amanuenses to copy drafts of their works-in-progress and completed compositions since medieval times.[2] The systematic analysis of an individual composer's use of amanuenses provides a heretofore-unseen glimpse into creative habits. Bach, it has been reported (*Bach: The Man, The Music*, Princeton Press, 1985), so trusted his son Karl Emmanuel that he "dictated" compositions to him without speaking a word, the master sitting at the keyboard while the keen-eared boy scored the arrangements as his father played. It is rumored—usually by jealous rivals—that some composers have, upon occasion, allowed favorite amanuenses to actually complete parts of important compositions. A closer evaluation of original texts may one day provide the evidence to prove or disprove these charges.

Imagine, to frame a hypothetical case, the analysis of the original score of Beethoven's Fifth Symphony leading to the discovery that credit for the sublime Fifth was in fact shared in significant degree with a precocious—and entirely anonymous—copyist who spent his life working in the great man's shadow.

Admittedly, this is stating the extreme case. However, until now scholars haven't *known* how big a role amanuenses have played in composers' work. The study of the amanuensis's hand is, as a scholarly pursuit, in its infancy. As research pro-

[2]See Dr. Milton Hasselbad's seminal article on the subject, "*Errors and Evolution: The Role of the Amanuensis in Liturgical Music,*" *Epoch*, January–February, 1978.

gresses, it is entirely possible that startling discoveries will be made.

Master painters ran schools where students learned to mimic the master's use of color, his brush strokes, his characteristic uses of perspective. Even today, art experts sometimes dispute whether a painting is a Rembrandt—or the work of one of his talented students. The heretofore-unexplored question of the role of faceless amanuenses will examine whether similar situations exist in the world of music.

My curiosity about the amanuensis led me to apply standard methods of handwriting analysis to original music scores.

I recently had the opportunity to survey the original copy of Tchaikovsky's Sixth Symphony at the Vocare Museum. I discovered most of the score was written in the composer's hand, with a single noteworthy and perhaps important exception: the *finale*. The symphony's dramatic climax, recognized as the work's crowning movement, is not in the hand of Tchaikovsky, but of an unknown, and until now unreported, amanuensis.

Did the composer revise the Sixth's *finale* so many times that, exhausted, he employed an amanuensis to recopy the clean final draft? We know from the accounts of Tchaikovsky's contemporaries that he was working on the *finale* during a time of great inner turmoil, so perhaps his emotional state was the reason for the sudden change in work habits. Or did the *finale* come to him in such a blinding explosion of inspiration that he called in a trusted assistant to set it all down to paper while he sat at the piano, anxious to complete the transcription before his Muse fled? Further analysis of other Tchaikovsky manuscripts will perhaps yield an answer.

I believe that a similar systematic analysis of other noted composers' surviving original scores and working manuscripts will provide scholars with a wealth of important new insights into composers and their art.

While the study of amanuenses opens the door on distilling intoxicating new brews from what has become familiar wine for musicologists, the handwriting analysis required to separate the composer's handwriting from others in a score is slow work for even the most talented experts. (See: "The Moving Hand: Opportunities and Obstacles in Handwriting Analysis," *American Forensics Review*, July 1989.) Nevertheless, today breakthroughs are occurring that allow computers to be used to speed the handwriting analysis process.

Characters written with quill pens consist of a relatively simple and systematized series of strokes and dots. My colleague Dr. Ling-Ling Tsu, chairperson of Computer Sciences at the University of Southern California, and I have written a computer program to translate these strokes and dots into corresponding numbers. Using a statistical technique known as cluster analysis, the computer is able to recognize the characteristics that distinguish one author from another.

The chief benefit of turning manuscript analysis over to a computer is, in a single word, speed. It would take a human expert many weeks to analyze a relatively complex symphonic score in its entirety; the UCLA Cray Supercomputer can complete the task in less than an hour.

As a follow-up to my initial work with Tchaikovsky's Sixth, Professor Tsu entered all of Tchaikovsky's original existing scores into the computer via an optical scanner. When the works were compared with one another as a body, a rather surprising discovery came to light. The same anonymous amanuensis who worked on the Sixth Symphony also scored key passages of the composer's best-known works, notably *Swan Lake* and *The Nutcracker.*

The amanuensis, whoever he was, seems to have been an especially trusted intimate of the great Tchaikovsky. . . .

IV

Rendezvous with a Vampire

CHRONICLE NOTES: Known in Jerusalem as "the last great Buchanan," Isaiah Buchanan was born in 1865, the year Lee surrendered to Grant at Appomattox Courthouse. He died in a nighttime fire that destroyed a stable on the family's estate, Arlington Plantation, in 1928. The Buchanans had been wealthy since the early 1800s, but the family's fortunes reached their zenith under Isaiah Buchanan's direction—and, following his death, shattered absolutely. The following passages are excerpted from Isaiah Buchanan's diaries.[1]

—Editor

November 22, 1928—The first true cold of winter has arrived. The wind is rapping at the door like Marley's ghost. This house, like any old house, is alive with creaks and moans at night—the more so when the temperature drops and the wind clocks around to the north. Northerly winds have never blown anything providential to the residents of Arlington Plantation.

The frost came as I slept, draping an autumnal pall across the countryside, weaving an icy winding sheet to veil and landscape. By the time I arose, the shroud cloaked each blossom and leaf with its death-bringing embrace. The black-eyed Susans and mums in the gardens have already taken on the brittle, papery appearance of dried flowers saved after a funeral. The four-o'clocks Camellia planted along the east side of the house have withered as if the life had been suddenly sucked out of them; by tomorrow, they will be shriveled, brown husks that show no hint of the explosion of late-afternoon color they've provided us.

I asked James to build a fire in my room to relieve the sharpness in the air and dressed with fingers numbly pressing buttons into their holes. I don't remember the cold bothering me this much before.

I am growing old.

I took my usual morning exercise. Senator's breath came in great steaming jets as we galloped through the orchard. The sky was brilliant; the air, bracing as a glass of spring water splashed in the face, a tonic for the body if not the spirit. Yet I was unable to escape a feeling of melancholy that settled into

[1]Carpenters working at Arlington Plantation in October 1991, removed a portion of wainscoting in the library and discovered a concealed cabinet fitted almost seamlessly into the woodwork, its existence long forgotten. Inside the hiding space were several very old, very excellent bottles of brandy and thirteen volumes of Isaiah Buchanan's handwritten memoirs bound in red leather.

my heart as we plunged across the frozen ground beneath the wintry sun. Mornings such as this will be rare. Ahead are gray skies, brown landscapes, months of chill.

Another year is dying.

We rode to the outskirts of Jerusalem, turning back as Father Michael began to toll the bell for morning worship. The bright chimes chased us halfway back up MacCullum's Hill, the sound running swiftly over the frozen field to find us, like the sound of the cannonade my father told me about from the time the Yankee cavalry menaced our town.

Tonight is colder still, a hard frost.

Why do I so often record observations about the weather?

Old habits bred in the bone, I suppose, linger long after the weather and land have ceased to be of any real importance to the Buchanan family. Our present interests are bank shares, railroads, industrial combinations—not temperature, rainfall, moisture in the fields. The plantation holdings have been sold off in pieces to raise capital for new ventures. Less than a thousand acres remain, most of it in the hands of sharecroppers. The plantation has not employed an overseer in nearly twenty years. Indeed, Arlington Plantation is not a *plantation* any longer in anything but name.

I wonder if it was wise for us to turn so much away from the land, which was so good to us for so many years. . . .

Of course, we Buchanans changed because we had to. There are seasons to more things than Nature. In fifty years nobody will remember that planters were once the richest men in this nation, not lawyers and speculators.

Yet this should not make me, of all men, sad. There are far worse things than forgetting—especially for the sole living guardian of the Buchanan Secret.

I've borne the Secret's weight long enough. I'm growing weary of carrying its deadening weight. While I've rebelled against the creeping infirmity of age—arthritic fingers, failing eyes—a part of me looks forward to the day when I will lay down my weary bones for the last time and forget *everything*.

But will it end there? Will taking the Buchanan Secret with me into the grave be the end of it? Will the forgetfulness of time obscure my family's crime, and make "the world forget," as Emerson promises?

The dead sleep in their moonless night. All history is an epi-

taph. A few days more, and idle eyes will run over your obituary, the world forget you.

The aching in my soul tells me the Secret won't pass from this world as easily as I.

The modern way of thinking holds that only the people directly involved in a crime are liable for punishment. That is not the traditional way of assigning guilt—especially not here in the South. Reading the Old Testament reminds me of a older, harsher justice: the sins of the fathers visited upon the sons. I pray that the Secret has not branded the Buchanans with a curse that will fall upon our children and our children's children. I pray for God's grace to cleanse my family of its sin; I pray to the Lord not to send devils to punish us, in this world and the next.

A group of fools in town Sunday were talking about the Old South, babbling about bringing its "faded glory" back to life. I would sooner go to the cemetery and dig up corpses! The old times are dead. They can no more be brought back by wishing than the sound of Andre's batteries on MacCullum's Hill. Let us forget them and be grateful for the forgetting.

God grant us the power to put the past behind us, and to forget.

And God forgive the Buchanans their sins.

December 1, 1928—I saw *him* last night.

I dare not write his name. I have no way of knowing into whose hands my diaries may fall. Only a braggart or a fool keeps a diary, Sam Chase once said to me. Perhaps that old cynic is right. I plan to destroy my diaries before I die.

Perhaps I should stop writing and burn them now. . . .

The fiend was standing outside the opera house tonight, a cigarette clamped in his teeth, its tip glowing like a signal from Hell. Not dead more than half a century, the way people think, but alive and unaged. And radiating unmistakable malevolence.

Which was, I realize, patently *impossible*. A hallucination—that is what I thought at first. My eyes were lying to me.

He smiled.

There was nothing pleasant in the fiend's grin. He drew in his breath. The cigarette glowed brighter. His eyes were like Mephistopheles's—impenetrably dark, except where they reflected the fiery ash at the end of his cigarette.

David DeWitt, our local apothecary, passed and tipped his hat to the devil. It was then that I knew that he was real, that he wasn't some fanciful bit of the Secret visible only to me.

I got into the car and came straight home, where I drank a bourbon, then another, and another, trying to convince myself I hadn't seen when I knew all along that I *had*, until I fell asleep at my desk.

I remain at a loss to explain the phantom. It is unquestionably *him*, or at least his face, yet he could not possibly remain alive and unchanged. Is it possible, given the infinite physiological combinations that God and Nature have worked over the course of seventy-odd years, that two men could share the same face? There must be a rational explanation—and perhaps this is it, though it does not explain the unbridled hatred in his eyes when he looked at me and let that ghastly smile play across his lips.

Perhaps I am losing my mind.

I pray that I am.

May God have mercy on our souls.

December 3, 1928—I saw him again tonight. He was driving out of town in a bloodred Auburn, taking the road toward Arlington Plantation, as we traveled the other way into town to call on the Culpeppers.

The fiend grinned at me as our automobiles passed, the same threatening leer he'd presented me outside the opera house.

He means us nothing but harm. That much I see in his eyes.

I started to order James to turn the car around, but I stopped myself mid sentence. I didn't want to alarm—or endanger—Camellia, who was accompanying me. The others are safely visiting our cousins in Memphis, thanks to my contrivance. If he did go to Arlington, I reasoned, he would find no one at home but the servants, and surely he could harbor no ill feelings toward them.

When we returned home, I, with a revolver cocked and ready in the pocket of my car coat, learned that a stranger in a red car had come down the lane to the great house, proceeded around the circle drive, and left again without stopping. The threat implied in this trespass seems clear: he knows where we live, and he is ready to come here, unwelcome, whenever he so desires.

What does he want with us? Why has the ghost returned—

* * *

I was interrupted briefly by Camellia, my baby, coming into the library to bid me goodnight.

It is sweet to have a young daughter to worry about me in my old age. But even this simple pleasure is made bitter when it falls beneath the threatening shadow of that grinning apparition. I clearly sense his malevolence toward me.

I should have insisted that Camellia go to Memphis with the others. The doctor was afraid that travel might turn her cough into pneumonia. I could not bear to lose her, so I let her stay, trading danger of one sort for another. Still, I can't help think she would be safer in Memphis. . . .

The thing that confounds me is how the fiend has managed to cheat time. He does not appear to have aged a day since 1865, although he's trimmed his mustaches and wears his hair neatly clipped and combed back in the modern fashion.

I would like to know the secret of his eternal youth. The pain in my joints as I direct this pen, the written lines that are no longer sharp to my eye—it would be wonderful to reverse this process by which we die a little bit with each passing year.

I remind myself that if he is eternally young, then there must be some unholy deed involved. I have never seen a man who looked so like he'd sold his soul to the devil. Perhaps that is exactly what *J. W. B.* has done.

December 6, 1928—I spoke to the fiend tonight.

We met in the most unlikely of places—at the Reverend George Hornsby's birthday reception in the rectory.

The fiend's back was to me when I entered, but there was no mistaking the evil emanating from his mere presence. Strange that no one but me seems to notice the malevolent penumbra that hangs around him like a shroud. The others were enormously charmed with his conversation—which was, I confess, both witty and learned, his remarks filigreed at judicious intervals with quotes from Shakespeare and the Old Testament. But then that is how I have always imagined Satan would appear to mortals—a charming, darkly handsome man, well traveled, sophisticated, erudite, falsely pious.

And beneath an urbane exterior, monolithic, impenetrable evil.

I caught B.'s eye as he conversed with three of the loveliest young ladies in our community, Amanda Chase, Ophelia

Hornsby Chase, and Maude Culpepper. The contempt and hatred he conveyed to me in a single glance explained more eloquently than words could have the harm he wishes us.

I walked straight across the room, interposed myself between B. and the ladies, and introduced myself.

The fiend offered his hand.

I paused a moment, then realized I had no choice but to accept the proffered claw. It was like shaking hands with Lucifer—firm, warm, yet unmistakably the touch of a remorseless killer.

For an incredible and terrible moment as I shook his hand, I found myself witnessing his past crimes as vividly as if I'd been recalling something burned into my own memory. The images remain as indelibly clear in my mind as if I'd actually seen them. I see them again now, as I write:

The fiend is looking at me with a sidelong glance, his expression an utterly blank mask. As he turns toward me—swiveling his head slowly, his jaw held firm and high—a depraved joy fills his merciless eyes. His lips twist upward into a leer—and as he grins, a copious amount of the blood he has been holding in his mouth spills out, covering his chin, dripping from it. . . .

The monster introduced himself. His name, he said, was Earnest Palmer. A lie, I knew, and his wicked grin told me he knew I was aware of his lie. Of course, I hardly expected him to publicly confess his true identity.

I told *Palmer* his face reminded me very much of someone else, someone who had come through Jerusalem a long time ago, a Shakespearean actor. When I mentioned the individual by name, he laughed and winked—mocking me to my face!

Mock me B. may, since there's no one with whom I can share my terrible knowledge. Even if I tried to convince Camellia—showing her actual photographs from the 1850s and 1860s—she would find it impossible to believe. *I* would find it impossible to believe, if I didn't *know*.

I've carried the accursed Secret with me since my twenty-first birthday. All those years, I expected some grim retribution to descend upon the Buchanans. And now, I fear, the time has swung 'round at last for old sins to be punished. . . .

One of the Culpepper girls made a grand entrance with her beau from New Orleans.

B. took advantage of the distraction. He leaned close to me

and admitted what I already knew, either to assure himself I knew or to magnify my distress.

"You know of course, that I truly am B—!" he hissed.

He pulled back and gave me a defiant look, challenging me to tell everyone so that he could see their reaction.

I could not find my voice, but I managed to nod my head dumbly. Yes, I knew who he was. I knew. And I believed. And I was afraid. . . .

The others soon returned their attention to *Palmer*, who remained, even with the arrival of the heralded fianncé, the center of attention. In the same voice I use to converse with any new arrival in our community, I politely inquired what business brought *Palmer* to our corner of Mississippi.

He'd come to "clear up some old business," he said.

I was anxious to be of service to him, if there was any way I might assist him, I replied, trying to draw him out.

"My business is of a rather confidential nature, but you could very likely assist me before I am through," he said, fixing me with a stare that sent a chill through my body. It was like conversing with Lucifer; every word had a double meaning, every nod and smile hidden significance.

B. excused himself early, pleading business elsewhere. But he'd only just arrived, the young people protested to their charming new acquaintance—Camellia among them, I despaired to see. He apologized, insisting he could not stay a moment longer. His business was quite crucial.

"You might say it's a matter of life and death," B. added, and winked at me!

A father's courage made me bold. I interposed myself between B. and the door.

"I look forward to conversing with you further, sir," I said.

B. said nothing, but smiled and bowed at the waist. I could not help but notice his teeth. Their whiteness was so perfect that they almost had the bluish tint of new-fallen snow. The upper incisors, however, ruined the effect. They were too long, almost like a dog's canines, and gave his visage an appallingly wolfish aspect when he smiled fully.

"I, too, have some old family business you might be able to help me settle," I said, determined to press the issue as far as I might. My comment seemed to amuse B. enormously, but then I saw that his good humor did not quite conceal the inner rage it was intended to disguise.

"Then I must do whatever is in my power to assist you," he said rather sharply.

A mutual challenge was offered and accepted in that brief moment. We stood staring at one another, the others looking on without understanding. But *Palmer* and I understood one another perfectly. I knew at that moment that B. has returned to Jerusalem to kill whomever was left in the old families he'd conspired with in 1865. And he knew that I am equally determined to stop him.

"I'm anxiously awaiting an invitation to Arlington," B. said, backing toward the door. "I'm so enthralled with your home's beauty that I might even decide to pay you an uninvited call some evening."

"I shall do my best to prepare a worthy welcome for you, sir," I replied.

He turned without another word and departed.

December 8, 1928—It has started.

Ophelia was attacked last night. I cannot bring myself to record here the condition in which her unclothed body was found, or the animal savagery of her attacker. The sheriff remarked that she looked as if a pack of wolves had taken her down. It has been fifty years since a wolf has been seen in this part of Mississippi. It seems the wolves have returned to Jerusalem—or one particularly dangerous wolf.

Camellia is prostate with grief. And poor Josephine. Ophelia's mother's nerves have never been good. I fear this terrible thing will unhinge her. Ophelia's husband—I should write "widower," although Adam is far too young for that gray word—is bearing up well, though he told me in a whisper that this was a judgment from God. Adam has an unfortunate tendency to see events great and small in Biblical terms. In this case, I fear, he is right, for we all are being made to pay for the sins of our fathers.

To think that it might just as easily have been Camellia . . .

I must confess that B. has already led me into blasphemy. I am mortally ashamed to admit it, but I prayed to God that it be anyone *but* Camellia when I heard that a girl had been unspeakably violated and murdered. It could have been Camellia—and it *will* be Camellia, if I do not stop the fiend.

Sheriff Fisher is of no use to me now. Nor is my good friend Dr. Culpepper. I must do the deed, and I must do it myself.

I sent a note to *Palmer* at his hotel, proposing we meet tomorrow. His response, delivered an hour ago by messenger, says he prefers night to the day—a legacy, he writes, of his early years in the theater. Here again he mocks me, taunting me with allusions to his true identity. Still, I wonder if there is more to it. The fact is that B. has never been seen in Jerusalem during daylight hours. Perhaps that is one of the conditions of his immortality—that he can never go out in the sun. I read a story once about a monster called a *vampyre*. Perhaps that is the secret of how he cheated death. Maybe *Palmer* is a vampyre.

No—too absurd.

There must be some rational explanation.

My plans turn upon an old story: During his final days, my father spoke of a manuscript or journal belonging to B. that had fallen into his possession. I do not know whether this document did, or does, exist, but I offered it as bait in the trap I've set. In my note to B., I reported that I had come upon a certain memoir of his that he might like to have returned. It struck a nerve, for his reply stated that he was "most anxious to have returned any of the property that had been *stolen*" from him. . . .

I've picked the perfect place for our meeting. The west stables are far from the house and in a very private location. I asked James to have the horses moved out. This afternoon I went down and looked after the final arrangements myself.

Speak hands for me.

My father and B. shared a passion for Shakespeare. As do I.

Speak hands for me.

There is irony in those words of Shakespeare's carved over the Buchanan family tomb. In 1865, it was not Buchanan hands but B.'s that spoke for four of the defeated South's most embittered families.

Speak hands for me.

Tonight, I will give real meaning to those hollow words. Tonight, with God's grace, I will bring an end to an evil that made a fractured nation weep and now threatens to wipe out the Buchanans and other descendants of the Founding Families of Jerusalem, Mississippi, although I know not what wrong we have done B.

Tonight, my hands will speak, and erase some measure of the *Buchanan Secret's* evil.

Tonight, B. must die.

V

Gracious Southern Living

CHRONICLE NOTES: The following article was published in the May–June edition of *Estates International* magazine, a slick, full color bimonthly devoted to mansions for sale around the world with prices starting at $500,000, but averaging much more.

—Editor

Jerusalem, Mississippi, may be less well known than nearby Natchez, but the quiet city overlooking the river is nearly as rich as its Confederate sister city when it comes to magnificent expressions of antebellum architecture. More than one hundred mansions built for wealthy planters, bankers, and merchants before the Civil War remain standing in Jerusalem, and a growing number are undergoing restoration as market forces drive prices upward in better-known Old South locations.

By far the finest of the historic homes in Jerusalem is Arlington Plantation, the city's crowning jewel, an immaculate storybook estate listed on the National Historic Landmark Registry. The property is currently owned by a religious order, which has carefully preserved the house and its original furnishings, outbuildings, and grounds.

Situated just outside the city limits, Arlington is one of the most outstanding expressions of Greek Revival architecture surviving anywhere in the nation today. Visitors approach the great house from an awe-inspiring formal drive overhung on either side with matched oak trees draped in picturesque Spanish moss. Surrounding the house like liveried servants waiting at attention are twenty-eight Doric columns that meet wrap-around porches trimmed in black wrought-iron railings on both the first and second stories.

A curved double staircase dominates Arlington's dramatic two-story entry hall. The home's interior features many expressions of luxurious hand-crafted workmanship unavailable in a new home today at any price. Floors are inlaid with wood parquet. Accenting the walls in the main house is beautiful wainscoting, the wood sawed and matched to grain. The interior walls and ceilings offer some of the finest ornate moldings found anywhere. Each room on the main floor of the great house is crowned with glittering eighteenth-century crystal chandeliers imported from Bavaria. Other features include antique Italian marble fireplaces in each room, a warmly paneled dining room with an oak-coffered ceiling, silver hinges and sash hardware, and beautiful Belgian lace curtains.

Arlington is offered complete with its exquisite collection of antique furnishings, many of the pieces dating back to the original residents. Fine examples of hand-carved English furniture abound. The formal receiving parlor is decorated with museum-quality Louis XV furnishings upholstered with immaculate Aubusson tapestry. A beautifully restored century-old Steinway grand piano is the focal point in the music room. The library shelves hold many fascinating antique volumes, including numerous matched collections, first editions, and other collectibles—a bibliophile's dream!

The estate for many years belonged to the Buchanan family, one of the South's wealthiest and most influential families during the nineteenth century. Construction of the great house began in 1830. Although work on the central mansion was completed four years later, major constructions to the house and grounds continued almost nonstop up until the start of the Civil War. Many of the South's leading historic figures, including General Robert E. Lee and Confederate President Jefferson Davis, have slept in Arlington's bedrooms, as guests of General Noah Buchanan, who lost an arm fighting for the Confederacy at the Battle of Antietam, and of his father, Senator Ezekial Buchanan.

A spacious addition at the rear of the main house was built in 1912 by Isaiah Buchanan, a banking and investment magnate. The "new" addition, as it is quaintly called, features such amenities as a third-floor ballroom and a fully equipped hotel-class kitchen capable of suiting the needs of the most ambitious host and hostess, with eighteen bedrooms, including the staff quarters—enough space for the most expansive type of Southern hospitality.

Once one of the largest plantations in the South, Arlington still boasts one hundred acres in grounds, pasture, timber, and wooded bayous. A private Mississippi River landing below the bluff behind the great house serves as a living reminder of the era when steamboats used to call at the plantation to load bails of Buchanan cotton bound for the market in New Orleans.

Beautiful formal gardens surround Arlington's great house. A greenhouse connected to the main house by a porte cochere is filled with prize-winning orchids, living artifacts of a time when the words "Arlington" and "orchids" were synonymous at the best gardening shows throughout the states of Mississippi and Alabama. Each spring the grounds explode with color as masses of tulips burst into blossom.

Arlington has been attended with loving care, and the mansion has been updated, with special attention given to preserving the home's historical and architectural integrity.

The great house offers all the modern conveniences. All bathrooms have been updated with the finest fixtures and appointments. There is a full-sized, heated pool outdoors with cabana. Heating and air conditioning were updated in 1980, a complete renovation of the mansion's electrical system having taken place a decade earlier. The numerous outbuildings include a caretaker's cottage, a stable converted into a garage with spaces for a dozen vehicles, and a former slave quarters renovated into office space. The only thing Arlington lacks is Rhett Butler and Scarlett O'Hara!

Arlington Plantation embodies the grandeur and gracious living that were characteristic of the Old South. The estate stands as a symbol of a lifestyle all but extinct in the modern age, a romantic dream preserved for the discriminating buyer.

$4,500,000 Furnished

Culpepper Realty

(Contact: Henry Culpepper)

Post Office Box 1533

Jerusalem, Mississippi 38641

(601) 555-6083

PART III

✧

Return to Mississippi

I
Rubber Playthings

CHRONICLE NOTES: "Becker Thorne's" diary, continued.
—*Editor*

Tonight, a great Revelation!

The Neon sign drew me off the road and into the convenience store parking lot. It was a cheap, mass-produced advertisement for wine coolers, hardly a fitting tabernacle for the Voice.

The Neon pulsed pale blue, the color of moonlight on newly fallen snow, light and cold as a marble slab. There was a brief moment, a faint flicker.

No, I was mistaken.

Then again, just *barely* there.

Ah, yes, the familiar calling, the seductive, secret whispering of the divine! The Spirit of the Neon was speaking to me. I bowed my head to the multiheaded seraph. (I would have put off my shoes in the presence of the angel and fallen to my knees, but I had to be careful; among barbarians, obsequies must be paid in small, inconspicuous ways, fuller honors and sacrifices put aside for private times.)

The Neon angel, hovering before me on electric wings, said unto me:

"Behold, I am coming soon, bringing my recompense, to repay every one for what he has done."

And I knew it was true, and it was good, for so it was written in the Book of Revelation. So sayeth the angel to the Fury. And so it shall be done, and done again and again in Neon, until they all have been punished for their sins.

Amen.

The night fell silent. I sensed the world tremble in the presence of a divinity that it knew not, but who knew the world and its many weaknesses most perfectly. I could feel all of Jerusalem crouching around me in the darkness, as mindless as a flock of sheep lost in dreaming while waiting to gain admittance to the abattoir.

And I thought: This town knows not what it *knows*, but soon it will *remember*.

I am happy to be back in Jerusalem. I regret the time *she* made me spend in New York to replenish our purses. Yet it had to be done. No one is more practical than Nicoletta. Our coffers had to be replenished before we could turn our attention to more important things—she in Bucharest, I in Mississippi. But I digress from the *Revelation!*

I thought the Neon angel had delivered its message, but there was more. The piercing brilliance of holy illumination froze me where I stood. Its power radiated through me like a bright lamp through a thin paper shade; when I looked down, I saw the bones in my chest and arms and legs as if I were a skeleton encased in translucent and insubstantial flesh.

A great Revelation was at hand.

Neon wrapped itself around my spine, turning me bodily around. My bones creaked and cracked. I could see them glowing with the Neon now, the marrow suffused with pale blue translucence. My nerves were splayed out, raw and full of searing pain, as the Neon intertwined itself with me and poured its message directly into my soul, electric fire pumping into my heart, mingling its ancient blood with mine.

A dull moan echoed in my ears. It was my own voice, agonized but distant. I paid the voice no mind. My body was behind me on the Earthly plane; I had been transported to a higher sphere, the realm of Neon, where portents were foretold to the Fury.

And I saw him for the first time: a man with the mark of the saber angled across his left cheek.

"You will know him by his sign and by his words," the Neon said.

And I heard the mortal man's words, not with my ears but with my heart: *"I am the Last Gray Ghost of the Confederacy."*

The phantasm hovered before me.

"Together," the Neon said, *"you will smite the malefactors."*

Then it let me go. I fell jarringly back into the phenomenological world, back to the parking lot in a city I had been away from for so many years. The angel had departed.

I moved my feet toward the store. I have learned to watch for signs, and to follow them.

A thin woman stood behind the counter. She squinted through the smoke drifting up into her eyes from the cigarette hanging from her lower lip as she regarded a tabloid newspaper. The cover story was about Princess Diana. There was a homemade tattoo of a cross in the skin between her thumb and forefinger. I smiled. Women with tattoos always interest me.

The clerk wasn't as old as I'd first thought. I guessed she was somewhere in her thirties. Too much fun—drink, cigarettes, men, and drugs, of course—had aged her prematurely. Her mouth was sunken as if to counterbalance her chin, which jutted out like the upturned toe of a boot. Makeup would have disguised her pasty complexion, but she was beyond caring whether she was attractive. Frown lines ran from the sides of her nose to the corners of her mouth. Crows' feet pinched her red-rimmed eyes. Her mousy brown hair needed to be washed; it hung against her head as shapelessly as her clothing hung on her body—a gray sweatshirt, maroon double-knit slacks, and black discount-store running shoes that fastened with Velcro straps.

Five years ago she must have even been an attractive little Kewpie Doll, especially for someone like me whose taste in women runs toward whores. She was, however, already well on her way to becoming the kind of hag men would never look past the countertop Redman Chewing Tobacco display to see. No one is as invisible as a plain, aging, lower-class woman.

We were alone in the store. The hag glanced up from her reading long enough to decide that I wasn't anybody who needed watching. I smiled, this time catching her eye. Evidently not interested in flirting with strangers, she frowned, propped a bony elbow on the cash register, and went back to her reading.

I could smell her blood—sour with nicotine, which stinks like sweat on a plow mule. I turned away from her and began to wander through the store. I couldn't get interested in *that.* It would be degrading to drink from such a vessel.

And then: *There they were!*

The rubber gloves spoke to me the moment I turned into the

aisle where they hung amid the boxes of Spic and Span, Drāno, and Johnson's Floor Wax. There were a dozen pairs of them, each encased in a plastic cocoon that hung from a stainless steel rod extending from the shelving. They were electric yellow beneath the glaring fluorescent lights.

The gloves called out to me.

They said: "*Come play with me.*"

I plucked a pair off the hook without looking and slipped them into my pocket.

The clerk paid no attention. I could feel her contempt for her job, her bitterness about her life. The store wasn't hers; she didn't really care whether people came in and stole things off the shelves. Which made me reconsider her. Not a Kewpie Doll, but a Rag Doll. Perhaps I'd been hasty. Her malignant heart would be delicious—tough, sour, flavored with the essences of failure, regret, and envy. I stood there clenching and relaxing my jaw, thinking it would be amusing to take her there, impulsively, drinking in all her wonderful hatred, and leaving her body sprawled pale and limp across the counter for the next customer to find.

"Show me a sign," I whispered, praying to the Neon for guidance as I began walking toward the door. I put my hand in my pocket and felt the purloined gloves in their plastic package.

The Neon told me nothing.

When I reached the door without eliciting any response, I even exposed them a bit, challenging her to catch me in the midst of my theft.

"Show me a sign," I repeated.

Still nothing, only the smell of floor wax, cardboard, plastic, preservatives, and the hag's thin, wormwood blood.

I put my hand on the door, opened it, and walked out.

I admit I was disappointed. Even without a sign, it would have been fun to have her catch me stealing the rubber gloves. I'd wanted to see what she would do, and what I, in return, would do to her. I do—as you well know, dear diary—enjoy my little games. But tonight it was not to be. There were more important things to accomplish in town, and I knew I shouldn't do anything that would make the residents unduly apprehensive. That was the mistake I made when I came back in 1928, and as a result, Nicoletta made me leave town after I'd only started to punish them for their sins.

I felt Rag Doll's eyes suddenly upon my back as I walked out. I didn't look over my shoulder. The door swung shut behind me with a *whoosh* from its pneumatic cylinder. I heard the Neon humming in the window, but it was telling me that all things would come to he who waits—and remembers. Besides, I had been delivered a prophecy. Somewhere out in the night, living amid the *underlings* who inhabit Jerusalem, Mississippi, was the last gray ghost of the Confederacy, who would help me punish the traitors.

I had to find the gray ghost.

But first, I had an appointment with Katharine *Culpepper* Simonette.

II
Dirty Jobs

CHRONICLE NOTES: "Becker Thorne's" diary, continued.
—*Editor*

I sat in the dark and tore open the plastic bag with my teeth.

The rubber gloves released a sharp, chemical smell.

I tossed the bag out the window. The breeze caught the plastic chrysalis before it touched the ground and carried it away.

I had to wiggle my fingers to get the gloves over my hands. They were a tight fit, made for a woman's hands. Protection while doing dishes, cleaning out the toilet, other dirty jobs.

I smiled to myself.

"Dirty jobs." Not that I was afraid to get *my* hands dirty.

Lights flashed in the rearview mirror. I didn't look. I knew it wasn't the right car.

The gloves were hot and made my hands sweat. I could feel the perspiration on the backs of my hands, in my palms. I rubbed my hands together, feeling the sticky mushiness of rubber against rubber.

"Squeak, squeak," said the gloves. Just the right thing for dirty jobs, for fun and games.

There are so many ordinary objects that become marvelous playthings in the hands of the creative person who understands how to unleash their real potential. The gloves, for example. Or a corkscrew. I have done some of my best work with a simple can opener. Not the electric kind, of course, but an old-fashioned manual one, the type that has a serrated metal wheel that twists against a sharpened cutting edge. The hooked bottle opener at the other end comes in handy, too.

A true artist can make do in any medium and on any stage. (As Zola said of Monet, I am "a man amid this crowd of eunuchs.")

The times we had in Bulgaria! No luxuries there, I can assure you, but great opportunities for an artist to exercise his creativity. But, unfortunately, no Neon. Bulgaria is a backward place, even if Nicoletta is right about primitive conditions affording *our kind* the best opportunities. Still, I managed to make do rather well with a simple razor blade, fishing hooks, a food grater, and piano wire.

Yet I have not come all the way back from Europe, via New York, simply for amusements. I have returned to Jerusalem at the direction of a Higher Power. I, the Fury, am on a holy pilgrimage, and my destination is Justice.

"And I will strike her children."

So it is written. So it will be done.

I caught my breath and looked up. She was coming. I could *feel* her. I strained with all my senses.

Headlights appeared, winked out, reappeared. The car kept coming toward me up the winding boulevard, past the street lamp glowing dimly where Jackson Street veered away to the right.

Jefferson Davis Boulevard was pleasantly dark. The boulevard started at River Street and followed a natural depression up through the bluff, which was made up of a series of sharply rising hills thrown together in the chaos that is typical of most things in nature. There were lights on in the houses, but they were set back from the street and above it, obscured by the trees and bushes that were part of the carefully, almost compulsively, well-kept lawns. The houses along the boulevard were large, a few of them nearly as big as the older mansions lining River Street, where they overlooked the Mississippi.

The car pulled over to the curb and stopped. The headlights went out but the occupant remained within the vehicle.

I opened the door to the rented Cadillac. While parked at the convenience store where I stole the gloves, I'd taken the bulb out of the courtesy light to keep the car dark. Now I slipped out, shut the door silently, and ran into the alley that led behind the houses along that side of the street. I cut through a yard, listening to children's laughter as I ducked under their dining-room window, and continued my looping path to get behind the car parked in front of the next house.

It was a cream-colored Audi. The driver was a woman—a delicious young woman. But I had known that. In fact, I knew everything about her. Her family. Where she'd gone to school. Her tee time at the country club. Her fetish for lacy black undergarments. Oh, we were going to have fun, she and I.

I closed my eyes and breathed in the cool spring air. I could smell her perfume, her subtle, sweet body odor, and, beneath that, the sublime fragrance of her blood. So unlike the prematurely old whore at the convenience store. Blood like young wine, bright, flowery, as sweet as nectar.

From my vantage point behind an oak I could see only the back of her head. Her hair was black and neatly trimmed in a longish page-boy cut, the tapering sides and back breaking just at her shoulders. I imagined her bangs drawing a sharp line across her forehead a finger's width above her eyebrows. It excited me to think of such fine, black hair wet with perspiration against a linen pillow case. Or, perhaps, the same locks contrasted against the electric yellow of the rubber gloves I still wore on my hands.

Dirty jobs.

My hands burned within their tight rubber casings. I flexed my fingers in and out, in and out. The heat from my body had made the yellow rubber flexible, like a second layer of skin. I crouched and lifted my hands to my face. The sweat that had collected in the gloves trickled down my wrists and soaked into the cuffs of my shirt.

In the Audi, Kewpie Doll glanced at her wristwatch and began to tap her manicured fingernails against the leather-wrapped steering wheel, alternating them in sequence from index to little finger, one-two-three-four, one-two-three-four.

Bent nearly double, I moved behind the car.

The woman inside continued to face forward.

I rubbed the palms of my rubber hands together.

"Squeak, squeak," said the gloves.

The woman's head jerked. I ducked down. She couldn't possibly have heard. Not with her ears, at least, although it was plain that she had sensed it somewhere, somehow, deep inside, responding to the same sense of primordial alarm that makes dogs begin to howl in the night seemingly without reason. But of course she sensed it. The Fury was near, and who could know where next It would strike? Sensed but not seen, felt but not understood—this is what I am. I clapped one of the rubber gloves over my mouth to keep from giggling. The noxious chemical smell assaulted my nose; I put out my tongue and licked the glove, running my tongue over the ridged rubber surface.

Dirty jobs.

The automatic door locks on the Audi dropped with a loud, metallic click. As if locks could stop me! I could go right through the window if I wanted, claw through the roof with my fingernails.

I took in a deep breath and held it. It would ruin everything if I allowed myself to get too excited and lose control. The Hunger was not strong in me. Indeed, it never is, since I keep it fed rather more often than is strictly necessary! Fortunately, there was no Neon anywhere along the comfortable residential street, nothing to put me into a frenzy.

And I thought: *I am in control.*

Perfect control.

For a moment I allowed myself to feel sorry for Katharine Culpepper Simonette and the other guilty underlings in the town. They were pathetic weaklings with no hope of protecting themselves against the Fury who had carefully learned all of their secrets, and who knew everything about killing. I can be savage and quick, or I can be slow, savoring the achingly sweet moments as the last drops of life drain away in the uttermost agony. Nicoletta has taught me well.

I lifted my head enough to see through the rear window. Kewpie Doll was looking ahead, peering into the darkness, no doubt telling herself not to be afraid, that she was a grown woman who had long ago stopped being frightened of the night.

Crouched over, I ran to the tree and slipped back behind. A moment later and I was racing back up the alley to my car.

I climbed inside, started the ignition, and put the Cadillac into reverse almost in a single motion. Backing up the hill, up the boulevard, away from Katharine Culpepper Simonette, I tore the rubber gloves off my hands and flung them under the driver's seat. I'd need them later when it was time to have fun, time to begin delivering justice to Jerusalem.

And as I drove to meet Katharine Culpepper Simonette—whose great-grandfather had watched my body, a bullet in its breast, fall backward into the river and then taken his share of the gold that was owed to me—I thought, this is like a *dream*, a wonderful dream come true.

Dirty jobs. That's how some would describe being compelled to carry out the sentences of an unforgiving justice. But not me. To me, the Fury of the Lord, it was something I'd dreamed about for more than a century of exile—my dream, my bliss, my joy.

I will bring Jerusalem, Mississippi, bleeding to its knees.

I will teach them to die like dogs.

The Fury has returned.

III

Let's Make a Deal

CHRONICLE NOTES: "Becker Thorne's" diary, continued.

—Editor

I pulled the Cadillac behind the Audi, braking hard.

Kewpie Doll's eyes were in the rearview mirror, not frightened but extremely alert. Shrewd, watchful.

I shut off the lights and the motor and climbed out.

She watched me in the driver's side mirror, a tall, whippet-thin man who wore his thick, dark hair long, brushed straight back to where it broke several inches past the collar.

I smiled toward the mirror. My appearance, many women have told me, is quite handsome. I possess what have been described as "chiseled" features, with a high forehead; dark, deep-set eyes; high cheekbones; an aquiline nose, and a strong chin. My complexion is quite pale, but then I *am* what they these days call a "night person!"

My clothing was, as always, black: a black shirt buttoned at the neck, a black cotton "duster" coat that reached well below the knees of tight black chinos, the black cowboy boots exaggerating my height. The only thing I wore that was not black—the color that best absorbs Neon vibration—was my Navajo silver belt buckle, which I had taken from a dead man in Taos to bring me luck, along with the finger I cut from his hand.

I began to walk toward the Audi. The woman moved her left hand. The electric window on the driver's side lowered a few inches.

"Katharine Simonette? I'm Becker Thorne."

"Hello," she said, unlocking the door with her left hand while with her right she pushed something under the seat. A can of Mace, maybe even a gun. I wasn't offended. One couldn't be *too* careful these days, not even in a backwater like Jerusalem, Mississippi.

Katharine dragged her briefcase out of the car behind her. I accepted her hand and held it for a much briefer time than I'd have liked, feeling the caress of her skin against mine that had so recently perspired beneath the artificial skin of the cheap rubber gloves I'd stolen.

Katharine pleased me very much. The only makeup she wore on her tanned skin was lipstick that matched the red lacquer on her long, manicured fingernails. She wore a navy sweater over a white blouse. A simple gold pin was fixed to the sweater over her heart. Her other jewelry consisted of a small gold braided chain on her right wrist, the gold Rolex on her left wrist, and on the ring finger—*a very well-formed* finger—of her left hand, a pear-shaped one-carat engagement ring and a wedding band. Her skirt and shoes were matching navy blue, conservative in cut and the best of quality. She was in every way the picture of a well-bred young woman who divided her weekdays between the tennis club and selling real estate. I knew that her father must be very proud of her.

"It's a pleasure to meet you, Mr. Thorne."

"The pleasure is entirely mine," I insisted. "I apologize for being late, Katharine. I promised to meet you at seven."

"Don't give it a second thought, Mr. Thorne. My secretary doesn't always give the best directions."

"It wasn't that. I was held up at the airport."

"You flew in on that dreadful commuter? You *are* a brave man, Mr. Thorne."

I tipped my head back and laughed. It felt good to laugh, especially when I thought about the yellow rubber gloves and the fun I was going to have wearing them.

"No, I flew in on my own plane."

Katharine's eyebrows arched.

"I got the impression they don't see many Gulfstreams at Jerusalem Flight Service. They made quite a fuss."

"The last person to land in Jerusalem in a private jet was the governor, if I'm not mistaken."

"I never use the commercial airlines. My schedule makes it impossible."

"Then you do a lot of traveling?"

"This week, I started in New York Monday, then went to Boston, Chicago, Minneapolis, Denver, Taos, Los Angeles, San Francisco, and doubled back to San Diego before coming here." I paused long enough to pull on an embarrassed expression. "I apologize. I must sound like I'm bragging."

"Not at all, Mr. Thorne." She touched my arm lightly to assure me. "I can't imagine what it must be like to be so busy. My life has enough stress as it is. To have to fly around the country like that—oh, my."

"You said the key word: stress. There is rather too much stress in my life. That's what my doctors say. They've told me—*warned* me—I must slow down."

I touched my chest with a long, narrow forefinger, indicating my heart, that ancient organ, black and cold, beating the slow, deep strokes of a deliciously monstrous immortality. Katharine looked at me with concern. It amazes me that mortals never see me as I am: the Angel of Vengeance, the *Fury*.

"And so you're coming to Jerusalem to slow down the pace a bit?"

"That is it exactly. I need to get off the merry-go-round. When I arrived in Manhattan, I thought the island was a gigantic diamond where one might achieve anything with hard work and perseverance; it is, but it's also an iceberg with extremely slippery footing."

Katharine smiled at my description.

"I wondered why a person like you would be interested in our quiet little corner of the world."

"I think the town is charming. I looked around quite a bit

when I decided to buy a hideaway. Palm Springs, Palm Beach, the Cape. Do you know what your small city has that those places lack?"

Katharine looked up at me and shook her head slowly, her lips parted slightly, her eyes intent on mine. This would be easier than I thought.

"Jerusalem has such a rich sense of the past." I gestured at the shadows sweeping down from the hills above us on either side of the road. "The past is always with you here, which is as it should be. The present can never outrun the past, no matter how hard it tries."

"You make it sound almost ominous, Mr. Thorne."

"I do not mean to."

"Maybe it's different for those of us who have lived here all our lives, Mr. Thorne."

I felt a dangerous urge, but pushed it down. It was not time. There would be ample opportunity to take care of dirty jobs later, after all had been made ready. Everything had been planned. There would be time for *everything*.

"Jerusalem, Mississippi, strikes me as being the kind of place the present hasn't caught up with yet—and please understand that I mean that as a compliment. Still, I imagine things must have changed a lot around here in the past fifty or sixty years."

"Not that much. We're just a little old quiet Southern town," Katharine said, not entirely pleased with the fact. She yearned for brighter lights than the rural lanterns cast. Yet something had held her in Jerusalem to await my arrival, and I knew what it was. Fate—the inscrutable force that binds us with cords of invisible Neon—had decreed that it would be so. Katharine Culpepper Simonette was born to serve the higher justice. As it says in Revelations:

The time is near. Let the evildoer still do evil, and the filthy still be filthy, and the righteous still do right, and the holy still be holy.

"I like this town just the way it is," I said cheerfully. "The people here are good and simple. And trusting. I want to settle down in a place where people can still trust other people, where they haven't learned to be instinctively afraid of strangers."

"Do you intend to live here permanently?"

"Yes, for whatever passes as 'permanently' these days. One

year, two—after that, who knows where they'll be or whether they'll even be alive three years hence? There's nothing that I can't do here instead of in New York, with a telephone, computer, modem, and fax machine. And maybe a satellite dish. Although I do, of course, plan to follow doctor's orders and slow down a bit."

Katharine Simonette looked at me in a way that told me she very much doubted that anyone like me could learn to lead a quiet life. Perceptive girl. Kewpie Doll was right, of course. I couldn't become a retiring bachelor even if I'd wanted to, there being so many *dirty jobs* to do.

"I'm grateful to you for coming out here to meet me tonight. I'm sure you'd rather be home with your family."

Katharine Simonette stared at me blankly for a fraction of a moment—just long enough to inform me that in fact it was no inconvenience for her to leave her husband and young child at home to go out at night and meet a handsome and wealthy man such as myself.

"I'd show a house at three in the morning if I thought I could sell it. Business is business, Mr. Thorne. I know that you, of all people, understand that."

"Indeed I do understand, Katharine."

The yellow rubber gloves were calling to me in a voice somewhere between pleading and desperate, but I paid them no heed. I was savoring my first taste of the magnificent revenge unfolding before me, a bloodred rose opening before the hovering wasp; I doubt even Pegasus himself could have tempted me to indulge too quickly in my pleasures, blasphemy though it is to admit.

Katharine's eyes were fixed on mine, two azure orbs that sparkled in the light they captured from the nearest street lamp. So easy, so easy. But I, the divine tool, would wait until the appointed hour, when each would pay the price.

As for the cowardly, the faithless, the polluted, as for murderers, fornicators, sorcerers, idolaters, and all liars, their lot shall be in the lake that burns with fire and brimstone.

"Let's get down to business." There was a hint of tease in my voice.

"Yes, business." Disappointment in hers, and then, brightening, the intoxicating twang of profit. She was her father's daughter, as the saying goes, and as driven by money as the

Culpeppers I had known during my own mortal time in Jerusalem. "You are going to love this house."

She indicated the steps that climbed the steeply terraced front lawn toward a sprawling two-story brick structure designed to resemble an English country home. Even in the dark it looked comfortable, although modest by my own admittedly baronial standards.

"You're very fortunate. Places like this are usually sold to friends over the supper table or drinks at the country club. If it weren't for poor Mrs. Foster's accident . . ."

"Yes, the automobile accident. I heard that her head . . ."

"She was decapitated," Katharine whispered.

"Quite tragic," I pronounced solemnly.

Katharine gestured toward the steps.

"After you, Mr. Thorne."

"I don't want to see this house."

I took a step toward her. Katharine caught her breath, but she did not move away. She did not fear me. Quite the opposite. Her eyes remained locked on mine, and the way she held her body betrayed not so much as a hint of defensiveness. Her inner voice had to be warning her of the danger, but she suppressed it. She was completely taken in by me, by my appearance, by the impressive reputation I had contrived, but most of all by my wealth. Money was an aphrodisiac for Katharine Culpepper Simonette. That is how it had always been for the Culpeppers. Katharine would do anything for money, if the price was right. Even commit murder, as her ancestors had done, killing—or rather *attempting* to kill—me that night at Arlington Landing.

I allowed my eyes to close for a moment and drew in a deep breath of the sweet Southern air. Her perfume—a brand called Opium—was delightful, even if it did obscure the infinitely more sublime scent of her blood.

"I'm beginning to think you lured me here tonight under false pretenses," she said without nervousness. "What exactly are you up to?"

"I have a confession to make, Katharine. I have not been completely honest."

"You, Mr. Thorne?"

She was so ready for me that I could hardly stand it. The blood teeth throbbed in my upper gum. I sternly reminded myself that I was in control, that waiting would only make our moment of passion all the more delicious when it came.

"I took the liberty of tapping into your local real-estate broker's network from my office in Manhattan."

"But that's a serious violation of our privacy code," she said, pretending to be scandalized.

"I did not get where I am by obeying rules, Katharine."

"No, I suppose not." She laughed dismissively and leaned against the Audi, her briefcase resting against her thigh. I moved a step closer, maintaining the small distance between us. In a tree across the road a little toward the river, an owl cried three times before I willed it to silence. A long time ago, before Neon, birds were my omens, my divine messengers; now they are merely—birds.

"The truth is that there's another house I'd like to see tonight."

"Something you saw in our listings?"

I nodded.

"But Mr. Thorne, I assure you No. 9 Jefferson Davis Boulevard is without question the finest executive home on the market in Jerusalem," she said, standing free of the car. "There's not another home that could do you justice."

I looked directly into her eyes with mine, but I did not exert the least bit of pressure against her will. Using my powers would have hardly been in the spirit of my little seduction.

"Arlington," I said softly, caressingly, as if the two of us were in bed instead of standing between two cars on a dark street.

Katharine Simonette stared up at me in mute surprise as if trying to make out the meaning of the three-syllable word.

"Arlington?" she said at last. Her expression went from stunned to surprised to amused. "No, no, no, Mr. Thorne, I don't think you'd be interested in Arlington Plantation. You've gotten the wrong idea about that place altogether. That house is just an old barn—an elegant old barn, of course, and brimming with antiques, but a barn nonetheless. Do you have any idea what it costs to maintain the gardens alone? I do. I've seen all the numbers on that white elephant."

"It's perfect. I need space. I may intend to lead a quiet, reclusive life once I set up in Mississippi, but my business interests will require me to entertain out-of-town guests. The expense will be worth what I save in hotel bills alone. My accountants will write it off. The Buchanan family built the plantation, didn't they?"

"You know our local history."

It seemed to surprise her. My smile contained, I suppose, a trace of the bitterness that had rotted in my belly for more than a century, but I don't think she saw it.

"History is a hobby of mine. The Buchanans were important people in the South."

"Yes, a long, long time ago. There are many prominent old families in the South, Mr. Thorne. Not to boast, but I come from one myself. My maiden name is Culpepper, and the Culpeppers and Buchanans were among what they used to call the Founding Families of Jerusalem. But I doubt anybody remembers much about the Culpeppers or Buchanans these days. The past is, well, past."

"It is very much alive to some people," I replied dryly.

My eyes dropped to Katharine's gently curving neck, then returned to meet her soft eyes. "Are you interested in history, Katharine?"

She smiled as she leaned forward and, for the briefest moment, her fingers again brushed the sleeve of my coat. "I'm interested in whatever helps sell houses."

Her feckless honesty made me laugh.

"The Buchanan family hasn't owned Arlington since the Depression. An order of nuns lives there now. The Order of Submission." She frowned. "I went to parochial school and had the sisters as teachers. They are indeed serious about submission, at least when it comes to children."

"How long have they had Arlington?"

"The plantation has been a convent since the 1930s. That's how big the place is—large enough to be a convent. The sisters can't afford the upkeep any more. Their order is dying out. I mean *literally*. There aren't any new sisters taking vows. Most of them are old and need medical care. That estate has eaten up their endowment."

"Sounds like a buyers' market."

"I shouldn't tell you this—you know that technically I represent the sellers, not the buyers—but they are desperate to sell. While I'm certainly not encouraging you to buy Arlington Plantation, you can steal the place, if you really want it."

"I would not be averse to stealing Arlington from the good sisters."

"I'm not particularly disturbed by the idea myself, except that I'd hate to see you get stuck with that old place. However, Mr. Thorne, I must point out that there is one group in particular that will have a good deal indeed to say about the sisters selling Arlington to you."

"Who could possibly object to me buying that old estate?" I demanded, my surprise genuine.

"The Jerusalem Historical Preservation Society. They have been working for a long time to get together enough money to buy Arlington. They want to use it as a museum and local history library. Most of the furniture is from when the Buchanans still owned the house."

"But it hasn't been sold yet?" I cringed to hear the edge in my voice. The last thing I wanted to do was appear eager, yet the chance to use the Buchanans' own home as my killing field was too delicious an opportunity to see escape.

"No. The do-gooders don't have the money. Between you and me, I doubt they'll ever raise that much, but you couldn't convince them. You know the type: long on dreams, short on plans, and completely bereft of common sense. Say, you really are serious about Arlington, aren't you?"

"I never joke about business." I folded my arms across my chest and took a step backward. "Arlington is exactly what I want, what I've always wanted. Now, what do you say: Are you going to help me buy it, or must I find another Realtor?"

Katharine smiled with the left side of her mouth.

"It will make a lot of people angry."

"At you, or at me, Katharine?"

"At the both of us. The preservationists . . ." She blew out an impatient breath. "They're difficult people who are always getting in the way of development in town. There's been a small amount of progress in Jerusalem in the past few years, and the preservation society has stood opposed to most of it. This wouldn't be the first deal of mine they've tried to sink."

"Then we shall move so quickly that they will not have time to call their nosy, noisy committees together and vote on a course of action. I'm sure your commission will more than adequately compensate you for any cold stares you might get around town."

"We'll have to act fast." She looked off into the darkness, calculating the odds—and the commission.

"Why don't we go have a look at Arlington."

"Tonight?"

"Why not? I think the sisters will be only too happy to accommodate an unexpected visit from a potential buyer. I just want to see the place, to confirm that it's as I remember."

"You've been to Arlington before?"

"I mean as I remembered it from the listing that I read. I've got my checkbook. We can seal the deal tonight."

"When you say fast, you mean *fast*, Mr. Thorne."

"Business is business, Katharine. I know that you, of all people, understand that."

Her laughter was so charming that it made it difficult for me to ignore the rubber gloves' plaintive appeal to pull them on and get down to the real work at hand. In my experience, the ones who are good at laughing are also good at screaming.

"You never intended to look at this house, did you, Mr. Thorne?" Katharine said, pointing. "You just didn't want to tip your hand about being interested in Arlington, not even to me. Very shrewd."

"I confess," I said, holding out my hands, palms up. "If word had gotten out that a wealthy Wall Street investor was interested in buying what's left of the Buchanan plantation, the price could have shot through the stratosphere. Also I'd have had to contend with your tedious, obstructive preservationists. Know what you want, and know the bottom line: those are the two keys to making money, Katharine."

"It is a true pleasure to do business with a professional like you, Mr. Thorne," Katharine said, and put out her hand.

"Call me Becker."

"Becker."

I shook her hand and continued to hold it, my head swimming with the intoxicating aroma of her blood. I had so much work ahead of me. She did not try to withdraw her hand. Neither did she give any indication my familiarity caused her anything but delight.

Somewhere down by the river, toward the old part of town, the low thermal growl of a powerful Neon sign switched on, making the darkness buzz and hum with its infernal majesty. But the Neon could wait, even as the yellow rubber gloves in the car behind me could wait.

This time, the cunning old Fury was going to take things a step at a time until they were *all* dead.

PART IV

En Passant

I
Police Report

CHRONICLE NOTES: The following accident report was filed May 15, 1991, by Mississippi Trooper Stephen Tippet.
—Editor

At 0115 hours 15 May 1991, the Jerusalem Police Dispatcher relayed to me a trucker's report of a vehicle off the roadway on old Highway 22 approximately five miles outside the city limits, just past Arlington Plantation. Arriving in the area at 0120, I spotted a late-model Cadillac in the field on the west side of the road. Extensive damage to the vehicle was apparent from cursory visual inspection.

Jerusalem Dispatch was notified of a probable 10-50 PI at 0121. I requested an ambulance and assistance at the scene.

The vehicle was a silver two-door 1990 Cadillac Seville, VIN No. 625311-A, Mississippi license CFH 229.

I searched the car and the surrounding area for the vehicle's occupant or occupants. A single individual was located approximately 20 yards due west of the vehicle. The subject, a Caucasian female wearing a nightgown and robe, had been decapitated. Bodily trauma was consistent with that typically seen when a passenger is thrown from a vehicle at a high rate of speed.

I left my flashlight to mark the location, returned to the cruiser and radioed in a confirmed 10-50 Fatality. Jerusalem Dispatch was instructed to notify the coroner.

I returned to the body and covered it with a blanket before resuming my search for possible other occupants.

The aforementioned subject's head was found approximately 20 yards west of the body, 40 yards west of the vehicle. I personally identified the deceased as Charlotte Hornsby Foster, approximately sixty years of age, residing in the 500 block of Jefferson Davis Boulevard in Jerusalem, Mississippi.

The ambulance arrived at 0125, escorted by two Jerusalem police officers.

The coroner arrived at 0152.

A second sweep of the area was made to determine if there had been any other occupants in the Foster vehicle at the time of the accident. None were found.

The distance between the highway and the impact area indicated the vehicle had left the roadway at a high rate of speed. (Measurements and other technical data are included in the supplemental accident report filed with this narrative.) Further inspection of the field, conducted with the assistance of Jerusalem Police Patrolman Ed Wilcox, indicated the vehicle had rolled over at least four times before coming to rest on its wheels.

The preliminary investigation at the scene turned up no apparent contributing factors to the accident. There was no outward indication that alcohol was involved. Inspection of the automobile at the accident scene revealed no indications of mechanical failure. Additionally, there were no signs that another vehicle or vehicles had been involved.

The highway was free of skid marks.

Conditions were dark but clear and dry.

See supplemental report for additional forensic details.

Respectfully submitted,

Trooper Stephen Tippet

Mississippi State Police
0625 hours
5/15/91

II

Victoria Writes to a Friend

CHRONICLE NOTES: Karen Hornsby Foster received Victoria Buchanan's letter in Oxford, England, where she had gone to spend the summer.

—Editor

Dear Karen,

I talked to Peter today, who said Liz spoke to you last night on the telephone.

I hardly know what to say, or write, about this catastrophe. When I think of the work we put into building support for our project, I could just cry. (In fact, I *am* crying.) To get so close only to have Arlington snatched away from us by a—forgive me—damned carpetbagging Yankee! Five years of work destroyed in the time it took to sign a check. Not to mention the greater loss: preserving the history of the South, and of Jerusalem's Founding Families.

I realize now that I've become too emotionally involved in the project. My family built Arlington, and I suppose I've always felt that I owned it in a way, even though the Buchanans haven't lived there for more than sixty years. The plantation's overnight sale to a stranger from New York has made my folly painfully obvious.

The man from New York is named Becker Thorne, as Liz surely told you. I've never heard of him, but he's apparently a well-known stock market wizard who flew to town in his private jet. Mr. Thorne—who Liz said usually doesn't talk to the press—told the *Gazette* he "always wanted to own a gracious Southern mansion."

Now he does.

Katharine Culpepper Simonette put the deal together in the middle of the night, behind everybody's back. (Who else, but the queen of the strip mall?) She drove Mr. Thorne to Arlington under cover of darkness, and—believe it or not—he bought the place without even seeing it in the daylight.

He'll get a surprise when he sees the roof in the light of day!

I'm so angry at Katharine that I could—no, I won't say what I'd *like* to do to her, Karen, but you probably feel the same. It's difficult to imagine that Katharine is one of *us*, but then the Culpeppers' primary interest always has been money.

Speaking of money, the preservation society has a new money problem: giving back what was donated to the Arlington Plantation Acquisition Fund. The big gifts ought to be relatively easy to return, but I can't think of a way to make amends with the countless small, anonymous donors who gave us a dollar or two because they believed in our cause. Do you have any thoughts on the subject?

I can't believe we were given no advance warning of the sale—no opportunity to respond, to present a check or an offer. The sisters knew we were within a few thousand dollars of having the money. If push had come to shove, we could have gotten on the phone and raised the money in a day or two, instead of letting the fund drive run its course.

I only learned that Arlington had been sold behind our backs when Phil called from the newspaper looking for a reaction to put in his reporter's story. I'm afraid I was less than diplomatic. Phil was kind enough to omit my most inflammatory comments, for which I will be eternally in his debt. I don't want to alienate Mr. Thorne. Maybe I can make him listen to reason.

I'm utterly disgusted with the sisters. I know it must be frightening to be old and have no one to look after you, but it's difficult to forgive their lack of faith in the community. The sisters had a commitment from us to buy Arlington before the end of the year, and, by my way of thinking, we had a commitment from them, too. They're taking over the Carmelite Monastery near Cheswick, you probably know. I have no idea where the Carmelites are going.

I fully intend to track down Mr. Thorne, if he's still in town, and have a serious talk with him. I'm not naive enough to think I can convince him to let us buy Arlington from him for what he paid, but I'll give it a shot. The mind reels to think what an unenlightened person could do to Arlington Plantation. With Katharine as Mr. Thorne's advisor, we should be prepared for the worst. She'll probably tell him to turn the north lawn into a trailer park.

I hope this business does not cause you too much grief, especially when you've only just gotten away from here. You've had your share of tragedy this year. Losing Arlington is nothing next to losing Charlotte. I miss her tremendously. She was a loyal friend. I'll never forget the support she gave me after Michelle was born.

Other than the debacle over Arlington's sale, things have been quiet here. We did have a bit of excitement at the college when Raoule Illosa canceled his summer residency, leaving Delilah Mills and the rest of us on the Visiting Artist committee hanging. Delilah has the name of a pianist/composer in New York whom she is going to try to convince to come to Jerusalem on short notice to be the college's Visiting Artist for the summer session. I'm sure it will all work out in the end.

Please write—or telephone—if you have any ideas about how to handle Mr. Thorne.

I suppose from this point the news from Jerusalem can only improve.

Your friend,
Victoria Buchanan

III

Interrogation

CHRONICLE NOTES: The following is a transcript copy of a taped interrogation David Parker stole from the Jerusalem

Police Department—a violation of *Illuminati* bylaws. The original recording has been anonymously returned to police files.
—*Editor*

HARLIN PLUMMER INTERROGATION

INTERROGATOR: Were you planning to leave town tonight, Harlin?

PLUMMER: I was before Billy picked me up.

INTERROGATOR: Leaving for any special reason?

PLUMMER: I didn't know I needed one.

INTERROGATOR: Did Billy remind you of your rights?

PLUMMER: I know my rights.

INTERROGATOR: Where were you fixing to go?

PLUMMER: Over to New Orleans.

INTERROGATOR: You got business there?

PLUMMER: I don't have business anywhere. You know that, Jim. I was just going. I've had a bellyful of this town.

INTERROGATOR: I guess I'm surprised you didn't leave sooner.

PLUMMER: What do you mean? After the accident? Or when Julia died? Or when I got fired?

INTERROGATOR: Harlin, I—

PLUMMER: Forget it.

INTERROGATOR: Tell me what you did tonight from about five o'clock on.

PLUMMER: I was sleeping one off at five. I got up and left the hotel between six and seven. I went up to Mosquito Park.

INTERROGATOR: What did you do up there?

PLUMMER: Christ!

INTERROGATOR: Come on, Harlin. You know the drill.

PLUMMER: I went through the Dumpster looking for cans. There'd been some high-school boys up there in the afternoon playing touch football. I got twenty-four dead soldiers. Budweisers. Football's a thirsty game. I cashed in the cans down to the convenience store.

INTERROGATOR: Did you buy a bottle?

PLUMMER: Yeah, what else. A bottle of 20-20. The clerk might remember, if she's any smarter than she looks.

INTERROGATOR: Were you alone?

PLUMMER: At the park. I met a lush named Wilson outside the store. It was starting to get dark. It must have been around eight-thirty.

INTERROGATOR: What's Wilson's full name?

PLUMMER: Just Wilson, as far as I know. He's from someplace up north. Pittsburgh, maybe.

INTERROGATOR: What did you two do?

PLUMMER: We went up and sat under the trestle there on the boulevard and got well. It's not martinis at the country club, but it passes for sociability among us winos.

INTERROGATOR: How long did you hang out with Wilson?

PLUMMER: You really shouldn't keep needling, Jim. Long, uncomfortable silences work better. Wait until I want to talk, until I need to talk, until I can't stop myself from talking.

INTERROGATOR: I may not be as smooth as you, but I still got a badge.

PLUMMER: Needlessly antagonizing your subject will only strengthen his resistance.

INTERROGATOR: Why you always have to do it the hard way, Harlin?

PLUMMER: Trade places with me and see how cooperative you feel. (Laughter.) Where the hell were we?

INTERROGATOR: You and Wilson were drinking under the trestle.

PLUMMER: Yeah. We drank the Mad Dog and a bottle of sherry he had. Then Wilson had a can of this hair spray he'd boosted somewhere. He gets out this goddamn hair spray and starts trying to pry the top off the aerosol can, using a church key, so that he can drink it.

INTERROGATOR: Hair spray?

PLUMMER: I mean, Christ! I've sunk pretty low, but I've never drunk hair spray.

INTERROGATOR: And you two got into a disagreement over it?

PLUMMER: That's right. I dumped the hair spray, figured I was doing the poor rummy a favor. He took a swing at me. I swung back. We could hardly stand up. Neither one of us did much damage; just a couple of drunks rolling around under a railroad bridge. Did something happen to that bum? He was on his feet and breathing when I left him.

INTERROGATOR: What was Wilson wearing when you were together?

PLUMMER: These stinking Texaco coveralls he scrounged somewhere.

INTERROGATOR: Where did you go when you left Wilson?

PLUMMER: Back to the Armstrong. Must have been about ten.

INTERROGATOR: Anybody see you come in?

PLUMMER: I don't remember seeing anybody at the desk when I came in, but I don't know. I was fairly well poisoned. (Long silence.) I slept for a little while. Woke up. The window was closed. There wasn't any air in the room. I was sweating like a mule. I opened the window, and the air cleared my head. I think it was that hair spray that cut it, to tell you the gospel truth. It wasn't a big thing, but it hit home. I decided it was time to get the hell out of Jerusalem. I don't know if I can clean up, but for the first time in about five years I'm going to try. I threw some things in a grip and left. The night clerk, the new kid, saw me go out. I gave him my key, said *adios*, walked to the bus depot. I had to stop on the way and get a pint because I was getting the shakes. I was sitting outside waiting for the bus when Billy pulled up and invited me to come to the police station.

INTERROGATOR: Did you go over to the old depot on your way to the bus station?

PLUMMER: No, it's not exactly on the way.

INTERROGATOR: You didn't go to the depot, either alone or with Wilson Holzinger?

PLUMMER: Wilson Holzinger? What were you asking me his name for if you knew it?

INTERROGATOR: Answer the question, Harlin. Did you go to the depot tonight?

PLUMMER: No.

INTERROGATOR: You ever flop at the old depot?

PLUMMER: You kidding? The place is crawling with rats. I think Wilson flopped there sometimes. I don't know how anybody could stand it. I hear you wake up sometimes and rats are literally crawling on you.

INTERROGATOR: Did Gregory Culpepper ever sleep it off at the depot?

PLUMMER: Gregory Culpepper? There's a name. This is all beginning to make more sense. What's up with Greg? Something happen to him? I didn't think you could really be interested in a scuffle between me and Wilson Holzinger—if that's his name and not just some alias he fed you.

INTERROGATOR: Wilson uses an alias?

PLUMMER: Jesus, Jim.

INTERROGATOR: Never mind that for now. I'm trying to establish something, Harlin. Does Gregory Culpepper ever crash at the depot?

PLUMMER: I heard that he did, but I don't know first-hand, which makes it hearsay. I kept away from the depot, Jim. I've got a thing about rats.

INTERROGATOR: Does Greg still get money from his family?

PLUMMER: I think they've pretty much washed their hands of him. I don't blame them. You can't do anything for a drunk who wants to keep drinking. You know Greg. He's a lost soul even by my modest standards.

INTERROGATOR: Didn't he get some money recently from his niece, Katharine Simonette?

PLUMMER: I heard he put the touch on her a month or so back. Story was she gave him two hundred dollars to get out of town. She didn't do it out of kindness, either. The Culpeppers would do anything to be rid of him. They think he detracts from their la-di-da social status in this burg. I'll tell you something about Katharine, Jim. That girl may be the coldest Culpepper yet, and that's saying something. It was damned irresponsible to give two hundred dollars to a drunk like Greg. It could have killed him.

INTERROGATOR: When is the last time you saw Gregory Culpepper?

PLUMMER: Hell, I don't know. It's one day into the next for me, Jim.

INTERROGATOR: Don't give me the runaround, Harlin.

PLUMMER: It isn't any runaround. I honestly couldn't tell you. Three weeks, maybe. That's a guess. He hasn't been around much. Somebody—I don't recall who—said he was staying in an old tobacco drying shed out on the edge of Arlington Plantation. Maybe it was J. B. McNaughton told me about the tobacco barn.

INTERROGATOR: Did Mrs. Simonette give her uncle a bus ticket along with the cash?

PLUMMER: You'll have to ask her.

INTERROGATOR: Did Greg Culpepper ever have any quarrels with anybody?

PLUMMER: Only every person he ever ran into.

INTERROGATOR: You remember hearing anything about somebody stealing a bus ticket from him back about the time he went to Katharine for money?

PLUMMER: My memory isn't so good, Jim. Maybe a glass of that Four Roses you keep in your desk would spark a recollection.

INTERROGATOR: Where'd you get the bus ticket to New Orleans, Harlin? Wilson Holzinger says you and Greg got into it a while back over a bus ticket. Holzinger says Culpepper had the idea that you stole a bus ticket to New Orleans from him.

PLUMMER: I'll confess to being a drunkard. I'm not a thief.

INTERROGATOR: That isn't what Holzinger says.

PLUMMER: Then he can go to hell and you can, too. He'll make a great witness for the prosecution. I can just see the faces in the jury when he gets up on the stand.

INTERROGATOR: Did you steal a bus ticket to New Orleans from Gregory Culpepper? Yes or no?

PLUMMER: No. I categorically deny stealing a bus ticket from Greg, or from anybody else for that matter. I've never stolen anything in my life.

INTERROGATOR: Then how'd you get it? That ticket is a month old. That would coincide with when Katharine Simonette gave her uncle money and a bus ticket to New Orleans—a bus ticket Gregory Culpepper accused you of stealing. I got to tell you, Harlin, this don't look good. This don't look at all good.

PLUMMER: Then that's bad luck for me, but it doesn't change the way things happened. I found that ticket while I was looking for cans in the alley behind Popeye's. I figured it could have been Greg's. He'd been hoarding it like an uncashed check while he drank his way through the money his niece had given him. But it wasn't like it had his name on it or was in a wallet with an ID. It was just there, lying in the alley next to the Dumpster.

INTERROGATOR: And you didn't give it back to him?

PLUMMER: Assuming it was his, what would have been the point of returning a lost bus ticket to somebody like Greg? He wouldn't have used it. He would have lost it again, or thrown it in a urinal and pissed on it, or figured out a way to cash it in or sell it so he could drink up the money.

INTERROGATOR: Did you and Culpepper argue about the ticket?

PLUMMER: It was nothing. Thirty seconds of drunken shouting. He was always losing things and accusing people of stealing them. There was a coat one time, some shoes another time, a ratty bit of blanket he'd snagged off a clothesline once. Every lush in town has stolen something from Greg Culpepper, to hear him tell it. I'll bet money I wasn't the only one he accused of stealing that bus ticket to New Orleans.

INTERROGATOR: You've seen dead bodies before. You know how quiet and still they are.

PLUMMER: Did somebody kill Greg Culpepper? Is that what all this clumsy waltzing is about?

INTERROGATOR: You should have seen him, Harlin. You never really know when somebody calls in on a transient. They think they're dead, but they're just dead drunk. But Greg Culpepper was dead. His skin was so white. Looked like his face was made out of eggshell. I thought it might shatter if I poked it with my finger. His throat had been slashed like a pig's.

PLUMMER: I'm truly sorry to hear that. I've seen men get their throats cut. Nobody deserves to die that way.

INTERROGATOR: You're right. Whoever killed him was a goddamned animal. You couldn't be completely human and mutilate a person like that.

PLUMMER: Mutilate? Christ almighty, Jim.

INTERROGATOR: Doc Chesterfield said he would've died about the time you say you were laid up at the Armstrong, sleeping it off. But you say nobody saw you come in or can vouch for you. And you're right. Nobody did see you come in. We've checked.

PLUMMER: That doesn't mean a damn thing and you know it. If you think I got something to do with killing Greg Culpepper, you're as wrong as he was. Who found the body?

INTERROGATOR: Holzinger.

PLUMMER: In the depot?

INTERROGATOR: That's right. He wasn't killed at the depot, though. It happened someplace else, and the body was dumped there. That's how it looks at this point.

PLUMMER: What's that supposed to mean?

INTERROGATOR: The evidence is contradictory. He was tortured at the depot. That much is obvious from the blood sprayed on the walls and ceiling. But there was nowhere near the blood there should have been with his throat being cut. Hell, Harlin, his neck was torn wide open. There should have been blood everywhere.

PLUMMER: What makes you think Wilson didn't cut Greg's throat? He wearing the same coveralls he had on earlier?

INTERROGATOR: You guessed it.

PLUMMER: That would put him out of it. It's impossible to cut a man's throat and not get bloody.

INTERROGATOR: That's pretty much how I see it. What were you wearing earlier tonight?

PLUMMER: You're looking at it. Been wearing the same clothes for two days.

INTERROGATOR: We're going to have to hold you on suspicion of murder, Harlin. The county attorney will decide whether to go to the grand jury.

PLUMMER: My brain may be pickled, Jim, but it ain't so pickled that I'd get in a public argument with Gregory Culpepper over a bus ticket, wait three weeks, cut his throat, then use the ticket to get on the bus out of town.

INTERROGATOR: People do crazy things, Harlin. They act irrationally. That's how murders get committed in the first place.

PLUMMER: You better get somebody out to Arlington to check out that tobacco shed.

INTERROGATOR: Harlin Plummer, you're under arrest for the willful murder of Gregory Culpepper. We're going to need your clothes for the lab. We're also going to need to take some samples from under the tips of your fingernails. If there's any blood, Harlin, we'll find it. There will be microscopic traces you couldn't wash away, no matter how careful you were. You sure you don't have anything you want to tell me?

PLUMMER: Just that you're wasting your time. Don't let the trail go cold on you. Those Culpeppers can make a world of trouble for you if you screw this up. That is, assuming they care somebody slit Greg's throat.

INTERROGATOR: It would feel good to get it off your chest, Harlin. I'd be willing to stand you a bottle to keep you from getting the DTs if you told us the truth.

PLUMMER: Go to hell.

INTERROGATOR: Officer Dunlap, take Mr. Plummer to his cell.

PART V

✧

Pursuit

I

Garden Party

CHRONICLE NOTES: In Jerusalem, Mississippi, David Parker met a woman capable of diverting his mind—which is to say his attention—from the job he'd been sent there to do. Parker's journal, continued.

—Editor

I was late for the cocktail party that Powell Mills was hosting, especially bad form since I was the guest of honor.

It was an almost unbelievably hot day. The sun was a white disk that burned the blue out of the Southern sky. The temperature would have been bearable but for the humidity that rose up from the river below town. Moisture hung palpably in the air. There was no breeze, just a quiet, heavy stillness.

The college is nearly deserted during the summer session, a quiet campus in an even quieter town. The only distraction all day was the blue jay perched outside the guest's apartment where I am lodging, complaining in a harsh voice until the rising heat drove him to silence.

And then the sun went down and everything changed. The evening was like an apology for the day. The heat broke as soon as the sun fell below the horizon, and a pleasant breeze rose that carried a hint of the salt air from the Gulf. It was quite pleasant by the time I left to walk across campus toward the college president's house, not wishing to be any later than I already was after becoming too immersed in rescoring the overture to my opera. The stars blinked in the gathering dusk. Behind me in the wooded campus a melodious song began—a nightingale.

Powell Mills, Morningside College's president, had his eye out and met me at the curb.

Mills is sixty years old and looks like a former coach—which he was before being put out to pasture as an administrator. Mills was a football player, a tailback at Purdue, who played two seasons for the Bears before his left knee gave out. His athletic prowess now is limited to the golf course, where he's a scratch player. I learned all of this between the front curb and his wife's rose beds on the side of the house, where the garden party was already in full swing.

The president lives in a well-tended mansion that predates the Civil War. General Nathan Bedford Forrest, the genius of the Confederate cavalry, once spent the night there, as did General Stonewall Jackson; both events are commemorated with a brass plaque beside the front entry. A Union general intended to burn the house and the rest of the town, but Forrest derailed the plan.

Strings of Japanese lanterns were hung across the garden for light, with a dozen tiki lamps that gave off a citronella smell as they burned. The bar—folding tables pushed together in an L and covered with white tablecloths—held an impressive array of bottles and hors d'oeuvres. The two bartenders wore the sort of crisp white jackets bartenders wear at college garden parties staffed by undergraduates on work-study.

There was a good crowd for the evening—most of the faculty, Mills said. I could guess their departments from their clothing. The English faculty wore jeans with black turtlenecks or tieless oxford cloth shirts and blazers. The business department wore suits. The engineers were the ones with plastic pen holders in their shirt pockets. The athletic department's members looked sporty in gold shirts, Dockers, and Reeboks. The art professors did their best to look avant garde. For the most part the guests stayed segmented in groups, like schools of fish swimming tightly together.

Mills, who seems more at home chatting up athletic boosters than visiting pianists, got me a beer and turned me over to his wife, Delilah, who brushed aside my apology for being late.

"We're the ones who should apologize," she said graciously. "We asked you to come to Jerusalem with precious little notice."

"It really wasn't a problem, Mrs. Mills. I'm honored to be here."

"Do call me Delilah. The violist we had originally arranged

to have come was detained in Chile. Something about a revolution."

I laughed politely and complimented her on her garden.

"Howard will be pleased to learn you like it." She indicated a workman in khaki pants and a khaki shirt at the center of a circle of men and women who seemed to be enraptured by the sound of his voice.

"He's dispensing advice on gardening. It's something of a passion in Jerusalem. We have such a long growing season. Howard Truman is head groundskeeper for the college and president of the Gardening Guild. The credit for my roses belongs to him."

As if sensing Delilah's appreciation, Howard Truman looked in her direction and smiled.

Delilah squired me around the party, introducing me to the other guests. This consumed the better part of an hour and a second drink. By the time we'd finished, the party had progressed to the next, more comfortable stage. Made bold by drink, even the more timid faculty members discovered they did, in fact, have opinions about music they deemed worthy of sharing with me.

Once Delilah saw that I was sufficiently comfortable, she excused herself to tend to her other guests. As I watched her leave me and continue working the crowd, it occurred to me that Powell Mills might well owe his position to his wife's social skills.

I spent a quarter hour chatting amiably with Dr. James Plant, chairman of the physics department, about the history of the Civil War, his hobby. Plant, a fellow Yankee, has fallen in love with Jerusalem's past, which, unlike that of his native Milwaukee, is rich with tales of bloody battles, sieges, and duels. He told me that several of the town's most influential old families played important roles in the Confederacy. Jefferson Davis visited Jerusalem numerous times during the war, staying just outside of town at Arlington Plantation, a magnificent old mansion owned by a Confederate general named Noah Buchanan who lost his arm at the Battle of Antietam.

I asked Dr. Plant how he came to be at Morningside College.

"Actually," he said, tugging at a beard that makes him look rather like one of the Confederate generals he reveres, "it was because of a woman." He cleared his throat and shrugged. "It didn't work out. I intended to move on but never achieved escape velocity."

There was an outburst of raucous female laughter where Powell Mills was holding court among coaches and trainers. The men formed a ring, and in the middle of the ring stood an attractive woman with bloodred lips and matching nails who obviously enjoyed being the object of male attention.

"She's drunk already," Dr. Plant said with some bitterness.

I looked more closely. The woman was wearing a tight black Anne Klein dress, which left her upper chest and back bare and could not have been cut an inch shorter. She was slipping into middle age, but not, it seemed, in a particularly graceful way. One of the men leaned toward her and said something that made her laugh loudly.

"Who is she?"

"Lydia Chase, she's calling herself again. She's been married and divorced three times but has gone back to using her maiden name. Her father is Lysander Chase. You know who he is? The president and majority stockholder in the Bank of Jerusalem. The richest man in town."

Powell Mills clasped his hands in front of himself and took a pantomime golf swing. The gesture must have played a part in a humorous story, because the whole group was laughing again, Lydia Chase the loudest. A cloud of fireflies rose into the air from the bushes behind Lydia and Powell's group like a startled flock of tiny luminous birds. A lovely night, but beneath the pleasantness I felt currents of underlying hostility, the tidal pull of old disagreements and rivalries hidden under a veneer of conviviality.

I could see both Delilah Mills and her husband from where I was standing. Delilah was at the bar, giving instructions to the bartenders, seemingly paying no attention to her husband's group. Lydia placed her hand on Powell Mills's arm—and Delilah's chin jerked up and her eyes focused sharply on the younger woman.

"If looks could kill," Dr. Plant said softly, a keen observer.

I gave a sideways glance at the bearded physics professor. "I gather you do not approve of Ms. Chase."

"Lydia's loose morals have caused much embarrassment and unhappiness."

A startled look crossed Plant's face as he heard the unhappiness in his own voice.

"Scandals are never forgotten in Jerusalem, Mr. Parker. However, one is expected to disguise one's disapproval. It's one of the cardinal rules of Southern manners. This is a small town, and within it one's circle is very small indeed."

With that enigmatic pronouncement, Dr. Plant excused himself and wandered away—though not in Lydia Chase's direction.

I helped myself to a glass of wine from the bar. Pretending not to see two matrons bearing down on me, I retreated to an arbor as if to better examine Delilah's garden by starlight.

The view from the garden was worth the social disgrace I risked by slipping away from the rest of the party. Seen from a distance, the lawn party resembled a portrait of a gracious Southern evening. Across the lawn of the college president's mansion, where Stonewall Jackson and Nathan Bedford Forrest had once slept, across the larger lawn of the campus itself, wooded with magnificent old oaks towering over an odd collection of nineteenth-century buildings and a few modern additions, the nightingale's song echoed.

The nightingale called to me. I answered it back with a verse of Keats's poem about a nightingale.

> *" 'O, for a draught of vintage! that hath been*
> *Cooled a long age in the deep-delved earth,*
> *Tasting of Flora and the country green,*
> *Dance, and Provençal song, and sunburnt mirth!' "*

The night had awakened something within me. I used to read poetry, back when I was first with the *Illuminati* and it seemed that life's most fabulous mysteries were being revealed to me. Then things turned bad, Tatiana left me, and my passion for verse withered.

Only to return, quite unexpectedly, on a summer evening in a rose garden in Jerusalem, Mississippi . . .

Perhaps Wolf was right, I thought—perhaps there would be time for new loves and new dreams. This set me thinking about another night and another garden and another woman, Princess Nicoletta di Medusa. Sadly, that garden and woman were imaginary, a figment of my dreams.

I lifted the glass.

A woman's voice spoke behind me, picking up where I had left off with Keats.

" 'O for a beaker full of the warm South,
Full of the true, the blushful Hippocrene,
With beaded bubbles winking at the brim,
And purple-stained mouth.' "

I turned, expecting Nicoletta. I was wrong.

Even by the light of the distant lanterns in the garden, Victoria Buchanan's eyes were the summer-morning-blue of a robin's egg. Long blonde hair. A patrician face with just the slightest hint of imperviousness in the arch of her eyebrows. She was tall, nearly six feet, with the long, well-formed legs that go along with a lithe, small-breasted body—a body I immediately wanted to enfold in my arms and hold against me.

She resumed before I could find my tongue.

" 'That I might drink, and leave the world unseen,
And with thee fade away into the forest dim.' "

Our eyes locked a moment before she lowered her gaze. A blush deepened the color in her high-boned face.

"I'm sorry to interrupt your privacy," she said with a shyness that contrasted with her bold recitation. "I couldn't resist. I adore Keats."

"David Parker," I said, extending my hand.

"Our guest of honor. I'm Victoria Buchanan. I'm afraid I was a late arrival."

"Then we have something else in common," I said, smiling. "I was late to the party myself."

Holding her hand, I felt her warmth and intelligence—and an unmistakable vulnerability. Poor Victoria: It was plain to my *Vampiri* eyes that she had suffered a great wound at the hands of love. I did not pry into the privacy of her thoughts, of course. I knew she would tell me, in time.

"It's rare to find someone who shares my appreciation for dead poets," I said.

"Dead poets are my profession," Victoria protested mildly. "I teach Romantic and Victorian poetry here at Morningside. We're fortunate to get you here with so little notice."

"No, I am the fortunate one," I said.

"You are a pianist and composer. Are you also a poet?"

"No, but I do enjoy poetry immensely. Music and poetry are more compatible than you might think."

"Oh, I quite agree," she said, beaming.

"And Keats is easy to like."

"My students are invariably attracted to his fascination with death." Victoria quoted a well-known passage.

> " *'Darkling I listen; and, for many a time*
> *I have been half in love with easeful Death,*
> *Called him soft names in many a mused rhyme,*
> *To take into the air in my quiet breath.'* "

"If I were you, I'd warn my students to be careful about falling 'in love with easeful Death.' "

"Without question. You know how it is with adolescents and young adults. Darkness attracts them. They all think Lucifer is the hero of *Paradise Lost.*"

"Yes, I remember my undergraduate days," I said, my tone more bleak than I would have liked. "I thought the same thing. Sometimes I still do."

We strolled along the far edge of the garden, Victoria pointing out different varieties of roses. She laughed at the absurdity of trying to show me flowers in the night, but I insisted that I could see them well enough—as indeed I could.

"Do you happen to know if Becker Thorne is here this evening?" I asked as we began to walk back toward the others.

Victoria's face became a neutral mask.

"No, he's not. Powell invited him. He apparently had the bad manners to accept and then not show up."

"I get the impression that you and Thorne are not exactly friends."

"We've never met, actually. I suppose that I hope we can become friends, but I'd say the chance of that is remote."

"Oh?"

"It's a little complicated, I'm afraid."

"I don't mean to pry." The truth was I *did*. I wanted to learn what I could about Becker Thorne. Thorne is one of five people who have moved to Jerusalem since the spring. Although I haven't checked out the others' stories, Thorne is the only new arrival who is supposed to have come from New York City. The odds are good that Thorne is the vampire I have come to Mississippi to kill.

"My difficulties with Mr. Thorne are hardly secret," Victoria said with an unsuccessful effort to suppress a sigh. "I'm president of the Jerusalem Historical Preservation Society. For the past five years, the society has been raising money to buy Arlington Plantation and preserve it as a house museum. Are you familiar with Arlington and its story?"

"Only vaguely. Are you related to the General Noah Buchanan who owned it during the Civil War?"

In the space of a pause, her chest rose and fell again in another sigh. Her eyes focused in the distance and her voice became soft as she spoke from someplace between a memory and a dream.

"My family built Arlington and owned it until the Depression."

When she paused I noticed that her upper lip was almost imperceptibly moving, the only outward sign she was close to tears.

"And the preservation society is buying Arlington?" I prodded when her voice trailed off.

"*Was* is the proper verb, Mr. Parker."

"I take it the sale fell through," I said gently. "Please, call me David."

Victoria told me the story of how Becker Thorne had come to town and bought Arlington out from underneath the preservation society.

"I have to be practical, David. My first concern is still Arlington. I have nothing to gain by antagonizing Mr. Thorne. On weekends, the sisters allowed visitors to tour the grounds and main part of the great house. I hope to persuade Mr. Thorne to do the same. It won't be much, but it will be better than nothing. Arlington is a treasure that belongs to the entire state—not just some Johnny-come-lately from New York City."

"Present company excluded, I hope."

"Excuse me? Oh, I do apologize." Victoria blushed again and gave my arm a reassuring touch, sending a tingle of excitement running through my body. "I didn't mean *you*, David. I'm sure that you are a gentleman. Judging from the underhanded tactics he used to get the deed to Arlington, I'm afraid I can't say the same about Mr. Thorne."

"What does he intend to do with Arlington?"

"God only knows. People say he plans to live there as soon as the sisters get out, though I can't understand why a Wall Street wolf like Becker Thorne would choose to move to Mississippi. He's not from Jerusalem and doesn't have any relatives here."

"He must have some connection with the town."

"None that anybody knows of."

Away in the darkness, the nightingale renewed its song.

"Beautiful, isn't it?"

"They're not native to the United States, you know. A blockade runner brought a pair of nightingales to one of my ancestors, Anna Lee Buchanan, during the War Between the States. She couldn't bear to see them caged, and so she set them free. There is a small population living around Jerusalem. To my knowledge, it's the only place in the country you'll find them."

A harsh shriek of female laughter turned heads toward Lydia Chase.

"Oh-oh," Victoria whispered, although there was no one near enough to overhear. "I hate to tell you to leave your own party early, but I guarantee there will be a scene later on if she stays and keeps drinking."

I thanked Victoria for the warning and considered offering to go if she would go with me. I decided against it. I didn't want to scare her away from me by demonstrating too much interest too early.

"I saw you talking to Jim Plant earlier. I suppose he's still mooning over Lydia."

"I wouldn't exactly call it 'mooning.' "

"Did he tell you he was Lydia's second husband?"

"You're kidding," I said, genuinely surprised.

"Speaking of the devil, here she comes!"

"Oh, my God, Victoria," Lydia cried as she broke away from the others, "please don't bore our guest of honor with talk about Arlington and the other decrepit old buildings in town! You'll scare him away from Jerusalem before he gets to know what it's really like."

I looked from Lydia—bearing down on us with a fresh drink in her hand—to Powell Mills. He read my look perfectly but gave a little shrug to explain that he was unable to control her, and to warn me that she was likely to say or do something unpredictable.

"Hello," she cooed, ignoring Victoria. "I am Lydia Chase."

"I'm David Parker. How do you do?"

"I'm a little loaded actually, not that it especially matters. Now you come along with me. I can't leave you stranded out here among the geraniums and poetry professors." She took my arm and began to pull me bodily back toward the party. "I want to introduce you to the man who has the best golf game in town. You do golf, don't you, David? You don't mind if I call you David?"

I looked back over my shoulder and smiled apologetically at Victoria. And I thought:

"Away! away! for I will fly to thee. . . ."

Victoria seemed amused to see me hauled off by Lydia Chase, but I could see she was also disappointed. We had so much more to talk about.

II
Auld Lang Syne

CHRONICLE NOTES: "Becker Thorne's" diary, continued.
—*Editor*

So much here has changed. Almost everything, in fact, except the old part of town and Arlington. And Jerusalem's Founding Families, who all still have representatives living here—living at least for the present.

The old spirit of the South is gone. Signs of our former greatness remain, but only as symbols of a past forever lost, the dying strains of a magnificent waltz that will be followed by only the most unsatisfying silence. Yea, the titans have fallen. Our heros and our chivalrous dreams of a second American Revolution together were murdered by Negro-loving Yankees and the traitors who betrayed us.

Treason and murder ever kept together,
As two yoke-devils sworn to either's purpose.

But now I have returned. I must find the man with the mark of the saber angled across his left cheek and fulfill the Neon prophecy: *"You will know him by his sign and by his words."* And the words: *"I am the Last Gray Ghost of the Confederacy."* And the promise: *"Together,"* the Neon had said, *"you will smite the malefactors."*

Once I find the Ghost, we shall enact a more suitable ending to this drawn-out play.

So shall you hear
Of carnal, bloody, and unnatural acts,
Of accidental judgments, casual slaughters,
Of deaths put on by cunning and forced cause,
And, in this upshot, purposes mistook
Fall'n on th' inventors' heads. All this can I
Truly deliver.

After dusk I drove to Arlington. The magic of that place retains its power still. An Indian sorcerer must have cast a spell over her lands before departing, leaving them to the white man. They say Jefferson Davis, as dour and relentlessly practical a Southerner as was ever born, proclaimed Arlington the only place he could love as much as his own home.

Ancient oaks surround the great house still, more ancient now than they were when I was a young man. Ezekial Buchanan told me some of the trees had been standing since the Spanish king gave the land to the bastard son of his favorite courtesan. At night the trees spread out their fingers like the skeletal hands of dead men. Gaunt fingers drip moss like tresses of human hair or the decaying fabric of a funeral shroud.

The property came into the Buchanan family in 1803. Daniel Barrow Buchanan held twelve thousand acres in his original deed. His son, Ezekial Buchanan, was a Beau Brummell character, a handsome and wealthy charmer famous for his prowess with hot-blooded horses and dueling pistols. The real Beau Brummell died a pauper, but not so Ezekial Buchanan. While serving in the legislature, Ezekial killed four men with his dueling pistols. The fourth such meeting was to settle a question of honor regarding the governor's daughter—said at the time to be the most beautiful woman in the South. Ezekial Buchanan survived to marry the woman. In 1830, he began building Arlington for his bride. In 1866, on his sixty-third birthday, an ill-tempered stallion rolled on him. His bones were laid to rest in the family mausoleum he began as the burial place for his second son, Colonel Thomas Buchanan, who fell at Gettysburg. But Ezekial Buchanan's real monument remains the Arlington great house.

I saw it again tonight as I did that first night, so many years ago.

Walking toward the manse in the dark, everything quiet except for the crickets serenading the crescent moon with their lovely song, I saw the massive Doric columns rising up out of the darkness, sepulchral sentinels garbed in priestly white that stand out with almost supernatural brightness against the weird shadows thrown by the moss-draped Spanish oaks.

The great house is an intimidating symbol of our extinct Southern culture, a monument left to remind later generations of the best blood spilled on battlefields like Antietam and Cold Harbor—leaving the weak, the wicked, and the treacherous to take over. Arlington sits on a raised porch that is nearly as high as a man. Twenty-eight fluted columns surround the house, each crowned with an entablature rich with mutules, triglyps, and guttae, art of forgotten artisans. Supported by the columns, halfway between the porch and the roof, a second floor gallery runs around the structure. The columns and the walls are brick covered with plaster bleached perfect and pure white by the sun.

The rooms in the great house are arranged in the classic style: four rooms downstairs divided by a great central hall that runs for a full one hundred feet. Rising gracefully up to the second floor is a mahogany staircase that seems to glow with a soft corona imparted by generations of careful attention with beeswax and cotton polishing cloth. On the south side of the house is a double parlor connected by sliding doors added late in the nineteenth century. On the opposite side of the hall is the music room and, to the rear, a walnut-paneled dining room. The second floor is a mirror image of the first.

do not, personally, like the addition Isaiah Buchanan built in 1912. It was cleverly designed to hide behind the original structure. Its kitchen, pantries, bathrooms, and bedrooms add to the great house's utility and modernity, but they distract from its spirit, which is pure and unadulterated Old South.

The greenhouse at the back of the 1912 addition indulged Isaiah's passion for orchids. It is still filled with the most deliciously monstrous specimens of the plant, which give off a sickening perfume and have skin like the flesh of dead men. I confess to being rather fond of orchids. The greenhouse is the one change to Arlington of which I approve.

Isaiah Buchanan is still referred to around town as the last great Buchanan, although this is rather comical because the family would still own the estate if his ill-advised investments hadn't forced his heirs to sell after his untimely death—dying in the stable fire he'd contrived to kill *me*!

The furnishings throughout the two wings are exceptional, though the furniture in the main structure, or "old house," as it is called, is just a bit older and finer. The fireplaces all have Italian marble mantels. The furniture in the dining and music rooms is hand-carved English oak. The parlor is decorated with a priceless collection of Louis XV rosewood furniture upholstered in Aubusson tapestry. The doors in the old house are constructed of cypress wood; the hinges, knobs and assorted hardware are silver. The curtains are Belgian lace.

It took nearly four years to build the old house. Another year went into construction of the plantation's other buildings, of which there were originally thirty-three, including sugar houses, cotton gins, a church, a hospital, two smokehouses, numerous stables, kitchens, and assorted other outbuildings. Plus nearly one hundred slave cabins. It was a miniature city, really, although if it still existed today, it would be considered something between a farm and a park—in short, a plantation.

Many of the outbuildings have not survived the depredations of time and the Buchanan family's slow but steady decline in fortunes. The stable where Ezekial Buchanan kept his favorite mounts—rebuilt after Isaiah set it on fire—is still in fine condition, though it is used these days to house a pickup truck, three John Deere garden tractors, and miscellaneous lawn and gardening equipment. The overseer's cottage has been kept in repair. It is now home to a Negro—the middle-aged caretaker.

How ironic it is that many of the slave cabins are still standing. Ezekial Buchanan had built them of brick for ease of maintenance. Almost one hundred and seventy years later, most of them remain, or their walls do—the wooden roofs and porches having rotted away, except for the cabins sitting on property that has since been sold to small farmers.

To the sides and rear of the great house are the formal gardens. Though not as immense as they were when there were slaves to tend them, they remain magnificent. Anna Lee would be dissatisfied with their present state, of course, but all things considered, they are remarkable.

All of it was so long ago, forgotten by everybody but me, the last Confederate alive to walk beneath the trees of Arlington, to gaze at the white pillars of what was a temple of Southern culture before it was betrayed by its highest priests. The priests are gone, but their children shall pay for their blasphemy.

Behold, I am coming soon, bringing my recompense, to repay every one for what he has done.

As I stood staring at Arlington, I thought about how everything would come right in time—and that I was time's master.

Arlington would look so beautiful in flames, the great house engulfed in a Hellish conflagration, pillars crashing to earth like Titans fallen in battle when the roof collapsed amid an explosion of sparks and licking flames, divine justice fulfilling the prophecy foretold in Revelations, in Shakespeare, in Neon.

I patted the inside breast pocket of my blazer to make sure the yellow rubber gloves were still there. Smiling the secret smile of the Fury, I set off toward the greenhouse Isaiah Buchanan had built to tackle the next dirty job.

"Who's there?"

I suppose that there is nothing new in this tired world. I've heard those same words countless times, on countless nights, in many different places and languages—a reflex reaction, a verbal tropism. Startle an animal and it runs; startle a bird and it flies; startle a human being in the night and most of them will lamely ask, "Who's there?" They hope that no one is there, no one at all, when they know that sooner or later the answer will be: "Death." People plan to be out when Death comes to visit, or at the very least asleep so that they won't have to look Death in the face and know at last what they have tried so hard to *not* know.

"Who's there?"

The voice repeated from amid the forest of orchids that turned the greenhouse into a jungle. The voice belonged to an old woman—weak, brittle, little more than a hushed whisper, a dying wind turning over dried leaves in the gutter.

The gorgeous orchids have grown to enormous size in the stifling humidity. Illuminated in the night by only a few small lamps, the greenhouse is primordial, a place where the growl and screech of ancient monsters would not seem out of place. But instead of the roar of the terrible lizards, there was only the voice of an elderly woman, tremulous and pathetic.

"Is that you, Thomas?"

No, not Thomas. He had gone away with the others. She knew that. She had to know that.

The plants touched my face like warm, damp fingers. My shirt was clinging to the small of my back, under my arms. A perfect atmosphere to keep an orchid alive—or a meddlesome old bitch so weak that she had to derive her bodily heat from an external source, like a spider living in a heat duct.

"Thomas?"

"No, madam," I said, coming into a little clearing at the center of the glassed-in garden. The old woman sat in the middle of the space in a wheelchair, surrounded by the overreaching plants and the shadows they cast. "It's Becker Thorne come to pay his respects."

She was no larger than a child. The years had reduced her small frame to an almost skeletal essence, made no more substantial by her black-and-white nun's habit—it retained a miraculous crispness despite the humidity—and the blue-and-green plaid afghan across her knees. She'd had a stroke a few years earlier, I'd been told, and could no longer walk.

"Devil!" the old woman hissed.

The strength in her voice was surprising. I'd guessed she might remember me, although after so many years, I could not be certain. Her body was ruined, but her mind was intact. I would have expected her reaction to be horror, not defiance. Unlike the others, she knew, or suspected, that I was the merciless Fury returned to Jerusalem to exact justice from the sinners.

"I've been expecting you," she said, keeping her hard, unblinking eyes on mine.

"Have you really?" I shrugged out of my jacket. She had been a spirited woman in her younger days, and time had not taken everything away from her. "Do you mind if I take off my coat?"

She didn't answer.

"I don't know how you can stand the heat in here. Especially dressed that way. Long-sleeved, ankle-length black dress, heavy cowl over your head; it can hardly be comfortable. But then the blood doesn't circulate very well at your age. You must be close to ninety."

The old woman stared at me for a long moment before beginning to move her bluish lips.

"I've lived a long life, and, with God's grace, I've endured many tests," she said in her quiet, fierce voice. "Fear, for example. I put my life in God's hands a long time ago. I'm too old to fear death, and I'm too old to fear even you, *Mr. Thorne*. You did say your name was Thorne, didn't you?"

There was sarcasm in the tone of her question that reassured me that she was not completely beyond my reach.

"Yes, that's right." I laughed merrily. "It's 'Becker Thorne' this time."

I draped my jacket over the back of a sweating Adirondack chair and looked around, raising up on my toes to peer over the plants.

"There doesn't seem to be anybody else around tonight. Where is everybody?"

"As you know well enough, they've all gone to see the new convent." The blue lips formed a tight smile. "In the van you chartered for them. Sister Ludmilla volunteered to stay with me, but I insisted she go. I wanted it to be just the two of us this evening."

I burst into laughter.

"You are an amazing woman," I complimented her. And I meant it. "If you were not so old and disgusting, I would consider making you one of us. You have spine. Unlike so many of the others who live in this town—mere *underlings*."

"Do not seek to flatter me, Devil. I'm no more susceptible to your brand of charm now than I was sixty-three years ago, when a good man might have meant something to me."

Her gray eyes became two dark slashes in her wrinkled face. She was too old for many things, but not too old to hate. And that was good. I was always happy to see pure hatred. It made me feel strong.

"I've always wondered one thing about you, Devil."

"You must be a woman of limited curiosity."

"What scared you away in 1928? You hardly started what you'd come to Jerusalem then to do. If you are as powerful as your arrogance implies, why did you lose your nerve and run away?"

I felt myself recoil from the sting of her words. I wanted to grab her by the throat and—but I forced my temper back down. It would have been a pity to let her provoke me into doing something rash. Besides, I reminded myself, the Fury had to handle these matters carefully to ensure that he could remain in Jerusalem long enough to serve justice to the fullest measure—*unlike the last time.*

"You insolent old woman. What makes you think you can dare to speak to me with such condescension? I confess that I left prematurely, but only because I was called away on urgent business. Now that I've come back, I assure you that nothing will induce me to leave this town until my work has been finished to my complete satisfaction."

I remembered something that made me laugh.

"It certainly wasn't the holy water you threw on me that made me leave Jerusalem. I am still amazed you dared confront me at my hotel. I was so surprised at the time that I could only stare as you ran out the door. Whatever were you trying to accomplish by giving me an impromptu shower?"

"I knew you were an unholy thing the moment I laid eyes on you. I had never seen a Devil before, but I knew you were one. I hoped throwing holy water into your face would burn you like acid and send you screaming into the night."

"You ruined my favorite doeskin vest. I still haven't forgiven you."

I laughed again.

"You pathetic old bag of bones," I said quite calmly. "You are not worthy of the Fury's rage. You realize that I did not come back for you, but the others. This time I shall kill them all—the Buchanans, the Culpeppers, the Chases, the Hornsbys—every man, woman, and child. For so it has been written, for so it shall be done. But do not flatter yourself by thinking that I came back for you, a mere *servant*."

"I am proud to be a servant of God," she said in a level voice. "And before that, I was proud to be a servant of Isaiah Buchanan's."

"God love the Irish! Isaiah Buchanan, the so-called last great Buchanan. What a laugh!"

"Forgetting my vows, I very much wish I could get up out of this wheelchair and slap your face, Devil."

I smiled, remembering Mary Helen's legendary temper.

"But surely you do not mean to imply that Isaiah Buchanan was indeed a great man. He certainly wasn't great at managing the Buchanan money. He lost the fortune the family had built up over four generations."

"The financial difficulties began after he died, not that it's any business of yours."

"He set it all up. He made the investments."

"Yes, but he was preparing to make changes. He knew what was coming. If not for you, the Buchanan family would still be in this house."

"Do you expect me to believe that Isaiah Buchanan confided his business secrets to you, his cook? Or were you more than the widower Buchanan's cook?"

The shriveled old woman stared up at me with such venom that I was almost glad she was unable to leap up out of her wheelchair. I could see it then in her mind. Her anger made her thoughts transparent.

"I can hardly believe it. You *were* his lover."

I doubt I've ever had someone look at me with such loathing!

"You were his lover, and yet you killed him. You locked us in the stable as he threw a lantern on the kerosene-soaked bales of straw."

I could see tears in the old woman's eyes. The real fun was finally beginning.

"I did as I was told, if he wasn't able to lock you in himself by the appointed time."

"You meant to murder us both!"

She looked at me very hard. "No, just you. There was a trap door in the floor. When the stable filled with smoke, Isaiah was going to slip out the trap door."

"Only the smoke overcame your lover. Meanwhile, I was the one who escaped."

The old woman sobbed a single time, then regained her expression of stoney contempt.

"How I wish that Mr. Buchanan had been able to send you straight back to Hell."

"*Mister*, is it? Still keeping up the pretense when we both know you used to fuck him!"

The old woman gasped with shock. I suppose she wasn't used to hearing that kind of talk. She was probably unaware of how far society had degenerated during her years of living in the cloister.

"Instead," I continued, "it was Buchanan who ended up in Hell."

"I am quite certain Mr. Buchanan is in Heaven."

"Less time in Purgatory for adultery."

"We must all atone for our sins, Devil."

"But it must have seemed like Hell for him—in the stables, I mean. They say burning is the worst way to die."

"Perhaps you would care to try it to see how you like it."

"No, thank you, I already have. Neither of you guessed that I could jump to the ceiling and smash my way out. But poor Isaiah. Left behind in the flames, trying to find his way out as the smoke clouded his senses, the windows nailed shut, the door barred from the outside—by you. You're lucky no one saw you. You would have hanged."

The old woman's chin dropped to her chest. For a moment I thought she'd fainted, but she was only grieving, grieving for her dead master, her dead lover.

"I wonder why he asked you to help instead of one of the men."

"They were all too superstitious." The old woman looked up at me again, hating me with every atom of her being. "We both understood that you were a Devil, that you might perform strange tricks to frighten anyone who helped Mr. Buchanan. But Mr. Buchanan knew that I was a good Catholic, that I'd learned about evil, and that I wasn't afraid to stand up to it."

"Bravo for you! Too bad you only managed to kill your aging lover."

I slipped back into the Adirondack chair across from her. The old woman's hands searched for something beneath the wool blanket that covered her knees. She was looking for the crucifix that all the members of her order wore looped through the belts of their habits.

"You opposed me buying Arlington."

"Yes. I will never abide evil in God's world."

"But you couldn't stop the deal."

Her eyes—the bloodshot whites spiderwebbed with blood vessels—regarded me with a cold, unblinking stare, and then broke off and looked away.

"You couldn't convince the sisters to sell Arlington to the local do-gooders instead of a shady character from New York with the ready cash in his hands."

"I spoke against it, but Mother Superior made the decision," the old woman said without looking at me. "I told them . . ."

"You told them what?"

"Not the truth, I'm afraid. They'd have thought I'd become senile. I told them that they should sell to the preservation society. Mother Superior was concerned that they would not be able to raise the money, that the society's directors were too proud to admit as much. So I told them God had sent me a vision telling me that you were evil, that the order should shun all contact with you."

"And did God really send you such a vision?" I asked, fascinated to know whether the Lord could actually chose me as His Fury and at the same time find me morally wanting.

Sister Mary Helen did not answer very quickly. "God will forgive me for molding the truth," she said finally. "My prevarication didn't do any good. None of them would listen. They think I've gone dotty on them. I might just as well have told them who you really are."

"They are greedy, aren't they? Those preservationists would have given you the money for Arlington, but your Judas sisters were too eager to get their hands on their pieces of silver to wait."

The tears in her eyes proved again that the old woman was not nearly so impervious to earthly concerns as she had earlier pretended.

"The church has a divine mission, but it is an institution made up of human beings with human failings. Taking care of Arlington has eaten up most of our financial resources. The others are nearly as old as I. They were afraid of what would happen to them. In my heart I know they really wanted to sell the plantation to the Jerusalem Historical Preservation Society, but at the same time they felt a measure of desperation that made them weak."

I laughed in the old woman's face. "Desperation—is that what you call worshiping Mammon these days. Tell me: Did Mother Superior wash her hands like Pilate after accepting my check?"

"Do not assume yourself fit to judge us, Devil."

"But that is where you're most wrong, my dear Sister Mary Helen. I have come to judge you all. Have you ever read *Alice in Wonderland*, perhaps back when you were rutting like a dog in heat with old Isaiah Buchanan?"

The old woman's blue lips trembled but she did not speak. I quoted in a child's singsong voice:

" 'I'll be judge, I'll be jury,' said cunning old Fury;
'I'll try the whole cause, and condemn you to death.' "

I could see that behind her pale gray eyes, she was beginning to take a more accurate measure of the extent to which my divinely appointed role as Fury would require me to act against the residents of Jerusalem, Mississippi.

"I've come here tonight, *Sister* Mary Helen, not to torment you, but merely to ask two simple questions. And make no mistake about it." I leaned forward and put my face very close to hers. "You are going to answer and answer truthfully."

I pulled back in ample time to miss the hand she threw at me.

"You're old!" I taunted. "Your reflexes are slow. You are, in a word, at my mercy. And, unfortunately for you, I have none."

Her hands clutched at the crucifix beneath the afghan. The blue lips began to move silently, though I could see the words they were tracing were the words of the Twenty-third Psalm.

Even though I walk through the valley of the shadow of death
I fear no evil; for thou art with me;
thy rod and thy staff,
they comfort me.

"My two questions are really quite simple, and I can't conceive any reason you will not be able to answer them for me when I put them to you. One, how much do you really know about what I am? I mean *really* know about what I *really* am. And, two, who else have you told? I'd like to think you've been discreet. It would be time-consuming and counterproductive for me to have to slaughter each and every person who lives in this convent to assure I have not been compromised. You see, there are so many people I need to kill during my time in Jerusalem that I hardly have time to go off and conduct the wholesale murder of a group of people who really concern me very little."

"The sisters know nothing about you except what you told them. I swear it. I know you, and I know your ruthlessness. The last thing I would do is endanger a group of old women nearly as defenseless as myself against the depredations of such a monster as you."

"Good." I smiled. "You've answered my second question, or at least partly, and I think I almost believe you. Now, before we get down to discussing me, let's probe just a bit further. Have you talked to anybody outside the convent about me?"

I could see that she was not going to answer, at least not without prodding. Which made me glad. I hate it when my opponents cave in too easily. I could trust the old hag to fight me with all her strength—all the more fun.

"I can see you're going to force me to resort to special measures for our discussion to be profitable." I got to my feet. "Scream as much as you like. I could keep you from screaming, but I won't. One of the things I like best about Arlington is the seclusion. It's so . . ." I looked beyond the overreaching orchids and out at the starry night beyond the greenhouse's glass ceiling. ". . . peaceful."

I gave Sister Mary Helen my most charming smile. "Shall we begin, then?"

The old woman jerked her right hand from beneath the blanket across her lap and thrust her fist toward me. Gripped in a hand that age and arthritis had transformed into a bony and gnarled claw lined with bulging blue veins was a golden crucifix. She pointed the cross at me as if it were a weapon.

The orchids and the humid air absorbed my laughter.

"That won't do you any good!" I snatched the cross from her with a sweep of my hand and hurled it backward over my shoulder. "This is not Hollywood! Crosses, holy water—what next? A string of garlic? Yet I see that you do understand a thing or two."

"I'm ready to die, if that is God's will."

"Your tone is not very pious, the way you spit your words."

I pulled the rubber gloves from the inside pocket of my jacket and began to tug them over my hands, wiggling my fingers, working my way in. The gloves were happy and caressed my hands with their clammy skin. I rubbed them together.

"*Squeak, squeak,*" the gloves told me. "*Squeak, squeak.*"

Ah yes, I couldn't have agreed more.

"These are just for fun," I explained, holding up my hands. "I don't usually bother with gloves. The Fury is much too careful when dealing with *underlings* to leave behind fingerprints."

The words the old nun said were so quiet that I could not make them out.

"I don't believe I got that."

The dry, cracked lips moved again, the voice louder this time and filled with venom: "I said, 'Go to Hell!' "

"When I do," I said with a big smile, "I'm sure you will be waiting there to meet me." I fished in the pocket of my jacket. "I'd like to begin by explaining that I prefer to work with common, everyday objects. Some torturers prefer exotic instruments made to fit special specifications, designed for special jobs, but not me. I think it is so much more creative to work from life."

I pulled out the transparent plastic bag, smoothed it, rubbed it against my face as if it were fine Persian silk.

"I love to improvise. Ah ha! I see someone has been kind enough to leave a broom propped up against the windowpanes."

I retrieved the broom and slipped it between the spokes of Sister Mary Helen's wheelchair. She looked straight ahead, refusing to meet my eye, while I bound her arms to the padded armrests with some torn sheets kept for tying up plants.

"The restraints are merely for your own protection," I said, passing behind the chair. I sank to my knees and put my mouth near the back of her head. "I wouldn't want you to hurt yourself. Old bones are so brittle. They will shatter if you hit them with almost anything."

She continued to look straight ahead. I listened closely to hear her thoughts. She was praying, of course, which was smarter than she could know; praying blocked out the other thoughts that would reveal what I wanted to know.

"You used to be such a lovely, high-spirited young woman, even if you were just a working-class Irish Catholic. I don't know how you feel about it, but seeing you again has made me almost breathless."

I caressed the edges of the cowl covering her head with my fingers. (The gloves did not much care for the feel of the starched material, preferring naked flesh.) I slipped the cowl and the cap beneath it off. Her head was covered with a few strands of sparse hair, shock white.

"Why, Sister, years of covering your head have made you almost bald. And you had such beautiful red hair."

She trembled momentarily, stirring fear, and memory, and—yes!—regrets. A bit of an image popped from her mind into mine: Isaiah Buchanan brushing her long tresses with a silver brush. The romantic old dog!

"Now, allow me to remind you what you're going to tell me," I said gently. "What do you know? And who did you tell?"

The old woman began to pray out loud, trying to block out the sound of my voice—rather rude of her after I'd come all the way out to Arlington that evening just to converse with her.

"You know, I've already done one of you in. A neat little job. I doubt anyone noticed."

"Who?" Sister Mary Helen demanded. She was worried. She was thinking about her closest friends, the other sisters.

"No, none of them. Charlotte Hornsby Foster. I'm afraid I pulled her head off. Fortunately, I was able to make it look like a rather credible car accident. The Fury exacted his measure of justice, for as it says in Scripture: *'But these enemies of mine, who did not want me to reign over them, bring them here and slay them before me.'* "

She gasped at the revelation and, before she could resist, I whipped the plastic bag over her head with a quick, practiced movement and gathered it around her neck with my hands.

At last! I could see it in her eyes. She'd shown a remarkable amount of courage, but the *dread* was in her now. I've never known a person—no matter how brave or obstinate—who didn't feel the dread when they realized death was upon them.

I closed my eyes and smiled, joyful that I could still delight in the act of killing after so many times.

"I have a confession to make, Sister, and I'd like to make it to you since I don't get to church much any more. I used to dislike doing what had to be done. Yes, it's true! I was weak. I was in a state of mortal sin, because weakness is the only real sin. But I became strong. And for my devotion, I was given Neon, and it transformed me into a Fury whose job is to smite the wicked. Killing has become my highest pleasure, my art. And it only gets better, time after time. I was like a virgin, forced to submit the first time, who learns to love it, to crave it, and to be wildly and indiscriminately wanton."

The plastic crackled as it expanded and contracted with each breath. She had remarkable control, especially for someone so elderly. Some people panic, which makes them pass out too fast.

I had several yards of twine in my pocket. I took it out and began to wrap it around and around the old woman's neck. Her breathing was picking up its tempo now. In and out, in and out. The clear plastic had clouded with water vapor, but I could see her eyes fluttering and beginning to roll up in her head. I didn't want it to go too quickly. I undid the twine and pulled the bag off.

"Palmer," she gasped.

"What?"

"The last time." Gasp. "You were here." Gasp. "You called yourself Earnest Palmer. You killed Ophelia and—"

"You have an excellent memory, Sister, but you needn't bore me with reminders of the good times I had in the past. I am here on holy business. Now, pray tell me what I have come here tonight to learn: What do you know about what I am, and who did you tell?"

" *'I know your works: you have the name of being alive, and are dead.'* "

"Revelation 3:1. Very good, Sister. Quote all the Scripture you like. I love to read the Bible, and I'm especially partial to the Book of Revelation."

"Your name isn't any more Thorne than it was Palmer. Mr. Buchanan told me who you are. I know, Devil. You're J—"

I whipped the plastic bag over Sister Mary Helen's head, holding it lightly around her neck with my hands.

She began to twitch and shake, first with her shoulders, finally with her entire body. Her struggling was pathetic. I giggled at the comical way her bound arms and legs jerked, as if she were dancing a little Irish jig in her wheelchair.

"Calm down, Sister. A woman in your medical condition should guard against unnecessary excitement. I simply want to know what you know and who you told."

She stopped struggling.

"That's better." I put my lips against her ear. "Now, I'm going to remove the plastic bag, and I want you to tell me everything."

I pulled off the plastic.

"What do you know about me, Sister? Who have you talked to about me? To whom have you confided your deepest, innermost fears?"

She did not answer. I touched her face and it fell forward.

"Sister Mary Helen?"

I touched my fingers to her jugular.

"Sister?"

She made no answer. Indeed, she was incapable of answering me. Her struggling apparently had been a seizure. She had died, and, in dying, she had beaten me before I ever really got started. A weak old woman had beaten me, in spite of my strength, in spite of everything I knew about bringing on death slowly and skillfully.

I looked down at her limp body and envisioned her as the others would find her. She died peacefully, they would say, here in the home she loved. Then they would reflect on how she had opposed selling Arlington to Becker Thorne—the only sign that her mind was beginning to go, that she was becoming irrational.

It made me so *angry*! Isaiah Buchanan's whore had cheated me. I wanted to rip her body to shreds, to commit outrages to it and crucify the corpse, so that the others would know that she had not escaped the world so easily.

But I couldn't.

A Fury had to serve the Higher Purpose.

I peeled the yellow rubber gloves off my hands, jammed them in my pocket, and turned to leave.

Life can be so unfair.

III

Pennies for the Poor

CHRONICLE NOTES: David Parker's journal, continued.

—Editor

The strangest thing happened today . . .

Wolf was right. I *should* pay more attention to my dreams, especially with such bizarre developments here in Jerusalem.

But I'm getting ahead of myself. I need to slow down and report it the way it happened, keeping a dispassionate record, as the *Illuminati* insist . . .

* * *

I went to Culpepper Realty looking for information on Becker Thorne.

The business is at 1313 Front Street on the southern edge of the downtown, just inside the downstream floodgates. Entry is made through a small stone cottage connected with another nineteenth-century building to its immediate south by a new addition constructed behind the two older buildings. The addition is a slanting modern affair with big smoked-glass windows and skylights set into the angled roof—a not-altogether-successful attempt to marry the old with the new.

The sidewalk leading to the entry is hemmed in by carefully tended flower beds. Gardening is a passion in this town. I climbed the steps and let myself in. The Southwestern furniture is a little incongruous, but then owner Henry Culpepper's tastes do not run toward the antique, nor do the tastes of his daughter and sales manager, Katharine Culpepper Simonette.

The Culpeppers comprise one quarter of Jerusalem's patrician "Founding Families"—the Buchanans, the Culpeppers, the Hornsbys, and the Chases. I gather that there is something of a rivalry between the Buchanans and Culpeppers, at least from the Culpepper perspective. The Buchanans were the first to settle the area, and were fabulously wealthy until their fortune was wiped out in the Depression. Some say the Culpeppers have never overcome a sense of inferiority to the Buchanans, which has led to a measure of subtle hostility in their relations.

Katharine Culpepper Simonette's role in seeing Arlington Plantation sold to Becker Thorne—which was what took me to Culpepper Realty today—has perhaps put the breach between the two families beyond mending.

Henry Culpepper lives in the finest mansion on the bluff, which he openly loathes, and when he dies, it is understood that his daughter Katharine and her family will move into the house and loathe it equally. It is a poorly kept secret that at least two generations of Culpeppers have grown up planning to leave Jerusalem, though none of them have yet escaped. Perhaps they are held in place here by the same inexorable fate that brought me to town.

The receptionist slipped a copy of *Cosmo* into the center desk drawer as I entered. I asked to speak with Katharine Simonette.

"May I ask your name?"

I told her.

"Do you have an appointment, Mr. Parker?" she asked, frowning as she looked into the leather appointment book on her desk. I shook my head.

"Mrs. Simonette keeps a busy schedule. I could pencil you in for tomorrow and confirm in the morning, if you'd like."

"I'm not sure what my own schedule is going to be." I glanced at the name tag pinned to her blouse. Amanda.

Amanda picked up a pencil. "I'd be happy to schedule you in. Let me see. Mrs. Simonette will be playing tennis tomorrow morning. Maybe in the middle of the afternoon? Or the following afternoon?"

"I'll really have to catch up with her at a later date. That was quite a coup Katharine had with the sale of Arlington Plantation."

"Wasn't it fabulous! It will be nice if the new owner keeps it open for tours on weekends in the summer."

"Any reason he wouldn't?"

"I can't think of any reason that he *would.* If I lived in a place like Arlington, the last thing I'd want would be strangers trooping through my living room every Saturday and Sunday."

I smiled sympathetically. She had a point.

"What sort of person is Becker Thorne?" I asked casually, glancing toward the door. Outside, across Front Street, I saw Victoria Buchanan striding up the sidewalk, swinging a thin, burgundy-colored leather briefcase, no doubt filled with her students' poetry. Or perhaps her own.

"I wish I knew. I've never met Mr. Thorne personally. Mrs. Simonette says he is incredibly handsome and even more incredibly rich." She pretended to pout. "It's not fair for her to keep him to herself. Mr. Thorne would be quite a catch."

"I suspect so."

"Have a good day," Amanda called after me.

Victoria went through a door beneath a swinging wooden sign saying PUBLIC HOUSE.

I followed.

The window seats were all taken by people who looked like they were still in college. Some had glasses of beer in front of them, others cups of coffee. Many of them, even the ones who were not alone at a table, had a book, magazine, or newspaper in front of them, and were pretending to be reading and not watching the people pass by on the sidewalk.

The walls were stripped down to bare brick and mortar and

hung with a series of enormous abstract paintings. On the right-hand wall was a big neon sign saying POPEYE's. Red fluorescent lights mounted in fixtures that blocked the light from going anywhere but up, ran around the room's circumference, throwing a soft, ruby glow on the upper part of the walls that spilled onto the old-fashioned tin ceiling. The bar, a huge oak piece with ornate filigreed carving, stretched the entire length of the left wall. Subdued jazz played through the house sound system, the soft volume just loud enough to be heard over the murmur of conversation.

Victoria was in one of the booths against the rear wall, taking a pen and comp book out of the briefcase on the seat beside her.

I recognized several faces from the Millses' party. Dr. Martin Chesterfield, one of the town's physicians, nodded. Dr. Chesterfield was at a table of men who shared the same vague air of money and self-assurance. Powell Mills was seated at the table, his back to me until Dr. Chesterfield nudged him. Mills turned, smiled, then returned to the conversation at the table.

Dr. James Plant was also at Popeye's, seated at a table for two near the door.

"You've discovered our little sanctuary," Plant said, rising to shake my hand.

"Quite by chance, actually."

"This is Cynthia Morris."

The young woman smiled.

"Cynthia is my star physics pupil. Cynthia, this is David Parker. A remarkable pianist. Our Visiting Artist for the summer."

"Nice to meet you."

She nodded, then transferred her attention back to Plant. It was plain the two were involved. I was still having trouble imagining Dr. Plant as Lydia Chase's second husband, and here he was with a girlfriend who couldn't have been much older than twenty-two. I was going to have to revise my idea of what tweedy, pipe-smoking professors were really like.

"Mr. Parker writes operas," Dr. Plant said, trying to spark some interest in his young companion, a gesture that I took as especially graceful, since Cynthia Morris was much closer to me in age than to the good Dr. Plant.

"I've only written one opera, actually, and I'm not sure that counts until it is actually staged."

"But the college is going to produce it at the end of the summer. Or doesn't that count? I've always thought these summer productions the college does are quite good. Musicians come from all over to take part."

"Yes, of course it counts," I said, feeling somewhat more cheerful about the subject. "I was just trying to be, you know . . ."

"Humble," Cynthia said, and gave me a sweet smile.

"Well, I'd invite you to join us, but . . ." Dr. Plant waved a hand at the table for two.

"No, really."

"They'll let you eat at the bar, if you've come for a sandwich," Cynthia said helpfully.

"Popeye's reubens are the best in town," Dr. Plant said, "and not just because they are the *only* reubens in town."

"Surely you're not that provincial."

"Almost," Cynthia said with undisguised ruefulness.

"In most things," Plant agreed.

I glanced at Victoria Buchanan. Her head was bowed as if in prayer. She was writing.

Look up!

She responded to my silent request. I smiled and raised my hand in half a wave, pretending at the same time to look around, as if only then realizing there were no tables available.

"The secret is to get here before four-thirty," Dr. Plant advised. "There's usually nothing left by five."

Victoria's eyes scanned the room before returning to mine. Closing the comp book with her right hand, she motioned for me to join her.

"Nice to meet you. And good to see you again," I said to Dr. Plant. He seemed stunned to realize I'd been invited to join Victoria Buchanan at her table, though after a moment his startled expression gave way to one of envy.

The waitress and I arrived at Victoria's table simultaneously. She asked for tea. I ordered a bottle of Anchor Steam beer.

"I survived."

"Excuse me?"

"My encounter with the formidable Lydia Chase."

Victoria's smile was even more lovely than it had been that night in Delilah Mills's garden.

"I'm happy to see it," Victoria said lightly.

"I really don't think Lydia is my type."

"I should think not. A man who recites poetry to himself at garden parties," Victoria said, teasing and serious at the same time.

"And you, a kindred spirit." Victoria blushed. "I feel like I already know you quite well."

"You flatter me."

"But I do. You're president of the local historical preservation society. Your family built Arlington Plantation. You teach Romantic and Victorian poetry to undergraduates, who are either bored or confused by it. Tell me more."

Victoria laughed. "That's about all there is. I'm a fairly boring person."

"I can't agree with that."

The waitress arrived with our drinks. She wanted to be paid immediately, the custom in college towns, and I paid for us both over Victoria's protest.

"You don't have a Southern accent, if you don't mind my saying so."

"I lived in Iowa for a few years."

"College?"

Victoria studied her tea, as if she would see something important if she looked hard enough. "That's right," she said finally.

"And your family lives in Jerusalem?"

Victoria lifted the tea bag and watched the water run out of it and back into her cup.

"There's only my daughter. My parents are dead. We're the last of the Buchanans, Michelle and I."

"How old is she?"

"Fifteen. She's rehearsing for a school play, so I'm on my own for supper."

"You don't look old enough to have a fifteen-year-old daughter."

I'd intended it as a compliment—what I said was true—but my words made Victoria visibly cringe.

"What about your family, David?"

"My parents live in Chicago."

"And your wife?"

I'd left my wedding band behind in New York. I don't know how she knew. Maybe it was just a guess.

"We're divorcing."

Victoria picked up the cup and brought it to her lips. As she sipped, her eyes looked up and met mine—but only for a moment—with a look that contained equal measures of disapproval and relief.

"I've never married," she said, closing watching my reaction.

"It must be difficult to bring up a child alone."

"Michelle is my greatest joy," she said, and went on to talk for some time about her daughter. She eventually told me how she'd gone away to school at the University of Iowa and gotten pregnant when she was only eighteen. At first it surprised me to hear her speak so freely, but then I realized this was her way of laying her cards on the table. She was testing me—or trying to scare me off.

She'd fallen in love with an English professor at the University of Iowa, a poet whose slim volumes of verse had received tremendous critical acclaim. He was married. When Victoria became pregnant, he wanted her to have an abortion. Victoria was Catholic and couldn't bring herself to do it. The father refused to provide emotional or financial support, or to have anything else to do with her or the child.

"It was a scandal, but the kind of scandal that the English Department loved, because it supplied them with months of gossip. It only enhanced Baker's reputation—Paxton Baker was his name—because he had done what poets were supposed to do: be a drunk, which he was; and a womanizer, which he was; and morally bankrupt, which he was. And in the end he stiffed us all: me, his daughter, his wife, the university. He ran off to Jamaica in the middle of one semester when a wealthy patroness offered the free use of her winter home there as a writing retreat. I never saw him again. And he's never seen his daughter.

"I quit school as soon as I got pregnant, but I stayed in Iowa City. I couldn't come home. Not then. I went back to school after Michelle's third birthday. My father was fifty when he died of a heart attack. I was finishing my dissertation when my mother became ill. Cancer after years of smoking. I don't think I could have ever come back if she hadn't gotten sick. Powell Mills and my dad used to play golf every Wednesday. Powell was kind enough to give me a job. So here I am."

"It must have been hard to come home."

"Only because of my false pride. People are more supportive than you might expect. In a town this size, everybody knows everything about everybody. It goes beyond even that," she added with a small laugh. "Everybody in this town—the old families, at least—are related to one another through marriage and birth. When I was growing up, we had what was called the Cousins Club made up of the members of Jerusalem's Founding Families—you know, the Buchanans, the Chases, the Hornsbys, and the Culpeppers. The joke was that when the Cousins Club held its annual July picnic, the entire town would come because everybody was related to the old four families. They had to accept me. I'm one of them."

A faraway look came into Victoria's eyes.

"And besides, my daughter and I are the last of the Buchanans. That means something in a town like Jerusalem. The past never dies in the South. A Southerner never forgets."

Victoria lapsed into heavy silence, which I broke.

"So you're related to your nemesis, Katharine Culpepper Simonette."

"Families don't always agree, but we generally try to be civil with one another. No one wants to cast the first stone."

" 'Judge not . . .' "

" 'Lest ye be judged.' That is it exactly. You're welcome to come with us to church Sunday."

"Thanks for offering. I'm not a church person."

"Then I shall have to save you from wickedness, David Parker." Victoria gave me a friendly smile, but I could see that she was serious.

"And what about Becker Thorne? Will you try to save his soul as well?"

"You asked me about him at the Millses' party. What makes you so interested in Mr. Thorne?"

"I'm just curious about him, and Arlington, I suppose. I'd like to see it."

"Poor Arlington," Victoria said with a heavy sigh. "The old place has had a streak of bad luck lately. First, Becker Thorne. Then, Sister Mary Helen's death."

That's when everything began to get strange . . .

The nun's death was not what I had feared. She was quite elderly, apparently, and passed away peacefully while sitting in the greenhouse at Arlington where Victoria's grandfather's orchids still grow.

Victoria was telling me all this when a familiar woman's voice said: "Excuse me, sir, would you care to make a donation to the poor?"

I turned around and saw a woman I had seen before in a dream. Princess Nicoletta Vittorini di Medusa was her name—or at least it was in my dream. It was a good thing I was sitting down. Seeing her standing beside me in the pub stunned me as much as being hit in the head with a plank.

"Would either of you care to make a donation to help the homeless?"

She wore a Salvation Army uniform, her jet hair coiled up under her cap. She wore no makeup on her pale, perfect face, but she was one of those women who are beautiful with or without using cosmetics.

"The money will be used for our work with the homeless." She had the same voice as the woman in my dream, an upper-class European voice with a trace of Italian in her accent.

Victoria put a dollar bill in the donation box. The woman offered the box to me, smiling. Our eyes met. I had an almost irresistible urge to stand up and kiss her.

"Do you mind me asking your name?" I managed, removing the wallet from my jacket and getting out a ten-dollar bill.

"I am Captain Vittorini. Captain Nicoletta Vittorini."

"You're not from here, are you?"

"I was born in Sicily."

"How did you come to be in Mississippi?"

"We go where the Salvation Army and the Lord send us, sir."

"Hey, you!" A middle-aged bald man behind the bar was pointing at Captain Vittorini. "There's no soliciting allowed in here."

"I beg your pardon," Captain Vittorini replied with a slight bow. "Thank you, ma'am. And you, too, sir."

The bald man was beginning to come out from behind the bar, a scowl on his face.

"Thank you both. And God bless."

She retreated out the rear door, moving just quickly enough to keep away from the bald man.

"What's the matter, David?" Victoria asked. "You looked as if you've just seen a ghost."

I suppose that in a manner of speaking I had.

* * *

A footnote to today's events . . .

I've written a letter to Wolf asking him to run Becker Thorne's name through the *Illuminati* databases and see what turns up. I'd do it myself, but I'm hopelessly inept when it comes to navigating the *Illuminati*'s Internet blind gateways. (I can't even cope with our E-mail system! I'm amazed Wolf has so little trouble with computers. I'm from the twentieth century, but they confuse the hell out of *me*.)

I'm interested in the obvious things on Thorne: the nature of his business in New York; his partners, if any; whether he can be traced to other cities where there have been killings; verifiable background records; et cetera. I don't want to waste time on him if he's just a wealthy-but-eccentric mortal.

I've also asked Wolf to sweep the databases for anything we might have on Captain Nicoletta Vittorini of the Salvation Army. There's something peculiar about Nicoletta. She might be mixed up in this somehow, perhaps without realizing it. However, I won't be surprised if we don't find anything on Nicoletta.

IV
Night Ride

CHRONICLE NOTES: "Becker Thorne's" diary, continued.
—*Editor*

It has been a most stimulating evening, my dear diary, a sweet song begun simply that before it ended soared upon the wings of inspiration most high. A grand performance, though not without cost. Neon commanded me and, like an obedient bark responding to the confident hand upon its tiller, I tacked the appointed course. My own small rage is but of little consequence beside the roaring anger of the *Eternal*.

Katharine Simonette came to see me tonight at Arlington. It was only twenty-four hours since she swore she would never do so again. How weak some women are, especially the ones who pretend to be strong. She came back on her knees, begging, promising that she would do anything to be with me—leave her husband, her child, even *die* for me.

Foolish woman. She could scarcely imagine what such offers mean to the Fury.

After an hour's diversion—I forced her down on a table and took her from behind—I told her to arrange her clothes, that there was something I wanted to show her in the carriage house. I observed her nipples become hard the moment she saw the 968s Porsche. I was familiar with her fetish for fast, expensive automobiles. She'd traded a Corvette for the Audi when she was pregnant.

"It must have cost a fortune," she said, caressing the hand-finished black paint, a gesture she made seem sexual.

"You always want to know the price of things."

"Money is the best aphrodisiac." She leaned her rear against the hood, hands on either side, legs apart, her eyes inviting me to do anything I wanted. But then I always did.

"How fast will it go? I like to go fast."

"One hundred and fifty at least. I had the catalytic converter removed and a few other special adjustments made. I really don't know yet."

"As if you could go even one hundred and fifty miles an hour on a two-lane highway in Mississippi."

I stepped between her legs.

"We can try." I put one hand on her breast and slipped my tongue into her mouth.

We drove south out of town on a state highway that climbed up and down the wooded hills stretching between the bottom lands and the plains. The road was a series of peaks and valleys that kept your stomach in your mouth. Up and down, streaking along S curves that snaked left or right—the mostly deserted road was a perfect place to put a new Porsche through its paces on a moonlit night.

"Can you feel its power?"

Katharine nodded. She was smiling, but I could see she was

a little frightened. Her idea of speed was a fast mile or two on a clear stretch of straight, wide road on a Sunday afternoon. Anything truly dangerous made her nervous.

"It's like plugging the base of your spine into a massive electrical current."

"Becker," she said between clenched teeth, "please don't go any faster."

"It puts you right here, right now. The past and future no longer exist at this speed."

"Becker . . ."

"There's no room for mistakes."

"Becker . . ."

"No margin for error."

"Becker, this is beginning to really frighten me."

The speedometer showed past one hundred, but there was no real danger. The car was engineered to take it and a lot more.

"It gives you such a rush of adrenaline. I don't think you could get this big a kick from drugs." At least I couldn't. I knew; I'd tried.

We crested the hill going one hundred and ten. I expected the speed to throw the Porsche into the air, but it held the highway in seeming defiance of the laws of physics.

That's when we saw the old truck with wood railings around its cargo box and one taillight burned out stopped in the right-hand lane on the near side of a narrow iron bridge in the hollow below us. The truck's front wheels were cranked hard over for a left turn, waiting to turn for the car coming down the opposite hill toward the bridge.

Katharine screamed.

I saw that there was only one way to avoid a terrible collision. As I'd learned through painful experience on horseback, only daring and audacity can save you from "impossible" situations.

I dropped down a gear and pushed the gas pedal to the floor. Even at the speed we were traveling, the acceleration pushed us back into our seats.

Katharine threw her hands up to cover her face. Through the truck's rear window, I saw the driver wave his arms frantically over his head, as if that would protect him.

I whipped the Porsche into the left lane. A lesser car would have rolled, or oversteered onto the shoulder, which would have been equally disastrous, but the 968 responded with its advertised precision. The truck shot past on the right.

We were instantly onto the bridge, which was even more narrow than the highway—so narrow that two semitrailers could not pass in opposite directions without smashing mirrors. The driver of the oncoming car, a Ford sedan, had slammed on his brakes; the car began to skid, sliding sideways to take up more and more of the lane I was supposed to be in. I eased the Porsche as far to the right as I dared. The Ford flew past with no more than a breath of space between the two automobiles.

I looked in the mirror and laughed. The Ford managed to avoid hitting both the bridge and the truck—no small accomplishment for such a plebeian vehicle!

"Yes!" I lifted my head and shouted out the open sun roof.

Katharine shouted, too, but not in exultation. "You son of a bitch! You nearly killed us!"

"Yes, I did. But you have to agree the Porsche passes muster."

She looked at me with astonishment and started to laugh, her laughter becoming almost hysterical. She was like a teenage girl on a roller-coaster, reveling in her own terror.

"I don't know how you kept us from dying back there."

"You must learn to trust me, Katharine. I have superhuman reflexes."

"You're dangerous, Becker. I knew you were dangerous the first time I saw you." She leaned across to kiss me. "I think it's tremendously sexy."

I pushed the CD into the player and settled back in my seat, enjoying the fine adrenaline high as we continued down the highway, the wind in my hair and the night in my heart.

"Turn left here, and we can drive along the river."

I took Katharine's recommendation, and within a few minutes we were tracing the line between the bluffs and the river. In some places the highway was no more than the flick of a cigarette from the Mississippi. The running lights of a barge plowing the black water were nearly as close as the lights of the traffic in the opposite lane. After a few miles, the road broke away from the river, climbed the bluff, twisting and turning as it followed the contour of the land, finally breaking free several hundred feet above a magnificent expanse of river.

The beauty of this land still moves me, dear diary. Some things never die inside a person, no matter how much they change, no matter how completely they leave their old selves behind. This was the South that I love, a country so precious that men were glad to give their lives to keep it free from Yankee oppression. I shall always remember watching those eleven thousand proud men as they marched across the broad, open valley, stopping to dress their lines torn asunder by the raking fire of the blue-bellies and the enfilading artillery. No one who saw Pickett's Charge will forget. The world would not see the likes of such heroes again. How shameful to think they were betrayed, as I was betrayed, like Agamemnon upon his homecoming.

There were worse enemies than the ones we fought. Can there be any evil greater than the viper that turns back to bite the breast that has suckled it? Let them continue to be at their ease, for the day of reckoning will come soon enough.

The time is near. Let the evildoer still do evil, and the filthy still be filthy.

We rounded a curve. The headlights danced across a deserted homestead. The house and outbuildings had long since perished, but the property's outlines are still marked with carefully spaced trees that now shade nothing. The remains of a fieldstone foundation poked out of the ground, little more than a few lines that created the impression of what once was.

Such things that remind us of the past can be dangerous.

I ejected the CD and slowed the Porsche to sixty miles an hour. The sound of the wind dropped to a whisper.

"I need you to help me buy some things."

"More property?"

"No, artifacts. I want to begin collecting artifacts from the War Between the States. The period I'm interested in is, say, roughly 1840 to 1870."

"Artifacts?" Katharine said derisively; she hates antiques and abides Arlington only because it is a symbol of wealth and power. "You live in a house full of them."

"I'm not talking about furniture. I'm interested in things that tell the story of the people who lived at Arlington at the height of its importance and power in this part of the country. Portraits. Old photographs. Military records. Scrapbooks. Diaries. Old diaries and manuscripts from the war are what I'm interested in more than anything else."

Of course, dear diary, I was thinking primarily of my lost

manuscript, *A True Patriot*, stolen along with my other property during that treacherous night at Arlington Landing. I suspected the Buchanans and the other curs would have been careful to destroy anything that might incriminate them in the assassination, but Nicoletta said I should make sure as long as I was in town. The last thing I wanted was the world to get interested in a new conspiracy theory that would result in my old portraits being published in dozens of newspapers and magazines. I also needed to make sure that none of my correspondence with Anna Lee or the others remained to pique the curiosity of prying eyes.

"I want you to contact the usual dealers, and tell them that I am ready to pay top dollar for anything and everything that had to do with the history of the people of Jerusalem during the war. These things are of immense significance. They must be"—I smiled to myself—"carefully preserved."

"I never suspected that you cared any more about history than I do."

"Why do you think I bought Arlington?"

"Because it's one of the most elegant homes in the state, and the only antebellum mansion you had a prayer of getting the owners to part with."

"Well, you're wrong," I said, pretending to be offended. "I don't want to just preserve Arlington. I want to fill it with artifacts that are indisputably of the first caliber both in terms of quality and historical significance. I want the library to serve as the repository for documents from Jerusalem's Golden Age. I may even open the grounds to visitors when I won't be bothered by the interruption—for a fee."

"When Victoria Buchanan hears about this, she'll want to French kiss you in the town square at high noon."

"Why? I thought you told me she is the most extravagantly chaste woman in town."

"Because you're planning to do exactly what she wanted to do with Arlington. And the best part is you'll do it with personal funds. It would have taken a lot of grant-writing and fund-raising before Victoria's preservation society could have afforded to do what you're talking about. I'd be willing to bet she'll try to talk you into donating the plantation to the state when you get bored with it or die."

"There's very little chance of *that*."

"It would have its tax advantages, Becker. You shouldn't be

so certain you'll want to stay here forever. You haven't lived here long enough to get truly bored."

"We shall see. I suppose that's why Miss Buchanan has been calling me every few days."

"I understand that she's quite distressed that you've closed the plantation to visitors. You won't take her calls?"

"The only calls I take that aren't from New York are yours," I said, and squeezed Katharine's thigh.

She returned the gesture, sliding her hand higher, her fingers caressing.

"Go this way," she breathed into my ear. "I know a place."

I followed her instructions, stroking the inside of her thigh with my hand. We drove another five minutes and turned into a park with narrow, one-way roads with fieldstone retaining walls on either side.

"Just ahead."

"This seems to be a familiar place to you."

"I used to fuck here every Saturday when I was in high school."

"I don't want to be around other people."

"Not tonight." She nipped at my ear. "They only come out on the weekends."

The road looped to the right, went down through a hollow dense with trees, then climbed a steep hill and curved around a picnic shelter until we broke into the open.

"Here."

Beyond the road on the right was an exhilarating bluff-top view of the river valley. The Mississippi stretched out in a slow, arcing curve toward the north in the moonlight. The flat land beyond sparkled with the lights of scattered farmhouses that glittered as if they were reflections of the stars in the sky. Everything was silent and peaceful. A beautiful night, all moonlight, stars, and river.

"I want you to do it to me really hard, Becker," Katharine said in a husky voice, and ran her hand down my belly. "I want you to fuck me until I can't walk. I want you to fuck me until I can't talk without stuttering."

She liked gutter talk, and so did I. It made her remind me of one of my Kewpie Dolls.

I got a blanket from the boot and followed Katharine down a path that led to a grassy open area at the edge of the bluff.

Katharine pulled off her shirt while I spread out the blanket. She unfastened her bra, took it off, and dropped it over her shoulder with a coy expression I found rather irritating. She pulled down her skirt and stepped out of it. Wearing only her panties, she made herself comfortable on the blanket.

Below us downstream, tucked into a cleft in the bluff, was a hamlet—a few houses, a trailer, and a filling station, and a sight that made me shiver.

And I saw, and behold, a pale horse, and its rider's name was Death.

The horse was pale, just a jagged outline in the moonlight.

I sank down on the blanket, my eyes locked onto the glowing seraph, feeling the Neon flow into me, mingling its electricity with my blood.

Katharine ran her tongue down my neck and began to bite and suck at the skin at the base of my neck.

"Be careful, my love," I whispered. "The way you're biting my neck, I might get the idea you're a vampire."

"You're the vampire," Katharine smiled.

"What did you say?" I asked, startled out of my Neon epiphany.

She pulled up my shirt and ran her tongue across my belly. "No criticism, darling, but you could use a little sun. You're pale as death, pale as a vampire."

I did not answer but went back to listening to the more important message. I could no more ignore the winged horse than I could choose not to breathe. And I was torn between anger and joy, for Pegasus might lead me to abandon my careful scheme. But then I realized I would just have to put my faith in Neon. It would all work out. This night had to be part of the greater, divine plan.

"What are you looking at?"

The secret message was beginning to become clear. I was beginning to see it clearly. And the Neon said:

But I have this against you, that you tolerate that woman Jezebel, who calls herself a prophetess and is teaching and beguiling my servants to practice immorality and to eat food sacrificed to idols. I gave her time to repent, but she refuses.

And the words were *exactly* the same as in the Old Testament! Could there be any mistaking the divine hand in this glorious undertaking?

"What are you looking at?"

"The sign down at the gas station."

"What's so interesting about it?"

"It's Pegasus."

"Greek mythology, right? I learned all about it in school and promptly forgot it, and I wish you would do the same. Why are you acting so strangely?"

"It's a beautiful myth, Katharine. And, like all beautiful myths, it's steeped in blood."

There was confusion in Katharine's face when at last I lowered my eyes toward her, and, beneath the confusion, the hint of something infinitely more satisfying.

"Pegasus sprung from the blood of the monster Medusa, a fabulous creature born from the purifying blood. Do you know who Medusa is?"

"The only monster I'm interested in is the one in your pants," she said, her tone halfway between teasing and exasperation.

"You don't know who Medusa is, do you?"

"No, and I don't particularly care. I only care about fucking. If you're not interested," she said, sitting up, "just say so, because I'm getting cold."

"I've been wondering how ignorant you really are," I said with a sad smile.

Katharine looked at me hard. I could see the wheels turning. Her first impulse was to try to slap me, but she was calculating what it might cost compared to what she had to gain by fucking her way into my life and fortune.

"Medusa is the one with snakes for hair."

"That's right. And do you know how she got them?"

"No," she said in the same voice she would use to indulge a child. "I bet you're going to tell me."

"She gave her favors to Poseidon, who admired her lovely hair. Athena was jealous and changed her locks into snakes. Medusa was a very great terror, until Perseus cut off her head."

Katharine crossed her arms over her breasts, which were lovely in the moonlight and covered with goose bumps.

"It's one of the oldest myths: a woman whose beauty turns her into a slut, and her sluttishness ends in her becoming something repulsive and hideous, so she must die. Almost biblical."

Katharine was watching me very carefully now.

"But if you slay the monster, if you take off her head, something wondrous springs forth from the steaming blood. A magnificent winged horse that you can ride all the way to Heaven. But first the whore must die."

"Becker, this talk about monsters and cutting of heads and blood is beginning to disturb me."

"Becker, this talk is beginning to disturb me," I mocked.

"All right, I want to go home," she said, and got up, bending to snatch up her skirt, bra, and blouse with such anger that the clothing made a snapping noise.

I smiled, slowly, broadly, showing her *all* of my teeth. I knew the words by heart so that I could recite them even without the angel Pegasus whispering them in my ear from behind. I'd read that Book thousands of times.

" 'Come, I will show you the judgment of the great harlot who is seated upon many waters, with whom the kings of the earth have committed fornication, and with the wine of whose fornication the dwellers on earth have become drunk.' "

Katharine bolted for the car. I let her run. I let her get all the way there before leaping up. I'd left the keys in the ignition. I could hear her thinking: *He can't humanly catch me now!*

She was right. I couldn't *humanly* catch her.

I reached out to grab her but used a bit too much force. Rather careless, I'm afraid. My fingers pushed effortlessly into her skin—the rubber gloves would be jealous!—and slipped around her spine.

For a sudden moment we were both absolutely still, panting, joined together like lovers—and how similar to love, me inside of her, feeling her hot juices! Her face was reflected in the car window, her eyes open very wide, and her mouth, an expression of profound surprise, as if something of vital importance had suddenly become unmistakably clear to her.

She began to draw in a breath—a harsh, ugly whisper that then came into her lungs in a series of short gasps. I began to lift my arm—and Katharine—into the air, higher and higher, turning her until her face was only a few inches from mine, her eyes looking directly into mine. There is a special knowledge in the eyes at such a moment, a communication that takes place directly between souls. Now, at last, she understood that a Fury had come to town to judge the wicked for their sins.

"Easy now, my love," I whispered reassuringly. "I don't think the damage is too serious. Not yet."

Her lips moved but no sound came out. It was rather comical, like watching someone imitate a fish.

"I'd planned to postpone this evening for some weeks, but Pegasus commands me. You have been condemned. You were born condemned. You are guilty. You all are guilty. The sins of your fathers will not go unpunished."

Katharine's hands began to work back and forth in the air but accomplished nothing. She reminded me of a battery-operated doll that has fallen on its side but continues to move without purpose. The horror in her face was wonderful. She was going to be so much more fun than that dried-up old bitch in the greenhouse or that slut Foster, whose whining infuriated me so much that I rushed my work. Katharine would be as fun to kill as her Uncle Gregory had been, but she was younger and stronger and I knew our playtime would last longer.

"Before we begin, dear Katharine, I'm feeling a bit hungry. Would you mind if I had just the tiniest taste to fortify myself?"

Her mouth continued to work. Perhaps there was some nerve damage, I thought, opening my mouth wide and distending my blood teeth. Katharine at last found her voice, but she had only one thing to say: "No, no, no—"

"It's all been prophesied, my darling. There is no escape." Again I quoted Scripture to prove to her that I did not lie.

"They and the beast hate the harlot; they will make her desolate and naked, and devour her flesh and burn her up with fire."

She looked back at me with the most mindless sort of animal terror. I pulled her gently toward me and sank my teeth deep into her neck.

V
Cocktail Party

CHRONICLE NOTES: David Parker's journal, continued.
—Editor

I have two momentous events to record in these pages tonight, the first much anticipated, the second much dreaded.

At long last I've met Becker Thorne. If he is indeed the vampire I've been seeking these many months—and *Vampiri* intuition tells me he and the blood-soaked daemon are one in the same—then he is more powerful, and dangerous than I feared in even my bleakest moments.

I note the second development with profound physical revulsion. The killing has started in Jerusalem—the slaying committed with an uncontrolled animal savagery that leaves no doubt "Dracula," whose exploits were luridly chronicled in New York's tabloids, has come to Mississippi, for his own dark reasons, as Wolf *dreamed* he would.

I should also note that a third significant (at least personally) event occurred tonight. I had my second waking encounter with the woman about whom I had vividly *dreamed*—the beautiful Nicoletta Vittorini. Between Nicoletta and the poetess Victoria Buchanan, I find myself bewitched at a time I should, I fully realize, focus my attentions entirely on stopping Thorne, if he is in fact the fiend.

Women have always been my weakness.

I cannot imagine Thorne and Nicoletta have any connection with one another, except perhaps through me. Thorne is a creature of consummate darkness, while dear Nicoletta embodies nothing more sinister than a moonlit night.

(Wolf has yet to respond to my request for any information the *Illuminati* may have on Thorne and Nicoletta. I wonder if he has gone back to Europe? Or perhaps he is off struggling with his mysterious "problem." I am distressed that he has been so little help in this case, even in such a trivial matter as retrieving files from the brotherhood's databases.)

But I get ahead of myself, as usual.

For the official record, this is how the night unfolded. . . .

I went to Oscar Sanchez's party with Victoria Buchanan, who'd at last agreed to go on a "date" with me.

It's a steep climb up the stairs to Sanchez's house, which sits upon a hill blocked off in steep, rising terraces held back with tiers of interlacing railroad ties. The planting beds at each level are filled with flowers, bushes, and small ornamental trees. Viewed from the street below, the square house crowning the terraces resembles a temple atop an Aztec pyramid that has been half reclaimed by jungle.

Our host met us at the door. Oscar Sanchez greeted Victoria more warmly than she would have liked, judging from her surprise when he kissed her cheek. Sanchez shook my hand, his grip firm, and looked me straight in the eye with a frank, appraising look, sizing me up against the other luminaries who had come to Morningside College, assigning me a preliminary ranking.

The whippet-thin Sanchez looked every bit the successful artist in a simple cotton shirt, French blue jeans, and sandals. He's more Italian than Hispanic in appearance, this from his mother, also an artist, who was born in Naples. Sanchez's hair is shot through with gray, and he wears it pulled back in a tight ponytail. His beard, also graying, is trimmed close. His brown eyes look at everything carefully, as if recording line and color for later translation to canvas.

"I've been wanting to meet you, David. I was disappointed I couldn't attend the party Powell and Delilah Mills gave for you. I was completing a commission at the governor's mansion."

Sanchez had once been chairman of the Morningside College Art Department, but he quit when his career as a painter took off. Sanchez is known for his huge, hyperrealistic pictures of scenes in rain forests. One of the paintings, a six-foot-by-six-foot swatch of jungle foliage, dominated the foyer at the Millses' house. Delilah Mills paid eight thousand dollars for it; her husband nearly had a heart attack when he found out about it, Victoria told me during the drive over.

Sanchez got me a glass of good champagne—mineral water for Victoria, who doesn't drink—and led us in to meet the other guests.

"Captain Vittorini," I said with surprise when we entered the room.

Nicoletta sat on the edge of an ottoman, a gold-rimmed china cup in her delicate, ivory white hand.

Nicoletta wore the usual severe blue uniform, unadorned except for the few sober, quasi-military embellishments. She wore no makeup. Her hair was drawn tightly back from her forehead and gathered into an austere bun. Her bearing was grave, almost stern. All of this did nothing to disguise the stunning beauty of her face or a figure that, in slightly less repressive clothing, would draw stares from men and women alike. Nicoletta may have taken a vow to lead an ascetic life of religion, social work, and unbending self-discipline, but she was blessed with qualities that must have provided more than a little temptation for the men she worked with in the Salvation Army. Little wonder I dreamed of this simple woman as a voluptuous Mediterranean princess!

"We met once before," Nicoletta said, extending her small hand as she looked up at me with her Tyrrhenian eyes and smiled.

"But our introduction was interrupted." Her hand was like a child's in mine. It felt feverish—from holding the teacup, I thought. "I am David Parker. I'm at Morningside College this summer on a music residency."

"David is the distinguished composer and pianist I was telling you about," Sanchez interjected.

Nicoletta Vittorini's eyes looked deeply into mine. Although I did not use my powers to push into her mind—which always makes me feel more like a voyeur than a fledgling psychic—I again sensed that there was some special bond between us. I felt an unmistakable harmony of purpose between us, almost as if she were one of the *Vampiri*.

"And this is Victoria Buchanan," Sanchez said. I could see from the laughter in his eyes that he recognized the attraction—entirely inappropriate, I confess—I felt for Nicoletta.

"And you, too, are at the college?" Nicoletta asked Victoria, who seemed not to have noticed my inexplicable enchantment with the other woman.

Fortunately, the two women and Sanchez began chatting

about the college, leaving me free to flounder in the crosscurrents of emotions swirling through my heart. I am, as I have confessed in the privacy of these pages, half in love with Victoria. So why did I feel such an inexplicable attraction for the pretty Salvation Army captain? And why had I dreamed of her—instead of Victoria?

But then there is no logic to matters of the heart. I can control my actions, but not my passions. It is an old story, especially with me. As the poet said, *Agnosco veteris vestigia flammae*—I feel again a spark of that ancient flame.

"Do you know Dr. Martin Chesterfield?"

I'd met the physician at the Millses' party. Dr. Chesterfield looked up from the pair he'd been talking with: Lysander Chase, the wealthiest man in Jerusalem, Mississippi, and his libertine daughter, Lydia.

I shook hands with Dr. Chesterfield, who is about sixty and looked extremely tired, and Chase. Lydia offered me her cheek, as if we'd become close acquaintances at the Millses' party, and I dutifully kissed it.

The doorbell rang. Sanchez left the room to admit the new guests.

"Are you all right, Martin?" Victoria asked.

"I'm afraid I've had a rather bad day. I'll be fine with a little rest."

The greeting Victoria exchanged with Chase was friendly if a bit formal, which didn't surprise me; there could hardly be two more opposite women in town.

"Here's Olivia," Dr. Chesterfield said as a woman entered the room with a silver tray bearing hors d'oeuvres. Olivia Sanchez was an attractive woman, somewhere in her early forties, who appeared to take quite good care of herself. She smiled hello but did not speak. She is the opposite of her husband in several respects: she is an introvert, her skin is fair, and her hair blonde nearly to the point of whiteness.

Sanchez returned to our group, bringing with him Bob Fitzer, a local lawyer. The conversation focused on me and my work for ten or fifteen minutes. The conversation would have remained superficial, if not for Sanchez, who had done careful homework and knew much more about me than he could have without having made a special effort. He was aware not only of my musical leanings and influences, but also of details of my personal life I'd just as soon have left undiscussed. It was Sanchez who brought up the subject of my wife, Tatiana, who had been much in the papers the past year as a consequence of her role as a prima ballerina.

The mention of Tatiana's name seemed to startle Victoria, as if it reminded her of a fact she'd worked very hard to forget.

Sanchez's eyes flitted from me to Victoria and back. I could see that he'd gotten the reaction he'd expected, and confirmation that Victoria and I had at least the beginning of a relationship. I explained—somewhat pointlessly, I'm afraid, the damage being done—that the relationship with Tatiana had sadly but inevitably dissolved.

Dr. Chesterfield gracefully changed the subject, asking Nicoletta if she regretted leaving Omaha, where she'd been previously posted. Winters in Omaha were cold, Nicoletta said; she wouldn't miss them.

"Actually, Captain Vittorini is the reason for this little gathering tonight," Sanchez said, again commandeering the conversation. He stood up as he spoke. Though Jerusalem was thankfully free of many of the crises found in larger cities, he said, their town was not immune to the problems of the world.

"Homelessness, for example," he said.

Olivia looked up at her husband and nodded, as did several other heads around the room.

Jerusalem needed a homeless shelter, Sanchez said, and went on to outline the preliminary aspects of what it would take to open such a facility.

"I've asked you here tonight not only to meet Captain Vittorini and one of our other new arrivals, David Parker, but also to ask you to serve as the nucleus of the group that will get this project off the ground. Victoria, as president of the historical preservation society, you know more about raising money than anybody in town. And Lysander, as bank president, you know more than anybody else does about money."

There was polite laughter.

"And the center, when it opens, will be run by the Salvation Army." Sanchez looked at Nicoletta, who nodded to indicate her organization was behind the project.

For the next hour, we ate crab-stuffed mushroom caps and drank champagne—or tea in Nicoletta's case, or mineral water in Victoria's—and discussed the shelter. Since I'd been on the board of directors of a homeless shelter in Chicago before I gave up being a lawyer for music and the *Illuminati*, I was able to add some important points. We'd just about exhausted the subject for the evening when the doorbell rang.

"A late arrival," Sanchez said, jumping to his feet, seeming not to mind at all.

Our host returned a few minutes later, grinning proudly. "I didn't think he was going to be able to make it," Sanchez said, his new guest behind him in the foyer. "As you all know, David Parker and Captain Vittorini are not the only new arrivals in Jerusalem this summer. I'd like to introduce you all to someone I'm sure you've been dying to meet."

Becker Thorne's entrance brought an electric charge to the air. The party rose as one to meet the reclusive billionaire, who had been a favorite topic of conversation and speculation ever since he appeared one night and bought Arlington Plantation with a personal check for $4,500,000.

Thorne is what I would term "darkly handsome." He's tall and rail-thin, with sunken cheeks and eyes that burn like coals from within the dark wells of their sockets. He wears his hair long and brushed straight back to make his carved features even more dramatic. The clothing Thorne wore to Sanchez's party made him look more like an actor than a wealthy stockbroker. Boots, trousers, shirt, and jacket—all black, except the silver Navajo belt around his waist.

Thorne looked around the room, certainly paying no special attention to me. He seemed most interested in two of the women present: Victoria and Lydia. Thorne seemed to avoid Nicoletta's glance, but I couldn't be sure.

But is Thorne a vampire?

It's usually obvious, especially to another member of our diverse and troubled race, but with Thorne I could not tell. He gave off none of the usual vibrations. His aura was that of a human, unusually dark, but with nothing that would indicate he was one of the *Vampiri*. Of course, I was fiercely masking my own presence, which made it impossible to reach out fully with my preternatural senses.

And yet . . .

A mysterious voice deep inside my soul warned me to stay absolutely on my guard. Thorne was marked by shadows and darkness—I realized this even though I can't explain *how* I realized it. There was a subtle, lethal quality to him, something that made me envision him as Death riding a pale horse, leaving behind in those places he visited corpses, grief, and the sort of horror that drives men to the brink of madness.

And I was afraid.

Observing Thorne from a distance, I thought that he *had* to be the vampire, yet if he was the monster, he was able to hide his nature from me, concealing it deep beneath the contrived persona of a mortal named Becker Thorne. If this was indeed the case, then it meant that he was extremely powerful—powerful enough to be a threat not only to the mortals in Jerusalem, but to me. . . .

"May I introduce Dr. Martin Chesterfield, Becker?"

"How do you do, Dr. Chesterfield."

The voice was deep and dramatic.

Thorne shook hands with the red-eyed doctor. The two men were a study in contrasts: the one young, tall, thin, exuding a sense of power and presence just short of menacing; the other old, short, portly, bowed a little with age, exhausted.

"How are you getting along out at Arlington?" Dr. Chesterfield asked.

"Splendidly."

"And this is Lysander Chase," Sanchez said.

"Hello, Lysander."

"How are you, Becker. I could use one more person to round out the foursome at the club tomorrow, if your morning is free."

"I'm afraid I can't, but thanks for the offer. I'm not much of a golfer."

"You'll become one in Jerusalem," the banker continued, still holding Thorne's hand. "There's damned little else to do in this town." Lysander Chase suddenly seemed to remember the women present. "Excuse my French, ma'am," he apologized to Nicoletta, who did not appear to be unduly shocked.

"She's a saint in a roomful of sinners," Sanchez joked, holding his arm out to draw the lovely Italian woman toward Thorne. "May I present Captain Vittorini of the Salvation Army?"

"You do me too much honor, Mr. Sanchez," Nicoletta said, extending her small hand to Thorne.

Thorne shook Nicoletta's hand with a taut smile on his face, saying nothing. He seemed to instinctively dislike Nicoletta, for which I was grateful—mindless jealousy, I suppose.

Lydia Chase, who had been prepared to follow her father in greeting Thorne before Sanchez summoned Nicoletta forward ahead of her, stepped to the fore, demanding Thorne's hand and his attention.

"I can't for the life of me understand why a man like you would want to shut himself up out in the country. Whatever is it you see in that place?"

"My accountant asked the same question," Thorne said, to everyone's amusement. "Actually, Lydia, I'm sure you'd change your mind if you'd let me show you Arlington. Do stop by for a drink. I'll give you a whole new appreciation for Arlington Plantation."

"I'll promise to take you up on that," Lydia said.

I knew as well as everyone else in the room did—except Thorne, apparently—that Lydia had been to Arlington numerous times when the sisters owned it and was not impressed with the plantation or anything else "old-fashioned." She had, however, gotten exactly what she wanted out of Thorne: an invitation—not knowing how dangerous a visit to his home might be.

Sanchez introduced his wife to Thorne next. Olivia smiled, simply said hello, and excused herself to get more champagne, the perfect self-effacing mate for her egocentric husband.

Victoria was next.

"Can you be the Victoria Buchanan who is president of the Jerusalem Historical Preservation Society?" Thorne asked with an ambiguous smile.

"There is only one of us in town," Victoria replied, her voice carefully modulated, her smile unwavering—a diplomat come to the first meeting with someone who might turn out to be either a valuable ally or an implacable foe.

"I'm afraid that you must be very angry with me, Miss Buchanan."

Every eye in the room was upon them. If there was going to be an ugly scene at Oscar Sanchez's party, this would be it.

"Not at all, Mr. Thorne," Victoria said levelly. "I was surprised when you bought Arlington." She paused for emphasis. "Yes, I think 'surprised' is the right word. And disappointed, of course. We had made elaborate plans."

"I did not fully comprehend the scope of your project. Otherwise, I never would have interfered, even though owning a place like Arlington has been an obsession of mine for many, many years."

"It's kind of you to say that." I could tell Victoria thought Thorne was lying. As did I.

"But I must confess that I am delighted to have been able to make my dream come true. Arlington is everything I'd hoped for and more. I believe it's important to fulfill one's dreams, don't you, Miss Buchanan?"

"Within reason," Victoria replied.

"Life is short. We must enjoy it while we can. One never knows when it will end. Take poor Katharine Simonette, for example. She was so young."

"What?" Olivia Sanchez asked, looking up at Thorne with startled eyes. "What was that about Katharine?"

"Oh, dear, I am sorry. I thought that you'd all have heard the news by now."

"What happened to Katharine?" Olivia demanded, her mouth trembling.

"Olivia, my dear," Dr. Chesterfield said, putting a hand gently on her arm. "I'd hoped to wait until after your guests had left. Perhaps I could have a word with you in the kitchen."

"Tell me!"

"A serious head injury of some sort," Thorne said, for it was to Thorne that Olivia looked as the clearest and quickest path to the truth.

"I'm afraid that Katharine is dead, my dear," Dr. Chesterfield said gently.

"The police apparently think she was murdered," Thorne added.

An awful quiet descended over the shocked people in the room. Olivia's shriek, when it came, was shrill enough to rattle the glass covering her husband's watercolors.

"Don't become hysterical," Sanchez snapped.

Olivia Sanchez appeared not to hear her husband. She stood, her spine rigid, her face drained of blood. Her jaw opened. I braced myself, expecting another scream, but instead she buried her face in her hands and gave herself up to wracking sobs. Victoria went and put her arms around Olivia.

I looked around the stunned room. Almost everybody seemed to be in shock, except for Thorne and Nicoletta, and myself. We were the newcomers in town and didn't know Katharine Culpepper Simonette. But then I realized that was wrong. Thorne knew Katharine; she'd helped him buy Arlington.

Realizing Olivia was beyond the point of controlling herself, Sanchez led his wife from the room. Dr. Chesterfield followed them up the stairs, motioning to Victoria to stay behind with a weary wave of a hand he seemed barely capable of lifting. The old doctor seemed at the point of collapse. I did not need to look into his mind to know that Katharine Simonette was the reason for his exhaustion and well-concealed depression.

"Olivia and Katharine were best friends," Victoria explained. She wiped away a tear with the back of her hand.

"We all were incredibly close," Lydia said as if to establish that she had as much right as Olivia to mourn Katharine Simonette.

"It's very sad, of course, but the living must carry on," Lysander Chase said with grim stoicism. He wasn't the sort of man who liked emotional displays. Olivia Sanchez's public grief offended Lysander Chase.

"When did it happen?" I asked.

We found ourselves looking again to Becker Thorne, who had sunk into a chrome-and-black-leather chair with his champagne glass. "Late last night, apparently."

"Last night?" I repeated. "Isn't it unusual that nobody has heard about this until now? Except for Mr. Thorne, that is."

"I knew," Lysander Chase said simply.

"I can't believe you didn't tell me," Lydia snapped.

"Henry called me around two this morning," Lysander said, ignoring his daughter's angry remark. "He said the police wanted to keep it quiet while they got the preliminaries out of the way." He glanced at his watch. "The chief should be having a meeting right now with Phil and one of his reporters. It'll be in the papers tomorrow."

"What happened?"

"I only know that Katharine has been killed. Apparently it was quite brutal. And, yes, murder."

"How horrible," Victoria said, the tears running freely down her cheeks now. "I feel so bad for her husband and little boy."

"They're beside themselves with grief," Lysander Chase said. "Martin was up most of last night, first with Katharine, then with the others. And, of course, he attended the autopsy early this morning."

"What a terrible time that poor family has had," Victoria said in a quavering voice. "Losing two members within such a short time."

"What's that?" I asked, a sinking feeling in my stomach.

"Henry's brother Gregory died about a month ago."

"What happened to him?" I asked, hoping my interest wouldn't seem morbid.

"He was a hopeless alcoholic," Lysander Chase said in a tone that signaled nothing more needed to be said about such a distasteful matter. The information relieved me somewhat. The killer's toll in Jerusalem stood at one—bad enough, of course, but still he'd claimed only a single victim.

"How did you happen to hear about Katharine Simonette?" I asked Thorne.

"Believe it or not, they were talking about it at the Amoco station where I stopped for gas on the way here."

"Good grief!" Lysander exclaimed.

"Bobby Hanson's brother is an EMT," Victoria said. "He must have heard about it from him. Bobby owns the filling station," she added for my benefit.

"Let us pray for Katharine," Nicoletta said.

"Poor, poor Katharine," Victoria said, bowing her head. Katharine and Victoria had been rivals all of their lives, yet Victoria's grief was genuine.

A long moment of silence followed, each of us thinking our private thoughts about Katharine Culpepper Simonette's death and what it meant.

I looked up and saw that Lydia Chase was not praying, and she certainly wasn't thinking about Katharine Simonette, either. Her eyes were fixed on Becker Thorne, a musing smile on her lips that left no doubt that she was marking him down as her next intended conquest. Thorne was returning her look and making plans of his own.

"Amen," Nicoletta said.

Nicoletta looked across at Thorne, and I saw the briefest flicker of loathing in her eyes. I suppose it is possible that Nicoletta was disgusted that Thorne could flirt with the vapid Lydia Chase at such a moment, but the condemnation in her eyes seemed deeper than that. I wondered whether Nicoletta's devotion to God had somehow given her the power to recognize evil when she encountered it.

Deciding to hazard everything, I let down my own psychic shield long enough to focus my energies on Thorne. I threw everything I had at Thorne's mind, intending to pierce his mental armor and get conclusive proof that he was the killer I'd followed here from New York City, and, no doubt, the one responsible for Katharine Culpepper Simonette's death.

It was like hurling my body against a brick wall.

Thorne's psyche was completely impenetrable. I've never run up against anything like it before in a mortal—if he is mortal, which I doubt most profoundly.

"I don't believe we've been introduced yet," Thorne said,

turning away from Lydia and smiling at me. I looked at Thorne's grinning face for a few seconds that stretched into an eternity. And then, repressing my loathing—and exerting every bit of my power to keep Thorne from seeing the fears that hide within the innermost corners of my own mind—I reached out to shake his hand, experiencing a moment of *déjà vu* that made me feel as if I were repeating something that had already happened.

VI
Fun and Games

CHRONICLE NOTES: "Becker Thorne's" diary, continued.
—Editor

I do not know why *she* had to come here now to cast her shadow prematurely over these joyful times. My ears still sting with her rebuke! She came out to Arlington and dressed me down like a schoolboy. She's never spoken to me like that—at least not since that time in Moscow, and before that in Berlin, and before that in Johannesburg, and before that in . . .

I must admit, dear diary, that I am a rather willful fellow. I *do* frequently need correcting, and she is the only one alive who can correct me, now that I have become the Fury. I did promise I'd return to New York after buying Arlington and amass still more millions, but how much money does even an immortal need?

She was very cruel, diary. She said I was insane, that I lacked all self-control, that I would not desist until the mortals in Jerusalem were howling for our flesh—instead of we for theirs!

And, of course, she's absolutely right.

She warned that it would be harder here to disguise my ways. I care not! Let them know of the glorious monster in their midst! All the better if they lie awake in their beds at night, shaking with terror.

She did relent after a bit and admitted she is herself planning something *special* for the guilty descendants of my enemies. What, exactly, I do not know. As usual, she will not let me in on her secrets, which is hardly fair, since she insists that I share mine—and manages to know them always. The only thing she would reveal to me about her plans is that she's planning a party at Arlington that will allow me to settle the score with the Founding Families forever. The only detail she would add was that the affair would be "something literary," something that someone who loved *Macbeth* as much as I do would relish.

In truth, diary, I'm rather surprised she is making such a special effort to help me. She's been telling me she's tired of me for the past fifty years, although only in the last decade have I begun to believe it's really true. As you know, my own passion cooled long ago. I am not the sort of man who likes to be dominated by a woman—yet she has dominated me, and there is nothing I have been able to do about it, because of her power.

The supreme irony is that she has developed an inexplicable fondness for that weakling David Parker. I would have killed him the first time I sensed him skulking after me in New York City, if she hadn't intervened on his behalf. What would Parker say if he knew her protection was the only thing that has kept him alive the past six months?

She can have the weakling, especially if a new plaything will get her off *my* back. And if she wants him, she will have him. If Nicoletta wants a powerless novice like Parker as her slave, nothing on earth will be able to save him from her.

My contempt for Parker is without bounds. He is too weak to kill for pleasure, yet he's irresistibly attracted to the hallowed act. My sacrifices in New York City drew him like a moth to a candle. Perhaps he felt a tingling hint of the Neon lingering behind me at the scenes of my work. Of course, he thinks me mad. And I *am* mad—but it is the madness of the prophets, the sacred lunacy of those touched by the gods.

How well I understand Parker and his pathetic soul! He is filled with weakness and indecision, and more beset with doubts than Hamlet. He allows himself to be controlled by women, not in the way I am (harried by a cunning and ancient enchantress) but by any woman, as long as she appeals to his infantile need to be loved. It goes without saying that Parker is a member of the wretched *Illuminati*. The worst vampires always are. He thinks I don't know about the *Illuminati*, and naively imagines his elders in the brotherhood to be the Brahmins of the *Vampiri* world. If he knew how often I have killed members of his self-important order. The conceit that they are the guardians of the mortal world is without parallel.

Let Parker delude himself. The *Illuminati* do not have the power to stop me from bringing Jerusalem bleeding to its knees.

I have already made progress in my work here. Charlotte Hornsby Foster was the first to die during my most recent visit. I will save the best for last, diary, and do my most inspired work on Victoria Buchanan and her lovely bastard daughter, Michelle.

Charlotte provided precious little fun. She started to screech, and I tore her head off in a fit of pique. Setting up the fake automobile accident was a shrewd way to conceal her murder, even if I did ruin a new pair of trousers leaping from the Cadillac at seventy miles an hour.

Of course, diary, you know all about Sister Mary Helen. It was a disappointment to see how badly the years had ravaged her. Once upon a time ago she was an arrestingly beautiful woman, a strong-bodied Irishwoman with brick red hair, high, fine breasts, and a temper even I would have thought twice about provoking. I argued with Nicoletta in 1928 over Mary Helen. I wanted to seduce Buchanan's servant, and so did Nicoletta, whose tastes in lovemaking are as varied as they are wild. We couldn't agree, so we decided neither of us would have her—when we should have taken her to bed together! Now I have learned Mary Helen was conducting a quiet affair with Isaiah Buchanan! She might even have married the old fool, if I hadn't steered him into Hell first. To think of Mary Helen locking herself up in a convent, and her delicious body, with its soft skin and thick red tresses, giving pleasure to no one. A waste, truly.

I made up for my two disappointments with Charlotte and Sister Mary Helen with the third object of justice, the sodomite Gregory Culpepper. He was alone in the abandoned Jerusalem depot when I found him. He offered to perform an abomination upon me for the price of a bottle of cheap whiskey. I was so delighted to see a Culpepper fallen to such ignominy that I could hardly contain my glee!

I instructed Culpepper to strip off his clothes. As he undressed, I pulled on the yellow rubber gloves. The gloves thrilled and tingled with expectation of the joyous moment that was at hand. The sodomite was excited, too, at the prospect of the new and utterly unexpected act of abasement he was about to experience. He was also flattered that anyone as beautiful as I could find his filthy and emaciated body attractive enough to illicit desire of even the commercial variety.

I asked Gregory if he minded being tied up.

No, he said, he rather enjoyed it.

As fate would have it, I'd brought a coil of clothesline with me for just such a purpose. I lashed him—his body reeked of vomit and piss!—to a cart once used to roll luggage to passenger trains.

And then I began to improvise.

I spotted a length of rusted wire amid the empty liquor and cough-syrup bottles in the corner. The wire was about four feet long, a little thicker than that used to make coat hangers, with jagged points at either end where shears had cut it.

I jabbed an edge of the wire into the flaccid skin of Culpepper's left leg. Gregory began to yelp, but I used my mind to stop his voice in his throat. I inserted the wire into Culpepper's body an inch at a time, until I succeeded in burying about two feet of it in him, his skin bulging upward in a misshapen ridge where the rusty catheter ran.

Gripping what remained of the wire, I jerked it in the opposite direction of the way it ran under Gregory's skin. At last, a bit of real fun!

There was a ragged tearing sound. Culpepper's body arched upward, straining against its bonds. I felt blood splattering against my face. His mouth locked open, and the veins bulged in his neck as he shrieked—yet no sound issued from his mute throat, only spittle and stinking breath! It would have been good to hear him scream in agony, to plead for me to stop, please stop, but I didn't want to attract attention to the abandoned railway station. Besides, diary, even a scream would have provided some small measure of relief, and it would have been wrong to have granted a Culpepper any degree of mercy, no matter how small.

I confess, diary, that I was rather impressed with my first bit of handiwork as I paused to admire it. It looked as if a vein had exploded in Gregory Culpepper's leg, blowing out the surrounding muscle and skin.

I picked another place, this time on his chest, and jabbed the wire into his flesh. . . .

I kept at it a long, long time. By the time I'd finished, he looked as if he'd been flayed alive. I confess that my work made me rather excited. In a frenzy I tore open dear Gregory's throat and gulped his blood in great, greedy draughts.

The police, who are, of course, beneath contempt or even notice, arrested some hopeless degenerate for Culpepper's murder. Then they did something surprising: they let the accused man go free just because he was innocent! What a curious idea of justice they have in America these days. In my time we would have lynched the odd darky or two if the real culprit couldn't be found, if only for reasons of preserving general respect for the law.

The fourth criminal to be executed was Gregory Culpepper's niece, Katharine Culpepper Simonette. I had fun with her—but not as much fun as I had with Greg and that rusty length of wire! But then I've told you all about my sweet evening with Katharine, diary.

Lydia Chase would have been next, except that I must postpone justice while Nicoletta makes ready her plans.

Lydia appeared unattended at Arlington last night and demanded I serve her a martini. She drank it and a second and offered to perform an abomination upon my person. I allowed her to—and repaid it in kind, much to her satisfaction! Needless to say, diary, I wanted to go on to give Lydia some of the very special attention I'd lavished on Katharine and Gregory Culpepper, but I refrained. Nicoletta is likely to become unreasonable if I do anything to upset her plans.

I have yet to meet the mortal the Neon prophesied would help me in my vengeance. *"You will know him by his sign and by his words,"* the Neon said. And his words will be: *"I am the Last Gray Ghost of the Confederacy."*

Where is this valiant warrior? I pray that Neon brings him to me soon so that we may make everything ready. I must consecrate this place to Neon. I must prepare a temple, a holy place. I will bring Pegasus to the temple and honor him with prayer and sacrifice. Jerusalem's sins will be cleansed in blood, for it is written:

But these enemies of mine, who did not want me to reign over them, bring them here and slay them before me.

And when all my work is finished, the Fury shall go wherever Neon sends me, for there is much wickedness abroad in the world, and I must punish it where I find it.

PART VI

Testimony

I

Marcus Cuttler

CHRONICLE NOTES: David Parker interviewed Marcus Cuttler a week before the dénouement at Arlington Plantation. Mr. Parker's journal, continued.

—Editor

"I knew the motherfucker was a vampire the first time I saw him."

The observation caught me slightly off guard. The language was unexpected, too, coming from a preacher's son. I reminded myself that Marcus Cuttler was at that age where young men are invariably contemptuous of the established order, if only covertly. Indoors, he continued to wear a black Malcolm X baseball cap, the solitary white X pulled low over his forehead.

"And how did you know he was a vampire?"

Marcus's heavy eyelids blinked.

"Who are you, man?"

"I told you, Marcus. I'm a member of a very unobtrusive, very private organization that studies unusual phenomena."

"I thought you were a musician."

"I'm a professional musician. My career affords me opportunities to travel. That, in turn, makes me useful to the organization I represent."

"What's it called, this organization? You didn't say."

"No, I didn't."

"And you think you might be able to help Eugene?"

I told him I thought I might be the *only* one who could help his friend. "So what made you think Thorne was a vampire?" I asked again.

"Shit, man, you're serious."

"You don't believe in vampires?"

"Don't tell me you do."

I shrugged. "If you don't think Thorne is a vampire, why did you say that you thought he was one when you first saw him?"

"I just meant he *looked* like a vampire. Tall, thin, sallow skin, too white for even a white man, dead eyes."

"But that's a strange way to think of him—as a vampire. Is that the actual term that came into your mind when you met Thorne? I'm curious."

"Yeah, I just flashed on it. I don't believe in vampires. That shit's crazy. But I remember he gave me this spooky kind of look and smiled at me, like he knew what I was thinking. That's impossible, isn't it?"

"Some are said to have such power. Tell me more about your first encounter with Thorne. Where did you meet?"

"At Eugene's. It was night. His mama had one of those mercury-vapor crime lights put up on a pole in the back last year. After Eugene came back to town for the summer, me and him would be out there most nights shooting hoops. Usually there were some brothers hanging out, but that night we were alone.

"It was about ten o'clock. I remember because Eugene's mama had the television on and I could hear through the window. I looked down the street and saw this big Mercedes coming toward us. I figured it must have been a fan or an agent or a coach come to visit their favorite basketball player. But then I thought about the time. It was pretty late for that. So I thought, look out, maybe it's a gambler or somebody who wanted to put Eugene together with some dope. I don't know how closely you follow basketball, but gamblers and coke dealers are two types of people Eugene has to stay away from no matter what."

I nodded, encouraging him to continue.

"One more mistake, even a little one, and Eugene is out for good. But if he keeps out of trouble, the future is wide open. That's the only reason a star like him came back to Jerusalem for the summer. You have any idea how much money a first-round NBA draft pick can expect to be paid?"

"Lots, I imagine."

"The driver got out first. He was short and powerful looking, about how you'd imagine a high-priced bodyguard would look. He was wearing a black suit, as if they'd just come from visitation at the funeral parlor. The driver gave me the look, you know, the quick glance that said, 'Don't even fucking *think* about fucking with me.' He kind of jogged around the Mercedes and opened the back door.

"The guy in the backseat—Becker Thorne—slowly rolled his legs out and climbed out slow and easy, like he owned the world and everybody paid him rent. That's when I had my flash: *vampire*. The cat gave me this slow kind of smile. His teeth were so white they were almost blue. Next thing I know, my feet were working backwards, getting out of this dude's way. He went toward Eugene with his hand out, said he'd come to meet The Man. And then I realized who it was. It had to be Becker Thorne, the man who bought Arlington."

"You'd heard of him?"

"Everybody in town was talking about Thorne. He's the only billionaire in Jerusalem. And he bought that old plantation outside of town where white people like to go to remember the romantic times when people with black skin were slaves."

"It doesn't sound as if you share the general nostalgia for Arlington Plantation."

"If I owned Hell and Arlington, I'd rent out Arlington and live in Hell. That place is an embarrassment to African Americans. Somebody ought to go out there some night and torch the fucking place," Marcus added with a surprising degree of venom.

"That's strong talk."

"Listen, Mr. Parker: When the Buchanans were living like kings at Arlington, my people were slaves there, picking their cotton, cooking their food, washing their clothes, taking care of their children. As a black man, I have a somewhat different opinion of the Old South than someone like Victoria Buchanan."

"I don't think you're being entirely fair to Victoria."

"I don't believe Victoria Buchanan is a bad person. I've known her all my life. She's an excellent teacher. I consider her a friend. But she's white, and the white people in this town have ideas about Arlington Plantation that I find frankly twisted. I guarantee you that Nathan Bedford Forrest Nightingale thinks Arlington Plantation is a mighty special place, too. Just ask him. He's working for Thorne now, you know."

"Isn't Nightingale the man who was accused of murdering your father?"

"Nightingale *killed* my father."

"My mistake. I thought he was acquitted."

"He was acquitted, not that that means anything. There was more than enough evidence to convict Nightingale. His fingerprints were on the rifle he used to shoot my daddy. Nightingale claimed the gun had been stolen, although he'd never filed a theft report. He'd threatened publicly to kill my father at least five different times, and there were witnesses, three of them white, who testified to it. It took the jury two hours to acquit. Yes sir, there was more than enough evidence to convict Nightingale, but the Klan intimidated the jury."

"Nightingale was in the Klan, as I remember."

"There was a time when he *was* the Klan in this state. He was Mississippi Grand Dragon. Even changed his name for the Klan. His real name is Shelby Robert Nightingale, but he changed it to name himself after Nathan Bedford Forrest, the Confederate cavalry general who was supposed to be the Klan's founder. He still calls himself the 'Last Gray Ghost of the Confederacy.' I think he's totally insane, but that wouldn't keep *me* from sending him to the electric chair."

"It sounds like a terrible miscarriage of justice."

Marcus took off his cap and turned it around so that he could look at the X. "If I had any guts, I'd have killed the motherfucker myself."

"You're showing more courage by leaving him alone. His own miserable, hate-filled existence is surely punishment in itself."

"No offense, Mr. Parker, but you don't know what the fuck you're talking about. Nightingale lives in a place guilt can't reach. He's a dangerous animal and should be put down." Marcus pulled the cap back on. "I know one thing. He'd better steer clear of Eugene. Eugene will hand him his fucking head—if Eugene isn't already too far gone on Thorne's coke."

"How did Thorne get your friend mixed up in drugs again?"

"He invited us to visit him at Arlington that night outside of Eugene's. Thorne gave Eugene the usual flattery. He said Eugene was the greatest, that he'd make Michael Jordan look like an old man, and so forth. Eugene had heard it all so many times that I was amazed that kind of talk could still make him feel impressed with himself.

"Thorne ended up asking Eugene to come out and see him at Arlington. He invited me, too, but probably only because he thought Eugene would be more likely to come if he brought a friend. Thorne said we could drink some beers and take a dip in his pool. Then his chauffeur interrupted, reminding Thorne that he had an appointment he had to make. Thorne excused himself, saying he had to look at some real estate. Pretty damn strange, I thought, looking at real estate at night.

"They got back into the Mercedes and drove two blocks up the street. Then Thorne got out again and met somebody I couldn't recognize in the distance and darkness. The three of them disappeared into one of the worst houses in the neighborhood, an abandoned wreck with windows all boarded up with plywood. I still can't imagine why Thorne would be interested in Gold Coast property. The house he went into must have been a beautiful place once—about a hundred years ago, when the Chase family owned it.

"Eugene and I went and bought a twelve-pack at the Quick Trip. Thorne and his man were gone when we returned."

"What do you think interested Thorne in Eugene? Was it because Thorne's a basketball fan?"

"I doubt it," Marcus said quickly. "Thorne knew a lot about Eugene, but it wasn't anything he couldn't have boned up on in a hurry. My impression was that Thorne wanted to draft Eugene for his entourage. There aren't any other famous people in Jerusalem, Mr. Parker. Eugene is the only sports star we have. That rich man was just adding my friend to his collection the way he'd buy a racehorse or a pedigreed dog."

Marcus looked at me sharply.

"Or maybe Becker Thorne is the kind of person who likes to ruin any goodness he happens to come upon in his night wanderings. He knew about Eugene's drug problem. He knew that Eugene's entire future depends on staying clean, yet he lured him out to Arlington and offered him coke. Thorne couldn't have done a better job of destroying Eugene's life if he tried."

I sat and waited, thinking Marcus might have something to add.

"Becker Thorne is evil," Marcus said at last, a frightened look creeping into his eyes. "And I mean *evil*. That's the only word for it. He is pure, undiluted evil. He's attracted to people like Nightingale because they're evil, too, and to people like Eugene because they're good and he wants to destroy them. Because isn't that how evil works, Mr. Parker—destroying whatever tiny pockets of goodness and light can be found to exist in this sorrowful world?"

"Yes," I agreed simply. Marcus Cuttler—son of a well-known civil-rights worker murdered by a man who went free because of, not despite, the fact that he belonged to the Ku Klux Klan—knew more about evil than most good men.

II

Ashley Prew

CHRONICLE NOTES: The following testimony was transcribed from a microcassette tape labeled "Prew" that was found in David Parker's rooms in Jerusalem. Mr. Parker left no notes detailing when the interview took place, or how he compelled the mortician to speak so freely.

—*Editor*

"I'd been at it all afternoon when he came by, asking to see her.

"Katharine was no small piece of work, I can assure you. Head all staved in on the one side, neck torn apart. She had wounds in her back from God-only-knows-what. They'd done an autopsy, of course. You used to be a deputy coroner; you know the business. Big, lazy S incision up her front. Not that I had to worry about anything people couldn't see, but it's a terrible thing to see someone so young end up like that. They'd stitched her up more or less. You know how it goes. They get in and get what they want and leave it to me to patch up the mess.

"Katharine didn't have much blood in her. Not hardly a drop. I got her out of the refrigerator and over to the embalming table and went to work. When I finished, you'd hardly known she'd been there. The white porcelain didn't hardly look like it'd been used. Wasn't hardly anything to flush down the gutters.

"I got her sewed up good and started running embalming fluid. It's only half a job when you don't have to pump the blood. The real work was making her presentable. Henry Culpepper insisted on an open coffin. To tell you the truth, it would have been a big job even if only the family was going to view her. I've seen bad car accidents do less damage.

"I used some wire, some wax, some latex, some plaster of Paris. I don't mean to brag, but I am pretty good at what I do, if I do say so myself. They always ask me to give a workshop at the state convention, but I don't like to reveal my methods. Any fool can embalm a body, but it takes an artist to make a trauma case look good. You don't work in the business as many years as I have without learning some tricks. I got some of mine from my daddy, who was in the business fifty-one years, and he learned his from his daddy. I don't just run them in and out, you know. I like to think of myself as an artist. And when I'm done, you know, my work goes on public display, so I take a lot of pride in what I do and how well I do it.

"I pulled out all the stops for Katharine. She was a lovely girl when she was alive, and I wanted her to look good when we wheeled her up in front of the church and opened the box. She never had the time of day for me when she was alive, but that didn't make no nevermind. I'm a professional. Besides, it's just good business. Every job is an advertisement.

"To tell you the God's honest truth, Mr. Parker, I don't know if I'll ever do better than I did for Katharine. She was my masterpiece. I don't think I've ever brought anybody so far. Of course, she deserves credit, too. The good looks were hers to begin with. She had beautiful skin tone, even postmortem. I just used what I know to try to give her looks back to her after everything that had been done to her, poor thing. I took before-and-after pictures for the next state convention, to show my colleagues what kind of magic old Ashley Prew can work. Yes sir, she was my masterpiece. I might not ever do better with another client.

"I got her dressed in clothes Henry's maid brought down and put her in the casket. A real nice one, too—a top-of-the-line bronze Eternal Slumber. Twyla came in and did her hair. Twyla always does my lady clients' hair. My wife used to do it, till she got busy with her bridge and the preservation society and all her volunteering. So I got Twyla. She does a super job, but I always have to check her breath when she comes in to make sure she hasn't been drinking.

"Afterward, I put the finishing touches on the makeup, put

the rosary beads in her hands. Her husband wanted that, although I don't know as they went to church much. I was just letting Twyla out when the bell rang. I looked at my watch. I remember that it was four o'clock on the dot. Visitation wasn't supposed to start until six. I hate it when the family gets nervous and comes too early, but what can you say? They feel like they should be there with the loved one, though they only get in the way when I'm trying to get things ready and grab a quick bite to eat before the friends call.

"I was alone, so I had to scramble out of my rubber apron and get my jacket on. I had a tie on, of course. That's one of the absolute rules my daddy taught me: an undertaker doesn't take off his tie until he gets undressed for bed. You never know when you're going to get called out.

"It wasn't any of the Culpeppers or Paul Simonette, like I thought. I'd ask you to guess who, but you wouldn't get it in a million years, being as you're new in town. It was Nathan Nightingale standing at my door. You've heard about Nathan? I don't suppose he's been to any of the, what do you call them, recitals you're giving up to the college.

"I've known that old boy all my life. He got himself into a peck of trouble some years back. Must have been, let's see—Lord, how time flies—twenty years? He was arrested for shooting that colored fella. Black fella, I guess we're supposed to say now. Or is it African American? I try to keep up with things, but they move too fast these days. At any rate, those people never come to me. They all go to Lee Nabolo, and probably just as well, as far as my customers are concerned. Nathan wouldn't worry about what to call somebody who was colored. They're all niggers as far as he's concerned. Yes sir, there are still a lot of them like Nathan around these parts. Me, I've tried to change. All that hate just takes too much energy. The South has changed, too. Had to. You either bend or you break, you know.

"Nathan went out to California after the jury let him off for killing the preacher. Starting up the Klan out there, I figured. Then I heard he was in the nuthouse there. Went loony. I expect living in California would drive me crazy, too. He come back to town a couple of years ago. I expected the same old trouble to get started again, cross burnings and so forth, but there weren't none of it. I guess people aren't so interested in that sort of thing anymore.

"Nathan seemed different when he came back. He used to

be a big, loud fellow who liked to drink too much Rebel Yell and get people stirred up. He was all quiet and sullen when he moved back to town. He keeps to himself now, not like the old days. Still hates Negroes—they're all 'mud people' to him, anybody who isn't white—but he doesn't say too much about it. Doesn't say much, period. Stays shut up in that big old frame house on the end of Beauregard Street where his family lived. Gets what little money he has off some property he inherited. It's kind of funny. It's kind of—what's that fancy word?—ironic. He has a dozen of those apartment houses up on the Gold Coast. You know the neighborhood up on the bluff, all ratty ass, rundown big houses. I'd call it a slum. I don't think there's anybody who lives on the Coast that isn't colored. I mean black. I'll tell you one thing: I bet Nathan's tenants pay their rent on time!

"Anyway, to make a long story short—or as the preacher said, it's too late to make the story short, just try to make it *interestin'*—I'd just finished working on Katharine, the doorbell rang, it wasn't any of the Culpeppers coming early like I expected, but Nathan Bedford Forrest Nightingale.

"I says, 'Why, Nathan. What can I do for you?' I was searching my mind, thinking who could have died that he comes to fetch me for, because all of his kin are dead and gone, long dead and gone and buried.

"And Nathan says, 'I come to pay my respects to Mrs. Simonette.'

"I wondered what in tarnation was going on. The Culpeppers and the Nightingales don't exactly travel in the same social circle. They did once, years and years ago. The Nightingales had a fine plantation a long time ago. Beauford, it was called. The Yankees burned Beauford. 'Spoons' Butler's soldiers burned it to the foundation, which you can still see west of town, if you drive out past Robert E. Lee Park. They called him 'Spoons' because when his troops occupied New Orleans, he stole everybody's silver. That's a historical fact. The Nightingales took what little money they had left after the War Between the States and built the house on Beauregard Street. They've lived there ever since. It was a fine house, too, back when my daddy, rest his soul, was a young man. I don't think there's been any real money in that family since the fifties. Nathan's daddy lost a bundle speculating in cotton.

"No, I never knew the Culpeppers to have any truck with

the Nightingales, not in my time. I know that none of the Culpeppers came around when Nathan's daddy died back in '68. And I know for a fact that Katharine Culpepper Simonette would not have spoken to Nightingale if he fell down in the mud so as she could walk over his face to keep clean those expensive Italian high-heels she used to like to wear. Not that Nathan thought any better of them. The Culpeppers are Catholic, you may know. He hates Catholics about as much as he hates his "mud people."

" 'Visitation is at six,' I says to Nathan. 'Why don't you come back then?'

"And Nathan says, 'Can't do it, Ashley. I got to see her now.'

" 'You come at six,' I says. 'Come back when you can pay your respects to the whole family.'

" 'I said I can't do it. I got to see her now,' he says. And then, for emphasis, he says, 'Now!' again real emphatic, and smacks his fist into his hand—*crack!*

"Well, it was just crazy to carry on that way. Nathan wasn't even dressed for visitation. He had on his work clothes. Jeans, soiled denim shirt, no tie. He hadn't shaved for a couple of days. His hands were dirty. He needed a bath. And you should have seen his eyes. I don't know too many people in town who could look Nathan Nightingale in the eyes since he came back from California. You ever see a dog with that wild, crazy look, like it's trying to make up its mind whether to attack you or go out in the street and get run over by a car? Nate's eyes are like that. He's obviously disturbed.

"I admit Nathan rattled me pretty damned good. I was still trying to figure out what to say next when he pulled open the screen and walked right in!

" 'Where is she?' he demands, craning his neck to look into the main visitation parlor. We've got three, but he knew where she'd be, right up front in the main parlor, the big one.

"I was about to tell him it would be wrong to let him see her before the family, but Nathan was standing there, looking down on me.

" 'I just finished getting her ready downstairs,' I says. 'I'll bring her up.'

"Maybe it was wrong to do it, but what the hell. Anyway, I thought it might have been better to let Nathan have a look and then get him out of there before the others arrived. The family would have enough on their minds without Nathan lurking around looking crazy and menacing. I admit I wasn't ready for any confrontation with Nathan Bedford Forrest Nightingale. He's already killed one man I know about, and the talk was there'd been more beside Preacher Cuttler, back in his Klan days.

"I came back up, and Nathan was standing right outside the elevator when the doors opened. Like to have scared me out of my wits. The casket was closed, of course. You always close a casket before you move it so the damn lid doesn't slam shut on your fingers. Nathan helped me wheel the box into the parlor and stood there, his hands folded in front of him, impatient for me to open it up so he could see her. I don't know what I would have done if the family had wanted a closed-casket visitation, which is what most people expected under the circumstances. It was plain that Nathan had come to *see* Katharine.

"I opened the lid, looked up at Nathan, and thought, Holy shit! Nathan's eyes were bugged out like there were invisible hands around his throat, choking him. I thought he was having some kind of seizure. His hands were working together, he was wringing them, and his shirt was soaking wet with sweat. The air conditioning was roaring, like usual, the big vent blowing right on him where he stood. I always put the coffin under that big vent. I like to give people a little extra shot of oxygen when they come up to pay their last respects, try to keep them from fainting.

" 'She's beautiful,' Nathan finally says in this hoarse whisper.

"I didn't say a thing. I didn't want to set him off. It was plain to me he was right exactly on the edge. No mistaking it. I've seen enough people fall apart to know that he was just shy of crossing the line. And the scary part was that I knew the crazy bastard was capable of anything if he flipped out.

"Nate just stood there shaking. It was the longest five minutes of my life. Then all at once the tension seemed to let go of him. He just sagged like a flag when the wind stops blowing. His shoulders and head kind of slumped down, and he let out a big sigh.

" 'Thank you,' he says and grabbed my hand so hard that it hurt. His hand was cold, but it was dripping with sweat. 'Thank you,' he says again. 'Thank you for letting me see her, Ashley,' he says, his breath like when you turn over a rock, and it's all damp underneath and crawling.

"Then he adds, 'Mr. Thorne said you'd understand.'

"Can you believe that? Becker Thorne! I heard Nate's been doing odd jobs for Mr. Thorne, but I can't imagine that loony sitting down to talk about poor Katharine with the likes of Mr. Thorne. But who knows? A lot of strange things happen in this world.

"And then he left. The front door shut. *Bang*, the screen slammed behind it. Let me tell you, I was relieved he was gone.

"I've been worried about Nathan and the entire situation ever since. The police haven't arrested anybody, so Nate's free like everybody else to wonder who did it. Knowing Nate, I figure he thinks some Negro killed Katharine. In the old days, Nathan was always quick to blame the coloreds for any damn thing that happened, and while he don't say much any more, I don't guess he's changed his way of looking at things. He still calls himself the Last Gray Ghost of the Confederacy. With a crazy man like that running around Jerusalem, there's bound to be trouble sooner or later.

"I'm also worried about that Becker Thorne. I wonder if Mr. Thorne knows about Nate? I've been tempted to call him up and warn him. I haven't, of course. It really isn't any of my business. But still, I wonder if maybe I shouldn't put a bee in Mr. Thorne's ear. When Nathan Bedford Forrest Nightingale starts to get wound up about something—like the way he was with Katharine's murder—people need to start worrying."

III

Nathan Bedford Forrest Nightingale

CHRONICLE NOTES: Independent filmmaker Ron Sisgold went to Mississippi in July of 1991 to make a documentary about the Ku Klux Klan. His video camera was found in October of that year in a cardboard box in the basement of Nathan Bedford Forrest Nightingale's house. The tape in the camera contained Sisgold's interview with Nightingale. Framed by Sisgold's stationary camera, Nightingale is a hulking man, with eyes that are large, blue-gray orbs protruding slightly from beneath a heavy brow, the whites yellowed from prolonged Chlorpromazine use. His hair, a black crewcut in photographs taken at the time of his murder trial, has turned steel gray. The large pores on his leathery face are visible, many filled with blackheads, indicative of the poor hygiene typical in schizophrenics. A scar runs from just below his left eye to his left earlobe. The filmmaker remains missing. A transcript of the video's audio track follows.

—Editor

SISGOLD: Tell me about what it was like to be the Grand Dragon and control the Ku Klux Klan in Mississippi.

NIGHTINGALE: Read the newspaper clippings if you want to know about how it used to be. It ain't the truth, but you wouldn't believe the truth if I told you.

SISGOLD: Give me a try, Mr. Nightingale. Tell me about what it was like back when the Klan still had the power to put a man in the governor's office.

NIGHTINGALE: What kind of name is "Sisgold"? Jew?

SISGOLD (with thinly veiled hostility): You've had some health problems, Mr. Nightingale. I understand you were hospitalized for a time in California.

NIGHTINGALE: I was in the John Greenberg State Psychiatric Hospital. I ain't ashamed to admit it. (Pauses to drink from a bottle of Pepsi.) That's where they put you now when they don't agree with your political views.

SISGOLD: I didn't think it had anything to do with politics, Mr. Nightingale. (Consults his notes.) It says here you were arrested in San Francisco for felonious assault with intent to commit great bodily harm. You nearly beat a man to death with a board, according to the police report.

NIGHTINGALE: He was an agent. He knew what to expect.

SISGOLD: An agent? What kind of agent?

NIGHTINGALE: ZOG.

SISGOLD: That's the acronym for Zionist Occupation Government.

NIGHTINGALE: I was ZOG's political prisoner. They held me in the John Greenberg State Psychiatric Hospital.

SISGOLD: If you were a political prisoner, why did they put you in a mental hospital?

NIGHTINGALE: I'm sure an educated boy like you knows all about how that works. They've been warehousing political prisoners in mental hospitals in Russia for years. Now they're doing it here, too. The same socialist cabal calls the shots here and in Russia.

SISGOLD: That sounds a little paranoid, Mr. Nightingale. What evidence do you have that a such widespread conspiracy exists?

NIGHTINGALE: The mud people are too clever to leave behind the kind of clues the average person could recognize. They're masters of deception. But a few of us know the truth.

SISGOLD: So you have no evidence.

NIGHTINGALE (angrily): I'm the evidence, boy, the living evidence. I was taken prisoner in San Francisco and locked in Reprogramming Facility 0399—that's the John Greenberg State Psychiatric Hospital's real name. They turned me over to Dr. Seti Jhabvala, their expert in thought programming. He weakened me with pills, turned me down to a whisper. A pill is small, and once you start eating them, they make you small. But now I'm big again, just like Becker Thorne said I would be if I quit taking my medication.

SISGOLD (surprised): Becker Thorne, the Wall Street investor?

NIGHTINGALE: No, no.

SISGOLD: I'd heard he'd bought an estate near here. Is he in the Klan?

NIGHTINGALE (shouting): No!

SISGOLD (alarmed): Calm down, Mr. Nightingale.

NIGHTINGALE (struggling to regain some measure of control): I want to talk about mud people. They've already got us outnumbered. They're going to wipe out the white race unless they're stopped. The white race needs to wake up. That's why I killed that preacher—to wake up my people.

SISGOLD (stunned): I beg your pardon?

NIGHTINGALE: The nigger preacher. You know the one I mean. I killed him to signal the others that it was time to rise up against the mud people. But I underestimated ZOG's power. They've implanted the webcore in too many of us.

SISGOLD (slowly): Are you admitting you shot Reverend Cuttler?

NIGHTINGALE: You got a hearing problem, boy?

SISGOLD: I'm—I'm surprised you're saying this.

NIGHTINGALE: Why? They took me to court for killing him once. I got off. They can't try me again. (Laughs.) That would be double jeopardy.

SISGOLD: But if you confess, they—(Tense silence.) No, of course, you are right. They can't try you again for Reverend Cuttler's murder.

NIGHTINGALE: My race has let me down, Sisgold. I led, but they didn't follow.

SISGOLD: Excuse me, Mr. Nightingale, but I'm not feeling very well. Could we continue this interview tomorrow?

NIGHTINGALE: Sit your ass back down, boy. I was about to tell you about my guerrilla war in California. You don't want to miss hearing about that.

SISGOLD (faintly): You committed similar, um, operations in California?

NIGHTINGALE: That's why I went to California. I took the battle to the enemy.

SISGOLD (even more faintly): What did you do in California?

NIGHTINGALE: I went underground. I'd kept too high a profile in Mississippi to be effective, so I took the fight underground. I got myself what they call a *nom de guerre*. I used my war name in all my military actions. That's how I signed my communiqués: Scorpio.

SISGOLD (stunned): You said Scorpio.

NIGHTINGALE (laughing): So you've heard of me.

SISGOLD (with extreme wariness): I've read about a Scorpio.

NIGHTINGALE: There's only one—me.

SISGOLD: But Scorpio didn't murder—didn't focus on civil rights workers.

NIGHTINGALE: The couples I did were zebra breeders. My single targets were either mud people or traitors to the white race. None of that has been made public. Ask the police. You'll see. You're talking to Scorpio.

SISGOLD: Scorpio never was caught, as I recall.

NIGHTINGALE: Oh, they caught me, but they just couldn't prove I was Scorpio. After the fight with the ZOG agent, they took my trailer and truck apart a piece at a time looking for evidence, but they didn't find nothing. I was too careful. Twenty-eight successful missions, and they couldn't touch me. So they rigged my arrest so they could lock me up in Reprogramming Facility 0399 and have Dr. Jhabvala scramble my brains.

SISGOLD (disbelief creeping back into his voice): I'm surprised they let you out if they thought you had something to do with Scorpio's serial killings.

NIGHTINGALE: The court appointed a smart Jew lawyer who got me out. (Laughs.) The police were very insistent about me coming back to Mississippi to live. The ZOG pigs who flew me back here said I'd disappear for good if I ever came back to California. I suppose I was lucky they didn't drag me behind a barn and put a bullet in the back of my head. That's what I would have done, had I been in their shoes. But they're weak. Our whole society has become rotten and weak. It's all part of ZOG's plan.

SISGOLD: Did Dr. Jhabvala know you were Scorpio?

NIGHTINGALE: Dr. Jhabvala knows everything. He reports directly to the webcore. There were times I could have killed him, but I knew it wouldn't do any good. You know that the webcore is like an octopus: you cut off a tentacle and it grows back. The only way to stop it is with extreme measures.

SISGOLD (interrupting, apparently wary of letting Nightingale become lost in his delusions): And so you came back to Jerusalem.

NIGHTINGALE (grinning): It was quite a joke for Dr. Jhabvala to send me back to Mississippi to serve as an example of what the mud people can do. But I'm going to turn the tables on them. There is no way Dr. Jhabvala can make me keep taking those pills, not with him in California and me in Mississippi. Mr. Thorne helped me throw away my medication, and now I'm almost well again. But I knew Dr. Jhabvala would find out. I knew the webcore would inform him, and that he would send an agent here under some false pretense to get me back under the webcore's control. I knew someone with a device like that fake camera would come here to put the webcore back into my head. (Nightingale squeezes his eyes shut and grasps his head between his hands as if in unbearable pain.)

SISGOLD: Mr. Nightingale, I hope you haven't gotten the mistaken impression that I—

NIGHTINGALE (screaming): ZOG bastard! (Nightingale leaps to his feet, hurling the Pepsi bottle at his interviewer. The camera tips sideways and crashes to the floor, its unblinking eye remaining trained on the ceiling while the sound of Sisgold being kicked is heard on the audio track. The filmmaker cries out in pain, but his voice is soon quiet. The sound of Nightingale's boots thudding against Sisgold's body continues for nearly five minutes.)

PART VII

✧

Letters and Documents II

I

Autopsy Report

CHRONICLE NOTES: This report is on file in the Coroner's Office, Keokuk County Courthouse, Jerusalem, Mississippi.

—Editor

Autopsy Report and Supplemental Record

Clinical Record

Date and hour died: 22 June 1991 12:22 A.M.
Date and hour autopsy performed: 22 June 1991 6:00 A.M.
Prosecutor: Louis Shaw, M.D.
Attending physicians: William Hume, M.D., and Martin Chesterfield, M.D.

Clinical diagnosis
Ht.—63 inches
Wt.—112 pounds
Eyes—Blue
Hair—Black

Pathological diagnosis
CAUSE OF DEATH: Massive trauma to head and neck; internal bleeding; loss of blood; shock.

Patient identification
Name: Simonette, Katharine Culpepper
Age: 28
Sex: Female
Race: Caucasian
Autopsy No.: F22-341

CLINICAL SUMMARY

According to available information, the deceased, Katharine Culpepper Simonette, was found on the sidewalk outside her home by her husband, Paul Simonette, at approximately 11:30 P.M. 21 June 1991. The subject's nude body was lying on its left side 12.5 feet from the front door of the Simonette family residence. Mr. Simonette observed that the subject's body was covered with so much blood that it made it impossible to make an initial identification of specific injuries. Mr. Simonette observed a rotary-shaped series of spherical sucking wounds in the subject's back, leading him to assume—incorrectly, the autopsy has determined—that his wife had sustained multiple gunshot wounds. Mr. Simonette, in his statement to the Jerusalem Police Department, also recognized the presence of a significant neck wound, and a large head wound, through which bone fragments and portions of the brain extruded. Mr. Simonette reported that his wife moaned on several occasions, but did not respond to questions or exhibit other evidence of consciousness.

Mr. Simonette summoned the Jerusalem General Hospital ambulance. The EMTs transported the subject to the hospital emergency room, arriving at 11:44 P.M.

Dr. William Hume attended Mrs. Simonette in the emergency room. (A copy of Dr. Hume's report is appended to this document.)

Dr. Hume identified the primary injury as a massive cranial wound, measuring 5 inches at its largest diameter, with the point of origin to the right and just above the external occipital protuberance at the back of the skull.

A secondary but equally significant injury resulted in extensive damage to the tissue on the right side of the subject's neck. Significant tearing was observed in the sterno-mastoid, to the extent that it was nearly severed, with damage extending deep into the trapezius. A small section of the clavicle was visible through this wound in the neck and upper torso.

Blood was observed bubbling from a series of five spherical wounds in the center of the subject's back, one on the left side of the spine, four on the right, in the area of the fifth, sixth, seventh, and eighth dorsal vertebrae. Dr. Hume initially suspected these indications represented entry points for gunshot wounds; he was, however, perplexed at the absence of the usual corroborating evidence, specifically the apparent lack of internal bleeding in the chest cavity associated with gunshot trauma.

In the course of cursory examination of the body during treatment, Dr. Hume observed a number of secondary injuries in the subject, including (citing the original Emergency Room transcript):

—Burns in the genital area apparently caused by the application of electrical current to the skin;
—The fingers and thumb on the right hand had been individually broken;
—A profusion of small wounds to the left breast had been inflicted with a pin or small, sharp knife;
—The nipple on the right breast was missing, the appearance of the remaining tissue indicating it had been bitten off.
—The ring finger of the left hand had been neatly severed by an extremely sharp instrument, possibly a surgical scalpel.

Dr. Martin Chesterfield, the Simonette family physician, arrived in the emergency room at 11:52 P.M. and assisted Dr. Hume in introducing an orotracheal tube, which was connected for ventilation. Dr. Hume concurred with Dr. Chesterfield's determination at this point that the back wounds had not been inflicted by gunshot and were more consistent with stab wounds introduced by a blunt tool.

Dr. Hume found no pulse or blood pressure at the time of admission, although a heartbeat and slow, labored respiratory efforts were present. The subject's feet were elevated for the Trandelenburg position. Dr. Hume performed a cutdown on the patient's right ankle, inserted a polyethylene catheter into a vein and began an infusion of lactated Ringer's solution, with 300 mg of hydrocortisone added to the IV. Dr. Chesterfield drew blood for type and crossmatch.

Because quantities of blood were present in the oral pharynx, Drs. Hume and Chesterfield began a tracheotomy. However, due to severe lacerations to the trachea, Dr. Hume elected to place anterior chest tubes in both the right and left pleural spaces.

Neurological examination found the patient's pupils to be fixed to light and dilated. The eyes deviated outward, with moderate skew from horizontal. There were no tendon reflexes.

A profuse amount of frank bleeding continued from the head wound. A considerable amount of scalp and skull plate were missing. Gross laceration and herniation of the temporal and occipital lobes of the right side of the brain were noted, with the cerebellum extruding through the wound.

Dr. Hume began an immediate transfusion of unmatched O Rh positive blood, although the extent of the trauma made it impossible to control the bleeding. An estimated 1400 cc of blood was later removed from the floor of the emergency operating room and draperies.

At 12:12 A.M., cardiac arrest occurred. Dr. Hume began external cardiac massage. This resulted in a renewed flow of blood from the cranium, evidencing extreme damage to the brain tissue and its vascular system.

There was no electrocardiograph evidence of heart activity, and a scan of electrical activity in the brain charted a consistent flat line. Dr. Hume continued cardiac massage without reviving pulse. This activity was carried out until 12:22 A.M., at which time Dr. Chesterfield pronounced Katharine Culpepper Simonette dead.

The body was cleaned and prepared for autopsy. A preliminary set of forensic color photographs and X rays was taken.

GENERAL DESCRIPTION OF BODY

The body is that of a slim and physically fit adult Caucasian female measuring 63 inches and weighing 112 pounds. Beginning signs of rigor mortis are present. The hair is of medium length, black, and abundant. The eyes are blue. The right pupil measures 7 mm in diameter. The left pupil measures 5 mm in diameter. There is extensive ecchymosis in the region of the right supra-orbital ridge. Distinct and abnormal mobility is present in the superciliary ridge, extending upward to the frontal bone and transversally to the temporal bone. (See later discussion of the skull and brain.)

Clotted blood is evident in the ears, nose, and mouth. The teeth are healthy and in excellent condition. The mouth is otherwise unremarkable.

There is extensive tissue damage to the right side of the neck. An irregular laceration 8 inches in length and approximately 7 inches in diameter at its widest point extends from jaw to sternum. The epidermis and subcutaneous cellular tissue is missing over much of this area, as is a portion of the platysma myoides and the underlying muscle. The sterno-mastoid muscle is close to being severed in two places, the first approximately 4 inches above the superior border of the clavicle, the second just below the mastoid process. The clavicle is visible through the lower portion of the wound. The trapezius also sustained moderate tearing, although it is primarily intact.

Damage to the major veins in the neck is surprisingly light. Despite massive trauma to the surrounding muscle mass, the external and internal jugular veins appear undamaged. There is, however, vague evidence of scar tissue on the external jugular, perhaps an indication of an earlier surgical procedure.

The upper extremities are otherwise unremarkable with the following exceptions:

1) The skin encircling the wrists and upper hands of both arms is discolored, the shading of the contusions ranging from pinkish red to deep purple, with the most profound area being along the back of each wrist/upper hand region. There is evidence of subepidermal bleeding. The wounds are consistent to those associated with rope burns, and are of an extent that is consistent with cases where subjects were tied at the wrists and hung suspended for an extended time prior to expiration.

2) Fractures are present in the thumb and each digital extremity of the right hand, as follows: thumb, first phalange; index, second and third phalange; middle, first phalange;

ring, second phalange; and little, first phalange. The usual contusions associated with simple fractures is present in each digit.

3) The ring finger of the left hand is missing. The wound is neat and clean, the apparent result of a pseudo-surgical action.

Surveying the upper torso, the left mammary is slightly larger than the right, as is typical in adult females. Wounds are present in both breasts, and are described as follows.

There are 32 punctures in the left breast, most of them of pinprick size. Six of the wounds, four of them within the nipple itself, are slightly larger, indicating use of a second instrument. Sections are taken and preserved for microscopic inspection and further analysis.

Damage to the right breast is more significant. There is a round, ragged laceration three inches in width, across the top of the hemisphere. The nipple and surrounding tissue are missing, as is a portion of the fatty tissue beneath. There is an indication of a human bite pattern in the wound. Two deeper punctures, both extending as far as the pectoral muscle, display characteristics consistent with an animal bite. Sections are taken and preserved for microscopic inspection and further analysis.

Continuing the examination from the dorsal side, there are five spherical wounds between the fifth and eighth dorsal vertebrae. Each puncture is approximately 1 inch in diameter. The condition of the skin surrounding the wounds as well as the subcutaneous tissue indicates that they occurred several hours before death. One wound is on the left side of the spine adjacent to the sixth dorsal vertebra. The remaining four wounds are on the right side of the spine, aligning with the fifth, sixth, seventh, and eighth vertebrae. The wounds penetrate all three layers of muscle. The wounds follow an irregular course, but curve generally inward to surround the spine. Each of the wounds is 4 inches in depth, with the exception of the one on the left side of the spine, which is 3 inches deep, and the one adjacent to the sixth vertebra, which is 4.5 inches in depth. The four deepest wounds puncture the right lung. These wounds are not judged to be serious enough in and of themselves to have been a major contributing factor in the death. The nature of these wounds is impossible to identify and inconsistent with common phenomenon. Sections are taken and preserved for microscopic inspection and further analysis.

The skin on two areas of the left upper thigh and one on the right labia majora display small, circular burn marks consistent with those typically caused by the application of electrical current to the skin. Sections are taken and preserved for microscopic inspection and further analysis.

The vagina shows evidence of recent intercourse. A sample of semen is taken and preserved for blood typing and DNA analysis.

Gross description of the skull and brain

The massive, irregular injury to the skull encompasses most of the upper right hemisphere, from just above the superciliary ridge through the frontal, upper temporal to the occipital region. Much of the bone and scalp are missing. Extensively lacerated and disrupted brain tissue is visible. Both the wound and brain are distorted to the extent that satisfactory verbal description is impossible. Photographs are taken.

The brain is preserved in formalin for further analysis and study.

Internal organs

The organs are removed and are unremarkable with the following exceptions:

1) There are four perforations to the right lung, described above.

2) Preliminary examination of the parenchymal cells of the liver indicate the presence of granular cytoplasm, consistent with a condition of high glycogen typical to cases of violent death.

Tissue samples of each organ are collected for further study and analysis.

FINAL SUMMARY

This autopsy confirms the attending physician's diagnosis as to the cause of death of massive trauma to the head and neck compounded by numerous contributory injuries.

Recommendation: The coroner supervising this autopsy recommends this report to be forwarded to a Grand Jury impaneled to bind over person or persons unknown for trial in the homicide of Katharine Culpepper Simonette.

Sworn this 22nd day of June, 1991.

Louis Shaw, M.D.
Keokuk County Coroner

Jerusalem, Mississippi

II

Dr. Oppenheim's Papers

CHRONICLE NOTES: The following documents were found in Dr. Joan Oppenheim's briefcase in her room at the Jerusalem Holiday Inn.

—Editor

New research[1] has discovered an important, unsuspected link between two giants of late nineteenth- and early twentieth-century music: Petr Ilich Tchaikovsky and Claude Achille Debussy.

For the past year, my colleague Dr. Ling-Ling Tsu and I

[1]Excerpted from *"Unbroken Chain: Copiest Proves to be Missing Link Between Tchaikovsky and Debussy,"* by Dr. Joan Oppenheim, published in *Epoch*, the journal of the Society of American Music Scholars, June 1991.

have been engaged in a project to use computerized cluster analysis to evaluate evidence of multiple-author scripting in original nineteenth-century music scores. (See: "Using Computer to Recognize Amanuenses in Composers' Scores," Dr. Joan Oppenheim, *Language and Culture Quarterly*, Fall 1990 edition.) We have used either original or photographic reproductions of original music scores and input them into a Cray supercomputer via an Apple Macintosh Quadra 950 connected to a Microtek scanner. Dr. Tsu has programmed the Cray to transform the strokes and dots found in standard musical notation into mathematical equivalents, which are, in turn, used to identify variations in the handwriting in the scores.

Our aim has been to analyze how individual composers used amanuenses—or copyists—to transcribe the scores of major compositions.

Evaluating the original manuscript of Tchaikovsky's Sixth Symphony, we discovered that all but one movement—the transcendent *finale*—had been penned in the composer's hand. The *finale*, however, was written in the hand of an anonymous amanuensis.

The work of this amanuensis—provisionally identified as Amanuensis 1, or A1 for short—appears in other notable Tchaikovsky works, including *Swan Lake*. A1's most pervasive work is found in the *Nutcracker* ballet, where his handwriting is present throughout the inspired score. Indeed, Tchaikovsky's own handwriting on the original *Nutcracker* orchestral arrangement is limited to scoring the counterpoint in a few inconsequential passages.

. . . Yet the bigger discovery was still to come. Our continued computer analysis of nineteenth-century scores discovered A1's hand scattered throughout the body of the French composer Debussy's work, indicating a heretofore unsuspected connection between Tchaikovsky and Debussy.

Where Tchaikovsky had tended to employ A1 (with the exception of the *Nutcracker*) to help with work on the climactic movements—which, we know from contemporary accounts, gave him the most trouble—Debussy used A1 much more sparingly. However, there are key instances when Debussy, too, relied heavily upon the ubiquitous A1. The haunting melody line in *"Claire de Lune,"* Debussy's best-known work, was also penned in A1's hand.

Our research, identifying A1 as the surprising and heretofore unsuspected bridge between Tchaikovsky and Debussy, has led to one of the most perplexing mysteries of musical scholarship in recent memory. Who was A1? And what unlikely set of circumstances conspired to have him present at those intimate moments of creative genius that saw Tchaikovsky and Debussy give birth to their most transcendent works, compositions that establish them for all time among the pantheon of immortal musical giants?

These questions make all the more frustrating our inability to discover A1's identity in our corollary research. If A1 was a minor composer—as his close professional association with these two musical geniuses seems to suggest—we have been unable to link him to any of the signed original manuscripts surviving from the period.

. . . Dr. Tsu and I continue our computerized search, confident that other traces will be found that will allow us to substitute a proper name for this individual we now know only as A1.

. . . The infuriating thing[2] is that I still can't find the damned mistake. I've looked through our research more than a dozen times, and the error—or errors—elude me.

A1's handwriting is all over Tchaikovsky's and Debussy's original scores. And Wagner's. And Charles Ives's. And Stravinsky's. And Mahler's. And Bizet's *Carmen*. And the opening movement of Beethoven's *"Moonlight Sonata."*

And, the most preposterous "finding" yet, *all* of Mozart's compositions were scored in A1's hand!

Which is patently impossible. It goes without saying that it would have been humanly impossible for A1 to have worked with all those composers, over two centuries. He would have to have been as immortal as the music Ling-Ling and I were misled into thinking he set down on paper for the geniuses who hired him as their amanuensis.

Plus, there is the well-known fact that Mozart scored all his work himself, composing in his head, transcribing the finished works to paper for the first time as miraculously completed works. That means—extending this insane logic to its "logical" conclusion—that A1 and Mozart are the same person, that Mozart didn't die in 1791, as any undergraduate knows, but lived on to work with Tchaikovsky and the rest.

[2]Material photocopied from Dr. Joan Oppenheim's research notebook, where she sometimes recorded personal remarks.

It is insane to even consider such a ridiculous possibility.

A1 *is* a ghost—a research ghost. The amanuensis A1 does not, did not, exist. He's a chimera, a bad echo hiding in the data, a mistake somewhere in our work.

I cringe to think how tremendously excited we were when A1 first cropped up. It was intoxicating stuff, a golden connection. It is an academic's dream come true when a modest research project turns out to be the gateway to a significant discovery.

But then Ling-Ling's computer started to find A1's handwriting *everywhere*.

As a final desperate test, I had Ling-Ling scan random composers' works into the Cray supercomputer—Wagner, Mahler, Beethoven—anything to prove the computer wasn't seeing A1's handwriting in places it couldn't possibly be.

The test failed miserably. A1's "fingerprints" were on manuscripts it was impossible for him to have touched.

I can't understand how this happened. Our methodology was sound. The only remaining possibility is that Ling-Ling's cluster analysis doesn't work properly—a possibility she angrily refused to consider when I broached the subject. She's furious I ever talked her into collaborating and has stopped taking my phone calls.

There's nothing left for me to do now but discard the work the computer did, drag out the manuscript copies, and start laboriously working my way through one at a time. A1 can't be found in all the places Ling-Ling says he is, and I'm going to prove it. Maybe that will make it easier to think of a credible defense for having published our research results prematurely.

Dear Joan,[3]

I was pleasantly surprised today to find your letter in my mailbox. Recognizing your familiar handwriting on the envelope immediately brightened my day. I wish we could keep in better touch. Why is it easy for friends to become lovers, but difficult for lovers to become friends?

I'm sorry to hear you're having so much trouble with your project. However, I think you might be taking it a little too much to heart. You're hardly the first academic to make a mis-

[3]A personal letter from Yale School of Music musicologist Dr. Eric Kell to Dr. Joan Oppenheim. According to Dr. Kell, Dr. Oppenheim never replied to his letter.

take. As long as there is no evidence you falsified data—I know there's no question of *that*—this will, I predict, prove to be nothing worse than a middling setback.

That being said, I must advise you to reconsider the conclusion that your research data is faulty. Yes, you read that right. I don't think your conclusions about A1 are necessarily false—I hope you're sitting down as you read this.

I know that seems like an absurd assertion to make, but bear me out.

To begin with, you have to agree that Ling-Ling Tsu knows what she's doing. She's one of the most highly regarded experts in her field. If she says she can program a Cray supercomputer to analyze handwriting in music manuscripts, my bet is that she *can*.

As for A1's handwriting showing up in so much music over such a broad stretch of time, I agree that it *seems* impossible, but that doesn't mean that it *is*.

I don't know a thing about handwriting analysis; that's your specialty. However, I do know how to look closely at the characteristics within a given score. Forget about the *handwriting*, Joanie, and look at the *music*. That's where you'll find the proof that A1 exists, regardless of who—or what—he is.

I've attached photocopies of seven of the passages you mentioned in your letter. Look at the ways major and minor themes are interwoven. Look closely at the counterpoint. The best illustrations are highlighted. There's no question in my mind that these passages were written by the same person.

I don't pretend to have an explanation. I'm not superstitious. I don't believe in ghosts. You know I'm not sure I even believe in God. I do, however, think some power or agency beyond our understanding is at play here. I think it is entirely possible that finding that Mozart's manuscripts were written entirely in A1's hand is not where your research project collapses in a heap of procedural failure, but the point from which your diligent work slingshots forward into the realm of unimagined and unparalleled discovery.

I agree wholeheartedly that A1's existence *seems* an impossibility, but look at the music. Study it closely. Show it blind to other musicologists. You'll see. The proof is there.

The only matter of real consequence now is finding A1. I wouldn't waste another minute looking backward in time. Forget about hunting for A1's footprints among dead composers. You need to get your hands on copies of as many *contempo-*

rary manuscripts as possible from ASCAP and try to find the music A1 is collaborating on *today*.

Just be careful.

You're obviously dealing with something beyond our present understanding. I don't have any reason to think it might be dangerous, but I have no way of knowing. If you have discovered the first scientific evidence supporting reincarnation, putting A1 in touch with past lives could be a bad shock. (I'm embarrassed to even suggest reincarnation could be at the root of this, but there's got to be *some* explanation!) Or A1 could be something unique and wholly unsuspected—an ancient entity who has somehow defied aging and death. He might not even be human. We don't know—and we won't know, until you find A1.

Of course, if A1 is conscious of his "past" lives, he may have very good reasons for wanting to keep the world from finding out about them—and him. So proceed slowly and carefully, Joanie.

If I can assist in any way, please do not hesitate to phone, night or day. You can no doubt tell from the tone of this letter that I would love to help you. Please call or write as soon as you have had a chance to take a look at the way the music in the A1 scores is constructed. I know that's all it will take to convince you.

Until then, I remain,

Your devoted friend,
Eric

III
Cuttler-Mozart Correspondence

CHRONICLE NOTES: Marcus Cuttler disappeared after the dénouement in Jerusalem, Mississippi. Wolfgang Amadeus Mozart eventually located the young man in Paris, France. Mr. Cuttler corresponded with Herr Mozart for a brief period before the young American vanished a second time. His status is listed as "missing" in the *Illuminati* master files.

—*Editor*

Marcus Cuttler–Wolfgang Amadeus Mozart correspondence
Letter No. 1

Dear Mr. Toland,

I hope you won't be disappointed if I ask that you *not* come to Paris to meet me next Sunday. It'll be a while before I'm up to talking about what happened at Arlington Plantation.

Sincerely,

Marcus Cuttler

Marcus Cuttler–Wolfgang Amadeus Mozart correspondence
Letter No. 2

Dear Mr. Toland,

Thanks for the understanding expressed in your latest letter.

I decided to take your suggestion and talked to Dr. Rittenheur here. I'd given some thought to seeing someone like her, though I thought any psychiatrist I saw would conclude I was a delusional paranoid and have me locked away. Dr. Rittenheur was quite understanding, and her English is excellent. She seemed more than a little familiar with your line of work.

You were right. Talking helps.

You asked about the first trip Eugene and I took to Arlington Plantation, the time Thorne asked us to bring him the neon sign. . . .

Thorne had invited us out to take a swim. Eugene wanted to just show up, but I said we should call first. I did. Thorne wasn't home, so I left a message. He called me back that night and said to stop by the next evening. He said we could each make one hundred dollars by helping him move some sign he'd bought over in Crawfordsville. I said we would. I was broke and needed the money.

Eugene drove us out to Arlington the next day in his BMW. Thorne wasn't around when we got there. Zaharim, his butler-chauffeur, met us at the door and handed me a set of keys. He said the sign was crated up and ready for us to pick up in Crawfordsville. There was a forest green Ford F-150 parked around back by the kitchen entrance. It was a real cracker-mobile—four-wheel drive, gun rack in the rear window, Confederate flag flying from the radio antenna. Eugene refused to ride in the truck, so I had to drive it. If I'd known who the truck belonged to, I would have refused to ride in it, too. Eugene followed in his car.

Crawfordsville isn't a town in the proper sense, just a couple of houses and Shoetree's, a tumble-down business that's one-third gas station, one-third grocery, one-third liquor store. The crate was waiting for us over to the side of the business. It was about five feet high, six or seven feet long, and a foot across.

I could see the sign inside through the open slats. It was a tin horse with wings, its form outlined in glass tubing. It was weather-beaten as hell, its tin skin pocked with rust and hail dents, the red enamel paint cracked and chipped and faded by the sun. The winged horse stared out of its box at me with one wild eye, its head reared back, its front hooves pulled up to tear at the air. I didn't like it, and I couldn't imagine what Thorne would want with such a weird piece of junk.

Eugene and I got on the opposite sides of the crate, which was as heavy as it looked. We wrestled the front end into the truck first, then managed to slide it forward, but not without a lot of pushing and swearing that greatly amused the toothless old man who came out of Shoetree's to watch.

We got back to Arlington and unloaded the crate. Thorne still wasn't anywhere to be seen. Zaharim said there were swimsuits in the cabaña for us to use. Eugene and I had our trunks on under our shorts, but we didn't say so. Zaharim brought two bottles of beer—Dixie Blackened Voodoo Lager, I remember—and towels while we changed. Zaharim said Thorne was on the telephone, conducting overseas business, and would join us later.

We swam for about a half an hour and drank a second round of beers before Zaharim told us we should get dressed and join Thorne in the game room.

Five minutes later Zaharim ushered us into a room that was completely dark except for the matching Tiffany lamps suspended over the pool table. The table's green felt covering reflected upward on Thorne's face as he leaned forward to make a shot, making his exceptionally pale skin cadavarous.

"Welcome to my humble home, gentlemen," Thorne said without looking up.

It was a difficult shot but Thorne made it. Off the bank, hitting the eight ball, which tapped the fifteen, which cut the three with just enough of a nick to drop it into the side pocket.

Eugene told Thorne it was a nice shot.

"Why, thank you. That's quite a compliment coming from such a sportsman, Eugene."

Thorne straightened and let one hand fall into the pocket of his velvet smoking jacket.

I thanked Thorne for the swim.

"Not at all, Marcus. You're welcome to use the pool any evening. Bring your girlfriends." He leered. "A house like this is particularly empty without young ladies. Just call ahead and make sure I'm not already entertaining. Zaharim! Champagne for my new friends. Champagne is all right with you both?"

We nodded. I'd never had champagne before, though Eugene had after championship games.

"You picked up my little parcel without any problem?"

I said we'd unloaded it in front.

"What good is that old sign?" Eugene wasn't too shy to ask what I'd been wondering about, too.

"Anything becomes collectible if it is scarce, Eugene. Old coins. Bottles of wine. Stamps. Paintings by insane artists who kill themselves. Even neon signs. With careful restoration, it will be quite valuable."

Thorne chuckled.

"I paid the owner one hundred dollars for it, a laughably small sum, even considering its present condition."

"A real steal," I said. I guess I didn't do a very good job of keeping the sarcasm out of my voice.

"If someone does not know the value of his property, is it my responsibility to inform him of his ignorance?" Thorne said. "If I'd offered more, it would have only made the previous owner suspicious. If I'd made a fair offer—and 'fair' is an extremely slippery and relative term when one is talking about art—his ignorance and inexperience might have led him to believe it was worth a great deal more than it actually is. That, in turn, could have made a deal impossible, and the valuable Pegasus would have continued to sit outdoors and deteriorate beyond the point of salvage."

"Pegasus?" Eugene asked, as if he'd missed something.

"The winged horse on the Mobil sign is a representation of Pegasus," Thorne explained. "Properly restored, Pegasus will be worth at least a hundred times what I paid for it."

Eugene made a low whistle.

"More, if the market continues to improve. This particular model was built in 1955. It's the most aesthetically successful design. There are fewer than a dozen known left in existence. I would be happy to pay a finder's fee if there are any more in the area. So keep your eyes open, gentlemen. You will discover some amazing things if you pay close attention."

Zaharim served us champagne from a silver tray. There were only two glasses—one for me, one for Eugene. Thorne wasn't drinking.

"So tell me, Marcus, what do you think of my acquisition? I'd be interested to hear your opinion."

I muttered something polite.

"No, what do you really think?" Thorne asked a little more firmly. His eyes locked onto mine. I felt a little dizzy for a second. It must have been the champagne, I thought, blinking to try to clear my head.

"I think it's a little spooky. It reminds me of a—" I thought for a moment. "—It reminds me of a pagan idol."

Thorne burst into mocking laughter. "What do they teach in school these days?"

"They teach that Pegasus horse was born from the blood of Medusa after Perseus cut off the monster's head."

"You *did* get an education!" Thorne said, delighted. "But perhaps you're right. Pegasus does rather resemble an idol. I suppose the impression comes from the fact that the sign is rendered in two dimensions, like the idol unearthed at Ninevah—the winged bull with the head of a man with an elaborate, stylized beard. Have you ever seen the Babylonian idols in the Metropolitan Museum in New York? I went to see them myself after a policeman I knew—he's dead now, unfortunately—told me about them. Magnificent specimens."

I said I'd never been to New York, though Eugene had. Eugene answered Thorne's inquiring glance with a shake of the head.

"Your comment, Marcus, puts me in mind of a passage in the Bible:

"Go down; for your people, whom you brought up out of the land of Egypt, have corrupted themselves; they have turned aside quickly out of the way which I commanded them: they have made for themselves a golden calf, and have worshiped it and sacrificed to it."

I stood there with the champagne glass raised halfway to my lips, staring at Thorne in total disbelief. He was the last man on earth I expected to hear recite Scripture. Even the quotation itself was bizarre. My father had used it in the last sermon he preached before Nathan Bedford Forrest Nightingale murdered him—I don't pretend to remember actually hearing it, but I have reread my father's last sermon many times. For a few uncomfortable moments I was convinced that Thorne had somehow plucked the verse out of *my* mind—but I told myself that such things were impossible.

"I hope you don't mind that I'm not having a drink with you," Thorne said. "Alcohol does not agree with me. I prefer other recreational drugs."

I drained off my glass in a single swallow and put it down on a table. I told Thorne he would have to excuse us, but Eugene and I had to get back to town.

"That's too bad," Thorne said, his eyes on Eugene. "As the Fates would have it, I recently obtained an ounce of rather fine cocaine direct from Peru. Would you care to sample a bit before you leave?"

There was not the slightest resistance in Eugene's face, only stupid animal desire. All I could think about was what would happen if the NCAA called in the morning and told Eugene to report for a random urine test. But not Eugene. The only thing he was thinking about was putting cocaine into his nose.

"Eugene, let's go," I said.

"I'm sorry if I offended you, Marcus," Thorne said. "I didn't realize you were so puritanical."

"Fuck *puritanical*, Thorne," I said. "That shit don't do a thing for me. And Eugene can't afford to mess around with it. He'll be out of basketball if he messes up one more time."

"You leave worrying about me to my mama," Eugene said. The hostility in his voice surprised me so much that it took me a beat before I felt hurt—and another beat before my anger returned.

"Your friends worry about you whether you want them to or not, Eugene," I said. I shot Thorne a withering glare. "Your real friends."

Eugene said that just one line wasn't going to hurt him. I told him that there wasn't any such thing as just one line of cocaine for him.

He told me to fuck off.

I wheeled on Thorne. "Why are you fucking with my friend's life? Is this some kind of rich man's game?"

"Quite the contrary," Thorne answered. "I'm trying to help Eugene."

I told Thorne he had a strange idea of help.

"A man must learn to control his weaknesses or he becomes a slave to them. I know how to say yes and how to say no to cocaine. Why not teach Eugene the same kind of control over his appetite?"

"Junkies don't have any control, you ignorant white motherfucker," I shouted.

Eugene came at me, swinging.

"Nobody talks about me that way," Eugene tried to say, the words coming out in an angry tangle as he tried to connect with me.

"Boys, boys," Thorne said, forcing himself between us.

That was it. I never had liked Thorne, and he sure as hell wasn't going to call me *boy* and get away with it. I was about to put my fist in Thorne's face when somebody grabbed me from behind. It was Zaharim. I struggled, but it didn't do any good. The harder I tried to get away, the harder Zaharim squeezed.

"Like so many young men today, you're filled with anger," Thorne said contemptuously. "I'm sorry, *Mr. Angry*, but I find that I'm forced to ask you to leave and not come back."

Zaharim shoved me foward. One foot caught on a table leg, and I went down. Nobody helped me get up. When I turned and pushed myself up with my arms, I saw the three of them—Thorne, Zaharim, and Eugene—staring down at me.

"Come on, Eugene," I said as I stood. "This isn't any place you want to be. These people are poison."

"Eugene, *you* are welcome to stay," Thorne said.

Eugene tossed me his keys and said I could take his car. I could tell he was secretly ashamed, but he was staying nonetheless. He couldn't resist. I threw the keys back at him, hitting him in the chest. They fell to the floor with a jangle. Eugene's famous lightning reflexes had already gone to sleep, hypnotized by the prospect of the first rush of coke entering his brain.

Zaharim tried to take my elbow but I jerked free. His footsteps were close behind me all the way through the house, but I didn't turn around. He ran ahead of me when we got to the door and blocked my way.

"Mr. Thorne wanted to be sure you were paid for your work tonight," he said.

I wanted to knock the grin off Zaharim's face, but the anticipation in his eyes warned me that he was hoping I'd take a swing at him. He could have taken me apart with one hand. I snatched the new hundred-dollar bill from his hand, wadded it into a ball, and threw it on the floor.

Zaharim opened the door for me. I stalked out.

"Have a pleasant evening, *Mr. Angry*," he called after me, taunting.

I was walking down the lane toward the highway, too furious to think, when a big man stepped out in front of me in the darkness. I must have jumped two feet in the air. He started to laugh.

"I don't know who startled who the most," said a gravelly voice. "You know, you ought to smile when you go for a walk at night, boy, so folks can see your pearly teeth and know you're coming."

He struck a match and held it up to the unlighted cigarette

in his mouth. I stepped involuntarily backward. Jesus God in heaven—it was *Nathan Bedford Forrest Nightingale.*

"I'm just on my way back to pick up my truck. Mr. Thorne borrowed it so that he could send a couple of colored boys out to do a chore for him."

Nightingale exhaled a long plume of smoke toward my face. "He asked me if I had a problem with letting some coloreds drive my Ford. I told him, no, sir, I'm always glad to do my part to give Negroes gainful work, keep them out of trouble and off welfare."

And then he was past me, a big hulking figure stalking through the darkness toward the lights of Arlington.

I was too stunned to react. As I stood there in the darkness, watching Nightingale's silhouette moving toward Arlington, I realized I was trembling. There was a long time in my life when I would have liked nothing more than to meet Nightingale alone in the dark in an out-of-the-way place. Now that it had finally happened, I had been too startled to act.

I have to break off now and go to work, Mr. Toland. I'll continue in another letter tomorrow.

Sincerely,
Marcus Cuttler

Marcus Cuttler–Wolfgang Amadeus Mozart correspondence
Letter No. 3

Wolf:

You may not believe it, but I saw *her* here tonight—Lucretia Noire, if that's really her name.

I thought she was dead—I thought they were all *dead*!—but it's not so. She's alive, and here in Paris. She can only be here for one thing. I know she's come for me.

I was a fool to think I could escape them.

If I get away this time, you'll never find me again—and maybe *they* won't, either.

Wish me luck. And say a prayer for us all.

Marcus

IV

A Gathering of the Brood

CHRONICLE NOTES: This flyer was mailed to The Crystal Owl, a bookstore in Jerusalem, Mississippi, where it was found and photocopied by Victoria Buchanan.

—Editor

Come the dark star in its rage,
Symbol of the rising age,
Power to the Secret Ones
Who love Diane and loathe the Sun.

Lift high the jeweled chalice gold,
Drink libations to spirits old,
Before the Brood was torn apart
By Judas's children, with Judas's heart.

All will gather on that blessed night
To raise the fire that burneth bright
Within each soul lost to the light
But given Cain's immortality.

The Circle of the unseen few,
Princes, queens, ancient Druids,
Comes silent to the darkling wood
To renew primordial oaths in blood
And cause the mortal world to tremble.

—"The Prophecy of Ophelia"
From *The Secret Society*,
By Lucretia Noire
(Used with permission)

The Vampyre Guild of America is proud to announce North America's First Annual Vampire Convention: A Gathering of the Brood, Aug. 2–3, 1991.

The Vampire Convention will feature interactive role-playing based on the cycle of vampire novels by Lucretia Noire—*We, Vampires; The Vampyre Chronicle; The Secret Society; The Raven*; and *Lenore*.

For two nights, role-players will assume the identities of characters in Miss Noire's books. To avoid character duplications, role-players will be assigned the characters of their choice on a first-come, first-reserved basis. In other words, the first person registering to role-play as the character Princess Nicole will be the *only* Princess Nicole admitted to the convention, and so on.

Registration is strictly limited to the first one hundred vampires. Once all the major and minor characters from Miss Noire's vampire cycle are reserved, participants will be assigned characters belonging to the thirteen vampire Broods, or clans, in the series. Miss Noire has graciously agreed to write brief descriptions of each of these completely new characters, which will be mailed to participants before the Vampire Convention in time to afford players an opportunity to assemble costumes and develop roles.

Miss Noire has consented to participate herself, in person, in the First Annual Vampire Convention, and will be the guest of honor at the Vampire Ball. Miss Noire will be available at that time to meet her fans and discuss her books and sign autographs. Participants are asked to respectfully abide by Miss Noire's request that she *not* be photographed.

The First Annual Vampire Convention will be held in the Deep South in an authentic Civil War–era plantation, complete with Spanish moss–covered oak and a romantic, vampiric, nineteenth-century atmosphere.

On-site accommodations will be available to only the first twenty participants, so register soon! Only the first one hundred reservations will be accepted, due to the intimate setting for this Gathering.

The registration fee for costumed role-players (no others will be admitted) is $100 for the Vampire Convention. Accommodations at the plantation are $150 per night. Participants also may stay at a nearby Red Lion Inn at a special $75 per night rate (double occupancy).

For additional information—or to reserve a character with a

$100 deposit refundable only to those whose reservations come in after all available slots have been filled—please write:

The First Annual Vampire Convention
P.O. Box 666
Atlanta, Georgia 30301

The First Annual Vampire Convention: A Gathering of the Brood promises to be an experience you will never forget.

V

Letter to Lucretia

CHRONICLE NOTES: A University of Iowa college student named Kurt Teameyer wrote the following letter to Lucretia Noire.

—Editor

June 3, 1991

Lucretia Noire
c/o The First Annual Vampire Convention: A Gathering of the Brood
P.O. Box 666
Atlanta, Georgia 30301

Dear Miss Noire,

Enclosed please find my $100 entry fee for the First Annual Vampire Convention.

I would like to reserve the character of Alcibiades Poe. I'm sure many of your readers will want to be Poe for the weekend, but I doubt anybody understands the vampire's character as well as I do or will be able to portray him as accurately.

I already have the costume I will need to be Poe. I own an

antique double-breasted black suit that was my grandfather's, and I recently bought a vintage black fedora that is an exact replica of the hat Poe wears on the cover of *The Raven*. I also have a silver skull ring. And I've been brushing up on all my favorite Poe lines—*"By the blood and by the prophecy, the Brood is mine to rule!"*

I'm well qualified to play Poe. I'm an experienced role-player. I've been into Dungeons & Dragons ever since junior high school, and I'm active in the university's chapter of the Society for Creative Anachronism.

I do not know whether you will get to personally see this letter—or any of the others I've mailed to you in care of your editor Mr. Zoltan—but if you do, I want you to know that I am your most devoted fan. I've read each of your books at least twice, and I've read my favorite, *The Secret Society*, six times—so many times that the binding broke and the pages began to fall out! I plan to write my master's thesis on *The Secret Society*, if the committee in the University of Iowa's English Department accepts my proposal.

It would be the honor of a lifetime to meet you, Miss Noire. Although I totally respect your unwillingness to grant interviews or be photographed, there are so many things I want to ask you about your books. The privilege of speaking to you for even a few minutes would provide me with invaluable insights for my prospective master's thesis.

I'm mailing this letter less than an hour after your advertisement for the Gathering appeared in the *Daily Iowan* newspaper. I'm sure Post Office Box 666—nice touch!—will be deluged with reservations. I hope my application will be in time for me to be included.

Your most adoring reader,

Kurt Teameyer
625 Hillside Ave.
Iowa City, Iowa 52243

[illegible]

I do not know whether you will ever personally see this letter—or a copy [illegible]

[illegible]

Kurt [illegible]
[illegible]
[illegible] City, Iowa [illegible]

PART VIII

✧

Intermezzo

I
Tocatta and Fugue

7 P.M., Thursday, August 1—David Parker was thinking about Victoria Buchanan when the clock on the mantel above the fireplace began to chime. He'd asked her to dinner, but she'd refused, saying she had to work on her manuscript. This admission in itself bespoke the deepening intimacy between them. Victoria was extremely reticent about her writing and never discussed it. The fact that she had mentioned her work at all was an indication that she was opening up to him. It was a small thing, but in its way significant.

David listened to the chimes from the clock over the mantel echo through the apartment. Each keyed a resonate hum in the Bosendorfer and remained there, humming softly in the piano's sound board, until overtaken by the next chime.

Perhaps, David thought, Victoria knew more than she realized. The *Vampiri* were not the only ones with psychic powers. David had known prescient mortals; they often were as incapable as Victoria apparently was of understanding the true meaning of the strange ideas that came into their heads.

What was *that*?

David cocked his head and listened.

Silence was draping itself over his rooms again now that the clock had marked six, the stillness broken by only the steady ticking of the works inside the mantel clock.

Had it been a sound—or something not heard but sensed?

David got to his feet and went to the window.

There was an ineffable *something* out there.

"What is it?" David asked himself out loud, mildly disturbed by the undefined presence.

No reply was expected, and none came.

There were still a few hours of summer sunlight left, yet the absence of electric lights in the elegant nineteenth-century rooms where Morningside College lodged its visiting dignitaries, even at that hour, left deep shadows in the corners furthest from the windows and their heavy velvet Victorian draperies. The dimness in the corners, behind the wing-back chairs, inside the closet door standing slightly ajar, had already begun to deepen and become crepuscular. The enormous rubber plant in the corner between two bookshelves assumed an ominous aspect, as if it were not a plant at all but a malevolent sentinel placed there, in an unobtrusive location, to silently watch the occupant.

David turned slowly around, reaching out with his senses. And then he *knew*: It was another vampire!

"Thorne," David said to himself, the muscles in his jaws becoming rigid.

The only response was the ticking of the clock on the mantel, the slow, steady measure of time running out.

The other of the *Vampiri* was not in the apartment, David knew, or in the building. He pulled open the front door and stood there, halfway into the hall. The presence was unmistakable. He stepped out and pulled the door closed behind him, not bothering to lock it. He turned to the right; the presence felt stronger in that direction. His footsteps down the long hallway quickened until he hit the double doors at the end of the corridor with such force that they flew back against the rubber-tipped doorstops on either wall, rattling the etched oval of glass set in each door. David took the steps two at a time, then three at a time, running by the time he reached bottom.

The campus courtyard outside Buchanan Hall is called the Pentacrest; it sits atop a knoll surrounded by five geometrically arranged faux Grecian buildings. Buchanan Hall and another dormitory are on one side; the English/Philosophy Building and Natural Sciences Building are situated opposite the dorms; the chapel stands at the western apex so that seen from an airplane the Pentacrest would resemble a square crowned with a peak, the peak being the chapel.

The vampire was there, toward the chapel. No, inside it. The other vampire was in the chapel, waiting for David.

The Pentacrest was deserted. The few students and instructors who remained bound to Morningside College for the first weekend of August were already in town, marking the end of the week at Popeye's or some other haunt. The sun was falling lower in the sky behind the chapel, the rays traversing it, causing the stained-glass windows to pulse with brilliantly colored light.

The thought of Thorne waiting for him in the sun-drenched chapel, calling him out to such a place at such a time, made David Parker's heart sink. David had thought—perhaps *hoped* is the better word—that Thorne had but limited access to the higher *Vampiri* arts, the highest of which is the ability to control the epidermal cells to repel the ultraviolet radiation that is deadly due to the vampire's hypersensitivity to light. David's experiences with the murderous vampire in New York had convinced him his adversary was powerful, yet David had reserved the hope that the *Illuminati* discipline had taught him secrets the outlaw did not know—secrets that would enable David to defeat the killer.

David struggled to keep his energy focused as he mounted the stone steps and stepped quickly through one of the two arched doors that were fastened open with a brass chain. He had been in the chapel only once, when Powell Mills took him on a quick tour of the campus shortly after his arrival from New York.

The sinking sun poured light in through the enormous stained-glass windows, brilliantly illuminating scenes from Christ's life. The air was perfumed with incense, and, beneath that, the more subtle smells of beeswax and polish.

The thunderous blast of organ music struck David like a slap across the face—the opening figure of Bach's Toccata and Fugue in G Minor.

The organ was to the right of the sanctuary, on a raised platform of heavily carved wood, its brass pipes rising upward toward the open-beam ceiling. The organist's back was to David, his hands a blur as they flew across the multiple keyboards, his feet working the pedals, his entire body set into play in bringing to life Bach's trumpeting melody and throbbing bass runs.

David began to smile.

It was not Thorne but David's friend and mentor, Wolfgang Amadeus Mozart.

David sat in a pew, relishing the music, his eyes following the bouncing red ponytail that hung down onto the back of the organist's midnight blue jacket.

The fugue finished. The organist stood and turned, looking down on David with his large, intelligent eyes.

"Wolf."

"Mein Herr," the slight Austrian said, bowing his head.

One look at the set of Mozart's mouth told David that serious trouble was afoot.

"I'm relatively certain I've identified the killer."

Mozart nodded, pleased that at least that much had gone right.

"His name is Becker Thorne, as I told you in my communiqué."

"Your communiqué?" Mozart gave David a sharp look. "I received no communiqué, and I check my electronic mail twice a day, no matter where I am in the world. Ach, David, do not tell me you *mailed* it."

David's face colored.

"How many times have I told you to use the computer? If someone of my generation can use such an elegant and infuriating contraption, you certainly can. It is bad enough that the mails are not secure, but they're not even reliable."

"I'm afraid I did. My letter is probably sitting on your desk in New York."

"As if we do not have trouble enough. *Du bist genau wie ein widerspenstiges Kind.*"

Mozart turned his face toward the massive carved crucifix suspended over the altar. David thought crucifixes were gruesome, especially crucifixes as realistic as the one in the college chapel, with the wounds in Christ's hands and feet split open like red mouths with iron spikes for tongues.

"Can you feel it?" Mozart said in a low voice, his back to David.

"Feel what, Wolf?"

"There is danger in this place." Mozart's voice had fallen to a whisper. "Great danger. I sense a primordial evil lurking in this town."

Mozart turned back to face his protégé. "Can you feel it? Do you know its source?"

David shook his head. "No, not really, but it must be Thorne."

"I do not believe so, *mein Herr*. There is more than one of *his* kind here."

David's eyes grew wide. Thorne alone was trouble enough.

"This town has much to conceal. I can see . . ." Mozart paused. ". . . the outlines of a tremendous darkness coalescing here. How is it that you do not feel it, David?"

David didn't answer. He couldn't explain this latest inadequacy.

"Try, David, try."

Again David Parker reached out with his extraordinary *Vampiri* senses. The only thing he felt was the sense of dread he'd been living with since New York. The image of Princess Nicoletta Vittorini di Medusa floated through David's mind like a silk veil dropped from a balcony that disappears without leaving a sign it has ever been there.

David looked at Mozart and shrugged.

"I fear you are indeed out of your depth here, my young friend. Perhaps I should have been more helpful in New York City. Or more aware. We must proceed with as much caution as the problems facing us permit," Mozart said, and frowned. "I feel like the fox beset by the pack of English hounds. Any one of these problems would be sufficient to occupy me."

"What other problems are there besides Thorne and his allies?" David asked, his voice anxious.

At first Mozart refused to meet David's eye.

"Tell me, Wolf. Tell me about whatever it is that's been dogging you."

"The matter revolves around a *Fräulein* named Oppenheim. Dr. Joan Oppenheim."

"A mortal?"

"*Ja.* She knows rather more about me than she should."

"What do you mean?"

"Dr. Oppenheim knows, or at least suspects, that Wolf Toland is, in fact, Wolfgang Amadeus Mozart. That I possess the gift of immortality. She may even suspect I am a vampire."

"How did she find out all of that?" David demanded loudly. Then, as if to wave off the matter entirely, he too quickly concluded, "She'll only get herself committed with that kind of talk."

"Nein," Mozart said, solemnly shaking his head. "You fail to understand. The *Fräulein* has assembled a convincing body of evidence to prove that I am, indeed, who I am. I fear that I made a foolish mistake, a very foolish mistake."

Mozart sat in the pew in front of David's and turned to face him.

"My weakness—no, David, my *sin*—is that I have not been able to turn my back on composing. Ever since I was a child, I have been greedy for the opportunity to create music. For all my life, David, as a mortal and as one of the *Vampiri*, I have lived only to hear my music performed by the best musicians and the best orchestras, and through it to mold the shape of their music. You are my confessor, David. I confess my sin to you."

"That's no sin."

"You do not fully understand, *mein Herr*. I have worked with the most talented individuals. No one knew. No one suspected. Indeed, most of the time I caused my pupils—I liked to think of them as my pupils—to 'forget' me and my role entirely. Not even my closest associates among the *Illuminati* suspected. And I, of course, never suspected it would become a problem. But now it seems my *handwriting* has been found on a number of original scores. Dr. Oppenheim has found my footprints, as it were, and followed them back to their source."

David stared at his friend for a long moment while the significance of what Mozart had just said sank into his mind. "Oh, my God, Wolf," David said finally in a stunned voice.

"I have looked into Dr. Joan Oppenheim's background. She is an entirely likable person: an attractive, bright, well-spoken, ambitious, hardworking university faculty member. She began a comparative study of composers' use of amanuenses on original scores. An equally gifted associate devised a way to use computers to analyze the handwriting on the manuscripts. They looked at hundreds of original scores. And they discovered something most interesting: the same copyist's handwriting was on the scores of several different composers. They named the fellow A1, research shorthand for Amanuensis Number 1. But then something even more interesting—and disturbing—happened. They began to find A1's handwriting everywhere."

"But logic would tell Oppenheim that such a conclusion was impossible."

"Again you are mistaken, my friend. Dr. Oppenheim has done exactly as logic required. When her empirical evidence no longer fit the old inferences, she constructed a new set of inferences. She applied Einstein's dictum to think in new terms. The conclusion was inescapable. She has found me out, David. Dr. Oppenheim knows that Mozart, the composer of immortal music, is himself immortal—and therefore something other than human."

"I can't believe this," David said bleakly, referring not so much to Dr. Oppenheim's discovery as to the fact that his brilliant friend had spent the past two centuries unwittingly constructing a dangerous trap for himself.

"I am afraid that it gets worse, *mein Herr*."

"That hardly seems possible."

"Need I name the composer I have worked with most recently?"

David's jaw dropped. "You don't mean *me*?"

Mozart did not answer.

"You made some helpful suggestions when I reworked the overture of *Vanity Fair*, but I wouldn't say—although you did score the woodwinds, and . . ."

David's voice lost its certainty and finally it faded away altogether. The original copies for the opera and a dozen more of David's compositions had been submitted for copyrighting. Mozart's handwriting would be found here or there on all of them—an insignificant bit of notation, a minor amendment to a harmony line, a bit of counterpoint he helpfully jotted down as David sat at the keyboard. At least, Mozart's help had *seemed* insignificant. Now David didn't know which disturbed him most: the fact that Mozart's handwriting would surely lead Dr. Joan Oppenheim to *him*, or the notion that Mozart might deserve at least partial credit for the best of David's recent work. It angered David to think that his friend and mentor may have manipulated him.

"I can see what you are thinking, *mein Herr*."

"Don't look into *my* mind," David snapped.

"But you know I would never do that," Mozart replied, embarrassed that David could think Mozart would violate his privacy. "You need not have any doubts about your compositions. As God is my witness, I have not abused my role to unduly influence your compositions. They are truly yours. Wagner and the others were mortals; you are one of the *Vampiri* and a friend. I would never take advantage. Never."

The two vampires looked at one another for a long moment.

"All right," David said finally.

"But Dr. Oppenheim will find my handwriting on your scores. She has been relentless. I know for a fact that she has obtained a facsimile of the original score to *Vanity Fair*."

David nodded grimly.

"And you fully understand the implications?"

"Yes."

David was too depressed to answer with more than a monosyllable. Despite the pleasant diversion of his flirtation with Victoria Buchanan, he recognized that his life had been in a downward spiral ever since Tatiana left him. He quickly cataloged his troubles: a failed marriage, the "Dracula" serial killings, Gianni Rourke's self-serving treachery over *Vanity Fair*, and now Mozart's miscalculation, which threatened to expose them both—and the *Illuminati*, and the entire *Vampiri* race—to the public eye.

"Something must be done about Dr. Oppenheim," Mozart said rather ominously.

"She could be made to forget."

"I am afraid it will not be that simple with Dr. Oppenheim," said Mozart. "There have already been complications. She has published several academic papers about her preliminary data. Even if she forgot everything, the references would be there, and so would her colleagues. Although she might think that she had suffered some sort of mental breakdown, chances are she would eventually review the data and arrive back at her original conclusion."

"Isn't she afraid of what you might be?"

"I have not had the pleasure of meeting Dr. Oppenheim, but judging from what I know about her, I do not believe she would allow fear to stand in the way of her passion to learn the truth."

"She would make a good vampire."

"The thought has crossed my mind."

David blinked. "You're not serious."

"It would be one way to ensure her silence," Mozart said. "Dr. Oppenheim could lead to the unraveling of everything. If she discovers what I am, what you are, it is impossible to know where it would end. The threat to the *Illuminati*, and to all *Vampiri*, is significant."

"Sometimes I think it would be simpler if mortals knew. These aren't the Dark Ages."

"It would be a catastrophe, *mein Herr*! It is a dangerous conceit to think the world is filled with others exactly like yourself—rational, educated, not ruled by superstition and clan loyalty. The world has come a long way in the centuries I have known it, David, but mortal and *Vampiri* are not yet ready to openly coexist."

"I'm not so sure," David disagreed.

"Do you really believe that jealous mortals would be content to live alongside immortal beings with the power to levitate, to read minds, to *kill* by the simple projection of their thoughts? Do you think human beings would be willing to accept creatures with the power, and the necessity, to compel them to offer up their blood to feed the Hunger?"

Mozart's smile was bitter.

"If Dr. Oppenheim proved the existence of the *Vampiri*, the resulting paranoia would consume the world. The witch hunts would seem mild by comparison. Many *Vampiri* would die, but not as many as the innocents who would perish, for it is the nature of pogroms that innocents always suffer the most. I've seen it happen before. I know. And unscrupulous mortals would seek to gain advantage by allying themselves with vampires to take advantage of our powers. The *Illuminati* would reject such temptations, but the criminals would find the opportunities irresistible. Can you imagine Becker Thorne as a high official in the CIA or KGB? Or pulling the strings of the warlords in Mogadishu and Beirut?"

"I'm surprised it hasn't already happened."

"But it has. Fortunately, the *Illuminati* have been able to keep the outlaws mostly in check. Remember that our first and most inviolable law is secrecy. Everything depends on that. There can be no epistemological breach in the wall dividing the mortal and *Vampiri* worlds."

"Are you saying," David said, pronouncing each word slowly, carefully, "that Dr. Oppenheim must die?"

Mozart looked up again at the crucifix suspended over the altar. David knew that Mozart was religious. Mozart had spent a month in contemplation at a monastery in Mexico earlier that year, when he'd gone there to buy paintings.

"I do not yet know whether Dr. Oppenheim must die, but it does seem the only way to stop this from going any further. Either that or inviting her to join with us. I do not know whether she would agree to undergo the transformation. She could well reject the opportunity."

"So what are you going to do? What are *we* going to do?" David quickly added, Joan Oppenheim being as much his problem as Mozart's.

"I have wired Geneva for instructions. The High Council meets tomorrow to try the matter."

"Without you?" David looked stunned. "Who will chair the session?"

"Da Vinci. It would hardly be ethical for me to rule on my own violation of *Illuminati* law, or to determine the best way to deal with the consequent damage." Mozart looked at David unblinkingly. "Our law prohibits the taking of an innocent life.

If Dr. Oppenheim must die to preserve our secrecy and prevent countless others from dying, then I will atone for the loss of her life by forfeiting my own."

"The Council would not demand *that*."

"They would have to. That is the law. And I would obey."

"But there has to be some other way to—"

Mozart put a finger to his lips. "Someone is coming."

David looked back toward the chapel door, reaching out across the Pentacrest with his senses. He immediately recognized the distinctly perfumed blood pulsing through the approaching mortal's veins, a fragrant mixture of roses and strawberries.

Victoria Buchanan appeared in the doorway a minute later, a silhouette against the sun.

David felt a pang of desire, and, beneath it, a different urge entirely. The Hunger.

"Excuse me for interrupting, David, but I need to talk to you. Larry said you were in here."

Larry Morgan was the campus weekend security officer. The closer Victoria came, the more David wanted her—and the more insistent the Hunger became.

"You're not interrupting, Victoria. This is my good friend, Wolf Toland. He's a musician, too, as fate would have it. We were just having a look at the chapel organ."

"Pleased to meet you, Mr. Toland."

"The pleasure is entirely mine," Mozart said, bowing from the waist.

"Is something the matter, Victoria? You look upset."

She glanced from David to Mozart and back.

"It's all right. Wolf is the closest friend I have."

"Have you seen this?" Victoria held out a crumpled flyer announcing the First Annual Vampire Convention.

"It's this weekend," Victoria said as David and Mozart scanned the paper.

David allowed his own mind to glance ever so lightly off Victoria's. The Vampire Convention—David thought it a juvenile, tasteless, and potentially dangerous conceit—was not what disturbed Victoria. The true source of her anxiety, and of the fear that hid beneath it, was a familiar subject: Becker Thorne.

II

Revelations

8 P.M., Thursday—Night came on fast now as they sat in the parlor, speaking in murmurs. Outside the screened windows, a pair of nighthawks crisscrossed the purple sky, their keening cries floating above the rhythmic cicadas.

David and Victoria were on the couch, Mozart across from them in an overstuffed armchair that nearly swallowed his slight frame. The only light burning in the room was the lamp beside the armchair. As the summer twilight deepened into night and shadows enveloped the room, the lamp's illumination increasingly concentrated on Mozart, who sat enveloped in a mantle of unperturbable *gravitas*.

Victoria had surprised David by accepting his offer of wine. She surprised him even more by consuming the merlot in several deep swallows. David refilled her glass, but she left it untouched on the coffee table beside her Hartmann briefcase. The briefcase was locked when Victoria brought it from her car; she kept it closed on the coffee table, opening it only long enough to withdraw, and return, documents she had brought David to examine.

"Rather strange, isn't it?"

David held the circular Victoria had delivered to him in the chapel. He read from it out loud:

> *"Come the dark star in its rage,*
> *Symbol of the rising age,*
> *Power to the Secret Ones*
> *Who love Diane and loathe the Sun."*

"What's the reference to 'Diane' supposed to signify?" he asked.

"The mythical huntress," Victoria said. "Her symbol is the moon. Lucretia Noire's implication is that Diane is sacred to creatures of the night—to *vampires*."

David and Mozart exchanged a glance.

"I've never heard of Lucretia Noire."

"I find that hard to believe, David," Victoria said, smiling.

Amazing as it seemed, David and Mozart protested that they were both ignorant of the author and her work.

"She's not as famous as Stephen King or Anne Rice, but she deserves to be. A wonderful writer."

"And she writes about vampires?"

"Yes, David, exclusively."

"I didn't realize you were interested in that kind of thing."

"Well, yes." Victoria blushed. "As a matter of fact, I am quite interested in Ms. Noire's work. Being an English professor doesn't require me to be a literary snob."

"Indeed not," Mozart agreed. "Dickens wrote for the masses."

"A point I have made myself upon occasion," Victoria said, pleased with her new acquaintance's empathy. "The fact is that I would like very much to meet Ms. Noire and express in person my admiration for her work. I would prefer, of course, to do so in circumstances other than these."

Victoria nodded at the flyer in David's hand.

" 'The Vampyre Guild of America is proud to announce North America's First Annual Vampire Convention: A Gathering of the Brood, Aug. 2–3, 1991.' "

David looked up from the flyer, mystified. "What is this all about, anyway?"

"It's a fantasy weekend, David."

David's eyebrows raised.

"Participants pay for the opportunity to dress up and impersonate one of the vampires in Miss Noire's novels. The major characters in all her books are vampires. Mortals only make cameo appearances as objects of, ah"—Victoria blushed again—"as objects of desire."

"You seem to think that this play-acting borders on the juvenile, *Fräulein* Buchanan."

"I don't wish to throw cold water on anything that encourages people to read, but the truth is, yes, I do find the idea rather ludicrous. However, for the opportunity to meet Miss Noire, I am willing to swallow my pride and play along."

"You plan to attend, *Fräulein*?" Mozart's concern was evident in his voice.

"Yes. I applied and was accepted. I know it is all very silly, David," she added when she saw his incredulous stare, "but I couldn't resist."

"The flyer specifies only a vague location," David said, trying to change the topic enough to relieve Victoria's embarrassment. "But if I had to guess . . ."

Victoria had already started to nod.

"I'm afraid you are right, David. It's supposed to be held at Arlington Plantation."

"And this weekend, *Fräulein*."

"That is correct."

David looked at Mozart, his mouth set in a grim line. There could be no mistaking the danger this "vampire convention" posed to Victoria and the others, assuming David was correct about Thorne being a lawless killer.

He is orchestrating a slaughter, mein Herr, Mozart told David telepathically. *He has devised an elaborate scheme to turn Arlington's great house into an abattoir. So fiendish—to advertise a gathering of vampires and then deliver unto the naive participants exactly what you have promised.*

You said Thorne is not the only one of his sort in Jerusalem. Do you think the others will be at this gathering? Can the two of us stop them without help?

We must deal with events as we best can. We lack time to seek an alternate course.

Why drag this writer into it?

Ach! It is the worst kind of renegade madness. He risks exposing us all. To lure someone as famous as Lucretia Noire and her fans to Arlington and then slaughter them at a macabre vampire ball. He is utterly depraved. We must do everything within our power to upset the killer's plans. But there is much evil in this town. Jerusalem possesses a great reservoir of darkness. The town has a history, my young friend, that is filled with many secrets. The after-images of what has gone on before linger still.

Does it have anything to do with Thorne?

I have a feeling Fräulein *Buchanan is about to tell us exactly that.*

Mozart turned to Victoria. "Is it not odd, *Fräulein*, that you only today received notification that your reservation for this affair was accepted? The event commences tomorrow. How, pray tell, were you expected to make travel plans with so little notice, assuming you, like the other participants, had to arrange to come here from another part of the country?"

"It's my own fault, Mr. Toland. I foolishly used my office address when I mailed my registration. The post office changed the college's zip code this spring, supposedly to make delivery more efficient. Ever since then we've had an atrocious trouble getting our mail. Half of the admissions applications were lost for weeks, arriving long past the deadline. Powell Mills was apoplectic."

"Your reservation was lost in the mail, *Fräulein*?" Mozart said throwing David a fierce glance.

"For more than a month."

"Which of Noire's characters are you going to portray?" David asked, not wishing to discuss further the efficiency of the U.S. Postal Service.

"Do not mock me, David."

"No, I'm genuinely curious, although you'll have to explain who the character is, since I haven't read any of Noire's books."

"I asked to be Princess Nicole," Victoria said in a quiet voice. "Nicole is the queen of the thirteen vampire Broods."

"Broods, Fräulein?"

"Lucretia Noire divides the vampire world into thirteen families, known as Broods or, informally, as circles. The clans are made up of vampires of different types. The Valkyries Brood, for example, is exclusively female; they revel in violence and battle and can be found wherever mortal armies engage in slaughter. The Athenians are interested only in art, music, and literature. Nicole was originally in the Athenian Brood, although she doesn't really belong to any of the circles anymore. Her aim is to unite the warring Broods so that she can combine and concentrate their power."

"Toward what end, *Fräulein*?"

David looked at Mozart, surprised he could manage even to feign interest in such nonsense.

"Why, to take over the world."

"Miss Noire has quite an imagination, *Fräulein*."

"Maybe not."

Mozart came slowly forward in the chair. "Do please elaborate, *Fräulein*."

"The world is a strange place, Mr. Toland," Victoria said, her voice trailing off. She sat with lowered eyes. Neither David nor Mozart pressed her to continue, sensing she was working up to something.

"Unfortunately, someone beat me out to be Nicole," Victoria said after a long pause, looking up at David with a sheepish smile. "Given the fact that I had to dress up and act like an idiot to meet Lucretia Noire, I thought I might as well go all out and portray the Queen of the Night. As it is, I was assigned Melinda Tranque. She was a vampire's mortal lover in *The Raven*, one of Noire's books."

"You don't like the idea of Becker Thorne allowing Arlington to be used for this gathering," Mozart said.

"That is not the half of it," she said heavily.

Victoria pinched the bridge of her nose between thumb and forefinger to alleviate her headache. Perhaps it was the wine. She had drunk it too quickly.

"This is precisely the kind of thing I was afraid of when Thorne bought Arlington. That he would, at the very least, open it up to the kind of people who do not appreciate its significance or its fragility. This sort of role-playing event appeals mainly to college students. I work with college students for a living. Take my word for it: it is not a good idea to turn over a museum-quality site like Arlington to a gang of students for a weekend-long fantasy game."

Victoria blinked her eyes rapidly.

She picked up her wine, her hand shaking a bit, and took a sip. She put the glass down quickly, as if shocked to discover herself using alcohol to steady her nerves.

"We want to help," David said, putting his hand lightly on her shoulder. Their eyes met. For a brief moment, they experienced the kind of intimacy they wanted to share but hadn't.

"I went to talk to my minister about it. I didn't know who else to talk to. Not the police, certainly. But Reverend Holister, he said, he said . . ." The words seemed to catch in Victoria's throat.

"He didn't understand," David helped.

"Reverend Holister told me I had opened myself to Satan by reading books by Lucretia Noire. He wouldn't even give me the opportunity to discuss my real concerns."

"What foolishness," Mozart said with disgust.

"Maybe it isn't," Victoria countered. "The truth is, I think that Becker Thorne is a devil. He might even be Satan himself."

"Surely you are speaking figuratively, *Fräulein* Buchanan."

Victoria shook her head violently. "If I tell you what I know about Becker Thorne, you'll both think I've lost my mind."

"Give us a chance," David said kindly. "Let us have an opportunity to hear what you know about Thorne. You can trust us."

Trust us, David projected his thoughts into Victoria's mind.

"The world is a more complicated place than most people appreciate, *Liebchen*. You will have to take it as a matter of faith that David and I know that better than most."

Mozart leaned forward and began to speak in a patient voice, as if he were addressing a favorite niece.

"You must not question your sanity simply because you see something you cannot explain by the standards of ordinary reality. There are things in this world that are beyond our limited everyday understanding. Yet we must do our best to comprehend these things, and to deal with them as best we can, no matter how difficult or frightening."

Mozart's soothing voice had a calming effect on Victoria. She relaxed visibly as she listened to him speak in his Austrian-accented English.

"There are few problems that cannot be dealt with if they are faced squarely. Reason can untie any knot. However, I must warn you, *Fräulein* Buchanan: the one thing we must never do is turn our back on the unknown. If we do that, we have no choice but to accept the consequences."

Mozart sat back in his chair.

"So let us face this thing," he concluded. "Together. The three of us."

"Wolf is a member of an organization that studies unusual phenomenon, Victoria. He can help."

"What kind of organization?"

"You may think of us as 'watchers,' *Fräulein* Buchanan. We watch for certain developments."

"And when you find them?"

"We try to make ourselves helpful."

"Is it just your friend who is a 'watcher,' David, or are you one of them, too?"

"It's a tiny organization," David said evasively. "It would be rare to have one of its members in a room with you, let alone two."

David briefly touched her shoulder again.

"Let us help you, Victoria. Please."

"All right," Victoria said finally, "I'll tell you everything. I'd might as well. It's what I came here to do."

"It's a puzzle more than anything," Victoria said. "I have some of the pieces, enough to get an idea of what the overall picture is."

She picked up the flyer advertising the ersatz vampire convention.

"This is the first puzzle piece."

She opened her briefcase and put the flyer away as if for further reference, removing something else in its stead.

"This is from the Jerusalem Public Library. The library has copies of the *Gazette* back to day one. Take a look at the advertisement in the lower right-hand corner of the page. I realize it's a bit hard to read. The microfilm copier needed toner."

David examined the document and passed it to Mozart.

"The John Wilkes Booth who came to Jerusalem in 1858 with his production of *Julius Caesar*—is he the John Wilkes Booth who assassinated Abraham Lincoln?" David asked.

"They are the same person. Booth was a well-known actor in the 1850s and 1860s. I also have proof he was actually here with the rest of his troupe. I have a copy of the review published after the production, if you want to see it. It's not especially relevant."

Mozart handed the photocopy to Victoria, who returned it to her briefcase. "Booth's name is familiar, as is Marcus Cockburn's," he said.

"Marcus Cockburn?"

"Like Booth, a noted Shakespearean."

"Don't look so surprised, Victoria. Wolf is a walking encyclopedia of the arcane."

"I was unaware of Mr. Cockburn's accomplishments," Victoria said. "We can keep Mr. Cockburn in mind, but I don't think he is of special interest to us. Booth, however, is."

Victoria next retrieved from her briefcase a piece of paper encased in a protective plastic sheath. It was a letter, the stationery yellow with age, brittle-looking. The writing was in a flowing black script, very elegant and antique-looking, which reminded David of Mozart's handwriting.

"This is the second piece of the puzzle. Please note the date—September 12, 1863. This was written by my great-great-grandfather, General Noah Buchanan, a little more than two months after the battle of Gettysburg. Noah lost his right arm in the Battle of Antietam. His brother, Colonel Thomas Buchanan, was killed at Gettysburg during Pickett's Charge. Noah wrote this letter to one of his closest friends, Titus Hornsby, while convalescing. Noah never recovered enough to report back to active duty after he was wounded. A persistent infection from the amputation troubled him until 1867, nearly killing him several times. It did finally heal."

David and Mozart took turns scanning the letter.

"Your observations?"

"There was no mention of Booth," David said.

"No."

"I'm surprised your relative knew the Confederacy's cause was doomed so early," David said. "The war went on another two years."

"It was obvious to anyone in the position to make simple, commonplace observations that the war was lost. As Noah spelled it out in his letter, the South had neither the factories nor the men to defeat the Yankees."

"What strikes me, *Fräulein*, is the radical bent of Noah Buchanan's rhetoric. He writes that the South had to be prepared to do whatever was necessary to turn back the Union forces, including terrorist attacks on Northern civilian targets. Forgive me for saying so, but the tone of the letter borders on fanatical."

"My point exactly, Mr. Toland. My family, and their closest friends and associates, *were* fanatical Confederate patriots. Jerusalem's politically influential Founding Families were among the first to call for succession. The Buchanans, Hornsbys, Chases, and Culpeppers were powerful, radical supporters of the Confederacy. They sent their sons to die for the cause, and they gladly died for it themselves. And when they failed to throw off the Northern armies . . ."

Victoria looked away into the shadows for a moment. David and Mozart waited patiently for her to compose her thoughts and continue.

"Anyone who decides to research their family's history must be prepared to discover things they might just as soon have left unknown. Time tends to idealize the positive and conceal the negative. Sam Chase's descendants, for example, remember him as a brilliant businessman who made a fortune they continue to live off of today. They have forgotten he was a drunkard and a wife-beater."

Victoria's breast rose and fell in a sigh.

"But the past has a way of making itself known. We have a saying in the South: The past can be buried, but it can never be forgotten. Southern dead do not sleep quietly."

With shaking hands, Victoria opened her briefcase and removed a second letter, encased, like the first, in plastic. The stationery had once been lavender-colored, although the years had turned it muddy pink. The letter, dated March 15, 1865, was written in a feminine hand, with large, looping ascenders and elaborately curlicued descenders. It was a love letter addressed: *My dearest John.* It was not the sort of "Dear John" letter people joke about, but one filled with expressions of passion—and a solemn oath that writer and recipient would "soon be together forever, God willing, at the completion of your most daring and dangerous assignment." The letter was signed, after a flurry of *X*s signifying kisses, *Anna Lee.*

David read the letter and passed it to Mozart. Mozart scanned the document and handed it back to Victoria, remarking, " 'Beware the ides of March.' "

"What?" David asked.

" 'Beware the ides of March,' " Mozart repeated. "Shakespeare's *Julius Caesar*, Act I, Scene ii."

"You understand the third piece of the puzzle perfectly, Mr. Toland," Victoria said grimly, and turned to David. "The author of this letter was Anna Lee Buchanan, my great-great-great-aunt, the sister of Noah and Thomas. Her portrait hangs in the ballroom at Arlington. She was by all accounts one of the South's leading belles. Anna Lee's letter to her lover was written March 15—the ides of March."

"And her lover . . ." David said, beginning to guess the rest of the story.

"The actor she met when he came to Jerusalem to play the lead role in *Julius Caesar*."

"John Wilkes Booth. The full name is on the envelope."

Victoria seemed on the verge of tears. David could see the shame in her eyes. She'd worked all her life to preserve Arlington Plantation and the memory of her family during its golden age, but now her work was culminating with the revelation that the Buchanans were at least indirectly involved in the most infamous incident of the Civil War—the assassination of Abraham Lincoln.

"No doubt there were a great many other letters like the two I have shown you. My great-great-grandfather, a good military man, burned sensitive correspondence during the war as quickly as he read it. Hornsby was not as careful. I found the letter my forebear wrote him in the back of one of Hornsby's account books. Apparently he'd inadvertently put it there and forgot it. It spent more than one hundred years in a box with other business records, waiting to be found."

"And Anna Lee's letter?" David asked.

"It was sealed in its envelope but never mailed. Her writing desk has a secret compartment for hiding valuables and love letters. The envelope must have been on the top of a stack of papers—probably other letters from Booth—and slipped backward when she opened the drawer. The rear of the channel in which the drawer slides is open; the letter dropped down a gap into the back of the desk. It would have been impossible for her to retrieve it without disassembling the desk, even if she realized it was there."

"You took the desk apart?"

"The sisters used to call me for advice or help with the facilities when they owned Arlington. The rear panel on the desk was held on with horsehide glue. With time and humidity, it started to work itself loose. The sisters asked me to fix it. I donated my time, of course. I've always been happy to spend time at Arlington, given the opportunity. Besides, I've been searching for something at Arlington for the past few years. Whenever I went out to the plantation, I'd manage to get away by myself for a little while and continue looking."

David and Mozart were both listening carefully now.

"My great-grandfather, Isaiah Buchanan, kept diaries. I only have one of them. The others were either destroyed or are hidden up at Arlington somewhere. The great house has four secret panels I know about, and there easily could be more. Or Isaiah's journals could be simply sitting, like the letter to Hornsby, amid the uncataloged material that it would have been my first priority to sort, if Becker Thorne hadn't managed to buy the plantation before the Jerusalem Historical Preservation Society."

The mention of Becker Thorne's name sent a chill through the room. The darkness seemed to become just a little bit darker, the circle of light on the ceiling above the lamp beside Mozart's chair measurably smaller.

"But I've also been looking for something that could turn out to be a good deal more interesting than Isaiah's other diaries. The journal of Isaiah's I have makes several oblique references to a document called *A True Patriot*, which is evidently some sort of manuscript about the War Between the States. Not written by a Buchanan, apparently, but possessed by the Buchanans. I have a theory about *A True Patriot*, a hunch really. . . ." The manuscript's author is identified only as "B."

"That it was written by John Wilkes Booth," said David.

"If it does exist, it's a million-to-one chance that it was written by Booth. But the way old Isaiah discusses it, as if it were a document written by Satan himself, leads me to believe Booth might be the author. It might be up there at the house somewhere, hidden behind a false panel."

"But why would your relatives have destroyed their correspondence while keeping something that would have been the most sensitive, and incriminating, document of all?"

"That's a question I can't answer, David. If my ancestors were involved in Lincoln's murder—and the evidence is only circumstantial—maybe they were actually proud of it. They were fanatics, and they believed Lincoln was the ultimate enemy. Maybe they kept the manuscript as a reminder, as proof of the role they played in history but could never share as long as their land was occupied by the armies of their conqueror.

"Now comes the part of the puzzle that will make you both think I've lost my mind."

"You can't stop now," David said with a smile.

"No, I can't. But I have to admit that I almost hope that I am mad, because that would be easier to face than the alternative. Yet the evidence is, I think, impossible to dispute. Each thing follows the next, and they all lock together, and still . . ."

Victoria paused. She glanced at her glass of wine, then seemed to think the better of it.

"I knew there was something familiar about Becker Thorne the first time I met him. I thought that I must have seen his picture in the papers or in a business magazine. He is, after all, one of the richest men on Wall Street. I did some research on Thorne. I discovered that I couldn't have seen his photograph published anywhere because he is extremely shy about publicity. He has a thing about not allowing his picture to be taken. It's almost a phobia. Nearly every story about him mentions it. The few times photographers have managed to get his pictures, there were scuffles and broken cameras, although Thorne always paid to keep it from becoming an issue. That's one of the worst things about people like Thorne: they think they can get away with anything, as long as they can pay."

Victoria's hands reached out for the briefcase. She began to open it, then stopped. She closed her eyes as if she could not bear to look inside.

"Yet you did manage to locate a photograph of Becker Thorne, did you not, *Fräulein* Buchanan?" Mozart said gravely.

"Yes, I did."

"May we please see it?"

Victoria looked at Mozart and shook her head. She had come this far, but she now believed that she could go no further.

David's hand was again on her shoulder.

Trust us, Victoria. Trust us.

Her hands shaking, she opened the briefcase and withdrew a page torn from an encyclopedia.

"I don't know what I was thinking of, damaging library property," she said in a distracted voice. "I've never done anything like this before in my life. I really must go back and tape this in. It was just that when I figured it out this afternoon, when I found the last piece of the puzzle, all I could think about was that I had to show this to someone else to prove that I wasn't, that I hadn't . . ."

"It's all right, Victoria," David said, putting his hand on hers until it stopped shaking. He gently eased the torn page out of her hands. His eyes widened.

"My God!"

"You see it, David, don't you?" There was desperation in Victoria's voice.

"Yes, yes, of course. It's unmistakable. He's thinner now. His cheekbones are more prominent, and he's shaved his mustache, but I would swear it's the same person. Becker Thorne and John Wilkes Booth—they could be identical twins."

"Then you see it, too!" Victoria cried, grasping at David's arm, a wild kind of fulfillment in her eyes. Her chest was heaving, her heart pounding. David locked his eyes onto hers; she instantly became less agitated.

"There must be some explanation," David said, but the sharp look he drew from Mozart told him there was no point in trying to delude Victoria. It would only make her mistrust them.

"I think he's come back for *A True Patriot.*"

"Your intuition tells you that, *Fräulein*?"

Victoria nodded.

"I believe that you may be at least partly correct. Your powers of intuition are quite extraordinary. Kindly tell me, *Fräulein*, why else you think John Wilkes Booth has returned to Jerusalem, Mississippi."

The question seemed to surprise Victoria. "Now that I think about it, I suppose there has to be more to it."

"What does your intuition tell you, *Fräulein*?"

"Maybe it has something to do with Anna Lee."

"What became of Anna Lee Buchanan?"

"She married a lawyer and moved to Atlanta, Mr. Toland."

"What about her and Booth?" David asked.

"I suppose she must have broken off their engagement."

"Do you think she rejected him?" David asked, remembering Tatiana walking out on him.

"Or did her family reject Booth, *Fräulein*?"

An expression of devastation swept slowly over Victoria's face.

Mozart continued to bore in on the subject, to Victoria's discomfort and David's displeasure.

"Booth was involved in a heinous crime. That much is known. You suspect, *Fräulein*, that your ancestors and possibly others in their circle were involved in the dark deed. So you see, the question of how Booth broke with his fiancée is of potentially central interest. Although it defies the usual verities, *Fräulein*, there is no mistaking this revelation you have come upon: John Wilkes Booth did not die after being captured by Union soldiers, the way the history books tell us. And now he has returned to Jerusalem after many, many years. Perhaps he has come back for this manuscript Isaiah Buchanan remarked upon. Or perhaps he has come back to revenge himself on this town. This is merely speculation, *Fräulein*. I do not pretend to know."

"It's bad enough that my family was deeply involved with Booth. I can hardly stand to think they used and abandoned him."

" 'Beware the ides of March,' " Mozart said once again.

"Why Booth has come to Jerusalem is important," Victoria said, her voice taught with stress, "but I'm equally concerned with the question of *what* he is."

The fear was evident in her eyes when she looked up at David. "Is he a ghost? A devil?"

"Perhaps a little of both, *Fräulein* Buchanan."

"You came here looking for him, didn't you, Mr. Toland?"

"Your intelligence and your ESP make a formidable combination, *Fräulein.*"

"ESP? I don't believe in ESP."

Mozart shrugged. "It does not matter what we believe, *Fräulein* Buchanan. The only thing that matters is what *is.*"

"And Thorne—Booth. Tell me the truth, Mr. Toland. Is John Wilkes Booth a vampire?"

The question made Mozart frown. "What makes you think that?"

"The fact that he has cheated death, and this vampire convention business at Arlington. I can hardly believe it's true, but it's as good an explanation as any." A shocked expression crossed Victoria's face. "You don't suppose he had something to do with Katharine Culpepper Simonette's murder?"

"I believe that he did, Victoria."

"I can tell you this much, *Fräulein* Buchanan," Mozart said. "The people coming to Arlington Plantation this weekend are in grave danger. You must promise us something."

Victoria looked across the coffee table at Mozart, who had leaned forward in the armchair and spoke each word with careful emphasis. His head eclipsed the lamp behind him, its light creating a reddish nimbus, almost a halo, around him.

"You must promise us, *Fräulein*, that under no circumstances will you go to Arlington Plantation."

Victoria looked directly at Mozart, her chin coming up, her back straightening.

"I don't think that's something I can promise, Mr. Toland. I will not agree to stay away from Arlington if Lucretia Noire is there. Whatever Booth is planning, I cannot let him harm her."

"Then promise you will not go to Arlington without us."

"All right, if you want to help."

"Of course we do, *Fräulein*. That is why we have come to Jerusalem."

"Do you understand how truly dangerous this will be?" David asked.

"I'm not afraid, David," Victoria said, squaring her shoulders.

"It would be far better for you to be afraid, *Fräulein* Buchanan, for I believe that John Wilkes Booth means to see you dead."

III
Romancing Amanda

9 P.M., Thursday—"It's fabulous."

"I was afraid you'd find it vulgar."

"I don't know how you could think that."

"Nineteenth-century taste does not suit everyone. It's so ornate. It's too much for some people."

Amanda Hornsby Foster looked around her at the drawing room, and a little shiver ran through her body. Arlington Plantation was like something out of a fairy tale.

"I don't know about other people, but I think it's magnificent. I was a child the last time I was here, touring with a school group. I've always remembered the visit, but I didn't think it would be as incredible as I remembered. Everything is bigger than life when you're a child."

The killer smiled thinly, smoothing the fringe on the antique carpet with the silver-capped toe of his boot.

"Is it everything that you remembered?"

"And more," Amanda answered breathlessly.

Much to his amazement, the killer felt his cold heart quickening beneath the warming heat of the young woman's attentive eyes. He had seen far too much of the world to be excited by simple beauty, usually relying on exotic, brutish acts to ignite his desire.

"Those dreadful nuns lived here when I visited. I particularly remember one of them, an overweight woman who reminded me of those women who work in jails. I remember she smelled musty, like a damp basement, and followed me around, even when I used the bathroom, as if she were afraid I was going to break something. I had nightmares about her for months. Now that I've grown up, I wonder if she wasn't interested in me for another reason."

The killer smiled wolfishly.

"The sisters are departed, and good riddance to them," the killer said. "Arlington is now a much more pleasurable place. In fact, the plantation is entirely devoted now to the unashamed pursuit of pleasure."

Amanda's sparkling laughter drew attention to the cavernous silence of the dimly lighted country mansion.

The killer led his guest into his library in the "new" part of the house, the wing built at the rear of the original mansion at the turn of the century. Unlike the rest of the house, where the furnishings were at least a century old, the library was entirely modern, with one whole wall dominated by an array of state-of-the-art stereo and video gear in an ugly brass-and-glass unit.

"This is really where I spend most of my time. I enjoy living in this house and collecting antiques, but I prefer to live in the present."

He selected a soft jazz album from the extensive collection of CDs and slipped it into the player. Zaharim had come into the room—how could he move so silently? Amanda wondered—and stood at the wet bar, uncorking a bottle of Chardonnay from a half-sized refrigerator cleverly hidden behind a false panel in the bookcase. Zaharim first served Amanda, then his master, and departed as quietly as he had appeared.

Thorne said nothing to Zaharim about fixing them something to eat—the pretext for inviting Amanda to Arlington—but she didn't give it a thought. She was content to sit and talk with her host.

"It's funny to think that as old as this place is, you're only the third owner."

The killer smiled as he settled back into a cotton chintz club chair:

"That's exactly right. The Buchanans, the sisters, and now me."

The killer swirled the wine in his glass, closing his eyes so that he could better appreciate the bouquet of Amanda Hornsby Foster's blood. He inhaled slowly, deeply, savoring its freshness. That in itself was a change. His tastes did not typically lie in the direction of innocence; the debauched and the degraded—that was what excited his fancy. But this, too, could be pleasurable.

"There is something I have been wanting to ask a lifelong resident of Jerusalem, if you don't mind."

"Ask me anything," Amanda said disingenuously.

"Does it bother people that an outsider bought Arlington?"

She considered the question a moment. "I don't think so. Of course, people in a town the size of Jerusalem are expected to be a little suspicious of someone from New York."

"As well they should be."

Amanda laughed, taking the comment as a joke.

"The only negative remark I've heard was from one of our local preservationists."

"Victoria Buchanan."

"How did you know?" Amanda asked, surprised.

"A lovely woman," the killer said absently. "I can empathize with how she must have felt, getting so close to her life's desire only to have it pulled away at the last possible moment. No doubt she thought the sisters had dealt treacherously with her."

He looked at Amanda and smiled. He could tell that Amanda was jealous of Victoria, that she considered the other woman a potential rival for his affections.

"I'm sure Victoria Buchanan is too much of a lady to have publicly accused the sisters of double-dealing."

Biting the inside of her bottom lip, Amanda Hornsby Foster said nothing. The killer knew he would have to work at it to get Amanda to play along.

"I understand Victoria is a single mother."

Amanda nodded.

"What's the child's name?"

"Michelle Buchanan."

"Strange that the girl doesn't have the father's last name."

"I don't think Victoria wanted to be reminded of him," Amanda said, finally warming to the game. "I'm not sure who the father is. Someone Victoria met when she was away at college. It was a long time ago. Michelle is fourteen or fifteen now."

"That hardly seems possible. Victoria is too young to have a child that age."

"She was young when she got pregnant."

"I can imagine how the people in Jerusalem must have reacted."

"It was quite a scandal. It's not the sort of thing that happens to a girl from a good family, especially not a Buchanan. They've always been very high and mighty."

"Still, Victoria seems to have achieved a measure of respectability in town. I've never heard of anybody speak of her as if she were white trash."

"The men call her the Ice Maiden behind her back. It seems cruel, but it's not as if she didn't bring it on herself. She's tried to turn herself back into a virgin to make up for getting pregnant—forgetting the obvious fact that it's too late for that now."

"That isn't hard to understand. Once bitten, twice shy," the killer said, grinning almost wide enough to show the tips of his blood teeth.

"She may be ready to be bitten again."

"Oh?" he asked, suddenly very interested.

"I hear she's been dating David Parker, the pianist who is the Visiting Artist this summer at Morningside College."

"Parker? What a joke." The killer threw the glass of wine down his throat in a single swallow. "I'm acquainted with him from New York City. He is distinctly second rate as an artist."

"Are you a musician?"

"Good Lord, no. But I was an actor once, a long time ago, and I've always been around music and musicians. I know whereof I speak."

"An actor?"

The interest in Amanda's eyes elicited an unpleasant mingling of gratification and fury in the killer. The egotistical vampire considered himself one of the greatest actors to have ever lived, yet he knew Amanda could only associate his profession with pathetic, wooden amateurs from Hollywood, whose puny talents were so far beneath his own that he could not stand to hear their names uttered in his presence.

"It was a long time ago."

"Before you got involved with the stock market."

"That's right. You have a famous name," he said, deliberately changing the subject.

The young woman blinked, her astonishment genuine.

"Hornsby is an old and established name in Jerusalem, Mississippi. You are, if I'm not mistaken, a descendent of the honored Founding Families."

"I'm flattered, but a little surprised, that you know about that. Not many people care about the past these days."

"Oh, but I do," the killer protested earnestly. "I care about the past a very great deal. You might even say I am obsessed by it."

"I suppose that's obvious," Amanda said, looking around her. "You did, after all, buy this monument to the Old South."

"Monument? I don't quite like the sound of that. It's so funereal, almost as if this were a mausoleum."

"I'm sorry."

"I'm only teasing. Let me see—Hornsby. You must be descended from . . ."

"Titus Hornsby. He was my great-great-great-great-grandfather."

"Then he must have been very great indeed."

"He served in Jefferson Davis's cabinet. He was the Secretary of Something-or-other. I used to know, but I've forgotten. Jefferson Davis was president of the Confederate States of America during the War Between the States," she added, in case Becker Thorne didn't know.

"Your ancestor was Assistant Secretary of War," the killer said professorially. "From 1863 to November of 1864."

"You do know history, Becker."

"We owe it to the dead to remember them and their deeds. Titus Hornsby—wasn't he implicated in John Wilkes Booth's plot to kill Abraham Lincoln?"

"Heavens, no! Wherever did you get that idea?"

The killer frowned, pretending to concentrate. "I must be thinking of someone else. Well, no matter. Are there many others left—members of the Founding Families?"

"Not many. I suppose it's something that there are any of us left after all this time. There are still a few of us. Victoria and Michelle Buchanan."

"The end of the Buchanan line."

"And the Chases."

"I've met Lysander and Lydia."

"Isn't she wild? Parties will never be dull in Jerusalem as long as Lydia Chase is around. I just adore her."

"No sons?"

"Just Norville. He's a disc jockey in San Francisco. I don't expect him to get married any time soon, if you get my meaning."

The killer smiled crookedly.

"Lydia has a daughter by one of her husbands, a girl about the same age as Michelle Buchanan, but her name isn't Chase, of course. Unless Lysander takes up with his secretary and has more children, Lydia and Norville will be the last of the Chases."

"It sounds as if the Founding Families are on the verge of extinction."

"At least in name. There are only girls in my family. I have two sisters, Susan and Karen. Susan lives in Boston. Karen is spending the summer in Europe."

"Are your sisters older or younger?" the killer asked, pretending he didn't know.

"Much older. Karen's next. She's thirty-four, almost exactly ten years older than I am. Susan just turned forty."

"Buchanans, Chases, Hornsbys—that leaves only the Culpeppers."

"The poor Culpeppers," Amanda said sadly. "It's the last of the Culpeppers, too, it seems. Henry Culpepper's grandson is a Simonette, of course. Poor Katharine was Henry's only child."

"Yes, poor Katharine." The killer wondered why people now invariably said "poor" Katharine, as if her name were Poor Katharine Culpepper Simonette.

"Doesn't Henry Culpepper have a brother?" the killer said after a moment.

"He's dead," Amanda said.

"What happened to him?"

"Nobody really knows."

"What do you mean?"

"I really shouldn't say. The Culpeppers are close family friends. And Henry's my boss. He gets furious whenever anybody mentions Gregory."

"Tell me."

The killer looked at Amanda, his eyes unblinking. She found it impossible to resist his command.

"Gregory Culpepper supposedly died from natural causes, but nobody really believes that. Greg had a lot of problems. He was an alcoholic, a bad alcoholic, the worst kind. They found him earlier this summer down at the railroad station. The rumor is that he hanged himself, and that Henry didn't want it to get out that his brother committed suicide. The uglier version of the story is that he'd been beaten to death."

"I find it hard to believe that Henry Culpepper could have a murder concealed."

Amanda flashed the killer a chilly smile. "Powerful people get away with things in a place like Jerusalem. Always have, probably always will."

"I find that rather shocking," the killer said, cackling to himself at the secret irony.

"They arrested a former policeman, a man named Harlin Plummer, for questioning in Greg's death. He had a problem with drinking, too. His wife was horribly injured in an accident and finally died. People say Harlin just fell apart after that."

"Then the authorities think Gregory Culpepper was murdered."

"That's what everybody says. The police let Harlin out of jail after a few days. They didn't have enough evidence to charge him."

"But do you think he did it?"

Amanda shook her head. "Nobody honestly believes Harlin had anything to do with it, even if he was a drunk like Greg."

"What aren't you telling me?" the killer asked after a pause.

"That's it, Becker."

The killer's stare was relentless. It was impossible for Amanda to resist the killer's will.

"I doubt the Culpeppers were either surprised or sorrowed by Greg's death," she said all in one breath. "As if being a drunk wasn't bad enough, Greg Culpepper was a homosexual. He was an embarrassment to his family."

"And to preserve what remained of the Culpepper family honor, Henry was willing to let his brother's killer escape justice just so the town wouldn't have to endure the sordid details that would come out in a trial?"

Amanda seemed to wither beneath the question, yet there was no escape.

"Yes," she said finally. "At least, that's what most people think. Henry Culpepper is a proud man."

"Henry Culpepper would do anything to preserve his family's honor."

"Yes," Amanda said.

"Just like his ancestors."

"This is the South, Becker. Honor is important. Maybe that's good, maybe that's bad. I don't know."

The killer smiled sympathetically.

"I understand perfectly. I'm a Southerner myself." He crossed his legs and sat back in his chair. "It sounds as if Henry Culpepper's life has been a living hell this summer. To lose his brother and his daughter."

Amanda nodded sadly.

"Two tragic deaths in the same family. Despite his attitude about his brother's death, I imagine Henry is anxious to see someone arrested for his daughter's murder."

"To put it mildly. His way of coping with it was to bury himself in his work. I have some idea how he feels. I lost my mother this year. We were very close."

"Murdered?" the killer asked with surprise.

"No," Amanda said, shocked by the suggestion. "She went out in the middle of the night on some errand. Exactly what she was doing no one knows. She must have fallen asleep behind the wheel."

The killer moved from his chair to the couch where his guest sat.

"I am sorry. I've made you sad."

"No, it's all right." Amanda forced a smile. "Really."

"I'd invited you here hoping you would enjoy Arlington as much as I."

He gently laid his fingers upon her hand.

"I adore this old plantation, but I know so few people in Jerusalem. I make it a point to never admit to negative emotions, but something makes me want to confess to you that I've been lonely. I hope we can become friends."

Thorne locked his eyes onto hers. They were beautiful eyes. The Hornsbys all had beautiful eyes, the killer thought.

"I'd like that very much," Amanda said in a voice that was barely more than a whisper. Her eyes closed as the killer lowered his lips to hers. His kiss was warm and passionate yet reserved, not greedy—the kiss of a gentleman.

"Becker, please," Amanda said weakly when their lips parted.

The killer returned to taste again her upturned mouth. He brushed his tongue against her lips. Her mouth opened like a delicious flower, wet with dew and overflowing with the delirious perfume of young life.

Amanda put one hand against his strong chest.

"You must think I'm awful," she said, gently pushing her body away from his. "I'm not the kind of woman who does this."

"I think you're wonderful. Would you think me too sentimental if I shared a few lines of poetry that are going through my mind right now?"

She shook her head, completely in his thrall.

" 'No love, my love, that thou mayst true love call;
All mine was thine before thou hadst this more.
Then, if for my love thou my love receivest,
I cannot blame thee for my love thou usest;
But yet be blam'd if thou thyself deceivest
By willful taste of what thyself refusest.' "

Zaharim chose this inconvenient moment to announce his return to the room with a muffled cough.

"Pardon me, sir, but there is an urgent telephone call."

"Not now."

The butler said a few gutteral words in a Slavic tongue.

"Damn it all. Pardon me, Amanda, but I will only be a moment."

"That's all right," she said, wondering what million-dollar transaction hung in the breach, awaiting the brilliant financier Becker Thorne's approval. Amanda Hornsby Foster found that even the interruptions at Becker Thorne's were mysterious and exhilarating.

"Zaharim, give Miss Hornsby Foster a little more wine."

The servant was already coming up behind her with the bottle.

The killer apologized as he returned to the library. "I am sorry. I'm hosting a weekend for an author named Lucretia Noire. Have you heard of her?"

"*The* Lucretia Noire?"

"You're a fan?"

"I adore her books."

'Then you'll have to come to tomorrow night's party."

Amanda was too stunned to reply.

"I've asked a few townspeople out. You're more than welcome. I warn you, though, that it's going to be a fairly strange affair. Miss Noire's publisher has set it all up. It's supposed to be a 'Vampire Convention.' It will be a costume party of sorts. Everybody who comes is supposed to adopt the personality of one of the characters of Miss Noire's books."

"Oh, what fun, Becker!"

"I'll give you the number of Miss Noire's personal assistant. Call her up and ask her which vampire you will be. She's coordinating everything. Everybody will impersonate a character from Miss Noire's fiction for the night. Lucretia and I are old friends. Very old friends. I've never actually read any of her books myself—horror novels are not my cup of tea—but she tells me Arlington Plantation is like something out of one of her stories."

"It is," Amanda said, glancing up at the long shadows thrown on the coffered ceiling, "if you take this wonderful old place and turn it around so that the elegance becomes sinister."

"The preparation has been a lot more involved than I suspected, even with Lucretia's assistants helping. I had to hire Nate Nightingale just to truck crates of wine out here in his pickup and cart them down to the cellar."

Amanda shuddered at the sound of Nightingale's name.

"Is something the matter?"

"You mean that you don't know about Nathan Bedford Forrest Nightingale, the Last Gray Ghost of the Confederacy?"

"The only thing I know about Nate is that he's amazingly strong for a man in his late fifties."

"Becker, I want you to listen to me: Nathan Nightingale is a killer."

"You're not serious."

"Yes. He shot a preacher. His lawyer got him out of it, but he was guilty as sin. He went away and lived in California for years. They say he was in a mental institution out there for a long time."

"I never imagined. So many secrets lurking beneath the surface of this little town."

"I warn you to be careful around Nightingale, Becker."

"Don't worry about me, my dear," the killer said, and laughed. "I can take care of myself."

The Spanish tile surrounding the pool had just been rinsed and glistened with light reflected from the house and the garden lights set into the ground, shining upward through the manicured foliage. The lights in the pool gave the water a Caribbean blue glow, the light flickering with the waves' gentle movement. Patches of starlight could be seen overhead, the constellations appearing to move as the gauze-thin clouds raced overhead in the moonless sky.

"It was a ruin when I bought Arlington. The nuns did not swim."

"Mmm. I love the smell of bougainvillea."

They were standing next to one another, arms touching, Amanda gazing up into the killer's dark eyes, which curiously reflected no light and revealed nothing, so that she might as well have been looking into expressionless sunglasses.

Impulsively, she pushed up on the tips of her toes and kissed him.

Somewhere behind them, a door latch rattled.

"I do apologize, sir," Zaharim said from the doorway. "It's Miss Noire again. She was quite insistent that she speak to you."

The killer sighed deeply.

"Go ahead," Amanda said, amused to see so self-possessed a man at the mercy of the notoriously eccentric Lucretia Noire.

"Tell her I'll be there in a moment."

"Are you sure that you and Lucretia Noire aren't something more than just old friends?" Amanda asked with a crooked smile. She asked the question jokingly, not realizing how seriously she wanted to know until she heard her own voice.

"I promise you, no," the killer lied. "There is no one special in my life." He paused, and in that pause, Amanda felt a tingle race through her body. "Or there wasn't, until tonight."

He kissed her long and hard, feeling her body cleave to his, melting, yielding, ready.

"I'll only be a minute," he promised, his lips moving against hers as he spoke softly. "I'll tell Zaharim to turn on the answering machine and retreat to his rooms until morning. If . . ." He kissed her. ". . . you'll stay with me tonight."

"You know that I'll stay, but not until morning. I wouldn't want to start a scandal."

After another kiss, he was gone.

Amanda finished the marvelous wine and slipped off her shoes. She undid the clasp in the back of her dress. Amanda lay her clothes neatly on one of the lounges as she took them off. She thought that Becker Thorne brought out the worst in her—and she was glad of it. Her mind raced with the things she wanted him to do to her, and she to him, things she'd scarcely imagined, much less fantasized about.

It gave her a wonderful feeling of freedom to stand naked in the night air. Then, experiencing a sudden flush of modesty, she ran to the pool on the balls of her feet and dived into the warm water. For a moment she'd had the keen sense that someone was watching her. Was it Becker—or Zaharim, the servant?

She crossed her hands over her breasts, but her feeling of shame passed almost as quickly as it had arrived. Becker Thorne's confidence was contagious. What did she care if his servant saw her naked?

She let her hands float free and drifted over onto her back. Slowly, languorously, she began to propel herself backward through the warm, soothing water, waiting for her lover to return.

The room was dark when Amanda awakened.

She stretched slowly, like a cat waking after a nap, enjoying the sensation of cool satin sliding softly against her flesh. Amanda pressed against the pillow wedged against her belly and moaned. Her desire was reawakening, too. Parts of her body throbbed from pleasant pain inflicted by her gifted lover.

Amanda began to smile to herself in the darkness.

She'd experienced a pinnacle of bliss that night so intense that she'd screamed when she climaxed for the third time. It was a little embarrassing to remember how she'd urged her lover to thrust into her harder and harder. He'd laughed and said if he did it any harder, it would split her wide open.

"Oh," she said quietly, touching herself. She felt as if he had split her.

Yet she wanted him again.

What animal passion had Becker Thorne ignited in her soul? She'd come to Arlington Plantation a proper if not altogether prim young lady; her lover had, in the course of a few feverish hours of carnal delight, transformed her into an insatiable woman.

"Becker?"

She reached out further, opening her eyes, pushing up on one elbow.

The killer was not in the room.

Amanda quickly decided she did not like being alone in the dark at Arlington Plantation. Everything about Becker Thorne's comfortable bedroom suddenly seemed sinister.

She sat up in the gloom, drawing up the black satin sheet to cover her breasts.

The carved posts at the foot of the bed looked down on her like gargoyles, and the swag curtains were transformed into enormous cobwebs that swept across the windows. This, she thought, is how the plantation might have looked if it had sat abandoned and moldering, like the ruins of Beaufort, the Hornsby ancestral home.

"This is the perfect place for a vampire convention," she muttered to herself, reaching for her lover's shirt among the pile of clothes beside the bed.

Amanda went out into the corridor. The darkness would have been impenetrable if not for the outdoor lights spilling dimly through the French doors that led onto the balcony at the front of the house. She went to the window. Her Volkswagen Rabbit was parked where she had left it in the circular drive below. She'd insisted on driving herself to Arlington Plantation. The car looked tiny and ordinary in the turnaround.

Amanda turned and went to the railing, leaning carefully forward, looking down past the chandelier, beyond the sweep of the staircase, into the darkness below. She did not think Thorne was down there, not with the lights turned out. It would be dangerous to try to navigate the stairs in utter darkness.

Fingers brushed against her shoulder.

"Jesus!" Amanda gasped, spinning to find the killer standing behind her.

He wore a black silk dressing gown that extended all the way to his feet. Amanda reached out and touched him—her other hand covering her pounding heart—and realized the gown was richly embroidered, although there was not enough light coming in through the windows for her to see the intricate design of the intertwining oriental dragons.

"Did I frighten you?"

"Badly."

"I apologize."

"I woke up and you were gone. I don't like being alone here in the dark."

The killer smiled. His teeth seemed extraordinarily white, almost luminescent.

"You get used to it. At least you do if you have insomnia, like I do. When I sleep at all, it's during the day."

"Poor baby." Amanda slipped her hand through the folds of the robe and gently stroked the killer's chest.

"I was just admiring my latest art acquisition. Would you like to see it? No, what am I saying—it's three in the morning. You'd rather go back to bed."

"I'm wide awake now," Amanda said with a nervous laugh. "I would like to go back to bed, but not to sleep."

When the killer reached up to caress her cheek, she covered his hand with hers.

"But first show me this new acquisition of yours. You didn't tell me you collected art."

He took her hand and led her down the dark hallway toward the "new" wing.

"How can you see where you're going?"

"I can see better in the dark than a bat," the killer said truthfully, and smiled to himself in the darkness. "Lately I've become interested in neon art."

"I've seen plenty of neon signs, but I've never seen any neon art," Amanda said dubiously.

"They can be one and the same. In fact, the most valuable examples of neon art are old signs from before the war—World War II, that is. My latest acquisition was created toward the end of the classical period for neon. It's a 1950s filling-station sign. It's badly in need of restoration, but it's still a beautiful work. You'll see."

The killer's hands found the door handles. Amanda felt air move as the double doors to Arlington's chapel swung away from them. The killer put one hand on her shoulder and moved her forward a few feet, reaching out with his free hand to flip the switch.

Pegasus was suspended over the chapel altar, wired to the mahogany cross. The neon sign came to life with the menacing sound of arcing electricity and several loud pops that subsided into an ominous hum. Only half the neon tubing was in working order, yet the former filling-station sign burned bright enough to fill the chapel with a red glow.

Amanda's mouth fell open as she stared at the pagan winged horse that filled the chapel with a hellish red glow.

"Isaiah Buchanan built this as a ballroom," the killer said in a matter-of-fact voice. "The sisters had it converted into a chapel. The stained glass windows, I'm afraid, are not very magnificent. Passable, I suppose, but unremarkable, as suited the humble tastes of their religious order. Between the windows, you'll notice, are the Stations of the Cross."

Amanda's eyes remained focused on Pegasus, whose single gimlet eye seemed to be staring malevolently back at her.

"The sisters wanted to have the chapel desanctified, but I talked them out of it. I wanted to be able to hold my own services here."

Amanda took a step backward, moving more by instinct than by volition. The vampire's grip tightened on her shoulder, stopping her.

"I rather like spending time in here. The chapel gives me a certain spiritual solace."

Amanda tried to pull free, but the killer's grip only tightened.

"You're hurting me."

"God is in this room tonight. Can you feel it?"

"Let go of me!"

"Neon is in the room tonight," the killer said dramatically, nearly shouting. "He is moving among us now."

Amanda began to scream.

"Kneel in the presence of the Neon, harlot!"

Thorne threw Amanda forward. She hit the side of the pews, spun crazily, lost her balance, and sprawled facedown in the aisle.

"Behold, Lord, your servant the Fury has done thy bidding."

Thorne lifted his hands, the palms up, toward the buzzing sign.

"As it is written:

"I have this against you, that you tolerate that woman Jezebel, who calls herself a prophetess and is teaching and beguiling my servants to practice immorality and to eat food sacrificed to idols. I gave her time to repent, but she refuses to repent of her immorality. Behold, I will throw her on a sickbed, and those who commit adultery with her I will throw into great tribulation, unless they repent of her doings; and I will strike her children dead."

Pegasus gave forth a burst of electric crackling, as if in approval of the killer's supplication.

Amanda got to her knees. The only way out of the chapel was past the killer.

"You are Jezebel's child," the killer said, pointing.

"Please don't hurt me," Amanda begged, and began to sob.

"Behold the Fury. I have come to punish the wicked, and their children, and their children's children, down through the seventh generation."

Amanda grabbed a pew and pulled herself up onto unsteady legs.

The killer began to come forward, saying, " 'I know your works; you have the name of being alive, and are dead.' "

Amanda turned to run—and almost collided with a tiny woman. The woman was nearly hidden within the folds of a hooded cape made from rich black velvet and fastened together under her chin with a simple golden pin inset with a single ruby the size of a nickel. The woman was petite, with beautiful, milk white skin.

"Help me!" Amanda said, grabbing the sleeve of the woman's cloak.

"Has he frightened you?" The woman's gentle voice had an Italian accent.

Amanda looked desperately over her shoulder. The killer had not taken another step. He stood there with a vaguely displeased look on his face, watching them. Amanda pressed herself close to the woman, who put her arm protectively around her.

"You mustn't let him frighten you. He gets like this sometimes."

"I just want to leave."

"Of course you do. My name is Lucretia Noire. What's yours?"

Amanda's eyes grew wide.

"We've got to get out of here, Miss Noire," Amanda whispered. "He must be insane. He threw me against the pews. He said things—crazy things."

"I warned you not to let things get out of hand," Lucretia scolded the killer. "They never listen when they become afraid, and then what good is it? Don't you want them to know, to understand? Isn't that important to you?"

The killer nodded sullenly, like a child being corrected by an adult.

Amanda looked at her protectress in bewilderment. What was Lucretia Noire talking about?

"Come here and tell this young lady you're sorry you lost your temper."

Amanda shrank against her protectress as the killer came toward them.

"Tell me your name, child."

Amanda's face and the woman's were so close together that it was almost as if they were about to kiss. It seemed strange that Lucretia Noire had called her child, since Lucretia did not appear to be much older than herself. Except for her eyes. Something about Lucretia Noire's eyes seemed older than the rest of her face.

"Amanda Hornsby Foster."

"Ah, yes, a Hornsby. She's a Hornsby, dear boy," she said, talking past Amanda to the killer, who now stood at Amanda's opposite side. "She is a direct descendant of one of the illustrious Founding Families."

The woman began to stroke Amanda's hair.

"Oh, yes, my dear, I know your little town's history quite well. Indeed, I fancy I may know it better than you. Do you know that John Wilkes Booth, the man who killed President Lincoln, used to visit this town quite regularly?"

Amanda shook her head.

"He did. Booth visited here on many occasions. He was a great favorite here at Arlington Plantation. Did you know he was betrothed to Anna Lee Buchanan?"

Amanda again shook her head.

"You see, my dear, the Founding Families were the real powers behind the plot to kill President Lincoln. They supplied the money. They hired Booth to be their captain and go to Washington City and kill the president. The Founding Families killed Lincoln."

"That isn't true," Amanda said, instantly regretting that she'd tried to reason with Lucretia Noire, who was showing signs of being every bit as disconnected from reality as Becker Thorne.

"I'm afraid the evidence is undeniable. The proof was suppressed, of course, to protect the guilty and shield them from justice."

"But justice will be done," Thorne said, his voice filled with insane hatred.

"Booth returned to Jerusalem after the assassination," the woman continued. "Federal soldiers killed a double in Virginia, but the real John Wilkes Booth escaped and came back to Arlington Plantation to meet the Founding Families. But instead of paying him his bounty, so that he and his fiancée Anna Lee Buchanan could start a new life in South America, they shot him and threw his body in the river. Booth issued a curse against the Founding Families as his body fell into the dark waters of the Mississippi River that night. He vowed he would come back one day and revenge himself on them all."

The woman smiled sweetly.

"And now, my dear, here he is."

Amanda could only stare. She didn't believe a word of it. Why was this woman saying these things?

"John Wilkes Booth did not die. He managed to cling to a piece of driftwood and was pulled onto a packet boat bound for New Orleans. He was nearly dead, but there was enough of life's spark left in him to survive the transformation from mortal to vampire."

Amanda pulled away from the woman and turned to face her antagonists. The neon sign, glowing weirdly, towered behind them.

"I suppose you both think this is funny."

"Funny?" the killer asked.

"This dress rehearsal for your weekend vampire masquerade is not the least bit amusing. I ought to call the police and have you charged with assault, Becker. And as for you, Lucretia Noire, I will never read another one of your books as long as I live. You are as twisted as he is."

The killer grinned broadly, the two blood teeth slipping down from their cavities in his upper gum, clicking softly as they locked into place. Lucretia Noire displayed a similar set of fangs that appeared, upon examination, even a bit longer and more pointed than Thorne's.

"Those fake teeth don't frighten me," Amanda said.

The killer grabbed Amanda and jerked her toward him.

"Let me go, you crazy bastard!"

The woman grabbed her other arm. Amanda fought against them, but this time she could not break free.

"I'm going straight to the police. Let me go. Help! Help!"

"This is no joke," the woman said, squeezing Amanda's arm fiercely. "I know because I, Princess Nicoletta Vittorini di Medusa, initiated the mortal John Wilkes Booth into the *Vampiri* race. The dull coals of revenge might have died out in that dark organ that was his heart, but I kept them alive, fanning them, nurturing them with the very breath of my own life, with my blood."

"Until I completed the first transformation and became a god!" The killer's breathing came in ragged gasps as if he had run a very long distance or was on the verge of rapture. "I became an angel of revenge, a Fury."

"You're right about one thing, dear girl. My poor John has quite lost his mind."

"Shut your mouth, witch!"

The woman raised one eyebrow. The killer flinched—and used his free hand to wipe away the trickle of blood that had begun to run from his nose.

"Alas, my love, it may prove impossible to make them understand you truly are John Wilkes Booth," Nicoletta said.

"The pathetically limited nature of mortal intelligence may make it impossible for them to comprehend."

"They will understand," he said, "if only just at the end." His eyes rolled up until only the whites were visible. "Thy will be done in Neon," he added hoarsely.

Amanda Hornsby Foster did not have time to scream again before the two vampires simultaneously buried their teeth in the opposing sides of her throat. Her life drained out of her faster than she could have imagined—and at the same time a flood of foreign memories and experiences roared into her as if to replace the vanishing blood.

It was only then, in the final moments of her life, that she realized the truth about John Wilkes Booth and the vengeance he was about to unleash on Jerusalem, Mississippi.

Booth had been right.

In the end, Amanda Hornsby Foster understood everything.

IV

Allies

10 P.M., Thursday—David Parker downed his Scotch all at once and looked wistfully at the glass. He had taken a certain comfort in liquor—among other intoxicants—when he was still living in Chicago and mortal. Now, however, his constitution was much too strong for a weak poison like alcohol to have any effect.

Mozart pulled up the gold chain connected to the watch he wore in the breast pocket of his jacket—an antiquated fashion he saw no reason to discard, even though it tended to attract attention in America, where pocket watches were invariably worn in trouser pockets.

"They're late."

"I don't understand why we have to involve them, Wolf. We're only putting them at risk."

"Everybody in this town is already mortally at risk. I do, however, confess to a degree of anxiety in relying on mortals, but they are our only avenue of support. I wish there were time to summon others in the *Illuminati* to help us. Ah, here they are."

David ordered another Scotch when everyone was seated, Mozart, mineral water. Marcus Cuttler asked for beer, Dr. Martin Chesterfield, a Manhattan. Victoria Buchanan had a diet Coke.

"So," Marcus said as soon as the waitress departed, impatient as always to get on with things.

"Thank you for agreeing to meet us tonight," David said. "As I told each of you on the telephone, we need your help. I was not being melodramatic when I said it was a matter of life and death."

Nervous glances were exchanged around the table.

"Inspector Wolf Toland will provide the particulars of why you've been asked here. He works for Interpol, the European police agency. He's in the United States unofficially and requests that you do not repeat the fact that he is a policeman. Please listen closely to what he has to say—and do not be too quick to disbelieve. Your lives may depend upon it."

David looked at Victoria and gave her what he hoped was a reassuring smile. She was holding on to the edge of the table with both hands. Her knuckles were white.

"Life is filled with the unexpected," Mozart began, allowing his Viennese accent to be a little more present than usual because he knew it lent his voice authority with Americans. "Sometimes the unexpected can be pleasant. Other times, the unexpected can be unpleasant. Most unpleasant indeed."

Marcus and Dr. Chesterfield simultaneously picked up their glasses and drank.

"We never know where the unexpected will lead us. Sometimes a pattern emerges. The chaos begins to take form. We begin to see it has shape, and substance, and causality. Let us say for the sake of discussion that our story begins with the theft of a particularly large and valuable ruby in Vienna. In the course of the crime, the jewel's owner, a duchess, is murdered. A seemingly random event. Jewels are stolen almost every day, and murders are hardly a rarity. But as it develops, my friends, the ruby theft is linked to an armored car robbery in Paris; the robbery to a prostitute's murder in Budapest; the murder to a forged passport and the late-night departure of a plane bound for America. The government official who issued the bogus passport is found with his head severed."

Every eye around the table was on Mozart.

"These incidents, which have become part of an established pattern of violent crime, lead us to New York City. Similar incidents occur there, increasing both in frequency and violence. But then there is an unexpected break in the activity. The crimes stop."

Mozart paused to sip his mineral water.

"But the criminal has not really stopped. He has simply changed his locale to deflect suspicion. He cannot stop killing—for that is his true compulsion, not theft. When the crimes resume, they are not in New York City but in a small town in the state of Mississippi, with certain characteristic flourishes. Unless the killer is interrupted, for example, he likes to sever his victims' ring fingers and take them away as trophies."

"Good lord," Dr. Chesterfield said beneath his breath.

Mozart folded his hands on the table. "Tell the others about Katharine Culpepper Simonette's left hand. They do not know."

"The killer cut off her ring finger."

David glanced at Victoria, who grew very pale but otherwise maintained her composure.

"Of course you understand what this means," Mozart said. "It is my unpleasant responsibility to inform you that you have a particularly brutal murderer living among you."

"But why are you telling us?" Dr. Chesterfield asked, wary.

"Because we've got to help David and Inspector Toland stop him," Victoria said in a quiet voice.

"You must understand that this is a particularly dangerous situation, Dr. Chesterfield," Mozart said. "Have any of you ever heard of Scorpio?"

Dr. Chesterfield nearly dropped his drink.

"Who?" asked Marcus.

"You're probably too young to remember, Marcus. There was a serial killer in California who called himself Scorpio. It was in all the newspapers."

"Scorpio was the name adopted by a serial killer who terrorized the San Francisco Bay area," Mozart said. "He killed at least twenty-four people, although some investigators think the actual tally may be as much as three times as great. There was great versatility in Scorpio's killing pattern, which helped make it difficult to apprehend him. Most serial killers concentrate on a certain group: young women, for example, or the elderly or homosexuals. Scorpio, however, preyed on a wide variety of people. He killed men as well as women, young as well as old. He also seemed to have a certain interest in couples. In six confirmed cases, he killed couples."

"I think I remember hearing about him," Marcus said.

"A bloodthirsty maniac," Dr. Chesterfield said. "As I remember, the entire state was on the verge of mass hysteria. He mutilated his victims," Dr. Chesterfield said with great disgust, thinking of how poor Katharine had been savaged.

"Thorne is Scorpio, isn't he?" Marcus asked Mozart in an excited voice.

"Slow down, my friend. You've quickly come to the wrong conclusion."

"Fine," Marcus said and sat back, impatient.

"You may recall the Scorpio killings were never conclusively solved," Mozart said.

"The police are incompetent," Marcus said bitterly, leaning forward.

"Not all police . . ." Dr. Chesterfield began, but Mozart cut him off.

"*Ja*, Herr Cuttler, the police are often incompetent. But serial killers are by their nature difficult to apprehend. Many are brilliant and exceptionally cunning; otherwise, they would not remain free long enough to take more than one or two lives. When they stop killing, the murders often ceasing as abruptly and mysteriously as they began, we have no way of knowing why. The experts believe a certain percentage take their own lives. Others are killed by their accomplices—assistants who may be only marginally homicidal and are led into the crimes after becoming psychologically enslaved to their more dangerous counterparts. The accomplices sometimes become afraid of their masters and kill them; then, without the motivation of the prime mover, these grim assistants do not kill again.

"Certainly, some serial killers end up incarcerated in prisons or asylums for lesser crimes, thus isolating them from the opportunity to kill, sometimes for years. One theory is that most serial killers lose the compulsion to murder as they approach middle age. Perhaps the sickness that leads them to kill is like schizophrenia, which doesn't manifest itself until adulthood, and can become a recessive trait, if the subject survives long enough."

"God only knows how someone like Scorpio thinks," Dr. Chesterfield said.

"*Ja*, or Satan. I discovered the connection between Scorpio and Jerusalem quite by accident. I was in Vienna, doing computer searches of the FBI's inactive files on serial killers."

"What connection?" Marcus asked.

"I learned that the man the California authorities suspected of being Scorpio was locked away for fifteen years in an institution for the criminally insane. The suspect had attacked a Hispanic man. He accused his victim of being an agent for a cabal of nonwhites to take over the United States. The victim was nearly beaten to death with a board. You understand that police seldom publicize all the details of a crime, at least not until they go to trial and sometimes not even then. One such secret in the Scorpio case was that they most often involved a racial component."

"Oh, God," Marcus said hoarsely.

"You don't mean . . ." Dr. Chesterfield began but his voice died away. He, too, had made the connection.

"The evidence the California authorities had against Nathan Bedford Forrest Nightingale was entirely circumstantial, but when they had the chance to lock him away after the beating, they did. They committed him and kept him pumped so full of Thorazine that he would have been incapable of working up enough rage to kill a fly."

"But they set him *free*!" Marcus said, hitting the table with his fist, making Victoria jump in her seat.

"*Ja*. His attorney was able to convince the Mental Health Review Board that Nightingale had been medicated beyond the bounds of anything that could be justified as psychiatric treatment. They ordered that he be set free."

"Motherfuckers."

"Marcus," Dr. Chesterfield said sharply. "There is a lady present."

"That's okay," Victoria said. "My reaction is about the same as Marcus's."

"The California authorities were rather cynical," Mozart said. "They deemed that justice required Nightingale be set free, but they took special pains to ensure that he should be freed in his former place of residence, where he would no longer prove a nuisance to authorities in California."

"So they sent him back to Jerusalem," Marcus said with great bitterness.

"And you believe that Nightingale killed Katharine Simonette?" Dr. Chesterfield asked Mozart.

"*Nein.* I do not believe Nightingale was responsible for her death. Although I cannot be certain, I do not believe he has resumed killing—though he will, since I *have* been able to learn that he has stopped taking his medication."

"Wait a minute," Marcus interrupted. "What did Nightingale have to do with stolen jewels in Europe? You have me completely confused. You said the killer went from Europe to . . ." His voice trailed off.

"New York," Dr. Chesterfield said, concluding Marcus's sentence.

"There are two murderers in Jerusalem, my friends. One used to call himself Scorpio. I believe the other is even more dangerous. He was responsible for killing Katharine Simonette. He convinced Nightingale to stop taking his Thorazine."

"Becker Thorne," Marcus and Dr. Chesterfield said at the same time.

"*Ja,*" Mozart replied. "That is the name of the beast. As unexpected as it may be to find two psychopathic killers in a city of this size, it is inevitable that they would find each other. The fact that Nightingale is working for Thorne at Arlington Plantation removes all doubt that they are in collusion."

Dr. Chesterfield fixed Mozart with a level stare. "Can you prove all of this, Inspector, or is it merely conjecture?"

"I assure you, I can prove it all. That is not the problem."

"The problem is that he can't do anything about it," Marcus said, jumping straight to the point.

"I have no jurisdiction in this country."

"Well, no matter," Dr. Chesterfield said phlegmatically. "Any one of us can pick up the telephone and tell the police about Inspector Toland's findings."

"I quite agree," Mozart said. "In fact, I already have done so. My report is on its way to Vienna by overnight mail. When it gets there, it will be reviewed and approved by my command superiors, then routed back to Washington, where it will receive another level of review, then—"

Mozart made a despairing gesture with his hands.

"The real problem is time, my friends. We have only until tomorrow night to derail their plans. That is when the slaughter will occur." Then he added, "I must confess that much is conjecture, but I cannot dare to stand by and see whether I am proven wrong."

"What's special about tomorrow night?" Dr. Chesterfield asked.

"Thorne is planning a 'vampire ball' at Arlington Plantation over the coming weekend," David said. "There will be a hundred guests from all over the country. Nightingale and Thorne's butler have been working furiously to get everything ready."

"It's true, Martin," Victoria said. "I have an invitation myself."

"But what makes you think . . . ?"

"We're talking about two killers working together to plan a night of the living dead," David said. "It's hard to imagine they aren't up to something bad—something extremely bad."

"The conclusion is inescapable," Mozart said.

"Wait," Dr. Chesterfield said, holding up his hand. "I have a solution. I'm good friends with the police chief. I'll simply take Inspector Toland over for an unofficial chat. Can't we do that?"

"But of course. Unfortunately, the local constabulary will be helpless to act quickly enough to stop tomorrow's bloodbath. By your country's laws, a grand jury will have to be convened and the evidence presented before the authorities can arrest Thorne. What are the chances of that happening before tomorrow night?"

"I know the county attorney is gone on vacation, but we'll simply have to try," the elderly doctor said, looking more befuddled with every passing moment.

"The police will be damned reluctant to offend anybody as rich and powerful as Becker Thorne," Marcus said.

"We have to notify the police," Dr. Chesterfield said, adamant.

"Stop it!"

The strength of Victoria's protest startled them all.

David and Mozart both looked at Victoria with veiled alarm, fearing she would say too much. Instead, Victoria surprised David and Mozart—and herself as well—by lying convincingly.

"You must listen to Inspector Toland. Everything he has told you is true. I know.

"I went to see Thorne myself at Arlington today," she began, her voice breaking. "If I seem on the verge of tears, it's because I consider myself lucky to have escaped with my life. Becker Thorne is mad as a hatter, although he can hide it perfectly when he wants.

"Nightingale was there, too. You already know that Nightingale is a lunatic. The talk about being the 'Last Gray Ghost of the Confederacy' isn't just Klan rhetoric. Nightingale thinks he *is* the Confederacy's last living soldier. He told me. It fits perfectly with Thorne's delusion. Thorne thinks the Confederacy can be made to rise again, but only if the grounds of Arlington are soaked with the blood of sacrificial victims. He's even more insane than Nightingale."

"My God," Dr. Chesterfield said in a low voice.

"Thorne told me everything. As a Buchanan, he thought I would understand and sympathize. The only way I got out of there alive was by promising to come back tomorrow night and help him. He also wants . . ."

Victoria's voice broke. ". . . he wants me to become his bride. He thinks that together we will rule over the new Confederacy. I know it doesn't make a bit of sense. It's pure lunacy. And believe me, Martin, it's frightening as hell."

Marcus turned to the doctor. "We've got to help Inspector Toland."

"But don't you see that what happened to you at Arlington is all the more reason to go to the police? That gives us something more to take to Turnbull."

"Do you honestly think you can take a story like this to Bob Turnbull and make him believe it?" Victoria said. "How anxious do you think he will be to make trouble for a man who has enough money to buy every police department in this state, along with the congressmen and senators to boot?"

"Come off it, Doc," Marcus said. "You know she's right."

"We can't stop the bloodbath without your help," Mozart said.

"It will be dangerous," David warned.

"*Ja*, it will be dangerous. I cannot assure your safety if you agree to assist me. At the same time, I cannot assure your safety if you do not. No one in Jerusalem, Mississippi, is safe as long as Nightingale and Thorne are at large. But with your assistance, I believe we can stop them from killing until Monday, which is all the time we should need."

Marcus slapped the table with his hand. "Count me in," he said. "Victoria, I know you're in. Doc, what about it?"

Dr. Chesterfield thought Marcus looked like a kid itching for a street fight, someone too eager to let his temper rule his fists. He looked at Victoria. She was as irrational on the subject of Arlington Plantation as Marcus was about the man who had murdered his daddy. He looked at Mozart. He never would have taken the confident little man with the elegant clothes and red ponytail to be a policeman, but then he was from Europe and no doubt things were different there. He did know one thing: Turnbull wouldn't listen to a damn thing Inspector Toland had to say. Dr. Chesterfield saw nothing to encourage or reassure him in David Parker's face. Dr. Chesterfield was, after more than thirty years as a physician, a good judge of people, and he was not fooled for one second: David Parker was afraid.

Dr. Chesterfield was no hero. He was not inclined to let himself become drawn into any policeman's dangerous plans, especially when the policeman was from Austria and wore a black velvet jacket and a ponytail. But seeing the fear incompletely concealed in David's face meant something. The predicament had to be desperate for them to turn to an overweight, sixty-two-year-old man for help. Besides, he'd known Marcus and Victoria all their lives. He'd delivered them both. It was difficult for him to feel much genuine concern for the strangers from out of state who would descend on Arlington Plantation the next night for the so-called "vampire ball," but it was impossible to deny that he cared a great deal about Victoria and Marcus.

"All right," Dr. Chesterfield said at last, shaking his head as if unable to make his body and words convey the same message. "What exactly do you need me to do?"

V

Unexpected Visitors

6 P.M. Friday—The motel was a low, ugly building on the edge-of-town commercial strip Katharine Culpepper Simonette had helped develop two summers before she was murdered.

The facade, with its fiberglass pillars and mirrored-glass windows, looked like an architect's halfhearted attempt to adapt a boilerplate design to evoke the atmosphere of a Deep South mansion. Inside, a planter filled with plastic ferns divided the reception desk from the sunken cocktail lounge, the Tara Room. The synthesized bleeps of a video game came from an arcade beyond the front desk. The pool was through a pair of glass doors, the maroon carpet inside wet from guests coming in to use the restrooms and Coca-Cola machine. The air in the lobby stank of chlorine.

Joan Oppenheim was in too much of a hurry to be particular about her accommodations. All she wanted after a second day behind the wheel of her Volvo was to shower and change into fresh clothes. And then, of course, to find David Parker. She couldn't sleep until she'd been to Morningside College to meet the one person who could help her solve the mystery of Al.

Joan parked in a space labeled FACULTY ONLY out of force of habit. The campus was deserted, which was hardly surprising on a Friday evening in August. She found a security guard loitering near the chapel and asked where she could find David Parker, the college's visiting artist for the summer.

The guard was a middle-aged man with a well-developed beer belly and a droopy mustache. He scrutinized Joan carefully before answering. She didn't look like a threat to campus security, but you could never know.

"You a friend of Mr. Parker's?" he asked in a thick Mississippi drawl.

"I'm a colleague of his," Joan answered, using her faculty-meeting voice.

The guard, whose name was Melvin Lewis, looked Joan up and down and nodded. He envied David Parker, who'd been dating Victoria Buchanan. In Melvin's estimation, Professor Buchanan was the most beautiful woman on campus—and in town. This woman was attractive, too, although in a different way. She was small and dark, with a pageboy haircut and deep-set brown eyes that made her look intelligent and sultry at the same time.

"You'll find Mr. Parker across the Pentacrest." Melvin pointed at an ivy-covered building with mullioned windows. "Use the door in the middle, go to the second floor, and turn right. His rooms are at the end of the hall. You want apartment number three."

"Thank you very much."

The guard touched the brim of his cap and stood watching Joan cross the Pentacrest, envying David Parker his good luck with women.

In her briefcase Joan carried copies of five original music manuscripts, Ling-Ling Tsu's computerized handwriting analyses, plus corroborating studies by Joan and an independent expert who did regular work for the FBI.

Joan's plan was guileless. She would walk David Parker through her research one step at a time, showing him the data and the supporting evidence. He would see what it all meant—if he didn't already know.

And then she would ask David Parker to tell her about A1.

She'd earned the right to meet the man behind so much brilliant music. After nearly a year of full-time research, she'd broken away from her life to drive halfway across the country, racing along in the Volvo with the radio off, stopping only for gas, not eating except for a hamburger at the hotel the previous night and a package of Oreo cookies from a vending machine for breakfast.

David Parker would *have* to tell her.

No matter how improbable, no matter how impossible for others to believe, no matter how it would affect her career, no matter how *dangerous*, she had to know the truth.

She was almost to the building when she noticed a man

watching her from a bench beneath a towering oak tree. He looked like a caricature of a Kentucky colonel, or an actor made up to play Big Daddy in *Cat on a Hot Tin Roof.* He wore a white tropical suit and planter's hat made from finely woven ivory-colored straw; his hands rested on the silver head of a cane propped between his knees. He had to weigh at least four hundred pounds. It was impossible to see much of his face, which was bearded; his eyes were shaded with horn-rimmed sunglasses.

Joan pulled open the door and stepped into the dim coolness. The door to David Parker's apartment at Morningside College betrayed no hint of the mystery it contained. It was an ordinary hardwood door, heavy and solid with four inset panels. The brass "3" on the door had been polished recently.

Joan knocked and waited. She knocked again, this time louder. A minute went by, and she knocked a third time. Still no answer.

"Goddamn it!"

The curse sprang involuntarily from Joan's mouth. She'd driven so far, and David Parker wasn't even home! Mastering her frustration after a few moments, she took a piece of paper from her briefcase and wrote a note, wedging it under one corner of the "3," asking David Parker to call her at the Holiday Inn at his earliest convenience.

"Pardon me, young lady. May I be of assistance?"

The man who looked like Big Daddy was standing at the end of the hall, panting from the climb up the stairs.

"Yes, thank you, if you can tell me how to find David Parker."

The fat man began to beam.

"Are you Mr. Parker?" Joan had expected a younger man.

"Good heavens, no!" He laughed with his entire body, ripples spreading outward from his torso to his arms, legs, face. "Allow me to introduce myself," he said as he came quickly toward her. He was surprisingly nimble for a man his size, the cane apparently more of a prop than a contrivance required for locomotion. "I am Gianni Rourke."

Joan caught herself staring in surprise.

"The conductor and impresario?"

"At your service," Rourke said.

She felt the thrill of excitement. Gianni Rourke, the late Leonard Bernstein's protégé, was famous among opera aficionados. She beamed as he took her hand, but instead of shaking it he kissed it, releasing it with a little flourish, as if he were a magician freeing a dove produced during an illusion.

"I'm Dr. Joan Oppenheim."

"Enchanté."

"This little town must be the nexus of musical talent in the summer, Maestro."

"Oh, no, my dear lady. I'm quite certain that, aside from myself, David Parker is the only noteworthy person in this cultural Siberia. I myself am here but temporarily on a mission of some urgency. Do you know where I might find Mr. Parker?"

"I was rather hoping you could tell me, Maestro."

"Dash it all!" Rourke exclaimed in his affected manner. He took out a silk handkerchief and mopped the back of his neck. "I can't imagine why Parker agreed to come here."

"The college is staging a workshop production of the opera Mr. Parker has written. I'm afraid I don't remember what it's called, but they told me it was in rehearsal when I called the school two days ago."

"*Vanity Fair,*" Rourke said irritably. "A workshop production does not constitute a genuine debut."

"No, I suppose not," Joan agreed, wondering why Gianni Rourke would want to minimize Parker's achievement.

Rourke studied Joan carefully. "So you, too, came a long way to see David. Am I to assume that he was not expecting your visit?"

"Not exactly," Joan said awkwardly.

"No need to feel embarrassed, dear lady. He is not expecting me, either." Rourke paused to appraise her with his shrewd eyes. "You don't actually know David Parker, do you, Dr. Oppenheim?"

Joan's face began to burn. "No, we have never been introduced, but I do know a great deal about his music. I'm a musicologist. I'm working on a research project that hinges on several of Mr. Parker's compositions. I was going to write him, but since we're between semesters at the university, I thought I might as well make a trip of it."

"Perhaps we can help one another, Dr. Oppenheim," Rourke said after a bit. "I am going to take you into my confidence, Dr. Oppenheim. I wish to produce David Parker's opera in New York next season." That small portion of the fat man's face visible between beard and hat flushed a shade redder than its usual hue when he thought of Pauline Bettendorf's treacherous betrayal. "I had intended to stage another new opera next season, but my narrow-minded board vetoed the libretto as unsuitable for our audience. Their myopia provides Parker with a tremendous opportunity."

"How exciting for him."

"Exciting is precisely the right word," Rourke said with a little huff. "I will make Parker famous. Unfortunately, I offended him a few months ago. It was a small matter, nothing of any consequence and quite unintentional, but David Parker is a proud man. I'm afraid he'll let his ego get the better of him. And so, my dear Dr. Oppenheim, I propose that we help one another."

"I'd be happy to assist you in any way I could," she said tentatively, not knowing what Rourke had in mind.

"David Parker can be difficult. I'm not at all sure he will be willing to discuss his work with you."

David Parker *had* to talk to her.

"However, I would be happy to prevail upon him to grant you an interview to discuss your project."

"I'd be in your debt if you did," Joan said gratefully.

Rourke smiled. "And you could repay the favor by helping me convince David Parker to act in his own best interests and let me produce his opera."

"But how on earth could I do that? I doubt Mr. Parker would pay much attention to advice from someone he has only just met."

"I am not asking that you argue my case, Dr. Oppenheim. Simply having you present will, I think, keep Mr. Parker from letting his temper run away with him."

"I see," Joan said dubiously. "I'd be honored to help you, Maestro, but I really don't think—"

"Besides," Rourke interrupted, "I do not have an automobile."

Rourke's *non sequitur* left Joan staring.

"One need not drive in New York, where limousines and taxis are plentiful. I rode here this afternoon in a taxi. At least that is what they called it. It was a battered old station wagon that smelled of wet dog. The driver seemed rather insulted that I recommend he purchase an air freshener for the vehicle. Indeed, dear lady, he drove off and abandoned me here. Do you know how many taxis there are in this town, Dr. Oppenheim?"

Joan began to smile.

"Exactly one. If you do not agree to join forces with me, I shall be stranded."

"Okay, Maestro, you've got yourself a deal—until we find David Parker."

"Rapture!" Rourke said, clapping his hands. "I am faint with hunger. Perhaps you could drive us somewhere for a bite to eat, and we could return later when David is likely to be home."

What Joan really wanted to do was find David Parker, but since he was unavailable, dinner with the famous Gianni Rourke would have to do. She was dying to hear about Bernstein and Cosima.

"Do you suppose this town has a restaurant worth patronizing, Dr. Oppenheim?" Rourke asked as he gallantly took Joan's arm and began to escort her down the hallway. "I have the profoundest of doubts."

A young man with wire-rimmed glasses was coming into the building as they left. Rourke positioned himself between the student and the entry.

"Pardon me, but could you recommend a reputable restaurant in this town?"

"Or tell us where we can find David Parker?" Joan added.

"He's going to the Vampire Convention tonight," the student said, grinning at Joan.

"The *what*?" Rourke imperiously demanded.

"The Vampire Convention." The young man seemed to enjoy Rourke's astonishment. "It's a role-playing thing. You know, like the Society for Creative Anachronism. But instead of pretending to be medieval knights and damsels, everybody dresses up like vampires. I heard David talking about it with Marcus Cuttler, one of the seniors. It's at Arlington Plantation, that place outside of town that looks like the mansion in *Gone With the Wind*."

"Can you give us directions?" Joan asked.

"Sure, but you won't be able to get in if you don't have an invitation. It's pretty exclusive. Lucretia Noire, the author of those bestselling vampire books, will be there. I think they should have had it here at the college, where there's more room. A lot more people could have come. I know I would have, though not unless they charged less than a hundred dollars to get in. That's pretty steep for a student."

Gianni noted the directions, writing with a gold pen in a

small leather-bound notebook he carried in his inner breast pocket.

"If you really want to find David tonight, be at Arlington at sundown," the student advised. "The fun starts at dark. Even if you can't get in, you'll probably be able to catch him as the guests arrive."

"A vampire convention," Rourke said derisively as he walked across the Pentacrest with Joan. "How patently childish."

"David Parker isn't a vampire, is he?" Joan asked the question jokingly, but for some reason hearing herself mouth the words made the hair stand up on the back of her neck.

For a moment there was no sound but the scrape of their shoes on the sidewalk and the clicking of the tip of Rourke's cane.

"Not unless vampires can go outside in the sunlight," Rourke said, wheezing a little. "I've had lunch with him in New York at midday at least half a dozen times. Parker may be a somewhat difficult man, but he is not a vampire.

"Besides," Rourke snorted, "there is no such thing as a vampire."

They walked the rest of the way without speaking. Rourke was thinking that he should have asked Dr. Oppenheim to drive the car around the Pentacrest so that he wouldn't have had to walk. Joan was thinking that Gianni Rourke was, of course, quite right—there was no such thing as a vampire.

PART IX

✧

The Vampire Convention

I

Desecration

8 P.M. Friday—Lydia Chase ignored the signs that directed guests to park on the west lawn, where neat white chalk lines had been drawn on the grass. Instead, she left her red Corvette outside the main entrance to Arlington with the keys in the ignition. If Becker's servants wanted the car moved, they could bloody well move it.

She gathered up the folds of her long skirt and hurried up the steps, sure-footed even though she had already had four cocktails. The black skirt was made of several layers of billowing, nearly see-through gossamer, which barely disguised the fact that she wore a black silk garter belt beneath the dress but nothing else. The beaded halter top was black, too, as were Lydia's matching clutch bag, spike-heeled shoes, and nylons, which had seams running up the back.

"Good evening, Miss Chase," Zaharim greeted Lydia in his Slavic-accented English.

"Hiya," she chirped, and hurried past the butler. "Where's Becker?"

"He is presently indisposed, madam." Zaharim frowned at his watch, his way of protesting the fact that Lydia was an hour early.

Lydia checked her makeup in a gilded mirror. "You know, Zaharim, when people call me 'madam,' it makes me feel like the keeper of a whorehouse."

"I'm sure I intend no insult, *madam.*"

Lydia daubed a touch of burgundy gloss on her lips and turned on Zaharim with a warm smile, her formidable temper held in check. She detested cheeky servants, but she was determined that nothing would spoil her elaborate plans for the evening. There would be plenty of time to give Zaharim his comeuppance when she was Lydia Thorne.

"You may go about your business," Lydia said, and waved one hand dismissively. "I suppose I'll just have to amuse myself until my host comes downstairs."

Zaharim bowed, looking up through his eyebrows with ill-disguised rancor. Lydia laughed merrily and turned away. There was no question in her mind: Zaharim would have to go.

Lydia floated into the music room. The candles were already burning in the rococo candelabra on either side of the pipe organ's keyboards. Kerosene lamps had been put out on all the tables. Apparently the Vampire Convention was to be illuminated without benefit of electricity. A cute touch, Lydia thought.

She wandered over to the bar set up on a collapsible table the caterer had brought. A little drink would have been nice, but she thought the better of it and instead inspected the elaborate array of hors d'oeuvres, pausing to lift the cellophane and pick a caper from its bed of cream cheese.

She sighed. She was already bored. Arlington's antiquarian splendors failed to impress her. She'd been coming to receptions at the plantation for as long as she could remember—the great house was a popular locale for charity teas during the sisters' tenure—and she had long since become inured to its charms. Besides, she loathed antiques. She could not fathom people like Victoria Buchanan who made a religion out of worshiping the past.

The front door opened and closed.

Lydia strolled back to the grand entrance hall, licking a trace of cream cheese from her forefinger, hoping to find someone to entertain her.

The foyer was empty. It must have been Zaharim going outside on an errand.

She looked down the hallway toward the kitchen wing, where the muffled banging of pots and pans was the only evidence of the caterers' presence in the mansion.

Lydia's eyes followed the staircase's sweep up toward the second floor. A deliciously naughty thought formed in Lydia's mind. With a quick glance backward—no sign of the disapproving Zaharim—she slipped out of her high heels, picked them up with one hand and her skirts with the other, and dashed up the stairs two at a time.

Lydia had to stop at the second-floor landing and wait for her eyes to adjust to the darkness.

The bedroom doors were all closed, and the windows were draped with heavy, old-fashioned velvet curtains that admitted almost no light. She pulled one of the draperies back and saw that the shade had been drawn, too. Looking behind the shade, she saw that the shutters were closed and latched, allowing only narrow yellow lines of the day's fading light to penetrate the louvers.

The darkness must be because of Becker's insomnia. Becker had told her it was impossible for him to sleep at night, that he spent the hours between sunset and dawn looking after his financial affairs and making trades on foreign markets in places like Tokyo and Singapore. In fact, being up all night made it possible for him to steal a march on his competitors, and was one of the secrets to his wealth, he'd confided. In the morning, when the rest of America was waking up, Becker would finally be able to sleep.

Lydia was sympathetic to Becker's strange sleep patterns. She, too, was a night person, and hardly ever dragged herself out of bed before eleven in the morning.

She moved to the master bedroom and put her ear to the door. She heard nothing. Becker had to be awake, she thought, since the guests would begin arriving within the hour. She imagined him standing before the mirror, a towel tied around his waist, taut over his rippling abdominal muscles, shaving with his ivory-handled razor.

Or better still, lying on his back in bed, naked . . .

Without bothering to knock, she reached for the oval doorknob, feeling the cool silver press against her palm as she tried to turn it.

The door was locked.

She tapped gently on the door, but there was no answer.

Oh, well, Lydia told herself, it would be a long night, and she was certain that it would end intimately, even if it didn't begin that way, as she'd hoped.

Lydia was about to descend the staircase, her high heels still dangling from her left hand, when she remembered the chapel.

At Oscar Sanchez's party, Becker had told her he was going to make over the chapel. Lydia said she thought the Arlington chapel would make a nice discotheque, especially since it had originally been a ballroom. Becker refused to say exactly what he planned to do with the room, except that Lydia would "find it extremely interesting." That set Lydia's imagination in motion. She'd read a book of Victorian pornography once in which a secret chamber made over for bondage and other games had played a prominent role. Had Becker turned the chapel into a "Snuggery"? It was almost too delicious to imagine.

Lydia knew the way well enough even though the hall was almost pitch dark. The chapel—if indeed it still was a chapel—was all the way to the end of the hall and through the double doors.

The chapel doors were closed. A faint red light came from the crack beneath the door.

Looking over her shoulder for Zaharim, Lydia opened the door and slipped inside.

"I'll be *damned.*"

Only a dim reflex kept her from dropping the high heels that dangled from her fingers.

The chapel had not been remodeled in any substantial way, although there was one immediately obvious—and disturbing—addition since the last time Lydia had visited: the neon Pegasus.

Lydia stood for nearly a minute staring at the glowing winged horse suspended above the altar by bailing wire. Even from where she stood she could see how the jagged sheet metal had gouged and scraped into the beautiful mahogany cross. The crackle of arcing electricity made her wonder how anybody could be crazy enough to plug the thing into a wall socket.

Maybe this was supposed to be some kind of New York City art statement . . .

Or a sick joke concocted for the so-called Vampire Convention . . .

Whatever the explanation, hanging the sign over the altar demonstrated a shocking lack of consideration for the people who took religion seriously—which Lydia guessed meant just about ninety-nine-point-nine percent of the population of Jerusalem, Mississippi.

No, Lydia thought, the neon sign was worse than just bad taste, even for a lapsed Catholic such as herself.

It was desecration.

There was no other word for it.

Desecration.

Lydia did not immediately realize someone had entered the chapel and was standing behind her. She did not know what gradually alerted her to the presence. At first she was afraid to turn around and see who was there. She did not like people to sneak up on her, especially not since what happened to poor Katharine—but *no*! She would not allow herself to think *that*. Lydia continued to stare at Pegasus, whose gimlet eye betrayed nothing. No, that wasn't exactly true. The angle of the tin horse's eye, the turn of the jaw—there was something unmistakably malevolent about the winged neon horse.

The tension increased past the point she could bear it.

"Becker," she said, turning, half expecting to discover she was alone, her mind playing tricks on her.

Lydia's high heels fell to the floor, the sound muffled by the carpet.

It was Nathan Bedford Forrest Nightingale.

"Hello, Nate."

Nightingale did not answer. He wore rubber galoshes, a long rubber apron, and yellow rubber gloves.

Lydia smiled weakly.

The sound of the organ drifted into the chapel. Becker had hired a church organist to set the mood for the Vampire Convention, instructing him to play only weird, discordant fugues. He was warming up the pipe organ in the music room downstairs. The sound was faint in the chapel, but Lydia knew it had to be roaring loud on the first floor.

Lydia took a step backward.

Nightingale took a step toward her.

She took another step.

Nightingale took another step.

Lydia knew it wouldn't do any good to call for help. Nobody downstairs would hear.

Acting on instinct, Lydia turned and ran up the aisle as fast as she could, unknowingly retracing Amanda Hornsby's footsteps. She could hear Nightingale running, too, his footfalls heavy on the carpet behind her.

Nightingale threw his enormous arms around Lydia from behind, lifting her from the floor.

Lydia screamed. She screamed so hard that it felt like the tissue in her throat was about to tear.

Slowly, lugubriously, like Cyclops moving across his bone-littered cave, Nightingale turned back toward the door with his struggling burden.

It was at that moment that Lydia saw the other woman. She was a tall woman, standing in the shadows in the far corner of the room.

"Help me!" Lydia pleaded, too frightened to realize that even two women would be no match for the hulking Nightingale.

The woman in the shadows did not respond.

Lydia began to understand that something was terribly wrong. The woman in the shadows could not be *that* tall. And there was something unnatural about the way her body swayed back and forth as though she were drunk, or standing on the deck of a ship at sea.

Lydia's eyes found the gleaming meat hooks hanging from the ceiling beam like well-polished ecclesiastical ornaments. These grim instruments were even more horrifying than the bloodless pallor of the woman suspended from the furthest hook—her shrunken, shriveled cheek, her eyes bulging grotesquely from their sockets, the expression of horror that remained fixed even in death. The dead woman appeared to have been mummified; she looked as if all the moisture had been sucked out of her body.

Lydia's abductor began to lift her into the air.

Lydia could guess what was coming next as she felt herself lifted past Nightingale's shoulder, her eyes helplessly focused on the neon Pegasus, its wings stretching out over the chapel's altar.

"No," she pleaded with Nightingale. "Nathan, please, no."

Lydia felt her body jerked sickenly downward. She felt the sensation of being pierced by something cold and smooth and long. It surprised her how little pain there was.

Lydia was vaguely aware that Nightingale was somewhere below, shuffling backward into the shadows, gazing up at her with an expression of worshipful rapture on his rough face. She could comprehend the rough outlines of what was happening. The neon horse was a kind of god, she guessed. And she, a kind of sacrifice.

And then, with the next breath, the initial shock of being impaled wore off, and the pain arrived—pain so blindingly intense that Lydia couldn't even cry out. Although her mind knew that it was pointless, that it would only magnify her suffering, she began to twist and writhe, as if she might miraculously lift her body off the steel hook piercing her spasming back muscles.

Every breath was mortal agony now. Lydia couldn't breath, in fact, except in frantic, shallow gasps that made blood bubble on her lips.

Someone else had come into the chapel. Lydia heard but couldn't quite see. Deep shock had set in, robbing her of her peripheral vision.

"Ah, yes, I see our guests have already begun to arrive."

It was Becker.

Becker!

Lydia managed to twist her neck so that she could see him.

Becker and Nightingale? It had to be a hallucination. But the pain was no hallucination. There was no point trying to explain the impossible. Becker was there, dressed for the Vampire Convention in an elegant black tuxedo, conversing with her murderer.

Help me. She did not have the breath to speak, but she mouthed the words piteously. *Help me.*

Thorne frowned.

Yes! she thought, and grateful tears welled in her eyes.

"You couldn't wait, could you, Scorpio."

Scorpio? A distant light of recognition flickered in Lydia's mind, and, drowned by so much pain and animal fear, died.

"You promised me souls."

"But not my special guests," Becker said angrily.

Downstairs in the music room, the organ music paused, then resumed with an equally macabre piece.

"There will be plenty of souls for you, Scorpio, but the children of Jerusalem are mine. They belong to the Fury."

Nightingale bowed his head. "Yes, my lord."

"You might as well finish the job. Your crude work has ruined my appetite."

"As you say, my lord."

Nightingale was grinning now. It was the same imbecile grin Lydia had seen on his face a hundred times. It had always given her a chill. Now she knew why.

A butcher knife materialized from beneath Nightingale's rubber apron. It looked like something that had been salvaged from junk hauled from an old garage.

"You're a lucky girl, although I doubt you can appreciate

it," Becker said lightly, looking up at Lydia. "The others won't get off nearly so easily."

Then he turned on his heel and left, leaving Lydia alone with Nightingale.

Nightingale came toward her, rolling the butcher knife in his sweating palm.

Lydia couldn't stand to look at Nightingale, so she focused her eyes on the only thing left to look at—the neon Pegasus.

Ten minutes later, Lydia Chase was dead.

II

The Vampire Hunters

9 P.M. Friday—The remins of the day faded quickly as they sat in Dr. Chesterfield's van and watched the guests' cars pull around the circular drive in front of Arlington's portico, following the signs that directed them to the parking area on the west lawn.

Dr. Chesterfield sat behind the wheel. Marcus Cuttler was across from the doctor on the van's passenger side. Behind them, David Parker and Victoria Buchanan shared the first bench seat. Mozart sat alone in the third row, looking forward past his small cadre—the only force he had to throw against John Wilkes Booth.

Mozart had warned them it would be dangerous, but he did not reveal how formidable the odds against them might be. He had witnessed many ominous signs in Jerusalem, not the least of which was that he, with all his advanced preternatural powers, was unable to identify Booth's *Vampiri* ally—or allies. Mozart could *feel* Booth inside Arlington Plantation, but beyond that he detected only hints of dim, ghostly presences.

Any vampire who could conceal himself—or herself—was by definition an extremely powerful being, perhaps even more powerful than the *Illuminati*'s champion, Wolfgang Amadeus Mozart.

Dr. Chesterfield had parked the van a hundred yards up the plantation's formal drive, pulling over beneath the shadows of the moss-draped oaks that lined either side of the lane.

The diversity of the Vampire Convention's guest list was apparent from the array of vehicles parked on the west lawn. Guests arrived in everything from an immaculate gray Mercedes-Benz limousine to a rusted yellow Volkswagen Beetle with a Grateful Dead bumper sticker. Most of the vehicles had out-of-state license tags, although Mozart had counted twelve from the county where Jerusalem was located—thirteen, including Dr. Chesterfield's van.

The guests wore a variety of costumes representing everything from ancient Egypt to the present—the span covered in Lucretia Noire's cycle of vampire novels. Some revelers were dressed in knee breeches and morning coats. Others wore Edwardian suits or looked as if they had stepped out of *The Great Gatsby.* A small percentage—including the passengers in Dr. Chesterfield's van—were dressed in formal evening wear: black tuxes for the men, long dresses for the women.

Lydia Chase's car was already there when they arrived.

Victoria Buchanan frowned when she recognized the red Corvette, thinking that Lydia was usually found wherever there was trouble in Jerusalem. Victoria knew it was petty to think such thoughts with so many lives hanging in the balance, but at least it relieved her from the burden of having to think about Booth and what he was—and whether her daughter Michelle, sent out of town to stay with friends, would be safe from the killer.

The irony was that no one would have been able to convince Victoria of the truth if she hadn't discovered it for herself, she thought, smiling bitterly. Wolf Toland had been exactly right: there was no way they could tell the authorities what was about to happen at Arlington; they would be laughed out of the police station.

If anybody was going to stop Booth that night, it would have to be them.

But what of Wolf Toland? Who was he *really*?

And was it just a coincidence that David was Morningside College's Visiting Artist in residence that summer, or had he been drawn to Jerusalem by the same power that brought the little Austrian with the red ponytail?

Victoria suspected David Parker and Wolf Toland were in fact vampire hunters who'd followed John Wilkes Booth to Jerusalem, Mississippi, to kill him.

Victoria had always been fascinated by fictional vampires. She wanted to know what Toland and David knew about the real vampires, but she doubted they would share their secrets with her. Such information was bound to be dangerous. She was probably better off not knowing.

Or maybe, Victoria thought, giving David a sideways glance, it wasn't just a matter of keeping secrets, but of covering up unpleasant truths.

David caught Victoria's eye and smiled reassuringly, briefly touching her hand.

It was almost as if he knew what Victoria was thinking and meant to put her mind at ease.

Which, of course, was exactly the case.

Mozart saw David pat Victoria's hand and nodded to himself in approval.

He was glad to see David was in love. His protégé was the sort of person who was never happy unless he was in love.

Mozart had been worried about David since Tatiana had left him. New York had been a fiasco for David, and Mozart had been only too happy to dispatch him to Mississippi for the *Illuminati.*

The old vampire was impressed with Victoria Buchanan. She was a brave woman to come with them to Arlington Plantation, knowing what she did about Booth. Mozart was uncertain what to do about her memories after it was all over—assuming she or any of them survived. He thought she might be the rare sort of mortal who could be trusted to keep the *Vampiri*'s secrets. He would leave it up to the *Illuminati* to decide.

Dr. Martin Chesterfield and Marcus Cuttler were courageous, too, but less complicated than *Fräulein* Buchanan. With luck, Dr. Chesterfield and Herr Cuttler would never know the truth about what they were about to confront.

"All right, my brave friends," Mozart said in a voice that managed to be confident without disguising the danger that lay ahead. "The Vampire Convention is about to commence. More than half of the guests have arrived. It is time for us to make our move, while there is still a certain amount of social confusion inside."

"You're certain you'll find evidence in Arlington you can use to put these two behind bars?"

It was obvious that Dr. Chesterfield had been thinking very hard about what they were about to attempt. Laws would be broken. He could be arrested, lose his medical license, go to jail, be disgraced. He, Dr. Martin Chesterfield, a man who had never gotten so much as a traffic ticket!

"I am certain of it," Mozart said, reading the doctor's thoughts. "And as I've pointed out, the evidence of Thorne's crimes will be found by three local citizens of unquestionable character: Dr. Martin Chesterfield, Victoria Buchanan, and Marcus Cuttler."

"If there's evidence of Thorne's crimes inside Arlington, why would he invite so many visitors into his house? Wouldn't he be afraid one of them would find something?"

"*Nein, Herr Doktor.* Do not assume Thorne's mind works the way yours does. Serial killers are risk-takers. Part of the reason Thorne kills is because it excites him to commit the most heinous crimes, to take the risk of arrest and jail and worse, and yet to always elude capture. Inviting so many people into his house is Thorne's way of mocking society. He is daring us to find him out."

Mozart paused a beat, then added, "I would not be in the least surprised, my friends, to discover at least one corpse on the premises, put there as a sort of challenge for his guests."

Victoria caught her breath.

"And even if we find no waiting evidence," Mozart continued, "this misbegotten gathering will undoubtedly prove too much a temptation for Thorne and the unspeakable Nathan Nightingale."

"All right," Dr. Chesterfield said heavily, "I'm convinced. I just wanted to hear it one more time. We've got to stop him," he added grimly, talking to himself more than anyone else, psyching himself up for the job ahead.

"*Ja, Herr Doktor.* That is precisely what we must do."

"That, and keep ourselves from becoming his next victims," David said.

Victoria, Dr. Chesterfield, and Marcus all looked at David with the same startled expression.

"I need not remind you again how dangerous these two individuals are," Mozart warned. "Whatever you do, do not under any circumstances allow yourself to be caught alone with either Thorne or Nightingale. Do you understand?"

Everybody but David nodded solemnly.

"And now, if we recall the roles each of us are to play, let us commence with this task."

Marcus reached for the handle to open the door.

"May God bless and protect you all," Mozart said quietly as the door opened.

"Come on, people," Marcus said. "Let's do it."

III

Necrophile

9:15 P.M. Friday—The killer was in the entry hall to greet his guests personally as they arrived.

Zaharim stood at the door, admitting "vampires" to the first night of the Vampire Convention, the Grande Reception. Zaharim collected the invitations. Each guest was presented an elaborate, leather-clad booklet delineating the fictional characters in attendance. At the end of the night, guests would receive a silver signet ring—decorated with the image of a skull wearing a crown—that would gain the bearer admittance to the second night of festivities planned at Arlington Plantation.

"Lord and Lady Darkmoor," Zaharim called in a stentorian voice, announcing the guests by the names of the characters from Lucretia Noire's vampire novels that they were to assume for the weekend.

"Professor Lazarus . . ."

"Margaret, Duchess of Angelrock . . ."

"Sir Forbes Gold . . ."

Lysander Chase came toward the killer, a slightly embarrassed smile on his face, and briskly shook his hand. Unlike some of the other guests, Chase appeared comfortable in formal evening wear, but then there'd been a tuxedo hanging in his closet ever since he'd attended his first debutante ball forty years ago. Chase had occasion to wear a tux at least once a month, as he was invited to every benefit and charity event of any significance in that part of Mississippi and had served as chairman or a committee member on more boards than he could have remembered if he tried.

"You know me, Becker," Chase said, holding the killer's hand in his strong, practiced grip and looking him in the eye. "I'm a practical man. Don't have much time for play-acting. Never have. Feel damned silly."

"All work and no play makes Jack a dull boy, Lysander," the killer said. "Excuse me, Lysander, but I should have called you 'Sir Forbes.' They want us to stay in character tonight."

"I'll try to remember," Chase said morosely. "I don't know a bloody thing about this Noire woman's books. I don't have much time for novels; when I do, I like a good Tom Clancy thriller."

"At least they came up with a good character for you—Forbes Gold, a mortal banker who specializes in vampires' financial affairs. It should be easy to fit your role."

"I *do* have some bloodsuckers for clients," Chase joked, and both men laughed. "Why the kerosene lamps and candles? Trying to cut down on your utility bill?"

"Atmosphere, my friend. Miss Noire's people thought doing without electric lights would make the event more—I believe 'vampiric' was the word they used, if there is such a word."

"Alcibiades Poe . . ."

The killer and Chase turned together to see the next guest make his way through the entrance. It was Kurt Teameyer, the University of Iowa student who had driven all the way to Mississippi in his battered yellow VW. He was almost deliriously happy to have gotten his wish: he was portraying Alcibiades Poe, the vampire protagonist of *The Raven.* Lucretia Noire's moody book was set in San Francisco during the 1940s; more than one reviewer had described it as a *Maltese Falcon* with vampires.

Teameyer wore a vintage double-breasted suit, black, with chalk pinstripes, and a well-blocked black fedora. He even looked a little like Sam Spade—the one in the book, not the Humphrey Bogart movie—with the hint of an incipient paunch on his six-foot-two frame, a blond mustache, and blond hair beneath the hat.

Chase gave the killer a look. The killer winked.

"Some people really put themselves into this," the killer said.

Chase just shook his head.

"I appreciate your coming tonight. Why don't you get yourself a drink at the bar? I'll welcome a few more guests, then turn this over to Miss Noire's agent and join you. I've got something special I'd like to show you, something only a man of discriminating tastes could appreciate."

"I'd be happy to," Chase said, clearly interested. He glanced around at the swelling crowd. "Where's Lydia? I saw her Corvette outside."

The killer gave Chase a friendly grin, seeing in the banker's mind that his daughter had told him about having designs on the wealthy Becker Thorne—a conquest he approved of, for once.

"Lydia was the first one here tonight," the killer said. "I'm sure you'll find her hanging around somewhere."

The killer extended his right hand to the next guest.

"Alcibiades Poe, I'd know you anywhere! Damned good to meet you. My name is Booth. John Wilkes Booth."

Thus the killer dropped his mask. Booth no longer needed to pretend. The pretense used to set up the Vampire Convention set him free to be himself in public for the first time in one hundred and twenty-six years.

"Booth?" Kurt Teameyer said, wrinkling his brow. There were historical characters sprinkled throughout Lucretia Noire's novels, but John Wilkes Booth was not one of them. Teameyer knew; he'd read each of Noire's books at least twice. A look of enlightenment came into his eyes as he thought he grasped the explanation.

"You must be one of Miss Noire's new characters. It was good of her to create so many new personas just for this weekend."

The killer smiled.

Teameyer held up the Vampire Convention booklet he carried in his left hand.

"I'll have to get off in a corner somewhere and bone up on who's who."

"Oh, I don't know that it's so important to read about who

the guests are supposed to be," the killer said. "The fun is finding out for yourself."

"You've got a point, Booth. I haven't heard much of you since you offed Lincoln."

"I've been out of the country mostly, traveling incognito."

"Smart." Teameyer looked around him. He thought the great house was magnificent in lamp and candlelight. He knew this was going to be a weekend he would never forget.

"This is some joint. How'd you like to be the fat cat who owns it?"

The killer shrugged.

"Dr. Caligari . . ."

Nodding to the killer, Poe wandered off to introduce himself to the other vampires.

"You and I are not like the others here tonight."

Thorne led Chase down the darkened hallway, carrying a flickering candle, which he shielded with his free hand. "I've perused the guest list. There aren't any other players here tonight except Culpepper. There's Miss Noire, of course, but her money comes from writing. That hardly counts, does it?"

Chase chuckled.

"You and I, we are players in the only real game. We understand what's important, and we're not afraid to do what it takes to get what we want."

Chase smiled to himself. It was flattering that Thorne thought of him as a peer. Chase was a wealthy man, but his fortune was nothing compared to the billions Thorne had amassed on Wall Street.

They'd stopped outside a closed door.

"I have a confession to make, Lysander."

Chase's eyebrows went up.

"I'm bored."

"Bored?" Chase echoed, not knowing whether his host was talking about the party or in more general terms.

"I needed to get away from the game for a while, but now I'm ready to get back to the wars."

"I can understand that," the banker said, watching a rivulet of hot wax trickle down the candle and pool against Thorne's finger. He would have thought it burned, but the killer didn't flinch. "My daughter Lydia wonders why I don't retire. What in blazes would I do if I did?"

"Exactly," the killer said. "Let me tell you something,

Lysander. I've been keeping my eye on you. I like the way you do business. Your bank is the most profitable closely held financial institution in the state."

"It's not for sale," Chase said too quickly, thinking he finally understood why Thorne had pressed him to attend the ridiculous party. His ulcer flared. He never should have agreed to attend such a preposterous affair.

The killer tilted back his head and laughed. Chase saw that the handsome billionaire was not the perfect physical specimen he appeared; Thorne had a dental deformity, a pair of extra canine teeth set into his gums just above and behind the normal set.

"Everything is for sale, Lysander. It's just a question of price."

"My family has owned the controlling interest in the bank since it was founded in 1840. It will never be sold as long as I'm alive."

"Never say never, Lysander."

Chase saw the undisguised amorality in Thorne's face, the animal cunning and ruthlessness—qualities the banker found easy to recognize since he saw them looking back at him from the mirror every morning when he shaved.

"Never," Chase said, almost spitting the word at his host.

"But you mistake my meaning entirely. I don't want to buy your bank. However, I would like to do some deals in this corner of the country, and I'd like to use your bank as the conduit. The advantages for me are obvious. I'd be working with you one-on-one, not a board of weak-kneed shareholders terrified of the prospect of anything that might reduce their annual dividend by a few pennies. I also wouldn't have to worry about keeping my plans quiet, because I'd be dealing with just you."

"Well," Chase said simply. This was a different matter entirely.

"The advantages for you are also obvious. It's well enough to have the most profitable bank in Mississippi, my friend, but the fees you'll generate working with me will make it one of the biggest performers in the southeastern United States." The killer smiled warmly. "I think we can work well together, Lysander. We have the same values. We think alike. We're both players. Interested?"

Chase looked up at the taller man, looking him straight in the eyes, seeing the candle flame reflected there. They *were* alike, Chase thought. Players. Men who knew the game and played it hard.

"I think it's worth pursuing, Becker," Chase said, smart enough after countless negotiations not to appear too eager. In his mind, Lysander Chase was thinking that an alliance with Becker Thorne would be the crowning glory to his already exceptionally successful stewardship of the family bank.

"I think so, too." The killer inclined his head toward the door.

"I've got to go back downstairs, but you go on in and have a look around. Help yourself to the perquisites of real power. I think a little celebrating helps cement a new agreement between two real players."

Chase's well-trained face displayed neither curiosity nor displeasure—though he was feeling equal measures of each. What the hell was Thorne up to? he wondered.

"Here." The killer handed him the candle. "You take this."

"Won't you need it?"

"I have excellent night vision. You go on in and enjoy yourself a bit. We'll talk more later."

Thorne was already walking away, disappearing into the darkness.

Lysander Chase stood holding the candle another minute, watching the blackness that had swallowed his host. He did not, as a rule, like surprises. He looked at the doorknob as if it might turn into a snake and bite him when he reached for it.

What was Thorne's angle? Was he really trying to do him a favor, or was this a way to gain an advantage? And, foremost, what, or who, was behind the door?

"Oh, to hell with it," Lysander Chase said to himself finally, his curiosity proving to be stronger than his native caution.

The candle was nearly extinguished from the draft when Chase shut the door behind himself. Thorne and the others might think it quaint to stumble around in the darkness, but he didn't, Chase thought irritably, looking for a light. The switch panel was by the door. He flipped the switch and nothing happened.

"For the love of Mike!"

There was a reading light on a table beside an easy chair, a ginger-jar lamp with a fringed silk shade. Chase pulled the chain. Nothing happened. He peered under the shade. The lightbulb had been removed. The banker began to chuckle in spite of himself. As much as he hated these kinds of childish games, he had to admire Becker Thorne for careful follow-through with the details. Chase would have bet that he could inspect every electric light in the house without finding a single lightbulb—and he would have been right.

He found a candelabra on the dresser and began to light the five candles. He could hardly see a thing with the single candle, but the candelabra would help considerably. He snuffed out the single candle and left it on the dresser to use later to return downstairs. And then, taking up the candelabra, he turned to inspect the room.

At first glance it was just a bedroom filled with antiques. Unlike his daughter, Chase found the symbols of old wealth comforting. By the window was a magnificent old writing desk. He ran his fingertips over the grain—walnut. The center panel in the desk's top was inset with leather circumscribed with a gold-leaf design and angled to make it easier to write. You never saw desks like that anymore. He picked up a leather-bound book. Charles Dickens. He flipped it open and saw that it was, as he suspected, a first edition. Stupid of Thorne to leave such a valuable object lying about with so many strangers in the house.

There was an oil painting over the fireplace in an ornate gilt frame with an oval opening for the portrait. Chase lifted the candles for a better look and saw some of the colors come back into the painting: blue dress, a rose held lightly in the hand before the breast, rosy lips and rosy sky. And, of course, the golden tresses, hair so blonde it was nearly white. It was not the first time that Chase had marveled at how the Buchanan women bore such a strong resemblance from generation to generation. The woman in the portrait could have been Victoria Buchanan, though the style of dress and the cracking paint on the surface reminded Chase that the picture of Anna Lee Buchanan was more than a century old.

A pine armoire stood beside the window. It was a plain piece, almost Shaker in its simplicity; it seemed a little out of place among the richer pieces in the room, which Chase guessed had their origins in European shops.

"Hmmm," he mused.

The armoire was big enough for a man to stand inside. He'd seen armoire reproductions used to hide everything from entertainment centers to wet bars. Perhaps this held what Thorne had wanted him to see.

Chase grabbed the knob on the right-hand door and pulled. The armoire was empty.

Chase snorted and slammed the door shut, turning and moving away with such sudden deliberation that he barked his shin on a chaise lounge lurking in the darkness. The candles flickered.

"Son of a bitch!" he cried, lurching toward the window. The silk swag and jabot half curtains left only a small, irregular piece of window visible. Chase pulled back the curtain as the pain in his leg subsided and looked down to see two figures in the garden shadows. The unsteadiness in their movements caught Chase's attention. The party had hardly started and it seemed there were already two drunks fighting.

Chase would have watched longer if he hadn't heard a quiet rustle behind him in the room.

He spun around so quickly that two of the candles in the candelabra—which was beginning to get heavy—sputtered and went out.

Chase swallowed dryly.

Someone was in the room. On the *bed.*

Angled into the far corner was a four-poster bed. A canopy arched over its top, and its four uprights were hidden by draperies that were tied to each leg, midway to the floor, with braided gold ropes. There was a second layer of drapery, a nearly transparent gauze, hanging inside the heavier velvet outer curtains. This inner curtain had been drawn closed around the bed, nearly concealing the outline of someone lying there. He could have kicked himself for not having noticed it before, but it was easy to miss in the darkened room, for the gauze curtains created a kind of illusion, veiling the occupant of the bed without doing so in an obvious way.

The banker chewed his bottom lip and thought hard.

He had two choices: he could investigate further, or he could walk immediately out of the bedroom.

The latter was clearly the prudent choice. Chase was no prude. Indeed, his sexual drive was every bit as strong as his daughter's, but whereas Lydia did not care who knew how much she slept around, the banker was discreet. A banker always had to be discreet.

But discretion wasn't Lysander Chase's only concern. Becker Thorne was a player, and this was all part of his power game. Chase knew that you should never expose a weakness in a business relationship, and sex was the only weakness Chase could claim. On the other hand, you had to know how to accept a gift from a business partner. If Chase refused a gesture of trust and hospitality, Thorne might take it as an insult.

Chase's mouth had become dry.

He decided to have a look, telling himself that he still hadn't made up his mind whether he *would* or *wouldn't.* He couldn't decide without at least seeing what Becker Thorne was offering.

Lysander Chase set the candles down on the night stand, afraid the gossamer curtains would explode in flame if he got too close with the fire. He stood there a moment, listening to his heart pound. By God, this sort of thing made him feel *young*—but then, it always did.

Someone sighed softly on the other side of the curtain.

Chase licked his dry lips and swallowed again to moisten his throat. He had changed his mind about the Vampire Convention. He was glad he'd accepted the invitation.

He reached for the curtain and pulled.

"Jesus!" Chase said hoarsely, feeling a commingling of shock, anger, and excitement. Who the hell did Becker Thorne think he was? Had he no decency? No morals?

The bed had been stripped down to the white linen sheet. Upon it was stretched a tiny woman who was fastened hand and foot to the bedposts with handcuffs. Chase doubted she was twenty years old.

She was beautiful. Chase had never seen skin so white or perfect. Not a blemish, not a mole, not a freckle disturbed its unbroken snowy whiteness. Her lips were painted a deep, vivid red that was echoed in the nipples on her breasts. (Chase wondered if her nipples had been rouged, like a geisha's.) The silky hair between her legs and the tresses tied up on her head washerwoman style were coal black. Several long tendrils had come free in her dishabille and fell across her face.

Chase's chest felt constricted when he drew in a breath.

Such breasts! Even when she was stretched out on her back with her arms pulled over her head, they retained their full, ripe shape.

Her eyes closed, the woman made a submissive sound deep in her throat and moved her body against the linen sheet. Chase felt the sinuous movement of her pelvis in the pit of his stomach. His heart was pounding so hard that he could feel each beat in his neck, a pressure against his esophagus.

He felt his hand reaching out. He was acting purely on instinct, not thinking about what he was doing.

Lysander Chase touched the woman lightly.

She moaned. She did not object to her bondage. Indeed, it seemed to excite her.

Chase brushed his fingertips across the nipple of her left breast. It felt hot, feverish. The woman arched her back, pushing her breast upward into his hand. Her veiled eyes opened, and she gave him a wanton look.

Lysander Chase tore at his clothing, throwing his jacket down, pulling at his tie, his belt.

He thought he would explode the moment he mounted her, but he held himself back. As they fell into their rhythm, the woman began to take control. She made him go faster and faster—and then made him slow at the last possible moment. She knew exactly how to make it last, how to prolong their pleasure. She led Lysander Chase up and down love's ladder four times, a delicious sort of torture. Only then—their bodies drenched in sweat, hearts pounding, breath coming in frantic pants punctuated with cries and moans—did she allow him to finish.

Lysander Chase lay there with his face in the crick of the woman's neck for a long time. Maybe he even fell asleep. He wasn't sure. After a time the thoughts began to turn over in his mind. He should have known Thorne would have the best women, too.

The better the banker got to know Becker Thorne, the better he liked him. And now the billionaire wanted to do some deals with Chase's bank. It was almost too good to be true.

Yet for all the potential for financial gain there was in Thorne, Chase found that his mind kept returning to the woman beside him in the darkness. She was brilliant! Even with his eyes closed he could see her perfect beauty.

Lysander Chase began thinking—he knew they were foolish thoughts, but he didn't care. He couldn't get married again, not to a woman young enough to be his granddaughter, not to a *whore* whose name he didn't even know.

Yet Chase couldn't stop the unwelcome thoughts from coming. By God, thirty minutes in bed, and he was besotted with her!

He wanted to get up, to have a Scotch, walk around, smoke a cigar, get some air, and come to his senses, but he felt his desire stirring. The woman laughed quietly and gently thrust herself upward toward him. And all without one word of complaint about the handcuffs, which had to be hurting her ankles and wrists after the pounding he'd given her.

"You're fantastic," Chase said, lifting himself up on one elbow to admire her beautiful face as he rolled back onto her feverish body.

Chase gasped.

"What is troubling you, *amore mio*?"

Lysander Chase looked down at the face inches from him. He could not explain how he had failed to recognize her before. It must have been the candlelight. Or the shock, and excitement, of seeing the beautiful woman chained naked to the four-poster bed, waiting for him to take her.

But how could he have failed to have recognized before this that his beautiful and skillful lover was the Salvation Army's Captain Vittorini?

And what was *she* doing at Arlington Plantation, acting the part of a whore?

Chase's heart started to pound again—not in excitement but in a most disagreeable, disturbing way.

There was a rattle in the distance.

The bedroom door opened and closed.

Chase turned his head to see Becker Thorne grinning down at him.

"Here, old man," he said, throwing a robe at Chase. "Put some clothes on."

Lysander Chase pushed himself up off the woman, grabbing the robe angrily.

"You might have knocked," he snapped. Deflecting Chase's temper was his concern about the uncharacteristic pounding of his heart. Pain radiated up and down his left arm. It was just angina, he told himself, although he had never experienced it before. Chase, who'd just performed like a man of twenty-five, suddenly felt old and foolish.

Chase glanced at the woman. There was ambiguity in her smile. Was she laughing with him, or at him?

"I trust you enjoyed yourself."

Chase's face burned. He pulled the robe's belt around his waist and knotted it tightly, not answering.

"I find that it's always wise to move quickly to consummate

a business arrangement," the killer said, smiling at his own joke.

Chase cleared his throat. "I daresay that Nicoletta Vittorini is not a typical Salvation Army officer."

"Nicoletta is not really in the Salvation Army," the killer explained.

"I'm not surprised to hear that." It was difficult for him to keep his eyes off the woman. She didn't seem the least embarrassed. "No offense intended, my dear," the banker added.

"None taken, *amore mio*."

Nicoletta moved her hips slightly and put the tip of her tongue against her upper lip. Chase began to wonder how long it would take for him to get Thorne out of the room.

"The Salvation Army uniform is a wonderful disguise," the killer said. "It makes her nearly invisible."

"I suppose that you sent her in to do reconnaissance when you started thinking about investing in property in this part of the state," Chase said.

The killer ignored Chase's statement. "I took the liberty of videotaping your little romp. I have the latest cellular cameras and low-light cassettes. There, there, and there. I wanted to get your best angle."

Chase looked at the places in the shadows Thorne had indicated. He couldn't see cameras, but he had no doubt that they were there.

"You bastard," Chase said.

"Insurance," Thorne said in a matter-of-fact voice.

"Come on, Becker. I'd have to be crazy not to do business with you."

"But I never do business unless I hold all the cards."

"You'll never get the bank, if that's what you're hinting at." Chase began to absently massage his left arm. The throbbing ached as much as if he'd been punched hard in the bicep.

"I don't want ownership, just control of the board."

"Fuck you!"

"Ah, but it is you who has been doing the fucking, Lysander. I hate to imagine what would happen if pornographic tapes featuring your latest sexual exploits begin to circulate around town. Imagine what it would do to your reputation, and to your bank's reputation."

"If you want to play hardball," Chase said, "play hardball. Go ahead and leak the tape. Twenty years ago it might have ruined me, but people are quite used to that sort of thing these days. It'll be embarrassing, but I'll survive. After my daughter Lydia's antics, I've become quite immune to embarrassment."

Despite the pain in his arm, Chase was able to give Thorne a calm, confident smile.

"I'll also throw every lawyer in the state of Mississippi at you," the banker added in a matter-of-fact voice. "I know that doesn't impress you, but think about it. It will be obvious to any number of people that the videotape was made here at Arlington Plantation, implying complicity on your part."

The killer sniffed at him and looked unimpressed.

"I'm well aware of the fact that you can hire the best Harvard lawyers, Thorne, but don't make the mistake of thinking you can fuck me over in my own state. Chases have been running Mississippi since before the War Between the States. I'll have you for lunch. You'll get into court and discover that I hold the mortgage on the judge's house, and that his son has a loan application pending with my bank. Ask your smart, expensive New York lawyers about getting 'home-towned.' "

The killer shook his head, chuckling.

"You've got balls of steel, Lysander. I'll give you that. You really are a player. Maybe we can do business—as equals."

"That's more like it," Chase said, thrusting his hands into the pockets of the robe. He forced himself to ignore the pain in his chest and arm. This was no time to show weakness. "I'll never trust you, Becker, but I understand you, and I think you understand me. I think we can do business. But I have one condition."

The killer's left eyebrow went up.

"The young lady. I want her."

"Nicoletta?" The killer looked surprised. "Fuck her as many times as you like and with my compliments."

"That's not what I mean." Chase smiled wolfishly. "I want her until I get tired of her. It could be awhile. Weeks. Months. Maybe even a year. I'll put her up in a house here in town at my own expense."

The killer moved to the bedside and reached down to caress the woman's face with the back of his fingers.

"It's rather irritating to be bested at my own game." There was more sadness than anger in his voice.

"I've been at it a few years longer than you," Chase said. He allowed the merest note of triumph to show itself in his voice, not to gloat, but to remind Thorne who had won.

"Still, I make it a personal habit never to get into a game unless I'm ready to go all the way."

The smile froze on Chase's mouth. The pain in his heart flared.

"Listen, Becker . . ."

"No," the killer said savagely, "you listen. I play to *win*."

The knife seemed to materialize in Thorne's hand. Whether he'd been hiding it there all along or pulled it from a pocket or sleeve was impossible for Lysander Chase to say, but suddenly it was there, a chilling symbol of Thorne's claim that he was willing to go however far was necessary to achieve his ends.

The pain in the banker's arm and chest was so great now that he involuntarily pulled his arm up, holding his wrist against his heart as if pressure would deaden the pain.

The bulging muscles in Thorne's face and neck relaxed. The anger left his face as it had appeared. Thorne looked at Chase and smiled.

"My God, Becker," Chase said. "I almost thought you were going to—"

The words caught in Chase's throat as he watched Thorne turn and plunge the knife savagely into Nicoletta Vittorini's heart, thrusting it in to the hilt.

Nicoletta's body convulsed upward from the bed. Her mouth opened as if she were about to scream, but there was no sound. A sickening tremor went through her body as her involuntary nervous system reacted to the lethal shock of having a steel blade plunged into her heart, the handcuffs that held her wrists and ankles making any defensive reaction impossible.

After a moment longer, Nicoletta's head turned to one side and she lay there very still, her sightless eyes seemingly focused on the flickering candelabra.

White and black spots began to swirl across Chase's field of vision. He clasped both hands over his heart. There seemed to be a fire in his chest, turning and turning, choking off his breath, making it hard to remain standing.

The killer ran back by the door. He took a remote control device from his pocket and waved it in the air.

"It's show time!"

He pointed the remote control toward the three places he said the cameras were hidden, pressing a button on the handheld device three times. Then he returned the controller to his pocket and rushed forward.

"Jesus Christ, Lysander," the killer said with mock horror, "what have you done to the poor girl? You've killed her!"

Lysander involuntarily moved backward until his legs bumped the chaise lounge. His knees buckled. He sat down hard.

"That ought to do it," the killer said, glancing at his wristwatch. "Out of tape, I'm afraid."

Thorne went to the bedside and touched the woman's face lightly.

"Your friends at the country club might be willing to overlook your sexual escapades, Lysander, but do you think they'll be as broad-minded when they learn that you handcuffed this poor woman to a bed, then raped and murdered her?"

Lysander Chase tried to speak, but he didn't have enough breath to get the words out.

"Of course, if you decide to be more agreeable, I can arrange for none of this to ever become known to the police. I can make her disappear." He nodded toward the corpse. "There're plenty of places on the grounds of Arlington Plantation a body can be made to disappear. It's happened before. Believe me," he added with heavy significance, "I know."

Chase looked at the killer with disbelief. He really would go to any lengths to win.

"But now my terms have changed. I don't just want to control the bank board. I'm afraid I'll have to have the bank, too. It seems only fair. Your recalcitrance has cost me the services of a valuable and talented employee as well as incurring certain other expenses and risks. Well, Lysander, what's it going to be? Do we finally have a deal we can both live with?"

"How could . . . you have . . . killed her?" Chase asked between breathless gasps.

"You can have anything you want in this world, Lysander, if you are willing to do what it takes. If you want to be a real player, you must forget the mindless taboos that keep most people from aspiring to true power."

The killer leaned down and licked the trickle of blood flowing down the dead woman's side.

"You must realize that the greatest and most powerful good is *evil*."

The killer ran a long forefinger through the blood pooling on the bed and drew an upside-down star—a pentagram—on her naked belly. Licking the remaining blood from the digit, he looked at Chase through his eyebrows and gave him a grin that could only be described as demonic.

"You should try some of her blood. I think you would discover it would serve as a powerful tonic for your tired heart."

He patted the bed.

"You do still want to fuck her, don't you? Please, do go ahead."

Chase had to put one hand down on the chaise lounge to keep himself from falling over.

"I'll leave the room, if it is your modesty that is holding you back. You'll like making love to a beautiful corpse. I know I do. And afterwards I'll tell you secrets about this town that even you don't know."

"Call an ambulance," Chase asked, alarmed to hear the weakness in his own voice.

The killer grasped the knife sticking from the dead woman's left breast and drew it out. It was like taking a cork out of the woman's heart. A thick spray of arterial blood shot upward, instantly soaking the canopy, staining the gossamer bed curtains.

Chase began to retch.

The killer bent double with laughter.

"If you could see . . ." Thorne collapsed into a chair, his face in his hands. "If you could see the look"—his entire body convulsed—"on your face."

Chase was still sitting on the chaise lounge, but he'd fallen forward, his hands clutching his chest so that his arms and upper torso rested against his knees. He looked up past his eyebrows at Thorne in mute horror.

"But what kind of host am I? This was all supposed to be for your pleasure. I seem to have ruined everything. If you don't want to fuck a dead woman, then perhaps a living corpse is more to your tastes."

The sound of creaking wood came from the four-poster bed, then a splintering. There was a sharp *ping!* followed by a startling *whoosh* when a link from one of the handcuffs broke free and shot through the air.

The dead woman sat up in the bed and smiled seductively at him. She was covered with blood, her hair matted with it. This was no illusion. Chase could see the gaping wound in her breast, a sucking hole in her heart from which blood continued to pump with each heartbeat. This last observation replayed itself in Chase's frayed mind: *with each heartbeat.*

But surely there could be no heartbeat. . . .

The skin on her wrists and ankles was raw and bloody. Chase thought he could see *bone* on her left leg. The cherry-wood uprights on the four-poster bed had been scarred and splintered from the superhuman strength used to break the metal handcuffs.

But something was happening as he watched—a thing that was at once miraculous and horrifying. The terrible wound in her breast began to close in upon itself. The shackle burns on her arms and legs began to disappear.

Chase's eyes locked onto hers.

Her hands came up, reaching out to him.

"Come to me, my lover," Princess Nicoletta Vittorini di Medusa said, blood bubbling on her lips. Her blood teeth, now distended, were plainly visible as she spoke. "Come to me and know the death that is eternal life."

Chase sat bold upright, his spine ramrod straight. His stare remained locked on Nicoletta, but then his eyes changed focus. An unnatural sound came from the banker's throat, something between a gasp and a rattle.

Lysander Chase fell backward, stone dead, his body tumbling onto the floor.

"Thus the Fury of the Lord struck down another of the children of wickedness."

Nicoletta hissed angrily and began to crawl across the floor toward Lysander Chase's inert form. John Wilkes Booth's delusions had become increasingly tedious during the past fifty years.

She grabbed Lysander Chase by the hair and dragged his body toward her, sinking her teeth in his neck, feeding greedily, drinking in the mortal's precious blood with great sucking swallows.

IV
Old Enemies

9:30 P.M. Friday—Marcus Cuttler whistled through his teeth as he approached the plantation great house, ignoring the Bach organ fugue coming at him from the house. Whistling past the graveyard, he told himself. Or maybe on his way to the graveyard.

He made a quick assessment of his courage. He admitted he was afraid, but anybody in his shoes would be. He was also ready for a confrontation. His father had preached nonviolence, but Marcus didn't believe in turning the other cheek. He'd never gone out of his way to avoid a fight. Still, he knew a readiness to fight was not proof of real courage.

What would his father do in his place?

Marcus knew his motives were less than pure. No, anything but. Not when Nathan Bedford Forrest Nightingale was involved.

Given the opportunity, Marcus thought grimly, he would kill Nightingale.

Marcus hung back at the corner, waiting for the arrivals in front of him to get through the front door.

The grounds of Arlington Plantation were festooned with Japanese lanterns. Tiny white firefly lights flickered in the trees and bushes. Illuminaria burned along the walkways. The air smelled of citronella from the candles. There were no mosquitoes, unusual for a hot August night in Mississippi.

The congestion at the doorway dissolved. Marcus waited a minute longer and then moved quickly toward the entry, taking the steps two at a time.

The double screens had been hooked open, and both double doors inside were pushed back, opening the foyer to the outdoors. Zaharim materialized just before Marcus made it through the last threshold, blocking the way with his body, which was nearly as wide as it was tall.

"Ah, Mr. Angry," the Slav said in heavily accented English. "I do not believe your name is on the guest list."

Past Zaharim, the entry hall was filled with costumed people drinking champagne. Marcus had to raise his voice to be heard over the organ.

"Eugene said he'd get me in," Marcus said, lying. He hadn't spoken to his best friend since the night he'd left him at Arlington to share Thorne's cocaine. Since then, Eugene had virtually lived at the plantation. "But never mind that. A woman has collapsed outside. I think someone may have attacked her."

"Not so loud," Zaharim hissed, already pushing his way past Marcus. "Come. You will show me now."

Marcus had to run to get back in front of Zaharim.

"She's over there," he said. "Around the corner. Beside the bushes. Shouldn't we call an ambulance or something?"

Zaharim didn't answer but continued toward the shape of a woman sprawled on the ground. Victoria Buchanan was stretched out beside the bougainvillea that surrounded the great house. She was on her back, both knees to the left, face to the right, one arm thrown up, the back of the wrist resting on her forehead. Her eyes were closed.

Zaharim planted his feet and scowled.

"Victoria!" Marcus cried in a low voice. "Is she . . . ?"

"Not dead yet," Zaharim said irritably, getting down on one knee. There was no neck trauma, and her color was good. She hadn't been bled. The Slav began to shake his head angrily. "Scorpio," he muttered to himself. The master would be displeased.

Marcus hit Zaharim from behind, slamming into him with his shoulder. Zaharim rocked forward but caught himself before he toppled over Victoria. Marcus threw his arms around the Slav and tried to wrestle him down, but Zaharim did not budge. The squat Bulgarian stood without apparent exertion, Marcus clinging to him. Zaharim lowered his head, like a bull concentrating its rage prior to the charge, then rolled his massive shoulders in a slow, powerful movement that ended with a snap. Marcus's legs flew but he kept his grip, feeling himself whipped like the tail of a kite.

Zaharim brought an elbow back sharply into Marcus's ribs.

The blow knocked the wind out of Marcus. Marcus had the brief sensation of floating before he hit the grass and rolled over twice. He scrambled to his feet without losing the momentum of his fall, his fists up, switching to a defensive posture.

The Bulgarian came toward him, lumbering in his side-to-side gait.

Something momentarily distracted Zaharim's attention—a flicker of light in the window above. Marcus followed Zaharim's glance and saw the silhouette of a man holding a candelabra in one of the windows on the second floor. He was just there a moment and then was gone. There was something familiar about the outline in the window. Marcus knew that shape. It was Lysander Chase.

Zaharim grunted and drew back a fist.

Marcus was bracing himself when David Parker finally materialized from the shadows. Like Marcus before him, Parker threw his arms around Zaharim from behind. Marcus was surprised to see that the Slav couldn't shake David, whose feet remained firmly planted on the ground. The Slav was unaccustomed to being bested in a contest of strength. His eyes were wild, and a film of white spittle gathered at the corners of his mouth, which was distorted in an animal snarl.

"Come on, Doctor!" David complained. "We don't have all night."

Dr. Chesterfield emerged from behind the tree where he had been hiding.

Marcus saw Wolf Toland come out of the shadows and help Victoria to her feet. The little red-haired Austrian watched impatiently as Dr. Chesterfield opened his doctor's bag and proceeded to fumble inside it. A syringe finally materialized in the doctor's hand. He jabbed the needle into Zaharim's shoulder.

There was a burst of laughter from within the house.

Ten more seconds passed. The Bulgarian's body went limp in David's arms.

"That should do it," Dr. Chesterfield said, stepping back. "Put him on his side. We don't want him to choke on his tongue." The doctor knelt beside the unconscious man and took his pulse. "He should be out at least three hours."

"That will be more than sufficient," Toland advised.

"I wish we'd brought a blanket. He should be kept warm."

"He'll be all right, Dr. Chesterfield."

"One down, two to go," Marcus said gamely, lightly touching his ribs where Zaharim had elbowed him. Nothing seemed to be cracked or broken, but it still hurt like hell.

"I regret that the other two will be less easily handled," Toland said.

"I'll see you inside," Victoria said, touching David's arm lightly as she passed him.

Marcus and the others stood and watched Victoria disappear around the corner, on her way into the Arlington Plantation great house, alone.

Marcus and Dr. Chesterfield skirted the pool behind the greenhouse, where Vampire Convention revelers in their time-fracturing costumes stood sipping glasses of champagne and chatting in the roles of whichever Lucretia Noire characters they happened to be impersonating for the weekend.

Marcus, who had been leading the way, turned and found that the brick path he'd been covering in brisk strides ended in a cul de sac of lilac bushes arranged around a small fountain.

"This way," Dr. Chesterfield said, indicating that the disoriented Marcus should follow.

The caretaker's cottage was situated one hundred yards from the back porch of the Arlington Plantation great house—past the summer kitchen, past the greenhouse, past the stables and kitchen garden, halfway to the slaves' cabins and the cotton fields that extended in every direction.

The caketaker's cottage—or "overseer's home," as it had been known when Victoria Buchanan's family owned the plantation—was constructed of brick, like the slave cabins that stood in the distance, their backs to the pine windbreak. The slave quarters lacked any kind of adornment, but the caretaker's cottage sported the modest degree of nineteenth-century filigree that befitted the status of the mulatto freedmen the Buchanans had once employed to oversee their field hands. The wooden railing running the length of the front porch had been intricately milled, and the posts had been similarly dandified.

Unlike the cabins—which had been unoccupied since the

Great Depression and were mere shells of themselves, their roofs and ceiling joists rotted completely away—the caretaker's cottage was well kept. The wood-shingle roof was in good repair. The mortar had been recently tuck-pointed. The bricks had been given a fresh coat of canary yellow paint the summer before. The cottage had remained continuously occupied since the Buchanans built it. The present resident was James Guy, an elderly black gardener who'd been a member of the church Marcus Cuttler's family belonged to since the days when Marcus's grandfather was the preacher.

James Guy was the best fisherman in Jerusalem, and Marcus, like half the people who'd grown up in town, had gone to the old man for angling advice more times than he could count. Marcus and Dr. Chesterfield had both assured the others that they could depend on "Uncle James" to help them lure Nathan Bedford Forrest Nightingale to the caretaker's cottage, where they'd get him out of the way as they had Zaharim.

There were two pickups outside the cottage. Nearer to Marcus and Dr. Chesterfield was Uncle James's old Ford, with the rack he'd built in the back to hold an assortment of rakes, shovels, and other groundskeeping implements. Marcus recognized the second pickup instantly in the light thrown by the lamp outside the cottage's back door. It was the same Ford he'd driven the night Thorne had sent him and Eugene to fetch the rusting neon Pegasus sign at the run-down little country gas station.

"Damn!" Marcus exclaimed under his breath.

Dr. Chesterfield recognized Nightingale's vehicle, too.

"What are we going to do now?" Dr. Chesterfield asked.

"Improvise," Marcus said, and started for the cottage.

Marcus rapped on the door, making it rattle against the frame.

Dr. Chesterfield gave the young man a warning look over the top of his glasses. Marcus took no heed of the doctor's reproach and knocked even more loudly.

"Uncle James?"

They peered through the screen, old and heavy, the metal mesh weather-blackened. There was a single lamp on in the living room but no sign of the resident—or his guest.

"Uncle James?"

Marcus pulled open the door and pushed it back far enough for the old man to follow behind him.

"Uncle James? It's Marcus Cuttler. Is anybody home?"

Dr. Chesterfield's chin tilted up as he looked around the room, and his nose crinkled. He reached out and touched Marcus's arm. He used his eyes to tell Marcus to stop.

The furniture consisted of second-hand items, clean and serviceable if a bit worn and unfashionable, the sort of cast-offs that people use to make habitable rooms for servants and hired hands. The only personal possessions in the scrupulously clean room were James Guy's sports books. Uncle James had once played pro baseball in the Negro league and baseball remained his passion, along with fishing. All of the books in the cheap fiberboard bookshelf beside the door were about baseball, Marcus saw, scanning the spines. Ted Williams's *The Season of the Kid* lay open on the coffee table. A baseball Jackie Robinson had autographed in blue ink sat on top of the television on a little wooden stand covered with a glass globe.

"He must have stepped out," Marcus said in his normal voice.

"I'm going to have a look in the kitchen," Dr. Chesterfield said in a low voice with a tone so serious that it startled Marcus. "You wait here."

The door to the kitchen was mounted on a swivel hinge with a spring so that it closed itself. The doctor pushed the door open a few inches with his fingertips and looked through the crack.

"Wait here," Dr. Chesterfield repeated, and slipped through the door, using his body to block Marcus's view of whatever he'd seen.

Without pausing to think, Marcus ignored Dr. Chesterfield's instruction and followed.

The nauseating stench in the kitchen was overwhelming.

"When you've been a doctor as long as I've been, your nose gets pretty smart," Dr. Chesterfield said with grim professional pride.

Marcus stood with his hand over his mouth, his eyes wide. He thought he was going to throw up, but he didn't.

"You going to be okay, young fella?"

Marcus nodded. "I was afraid it was Uncle James."

"So was I."

"Are those a duck's wings?"

"I'd say they were from a goose, judging from the size. They're held in place with surgical pins. I wonder where they came from. I don't think I've ever seen them outside of an operating room."

The goose's wings had been attached to the calf at the shoulders. Sheep's horns had been screwed straight into the dead brute's skull. The bloody drill lay on the floor against the wall next to a power screwdriver. The result was a sort of mythological hybrid—a winged calf with the horns of a ram. It reminded Marcus of the pictures of the idol Baal he'd seen in illustrated Bibles—and made him think of the rusty Pegasus sign Thorne had hired him and Eugene to move to the plantation.

"What does it mean?"

"I'm not qualified to say, Marcus. A psychiatrist who specialized in treating extremely disturbed patients might have a clue. I'd say it had some sort of religious significance—at least to Nathan Bedford Forrest Nightingale."

Marcus startled at the sound of his father's killer's name.

"It looks a little like an Old Testament idol, doesn't it?" Dr. Chesterfield said, echoing Marcus's own thoughts. "Pagan idols in the Bible were made out of gold, but this one is made of corruptible flesh. Good God, what a stench! Judging from the smell alone, it's fortunate the screens are in good condition or this room would be swarming with bottle flies."

"Where do you suppose Uncle . . ." The words caught in Marcus's throat as he followed the path of Dr. Chesterfield's eyes, which were trained on the pool of blood leaking from under the door of the old Philco refrigerator.

"Doc, don't," Marcus said involuntarily, but Dr. Chesterfield ignored the request. He straddled the pool of blood and gingerly opened the door, spilling a snarl of reeking intestines out onto the floor.

There was a casserole dish on the bottom shelf. A bit of something Marcus couldn't make out jutted from beneath the opaque lid. Dr. Chesterfield lifted the lid and quickly put it back down. Even Marcus, who knew next to nothing about physiology, recognized the organ in the casserole dish.

Dr. Chesterfield stepped back from the refrigerator, pulling a handkerchief from his pocket, with which he proceeded to wipe his hands. "It's a human heart. The viscera are human, too, I'd guess just from looking at them."

"Are they . . . ?"

"I don't think they belong to James Guy, if that is what you're wondering," Dr. Chesterfield said, putting away his handkerchief. "The heart belonged to someone much smaller than James Guy, most likely a woman."

Marcus's delayed reaction was as sudden as it was violent. He rushed past the doctor and broke into a run. He began to retch before he reached the bathroom.

"You go back and wait in the van," Dr. Chesterfield said from the living room a few minutes later. His tone was patient, even comforting. "I've got enough Demerol in this hypodermic to handle a dozen Nightingales."

Marcus came into the living room drying his face on a towel.

"I'm staying," Marcus said.

Dr. Chesterfield studied the young man's face a moment, then began to smile. "Good," he said. "See the job through to the end."

Marcus nodded.

Dr. Chesterfield found Uncle James's bottle of Echo Valley whiskey in the rolltop and made Marcus take a drink.

"Hear that?"

"Your ears are playing tricks on you," Dr. Chesterfield said, taking the bottle of Echo Valley and drinking.

"No, listen."

Someone was singing as he walked through the gardens toward the caretaker's cottage, his baritone voice carrying above the organ back at the great house. Marcus and Dr. Chesterfield looked at one another. They recognized the voice, and the song.

> *"I wish I was in Dixie,*
> *Away, away!*
> *In Dixieland I'll make my stand,*
> *To live and die in Dixie!"*

Marcus grabbed a baseball bat—a souvenir from Uncle James's days as a player—and headed for the door.

"What are you going to do with that?" Dr. Chesterfield whispered frantically.

"Insurance."

"Marcus! You follow him in and distract him, like the detective said. When Nightingale turns, I'll give him an injection that will have him out before he hits the floor."

"But what if he just gets into his truck and leaves?"

A frantic look crossed Dr. Chesterfield's face. "I'll call him from the porch. He'll come my way. You distract him. Same plan. Now outside! Quick, or he'll see you!"

It was such a simple plan that it had to work. Unfortunately, all the things they hadn't thought of began to become obvious as soon as Marcus dashed outside alone into the darkness. To begin with, there was no place to hide outside the cottage. Unlike the great house, which was surrounded by bougainvillea, the cottage sat in a neat square of lawn. There was not even a tree within thirty feet.

Marcus's shoes scraped against the pea gravel as he dashed for Nightingale's truck. He'd have to hide behind it, or he'd be too far away to keep a close eye on the only door in or out of the cottage. Besides, he didn't want Nightingale to come down the walk and spot him running for the nearest clump of trees.

The singing was close now.

"In Dixieland where I was born,
Early on one frosty morn . . ."

Marcus hefted the Louisville Slugger in his hands and flexed his shoulders.

The singing had stopped. Maybe Nightingale sensed something was wrong. Maybe, Marcus worried, the murderer had seen him running across the grass.

A stick snapped.

Marcus's heart began to pound.

Heavy footsteps came down the brick path.

A trickle of perspiration ran down Marcus's neck. The next thing he knew, his shirt was soaked with sweat. He held the bat so tightly clenched in his hands that it trembled. He twisted the bat, feeling the sticky tape grab against his palms.

The sound of boots on the cottage walk shook Marcus like a slap across the face.

Jesus, he moved *fast*! Marcus saw Nightingale in his mind's eye, his long stride biting off stretches of ground as he walked.

The screen slammed.

Marcus jumped up from his hiding place. Jesus God in heaven, the killer was in the cottage with Dr. Chesterfield! Marcus could hear their voices, indistinct and distant.

This was a *stupid* damned plan, Marcus thought, breaking into a run.

There was a loud crash in the cottage, the sound of furniture turning over and glass breaking.

"Please, God!" Marcus said to himself, already close enough to the cottage for his eyes to measure the distance he would have to jump to get past the steps and land directly on the porch.

Dr. Chesterfield cried out in pain. It was nothing intelligible, the anguished cry of animal terror.

The Louisville Slugger held in front of him with both hands, Marcus Cuttler hit the screen door so hard that the frame disintegrated. A piece of splintered wood extruding a bent nail and trailing a ragged edge of screen lashed Marcus across the face, drawing blood as he crashed by, but he did not even feel it.

Nathan Bedford Forrest Nightingale's enormous body seemed to fill the room. Nightingale's back was to the door. He did not turn to face Marcus. Indeed, he gave no outward sign that he was aware of Marcus's presence.

Dr. Chesterfield lay sprawled on the floor between Nightingale's straddling legs. The old man looked small and crumpled beneath his attacker, an aged David struck down by a vengeful Goliath. The doctor was unconscious, his arms and legs splayed unnaturally.

Nightingale's right arm was raised high, nearly high enough to reach the cottage ceiling with the weapon he'd just used to pummel Dr. Chesterfield. It was a squarish mallet made of light-colored wood, its face covered with rows of dime-sized pyramids—a kitchen meat-tenderizing tool.

"No!" Marcus shouted the moment he realized the mallet was already beginning its journey downward toward the supine old man.

Nightingale gave no sign he heard. The path his arm and the makeshift weapon made were a blur. Dr. Chesterfield's helpless body leaped into the air as if shot with a massive current of electricity, coming down on its side, resting limply against Nightingale's boot. Only Nightingale's legs prevented the doctor's body from rolling completely over from the force of the blow, which snapped the mallet head from its handle and sent it flying.

Nightingale half turned to look at Marcus with his yellow

eyes, the splintered mallet handle hanging in his hand as if he was unaware he had broken it against Dr. Chesterfield's head. And the doctor's head—even though Marcus tried not to look at the disfigurement the blows had caused, it was impossible to ignore the spray of blood on the rag rug and couch.

Marcus met and held Nightingale's stare. The young man's breathing was fast and shallow. The shock and incomprehension were leaving him, forced out by the rage that was building stronger with every breath.

"The nigger preacher's boy," Nightingale said in a mocking voice. "Thorne said it was a mistake to destroy the weed but not the seed."

"Where's Uncle James?" Marcus demanded through clenched teeth.

Nightingale grinned. "What's one old nigger more or less to the world?"

Marcus acted out of instinct and anger. He swung the bat at Nightingale as hard as he could, not trying to hit any particular part of his body, merely attempting to inflict whatever injury he could.

Nightingale tried to dodge, but there was no room. There was a loud crack when the blow landed against his left arm, sending him flying sideways. He crashed into the couch and flipped it over, along with an end table and the lamp sitting on it.

Marcus glanced at the bat, thinking he had broken it. He was wrong. It wasn't the bat that had broken, but Nightingale's arm.

Nightingale scrambled to his feet, his lunatic smile intact. The sickening bend in his left arm made it appear that he had two elbows, one in the usual place, the second midway between the first and the shoulder. Nightingale slowly raised his good hand. In it, he held the knife Uncle James used to fillet fish; the knife was sharp enough to shave with, Marcus knew.

"First thing I'm gonna do, boy, is I'm gonna cut off your balls and make you eat 'em."

Nightingale came across the upended couch with astonishing speed, considering his age, size, and injury. Marcus barely got out of the way of the flashing blade, whipping the baseball bat at his assailant to parry the attack as he spun away. The bat caught Nightingale in the ribs and sent him crashing to the floor, where the big man lay, panting.

Marcus wanted to smash the bat down on Nightingale's

head, but something kept him from killing Nightingale while he lay there, dazed and injured.

"Get up!" Marcus commanded, furious at himself for his strange inability to do the one thing he wanted to do more than anything else in the world—kill Nathan Bedford Forrest Nightingale. "Get up, you bastard."

Nightingale rolled to his right side and tried to push himself up on his good arm—the knife still gripped tight in his fist—but he collapsed after a few seconds of trying.

"Get up!" Marcus shouted.

"I can't," Nightingale said between gasps, a mixture of blood and spit drooling out of the corner of his mouth. "You fucked me up good, boy."

"Get up, you bastard, or I'll kill you where you lie!"

"I can't," Nightingale protested again. "I'm too busted up inside."

"Jesus Christ!" Marcus swore. This was not how he'd wanted it to end.

Marcus looked over at Dr. Chesterfield and winced. The doctor had a syringe of Demerol in his jacket pocket. Marcus would do as they'd originally planned and shoot the serial killer full of dope. That would get him out of the way for the rest of the night. He bent to pat Dr. Chesterfield's jacket pocket, hoping the syringe hadn't been broken in Nightingale's attack. It wasn't in that pocket. Marcus gingerly slipped his hand under the doctor to reach the other pocket in the tuxedo jacket.

Nightingale flew up off the floor and shot across the room at Marcus.

The young man's reaction was entirely automatic.

Marcus began to jump to his feet the second he saw Nightingale coming at him from the corner of his eye. He'd held the bat in his left hand while searching for the syringe. Now, as he stood, he started to swing the bat one-handed in the direction of the charging man. He got his right hand on the bat, too, as it came around in front, putting his shoulders behind it, uncoiling his entire torso as he turned toward his attacker, increasing the power behind the bat's sweeping arc at the moment of farthest extension with a snap of his wrists.

The bat hit Nightingale squarely in the forehead.

There was no question he was dead.

The Louisville Slugger had left an oddly regular depression

in Nightingale's skull that made it look as if his head was made of molded clay rather than bone. Nightingale's yellow eyes bulged grotesquely from their sockets, popped out of their orbits by the bat's impact. He was bleeding from his eyes as well as from his nose, mouth, and ears. Curiously, Marcus noticed, there was no little blood around the place where the bat had struck Nightingale's head, only a horrible purple bruise.

The bat slipped from Marcus's fingers and fell to the floor. He felt no exultation. Instead, a powerful wave of grief washed over him. Marcus had spent most of his life wishing Nightingale were dead, yet he would have never bartered the gentle old doctor for his father's killer's life.

Where was the justice in that?

Where was the justice in anything?

Marcus covered his eyes with his hands.

"Ohhhhh."

Marcus looked at Nightingale in horror before realizing his enemy was, in fact, quite dead. The moan had come from Dr. Chesterfield. Marcus hurried to the old man's side. He was afraid to do any more than put his hand lightly against his shoulder. Who knew what injuries he'd suffered and what damage Marcus might unwittingly do by moving him into a more comfortable position?

"Take it easy, Doc. You're going to be okay." Marcus cringed to hear himself utter such clichés, but what could he say for comfort?"

Dr. Chesterfield tried to tell him something, but Marcus couldn't make it out. He bent lower. The doctor's lips moved, and a flow of blood and broken teeth dribbled out.

"Hop tile," the doctor whispered.

"I don't understand," Marcus said gently.

"Gym me to da hop tile."

Get me to the hospital!

"Can I move you?"

The doctor moved his head slightly.

"Jaw," he said, the words barely intelligible. "Smash jaw."

"I'll get the truck."

Dr. Chesterfield grabbed the sleeve of Marcus's coat as the young man began to stand. Marcus didn't need to wait to understand the frightened question in the doctor's eyes.

"Nightingale is dead."

The look in Dr. Chesterfield's eyes changed to relief.

The keys to Uncle James's truck were hanging on the cupboard key caddie. Marcus would put Dr. Chesterfield out in back of the truck so that he would be more comfortable. He'd need pillows and blankets from the bedroom. Uncle James—poor Uncle James—wouldn't mind. Marcus wondered where they'd find James, or if they ever would.

Marcus opened the door to Uncle James's bedroom—the first door past the bathroom—and flipped on the light.

Eugene Jones was stretched out on the middle of James's bed, legs crossed at the ankles, hands at his sides, eyes closed. He looked like he was asleep, but Marcus knew he couldn't possibly have slept through the noise of the fight in the cottage. His skin had an unusual color, too. It looked chalky.

There was a dinner plate on the floor next to the bed. On it were a razor blade, a rolled-up dollar bill, and the biggest mound of cocaine Marcus had ever seen—maybe an ounce. Eugene had never made it to the last line he'd prepared, an enormous finger of white powder a half-inch wide and four inches long.

Marcus stood there for a moment and looked down on his friend. He was so tall that his legs hung off the edge of the bed. He was wearing a new Reebok warm-up suit and Air Jordans.

Marcus didn't cry. He had no tears for his best friend. Becker Thorne may have provided the drugs, but what had happened to Eugene Jones was something Eugene Jones did to himself.

Marcus closed the door and went to the second bedroom, feeling an inexpressibly heavy sadness weigh down on him.

Marcus's mouth set as he thought of Becker Thorne and his role in Eugene's death.

He'd get Dr. Chesterfield to the hospital, then he was coming back for Thorne.

He got what he needed from the bedroom and brought the truck around to the front. He made the back of the truck ready, ignoring the sound of the continuing party up in the great house, then went back into the cottage for Dr. Chesterfield.

Marcus carefully wrapped Dr. Chesterfield in a blanket and lifted him. The old man was even heavier than he looked. Since the doctor had passed out again, he was unable to do anything to make it easier for Marcus to carry him.

Marcus somehow got the doctor out to the truck. He was gently lowering the old man toward the bed he'd made for him in the rear of the pickup when Dr. Chesterfield started to wake up. Feeling himself unsteadily held in Marcus's arms, the doctor instinctively reached out and grabbed for Marcus. The syringe, which Dr. Chesterfield had held concealed in the palm of his left hand since Nightingale burst into the cottage, jabbed itself into Marcus's back.

"Ow!" Marcus complained, letting Dr. Chesterfield drop the last few inches toward the pillows, where he slipped back into unconsciousness.

Marcus grabbed for the hypodermic dangling from his jacket between his spine and right shoulder blade. As his hands clutched empty air, he felt the Demerol entering his bloodstream, filling him with an indescribable peacefulness.

He stumbled and caught himself on the truck with his left hand.

Marcus knew he had to resist the comfortable warmth spreading quickly through his body. He knew he had to struggle against the powerful compulsion to drift into a deep and dreamless sleep.

It was no good. Dr. Chesterfield had injected Marcus with too much of the drug.

Marcus collapsed into the back of the pickup next to Dr. Chesterfield, and there they both stayed, insensate to the darkness and danger surrounding them.

V

Vintage Wine

9:45 P.M. Friday—"I hope they let us in."

"Fear not, dear girl. Gianni Rourke is welcome everywhere."

Joan Oppenheim nodded, hoping he was right, and turned the Volvo down the tree-lined lane that terminated at the Arlington Plantation great house. Joan had doubts about the welcome they'd receive at Arlington. While most opera cognoscenti would be delighted to have the great conductor turn up uninvited at a party, Joan's experience with undergraduates had made her painfully aware that most people could barely identify Beethoven, much less Gianni Rourke.

"I only wish supper had been better," Rourke fussed.

Their meal at the finest restaurant in Jerusalem, Mississippi, was a disappointment for the epicurean, who'd suspected the coq au vin had been prepared with inferior cognac and pronounced his bottle of Fortant de France Merlot "pedestrian and astringent."

Joan had thought the food was rather good, although she would have scarcely tasted it if Rourke hadn't peppered her with endless inquires about such things as whether she agreed that there was a bit too much cilantro in the Santa Fe soup. She'd wanted to talk opera with Rourke, but his interest was so tightly focused on food that Joan thought it was more like having dinner with a famous chef instead of a famous maestro.

And now, Joan thought with a mixture of anticipation and apprehension, she would with a little luck learn the secret of the chimera whose presence was found throughout her recent research, the talented and mysterious entity A1.

Joan saw silhouetted bodies outlined in golden light against the mansion's windows. The light had a beautiful opalescent quality—candlelight. Guests spilled out onto the veranda, filling the night air with conversation and laughter. And music. The music would have been strange for anything but an ersatz Vampire Convention—Bach fugues. At least it wasn't Mozart, Joan thought.

Joan let Rourke take her by the arm and lead her gallantly up the front steps.

It was interesting to see the array of amusing costumes, some quite elaborate, worn by the guests. Rourke, of course, fit right in with his white Tennessee Williams suit and silver-headed cane. Joan was plainly underdressed in her suit, though she realized it would serve as a sort of camouflage amid so much fanciful plumage. Approximately half the guests wore modern evening wear—classic black tuxes for the men, long dresses for the women. A few of the men in short white tuxedo jackets wore opera masks—servants, apparently, she thought.

A servant was stationed inside the entrance. He stepped in front of Joan and Rourke as they entered and bowed formally.

Joan blushed when she realized the other guests were staring at them, curious about the latest arrivals.

"Good evening, sir and madam. Your invitations, please."

The smile froze on Joan's face. It was obvious they would get no further.

"Of course, my good man," Rourke said genially. "Here they are."

The rotund conductor handed the doorman not invitations but *money.*

The doorman discreetly crumpled the one hundred-dollar bill in his hand. He neither smiled nor frowned but slipped the money in his trouser pocket with a casual motion.

"Very good, sir." He stood to one side and indicated they could pass. "I hope you both enjoy the party."

"No doubt we will," Rourke said with a wink.

He took Joan's arm again and steered her into the crowded foyer.

Rourke snagged two glasses of champagne from a passing waiter and steered them into the relative quiet of a corner to plot strategy.

"Guttman!"

Rourke and Joan looked up to see a young man in a black pin-striped suit and vintage fedora bearing down on them. Kurt Teameyer was grinning broadly, as if the three of them were old friends.

"I'd recognize you anywhere, Guttman," the young man said. He patted Gianni on the shoulder.

Rourke stared back at the interloper with epic disdain. It didn't seem to phase Teameyer.

"Oh, come on, Guttman, you remember me. I'm Alcibiades Poe. You know, the vampire detective," he added, his voice rising hopefully.

The Vampire Convention involved role-playing, Joan realized, feeling herself slipping toward the verge of open panic. All she'd wanted to do by coming to Arlington Plantation was talk to David Parker. How was she supposed to participate in an elaborate fantasy she knew absolutely nothing about? She knew nothing of Lucretia Noire's novels—and Rourke had confessed at dinner that the same was true of him.

Rourke signaled Joan with his eyes that they had no choice but to play along as best they could.

"I haven't seen you since Rome," Teameyer said.

"Ah, Rome. Such a combination of ancient and modern. Moonlight on the ruined Coliseum, billboards advertising Japanese televisions."

"There was so much violence the last time."

Rourke's face became thoughtful. "Dicey business, that."

"A bad end."

"Rather."

"And unexpected."

"One never knows what the future holds," Rourke said sagely.

"There's something I've been wondering. What was it about Buxton's activities that tipped you off about him?"

Joan nearly choked on her sip of champagne. How would Gianni Rourke answer a question requiring specific knowledge of a book she knew he had not read?

"That," Rourke said, touching one forefinger to the side of his nose, "is a very long story. But you haven't been introduced to my traveling companion."

Joan looked at Rourke with astonishment.

"I'm Alcibiades Poe from San Francisco," Teameyer said politely. "And you are?"

"Dr. Joan Oppenheim," Joan blurted, her face turning cranberry red. Rourke looked at her with grave disapproval, as if her inability to blandly lie were evidence of a serious character flaw.

"Dr. Oppenheim?" Teameyer seemed to search his memory. "You must be another of the new characters Miss Noire's created expressly for the Vampire Convention."

Joan smiled vaguely.

"Are you vampire or mortal?"

"I'm quite mortal." Maybe she could do this after all, she thought. "I hope you will not use your powers as a vampire to take undue advantage of a hapless mortal, Mr. Poe," she added.

"You know I'm not *that* kind of vampire," Teameyer said, pretending to be shocked. "I never take undue advantage. I haven't taken a life since that incident in Shanghai, and that was an accident. Guttman here and I get along famously, even though he's a mortal." The young man winked at Rourke. "Of course, he is a mortal of somewhat questionable character."

"I beg your pardon?" Rourke said imperiously.

"Well, you know, from Miss Noire's books. Your job is—would 'procurer' be an impolite word, Mr. Guttman?"

"It's as good a word for what I do as any, I suppose," Rourke said, brushing a bit of imaginary lint from his jacket.

"I'd keep an eye on Mr. Guttman, if I were you, Dr. Oppenheim. As the princess's gamekeeper, he is chiefly responsible for procuring 'game'—which is to say physically attractive mortals—for his mistress and her friends to use for their enjoyment . . . and to satisfy their blood needs. But then, you no doubt know all that from reading Miss Noire's wonderful books."

Gianni snorted and downed his champagne.

"I think I have Mr. Guttman's number," Joan said, looking past Teameyer.

"My God, it's really her!" Teameyer gasped.

"Who?" Rourke demanded.

"Lucretia Noire!"

"The small woman in the black cape?" Joan asked.

Teameyer nodded.

Lucretia Noire did not look at all like what Joan had expected. She'd imagined the author of the bestselling vampire novels to be a middle-aged woman with a calculated, painted-on sort of glamour and a dramatic presence—a sort of literary Joan Collins. But Lucretia Noire was quite the opposite: small, young, understated, and extremely beautiful. Joan doubted Noire was five feet tall. Her face had a classic loveliness. She resembled a Pre-Raphaelite virgin, Joan thought. Her pale skin was flawless and nearly as white as a polished Carrara-marble bust of Venus. Her figure, which seemed every bit as slight as her stature, was hidden beneath her hooded cloak, black with a red satin lining.

"She's lovely!" Rourke said, clapping his hands together. "Her face is exquisite. She is like a Japanese porcelain doll."

"I don't believe it," Teameyer said, his voice pitched nearly an octave higher than it had been. "She's coming straight toward *us*!"

"Gianni Rourke!"

"I am enchanted, Miss Noire, utterly enchanted," Rourke said, lifting her tiny hand to his lips.

"I am one of your greatest fans. You are a fresh breath to the opera."

The Italian accent sounded authentic, Joan thought.

Kurt Teameyer watched with complete surprise. He had no idea who Gianni Rourke was.

"I apologize for not knowing your name was on the guest

list," she said. "I should have been at the door to welcome you personally. I shall have to have a word with my secretary for being so remiss."

Uh oh, Joan thought.

"I must confess, Miss Noire, that I took the liberty of turning up here tonight uninvited. It is unforgivable, I know, but when I heard that the two of us were, quite by chance, in this quaint little town, I decided that I must come by to pay my respects. I admire your novels enormously," he added, lying effortlessly.

"You do me a great honor, Maestro." She glanced briefly at Joan and Kurt Teameyer. "And these are your friends?"

"May I introduce the distinguished musicologist, Dr. Joan Oppenheim."

"Ah, another inhabitant of the ethereal realm of music."

"How do you do," Joan said, and accepted the woman's hand. The skin was soft and cool to the touch, the bone structure delicate, like a child's.

"And this . . ." Rourke's voice fell away in a subtle way intended to announce that while he and Joan were together, this third person was of no consequence.

"My real name is Kurt Teameyer. I'm a student at the University of Iowa and a devoted fan of yours."

"Alcibiades," she said in a chilly voice, "please observe the protocols for this Gathering of the Broods and refrain from referring to your former mortal existence."

"I'm sorry." Teameyer looked stunned and confused. He'd only been following the lead set by Gianni Rourke.

"I heard someone say David Parker would be here tonight," Joan said, hoping to get the miserable young man off the hook before he suffered additional humiliation. She'd already decided that she liked Lucretia Noire as little as she did Gianni Rourke. Perhaps there was something about celebrity that made people cruel.

"David Parker the composer? Then two musical geniuses will be here the same night. I have his *Preludes* recording. I adore it. Perhaps he will one day write something for the opera, Maestro."

"As a matter of fact he has, Miss Noire. I hope to produce his opera *Vanity Fair* next season."

The prospect seemed to genuinely please the woman.

"I shall have to be there for the premiere. Oh, Gianni, you can't know how much this news delights me."

"But if you didn't know Mr. Parker was coming, perhaps he isn't," Joan said, not wanting to waste time at the party if David Parker was not there.

"I didn't know *you* were coming, either. We shall simply have to see what the night brings us. My sixth sense told me this evening would be filled with surprises. Imagine: Gianni Rourke *and* David Parker here at Arlington. And something tells me there will be more surprises in store for us tonight."

She glanced at Joan a moment and then looked past them and out the window. The moon had risen and illuminated the gardens in silvery light. Although she had a dreamy smile on her face, something cold in her expression made Joan wonder if Lucretia Noire was as thrilled as she professed about her unexpected guests. Maybe she was worried about having the spotlight diverted from herself. The author needn't worry about that, Joan thought, looking at the worshipful way in which the young man pretending to be the vampire Alcibiades Poe watched her.

"Why don't you come with me?" the woman said, suddenly emerging from her reverie. "If you'll excuse us, Alcibiades."

"But of course."

Poor boy, Joan thought. Joan smiled at him sympathetically, but she followed Rourke and the woman in the robe out of the room, her eyes searching the crowd for David Parker, hoping Lucretia Noire would lead her to him, and he to Al.

"Do either of you care for turtle eggs?"

"I adore them!"

Joan smiled weakly and shook her head.

The walnut library table was laden with an exotic array of delicacies and savories. A bottle of Dom Perignon stood beside it in an ornate silver ice bucket.

"This room is my retreat from the crowd," she said, ushering Rourke to the turtle eggs. She seemed to relish the sight of him devouring them as much as he did the rare treat. "I'm afraid all the attention I am afforded at these affairs becomes stifling after a while. It is nice to be loved, but only to a point. Certainly you understand, Maestro."

Rourke popped another turtle egg into his mouth and nodded.

"Would you care to hear some music?" She poured champagne into three fluted glasses. "The pipe organ is incapable of penetrating this room, which has been specially insulated. Fortunately, I might add. I never could tolerate Bach."

She handed a glass to Gianni and one to Joan, looking deep into her eyes and smiling as if there were something she knew that Joan didn't. The look unnerved Joan.

Joan sipped the champagne. She'd never had expensive champagne before, but even so it was easy for her to tell the difference between this and what they'd been served with the other guests. The Dom Perignon was deliciously dry. The bubbles seemed to dance across her tongue as she swallowed.

"I'm afraid I'm a bit of a snob," their hostess said, reaching for the clasp that held the robe closed at her neck. "I cannot abide cheap champagne."

"I think your attitude is exactly correct," Rourke said, washing down another turtle egg with a glass he drained in one massive swallow.

Joan couldn't keep herself from watching as the robe fell open and the woman shrugged it back off her shoulders, catching it with her fingers as it fell down her back.

Lucretia Noire's arms and shoulders were naked to a black lace bustier and the red lycra shorts fit her hips like a second skin. She possessed a perfect female body—her petite frame perfectly proportioned, perfectly turned, with breasts, hips, and a waist any model would have sold her soul to possess.

She threw the discarded cloak onto a chair and walked to pick up her champagne, moving with the supple grace of a ballerina whose muscles are firm and perfectly toned.

"Please excuse my dishabille. The robe is my publisher's idea. It's wool lined with satin and wearing it is hotter than the fires of Hell."

"No reason to apologize, dear lady," Rourke said. "You are a vision of loveliness."

"Dr. Oppenheim? There's some delicious fruit here, if the turtle eggs and pâté do not appeal to the connoisseur in you."

The woman picked up a small clutch of purple grapes, large and ripe, glistening with water.

Joan shook her head.

The other woman brought the grapes to her mouth. She pulled one free and held it in her lips a moment before sucking it slowly into her mouth.

Joan experienced a wave of shame as she caught herself wondering what it would be like to take the other woman in her arms and press her lips against hers, tasting the sweetness of fresh grapes mingled with champagne, and the sweetness of her mouth. Feeling her face begin to burn, Joan turned away. She heard the muffled sound of Lucretia Noire's spiked heels on the carpeted floor. The back of Joan's neck began to tingle. She could feel the heat of the woman's body. If she leaned even the least bit backward, their bodies would touch. She closed her mouth and swallowed dryly, thinking she must be on the verge of losing her mind. That, at least, would explain everything, including A1 and now *this* . . .

"Here you are, my dear." Joan felt the woman's perfumed breath on the back of her right ear; it was not a disagreeable sensation—no, quite the opposite.

Joan accepted the second glass of champagne and chanced a sideways glance at the woman. Thank God Gianni Rourke had come to Arlington Plantation with her, Joan thought. If she had to be alone in the room with Lucretia Noire, she was afraid she'd be seduced into doing something she'd regret the rest of her life.

"Please sit down."

Rourke lowered himself into a club chair close to the turtle eggs. The woman indicated that Joan should be seated on the leather couch. Joan obeyed.

The woman slipped a CD into the stereo. The familiar opening bars of Mozart's Piano Concerto No. 21 in C Major floated out of invisible speakers.

"Mozart is always a safe choice," she said, her penetrating eyes again locking onto Joan's.

"Everyone loves Mozart," Rourke agreed, and reached for a turtle egg. "He is tedious but safe."

The woman fluttered her eyes, releasing a flock of butterflies in Joan's stomach. Joan lowered her eyes and tried to concentrate on her breathing, a trick she'd learned as a graduate student to help overcome her fear of public speaking.

The woman turned her attention to Rourke.

"I wonder if I might ask you to do me a very small favor?"

"As long as these turtle eggs hold out, beautiful lady, consider me your slave."

The woman's laugh was musical and strangely exotic.

"I've read that you are an accomplished gourmet, Maestro."

"I have been privileged to become acquainted with the work of the world's foremost chefs."

"And you are equally knowledgeable about wine?"

"That is also true," Rourke said, frowning a little at the memory of the Fortant de France Merlot.

"Would you consider giving me your opinion of a Bordeaux? The caterer claims to know the widow of a connoisseur in Natchez, who died and left her with a cellar filled with some extraordinary vintages she'd now like to sell. It could be quite an opportunity, but I'd like a second opinion."

"Very wise of you," Rourke said, dabbing his lips with one of the linen napkins that were neatly folded and stacked on the edge of the library table. "One can never be too careful, especially here in the provinces. Persons such as you or I provide a tempting target to unscrupulous purveyors."

"You will excuse us a moment, Dr. Oppenheim?"

Joan smiled weakly, relieved that the woman did not intend to send Rourke off on an errand, leaving the two of them alone together on the leather couch.

"Here we are."

Rourke picked up the bottle and scrutinized the label carefully, as if he were an art appraiser called in to inspect a suspected counterfeit. Rourke had to hold the bottle close to his nose; he was nearsighted but too vain to wear glasses. They were in a storage pantry down a side hall that ran in the direction of the kitchen. Noire had had to unlock the door before they could enter.

"It looks like the genuine article, although you must never judge a book, or a wine, by its cover. How much are they asking?"

"One hundred even per bottle, but I have to take all sixteen cases."

"That would be quite a bargain." Rourke did some quick calculating in his head, estimating the profit to be made if he could get in on the deal and resell his cases back in New York City. "If the wine is everything it should be, and sixteen cases are more than you want, I'd be willing to assume half the allotment."

"That's very generous of you, Maestro."

"You needn't thank me, dear lady. I would be only too happy to help a fellow artist. You would want to open each case and inspect each bottle to make sure you are getting what you pay for."

"But of course. I'm indeed fortunate to have your assistance." She gave Rourke a demure smile.

Rourke's tongue darted out of his mouth to moisten his lips in advance of the otherworldly experience that awaited him, if the wine wasn't spoiled. This could more than make up for the disastrous Fortant de France Merlot.

"Well," he said, and cleared his throat, "the proof is in the pudding, as they say."

"Here are two glasses."

"And the corkscrew?"

"I have it right here."

The woman flicked open the stiletto that Becker Thorne had thrust into her heart earlier in the evening for Lysander Chase's benefit.

Rourke looked down at the knife and smiled stupidly. The last time he had seen such a knife, it had been used to hoist several generous servings of cocaine to his nose.

"I have a confession to make."

"Think of me as your priest," Rourke said with a sly smile.

"My name is not Lucretia Noire."

"A *nom de plume*?"

"You might say that. My real name is Princess Nicoletta Vittorini di Medusa."

"At least you're not a vampire," Rourke joked.

"Oh, but I am."

"Politically, economically, or—you know, in the usual sense."

"The latter."

"How fascinating," Rourke said in a bored voice, looking morosely at the Bordeaux. This Vampire Convention play-acting bored him beyond belief. The Bordeaux, on the other hand, was more than worthy of his interest.

"As much as I love to drain mortals down to the last drop of their blood, I also find that the act of ordinary murder provides a certain pleasure."

Rourke blinked and glanced briefly at the knife again. Perhaps, he thought, his situation might be slightly more threatening than he had imagined.

Nicoletta's tiny left fist shot up and struck Rourke squarely in his larynx.

Rourke grabbed his neck with both hands. He tried to scream, but the only sound that came from his mouth was a harsh rasping.

"I've crushed your voice box," Nicoletta said, sounding pleased with herself. "It is a trick I learned from a sixteenth-century Turkish assassin. It took me quite a little practice to get so that I could do it properly."

Rourke fell back against the counter, his face a welter of pain and disbelief that he had been permanently disabled by a completely unprovoked—and disturbingly casual—attack.

"Do not worry too much, Gianni," Nicoletta said, reading his thoughts. "The loss of your voice is nothing compared with the loss of your life."

Rourke stopped trying to scream and looked down at Nicoletta with terror.

"Before we proceed, I must make a second confession." Nicoletta smiled. "I have always thought you were a second-rate, perhaps even a third-rate, conductor. You are not fit to shine Cosima's shoes. Everybody says so—behind your back."

Hot tears welled in Rourke's eyes, which he could not take away from the glittering stiletto.

Smiling serenely, Nicoletta thrust the knife into Rourke's lower belly.

His eyes grew wide. He could not believe what was happening—he simply couldn't believe any of it.

The knife was extremely sharp. Nicoletta gave a short, preliminary tug, then jerked the blade all the way up to Rourke's sternum.

Gianni Rourke sat down hard on the floor, looking at his wound with mute incomprehension. His intestines started to spill from his abdomen. He tried to hold them in with his hands, but it was a struggle he could not win even though it was obvious he would continue trying until he finally died.

Nicoletta rinsed her right hand in the metal janitor's sink. She'd managed to get very little blood on herself, evidence of her considerable experience. She'd been killing for hundreds of years and knew exactly what to do.

The princess leaned over Rourke on her way out of the room.

"You see," she whispered in her accented voice, "I told you my sixth sense told me this evening would be filled with surprises."

Rourke stirred a bit, but he was already beginning to fade. Nicoletta went out the door, locking it behind her.

"Where's Gianni?"

"The Maestro has his hands full at the moment," Nicoletta said without further explanation. She filled two fresh glasses with champagne, carried them to the couch, and sat beside Joan.

"Let's get to know one another a little better," the Italian said, "and then one of us can go to try and find David Parker."

Joan nodded, a tingling feeling in the pit of her stomach.

Nicoletta raised her glass. "To life," she said.

"To life," Joan echoed.

Joan brought the glass to her lips as Nicoletta did the same, keeping her eyes locked on the other woman's as they drank.

VI

Move and Countermove

10 P.M. Friday—It was only a hireling, David Parker *saw*, scanning the man's mind, someone who had come with the caterer from Vicksburg.

"Your invitations please, gentlemen."

Mozart gave the man a half smile.

The servant bowed and stood to the side.

There were no electric lights burning that night at Arlington Plantation. Antique kerosene lamps were stationed on the tables and sideboards, along with an array of candles, some in single holders, others in candalabra boasting a dozen dancing flames. The lightbulbs in the hall chandelier had been removed for the evening and replaced with long white candles.

The crowd parted before David and Mozart as they waded into the packed hallway. The guests' deference to the two vampires appeared to be natural, even though they were in fact clearing the way at Mozart's wordless command.

"Lovely party," Mozart said.

David did not answer. He was paying attention to Mozart, not the mortals, as the Austrian studied the room with a look of good humor on his face. He was depending on Mozart to make this turn out all right, but he was less than optimistic.

There was no denying the terrible foreboding he felt. And then it hit him. With a sickening feeling in the pit of his stomach, David's powerful *Vampiri* senses told him that the horror they had come to Arlington to prevent had already begun. The stench of death was strong in the mansion.

"The crowd is not as big as I imagined. I think there are only two others of our kind here tonight," Mozart said.

"What do you mean you 'think' there are only two? Can't you be certain?"

Mozart shook his head. "Nothing is very clear to me tonight, *mein Herr*. And you? What do you perceive?"

David shrugged sheepishly. "Nothing except the oppressive pallor of death. It pervades this place."

"Our adversaries are very powerful."

David started to ask another question, but Mozart raised a forefinger to his lips. Mozart was reaching out with his preternatural senses, probing the house for the presence of the other immortals.

"Thorne is here," David said, suddenly *feeling* his adversary.

"You mean Booth."

David nodded.

"I need to be entirely honest with you, David," Mozart said in a low voice. "I know that you have come to depend to a certain degree on my experience and abilities. But this may prove to be a challenge that even I cannot surmount."

"But who could challenge you?" David asked in complete disbelief. "You are the most powerful vampire in the *Illuminati*."

"There is at least one in our race who is more powerful than I. She is not a member of the *Illuminati*. Indeed, she is hostile to everything the *Illuminati* stand for."

"Who?" David demanded, his voice filled with disbelief.

Mozart looked acutely embarrassed. "The *Vampiri* woman who served as midwife to my rebirth into our race. The vampiress who transformed me."

"The vampiress who . . ." David's voice trailed off, leaving him staring at his friend and teacher. About all David knew of Mozart's transformation was that he had been thirty-five and dying when a vampire who appreciated his musical genius touched his blood and lifted him above the weaknesses of mortal existence. Unfortunately, Mozart was only able to continue the charade that he was still human until 1791, when circumstances forced him to feign his death and cease to be known—at least to the mortal world—as Wolfgang Amadeus Mozart.

David had always assumed da Vinci, Michelangelo, or one of the other supremely cultured members of the *Vampiri* race had transformed Mozart. Looking back, he realized his mentor had deliberately created that impression with him. And now the grim truth. Mozart, the supremely good and powerful vampire, was the spawn of a supremely evil and even more powerful creature.

"A creature who is now in league with John Wilkes Booth," Mozart said, guessing David's progression of thought.

"Perhaps she even . . ."

"Transformed Booth from mortal to *Vampiri. Ja, mein Herr*, that has occurred to me also." Mozart looked at David with a look of profound regret. "You and I are in extreme danger. I do not fully understand it, but I sense that we have an important part in what is supposed to happen here tonight. We have been drawn here unwittingly to serve a purpose—and not a higher purpose, but an infernal one."

Mozart's eyes began to follow the upward sweep of the staircase.

"We shall have to wait and see. By morning's light, my friend, many truths will be revealed." His eyes returned to David's, and he added, "For those who survive the night. Do you see him?"

With a start, David looked up toward the second floor.

John Wilkes Booth stood at the top of the steps, leaning with one hand on the railing, hip cocked, looking down on David and Mozart as if he were a professional gambler, they a pair of provincial bumpkins who'd bluffed their way into a private casino.

There was no mistaking the strength, or the animosity, in Booth's haughty smile. His tall, lithe body looked powerful even from a distance, and his confident sense of superiority appeared to have been unshakably cast. The killer was dressed in all black, now, in the style of a nineteenth-century Western gunman: long black coat, black shirt, string tie, vest, trousers tucked into the top of riding boots. The clasp on his tie and his belt buckle were silver. Booth's dark hair was oiled and combed straight back from his narrow temples. His eyes glittered like lightless mirrors. His face was handsome, though more gaunt than it was when he had been one of America's most prominent actors. It was a sociopath's face: open and friendly but manipulative, the face of someone who was capable of anything.

Booth ran one hand—he wore tight black kidskin gloves turned back at the wrist—against the banister, caressing it, before he began to come down the steps. His movements were fluid, his head held so perfectly still that a cup of tea could have been balanced on it without spilling a drop.

Most rogue killers would have fled at the first sign of an *Illuminati* member of Mozart's stature, but Booth just came toward them with no more concern than he would have afforded a mortal. David glanced nervously at his teacher and protector. Mozart showed neither anger nor fear to the criminal member of their race. The Austrian's face remained perfectly passive; he might as well have been sitting on a park bench, watching children sail boats in a lagoon, as facing up to a killer whose list of dark deeds far outstripped even the most bloodstained mortal psychopathic killers.

The crowd continued to mingle and swirl around the three vampires at a discreet distance. They were invisible to the others, three immortals within a bubble of invisibility Mozart had created. Booth could spontaneously burst into flames and no one would have noticed, David thought.

A waiter approached. David realized that Booth's telepathy was drawing the hapless mortal into their private circle.

Booth removed a glass of champagne from the waiter's silver tray. Without blinking once or taking his eyes away from Mozart's, the killer drained the glass, returned it to the tray, and sent the waiter away.

"I've always had a fondness for the grape," Booth said.

"*Ja.* I had a few minutes to read about you at the Morningside College Library."

"You flatter me, Mozart."

David blanched at the killer's use of his mentor's real name, but it seemed not to concern Mozart in the least. Of course, given the conceits operating during the Vampire Convention, Mozart, like Booth, could have openly admitted his identity without attracting undue attention or straining credulity.

"Whether with alcohol or the blood of life, you have always been too weak to control your compulsive thirst, Herr Booth."

The killer glared at Mozart. Mozart was too shrewd to allow his face to reveal what his mind was thinking. His expression continued to be one of polite interest.

"We all have our weaknesses, Wolfgang," the killer said acidly. "As it says in the good book, *'Let he who is without sin cast the first stone.'* "

"Do not quote Scripture to me, devil," Mozart replied in an almost casual way.

"Most people would say all three of us are devils," Booth countered.

"I would restrict such facile generalizations to your branch of our 'family.' "

"When it is your misdeeds, Mozart, that threaten to expose us all to the mortal world?"

"We didn't come here tonight to listen to your insults," David said.

"If the truth is an insult, then by all means do consider yourself insulted, Mozart."

"I wonder, Herr Booth, whether there is any substance behind your words, or if you are speaking merely to hear the sound of your own voice."

"I am talking, old chum, about Dr. Joan Oppenheim."

David looked at Mozart with alarm.

"What do you know of Dr. Oppenheim?" Mozart asked as if the subject had but little interest.

"I had the pleasure of meeting Dr. Oppenheim earlier this evening."

"She's here?" Mozart asked, looking surprised for once.

"She was looking for this buffoon." Booth nodded at David, grinning. "But it is you she really hopes to find, Mozart."

"Listen, you son of a—"

"Where is Dr. Oppenheim?" Mozart demanded, interposing himself between David and Booth.

"I sent her away before you got here, of course. I knew you'd kill her to keep her quiet."

"No, he wouldn't," David said, rushing to Mozart's defense.

"I gave her a list of *Illuminati* enclaves around the globe, along with the name of a particularly devious and energetic investigative reporter at *The New York Times*. I trust they'll end up causing a good deal of trouble for you and your little fraternity of *Vampiri* Boy Scouts. Nothing of lasting damage, perhaps, but a serious annoyance."

"Even you would never do something so pointless and damaging," Mozart said, unwilling to believe a member of his race could indulge in such a tactic.

"It really makes the most extraordinary story," Booth said, his eyes sparkling. "Imagine a secret cabal of scholars, a sort of cross between the Masons and the Jesuits, who have existed as a shadow government in most Western countries since the Renaissance. During that time, this hidden society—call them the *Illuminati*, for the sake of argument—have amassed a fortune in treasure and art, plus a level of political power that would be regarded as patently dangerous in any democracy. On the surface are the ordinary politicians and money men, seeming to pull the strings. But that's the illusion. The *Illuminati* are the real power; they're the ones who control the Western world by the fiat of their Ruling Council of Elders.

"There is, alas, a dark side to the story. The *Illuminati* have remained cloistered from the sunshine so long that they have become ingrown and infected. They engage in espionage and political murder, routinely trampling on the ordinary laws they consider too mundane to apply to their exalted activities.

"The worst thing is the religious aspect the group has taken on. Rumor has it that the *Illuminati* have dabbled in the occult, that they commit ritual human sacrifice and consume the blood of their victims, believing it can give them immortal life. Some say its members are not even humans. Some say the *Illuminati* is made up of vampires.

"It sounds incredible, I know, but Dr. Oppenheim believes it. She even believes the part about how drinking blood makes it possible for members of the *Illuminati* to cheat death. And why shouldn't she believe? She has the hard scientific evidence in her own hands, thanks to you, Mozart. It's all over the music you've written during the past two centuries.

"Fortunately, I have been able to provide certain corroborating evidence in the form of names, safe-house addresses, bank account numbers, and so forth. As I said, it will make one hell of a story for an enterprising reporter."

"I have been a complete fool," Mozart said bleakly. Then he turned to David and spoke with his usual resolve. "I am sorry, but I must leave at once."

"Leave?" David cried.

"I am left no choice. I must stop Dr. Oppenheim. The consequences of such knowledge getting out among the mortals reach far beyond what may happen here tonight, no matter how horrible."

"You're going to go after her *now*?" David asked, incredulous.

"I must."

"But what about all of this?" David waved an arm wildly at

the crowd of revelers surging around them. He only then noticed that Booth had slipped into the crowd and disappeared.

"This situation is dangerous, but difficult as it is for you to imagine, the threat Dr. Oppenheim poses is even worse. She is on the verge of unraveling the entire fabric of good the *Illuminati* have woven over the past two millennia. It is entirely my fault. I must stop her before it is too late."

"You're going to leave me here to deal with Booth?"

"I am deeply sorry, but I must."

"And what of Booth's ally? You say you think the vampiress who transformed you is here tonight. You hinted that even with your powers you doubt you are any match for her. How am I supposed to contend with such a force?"

"You could come with me and avoid the confrontation," Mozart said. "But that, of course, would mean leaving Victoria and the others to a most unpleasant fate."

"Damn you, Wolf."

"Again, *mein Herr*, I am eternally sorry. I did not plan for it to work out this way."

"And when you find Oppenheim, what are you going to do to her?"

Mozart did not answer.

"Wolf," David said slowly, "you know that you cannot kill her. You are sworn to protect human life. It would be murder. You would have to pay with your own life."

"*Ja,*" Mozart said, as close to despair as David. "I also know I must not let her expose the *Illuminati*. I must do whatever is required to ensure her silence."

Mozart squared his shoulders.

"I must try to overcome insurmountable odds, David. You must do the same. That is the prime directive of life, my friend, whether we are mortal or *Vampiri*."

"But what should I do?" David asked desperately.

"All I know is that you must try your best. I will try to stop Dr. Oppenheim. If I succeed, I will return to help you. If I don't, David, may God bless you and give you strength."

Mozart spun on his heel without another word and headed toward the door. The crowd split apart. He was at the door a moment later and then, without hesitating or looking back, he was gone into the night.

David stood in the entry hall, surrounded by guests at the Vampire Convention, completely and utterly alone.

VII
Close Encounter

10:30 P.M. Friday—This was how she'd always imagined it would be: the light dancing like fireflies on the wicks of a hundred candles and within the blown-glass globes of the kerosene lamps.

Such *light*!

This was how the Arlington Plantation great house was intended to be seen, by candlelight—the mansion and its furnishings suffused with a golden glow, the shadows as deep and rich as any in a Rembrandt painting.

Victoria had come inside with her mind tightly focused on the horror she and her friends had come to Arlington to battle, but one look at the light—the *light!*—blunted her purpose and stranded her in the midst of a waking dream.

She surveyed the scene spread out before her and realized she was looking backward in time. This was how Arlington must have appeared the night in 1866 when her family celebrated Anna Lee Buchanan's betrothal to Harper Neuport, the lawyer from Atlanta.

James Plant had told her once that when you look at a star you're looking into the past, since the light you see has been traveling many, many years through the cold darkness of space to reach the Earth. In some cases, he said, the star may not even exist anymore by the time you look up in the night sky and see it. Maybe the candles and lamps work in a similar way, Victoria thought dreamily, admiring the warm, platinum luminescence. Maybe candlelight and starlight possess the same power to deliver the past unto the present.

Tilting her head to one side, Victoria began to smile.

She'd never seen so many people at Arlington. The entry hall and parlors were filled to bursting with happily murmuring guests. There hadn't been such a party at Arlington since the dour sisters bought the estate from the suddenly penniless Buchanans during the Great Depression.

This made Victoria very happy. The light—the *light!*—and the people brought Arlington Plantation truly to life. Arlington had been built on a grand scale; it was intended to serve as the stage for grand events. It was a kind of miracle to be able to see the estate as it had once been and as she'd always dreamed of seeing it.

Victoria's fingers began to tingle. She felt a little faint, but somehow the sensation was entirely pleasant.

Arlington was a sleeping princess awakened from death's sleep by her lover's kiss.

Strange to think the lover's name was John Wilkes Booth.

The killer.

Victoria blinked her eyes several times. The noise of a hundred conversations and the organ, neither of which she'd noticed before, suddenly rose up in her ears.

No, Victoria thought, amending her previous notion, Booth was something infinitely more dangerous than a mere killer.

Yet the *light*!

Victoria had to admit she felt a certain gratitude to Booth. As wildly inappropriate as that was, she was grateful to him for letting her see Arlington like this. He had, for his own dark reasons, brought Arlington round full circle to relive its former glory, if only for that night.

Arlington had once been the most glorious residence in the South, a reflection of the Buchanans' glorious lives. But that was over now, Victoria thought soberly—all of it.

Booth had not been the only one cheated out of what was rightfully his, Victoria thought bitterly. By rights Arlington Plantation belonged to *her*. Victoria had been cheated out of her birthright, just as Booth had been cheated—

"Excuse me!"

A bright-eyed young man bumped into Victoria as he tried to squeeze past her from behind. He smiled and paused, but when she looked through him as if he were transparent, he shrugged and continued on his way.

What am I thinking? Victoria wondered, as frightened as she was confused. How had Booth been cheated? Where were these ideas coming from?

Her eyes settled on the flame burning in a kerosene lamp on

a side table. However, the spell had been broken. It was dangerous to have so many open flames in the great house. Anything could happen, Victoria thought, especially with so many people present—drinking, jostling one another, crowding into every free corner. Arlington had no sprinkler system. The sisters had kept a fire extinguisher in the kitchen, but Victoria doubted another could be found anywhere in the house.

But what did it matter as long as there was such *light*!

Victoria took a deep breath and slowly let it out, blinking her eyes again—not knowing whether it was to force back the tears or clear the exquisite illusion that seemingly had been planted in her mind. Slowly, like a dreamer awakening or a diver returning to the surface after a deep plunge to swim among the sea fans and shells on the distant and shadowy bottom, Victoria made herself rise up out of the shimmering trance once and for all.

Arlington was beautiful that night, but she knew the beauty was being used as a mask to hide an evil that menaced them all.

Lucretia Noire had circulated among her fans for a brief time before withdrawing—only temporarily, her fans hoped—from the party. Victoria learned this much within ten minutes of being inside the great house. Although she still didn't know what Lucretia looked like, at least she had a description of the author: a small, beautiful woman wearing a hooded cape.

The character Victoria was supposed to portray for the Vampire Convention—Melinda Tranque—required no elaborate costuming. Victoria wore a black evening dress, elegantly simple, her long blonde hair held up on her head with an antique tortoiseshell comb. The fictional Melinda Tranque was a vampire's mortal lover who met with a predictably bad end in *The Raven*. There was little about Melinda Tranque's character with which Victoria could sympathize; Melinda was the stock sort of victim found in vampire novels, and it had been obvious to Victoria from the first reference to Tranque in *The Raven* that the character would be horribly murdered as the plot progressed.

Victoria was equally unsuccessful at locating Booth amid the noisy crowd that jammed into the sitting rooms, drinking champagne and talking loudly to make themselves heard over the melodramatic organ. Victoria hoped Lucretia wasn't off somewhere with Booth—then remembered with a few moments of stark panic that she'd been explicitly warned to refer to Booth by his alias, Thorne, even within the privacy of her own thoughts.

"He is a powerful creature," Wolf Toland had told Victoria in his solemn, accented English. "The likelihood that he will read your thoughts when you are surrounded by a hundred other guests is improbable but not impossible. And should you meet him face to face, you must never allow yourself to think of him as Booth. He will feel threatened if he realizes you know his true identify. If that happens, he will move to protect himself."

Victoria didn't have to ask what that meant. She knew Booth—*Thorne*—would kill her in an instant for his own protection—or pleasure—and not give it a second thought.

Victoria checked her watch for the fifth time in as many minutes. She wasn't going to wait any longer. She had to find Lucretia Noire.

Victoria had been cautioned not to wander off by herself, which might give Booth or his nameless, faceless vampire ally the opportunity to corner her alone. Nightingale, Victoria assumed, had already been lured out to the caretaker's cottage by Marcus and Dr. Chesterfield and drugged, like Zaharim, and so he was no longer a threat.

Unfortunately, Victoria thought, she could no longer heed her friends' warning to stay in the protective company of others. She was determined to find Lucretia Noire and get the author out of harm's way, even if she had to put her own life at risk to do so.

But where was Lucretia Noire?

Victoria didn't have to think very hard to come up with a guess. Lucretia would be in Arlington's library, she thought, hiding from the crowd—the very place Victoria would be, were she in Lucretia Noire's shoes.

The library was beyond the silk cord that roped off the corridor into Arlington's "new" addition. There were no candles burning in the hall. This struck Victoria as odd, since every few minutes a servant hurried to or from the kitchen at the far end of the hall, carrying a tray of champagne glasses or hors d'oeuvres. She decided the hall was being kept dark to discourage guests from doing what she was about to do: release the cord's brass latch and pass into the forbidden zone.

Someone had removed the oriental runner from the hall to

protect it from the traffic and spills. Victoria nodded to herself. She knew it was absurd for her to notice housekeeping details with so many lives at stake, but a lifetime of fretting over Arlington Plantation made it impossible for her to fail to register such observations.

Victoria stopped midway to the library when she saw the pool of dark liquid leaking from beneath the door of the butler's pantry. The floorboards in the pantry would be permanently stained if the spill—red wine, by the look of it in the dim light—were left to sit.

Victoria reached for the door handle. It was locked.

On the other side of the door, inside the butler's pantry, Gianni Rourke's body lay slumped to one side, his dead hands still clutching at his spilled intestines, a thickening lake of blood spreading out from his body, extending beneath the door.

Victoria frowned and wrinkled her nose. There was a peculiar odor coming from the pantry, a vile, rotten smell, like raw sewage. She rattled the handle a second time, but it would not open.

"Damn," she said under her breath, and carefully stepped over the pool of blood.

Even though the door to the library was closed, Victoria could see from the half inch of darkness between the bottom of the door and the floor that there was no one in the room. Victoria had guessed wrong about Lucretia Noire.

The sound of breaking glass came from the direction of the kitchen, followed by an exchange of angry oaths. A foot slammed against the kick panel, and the door swung open a foot.

"Everyone is capable of making mistakes, Mr. Overstreet," said an angry voice.

Victoria took a quick step backward, slipping around the corner just as a waiter carrying an empty silver tray came out of the kitchen. She flattened herself against the wall as the man passed her, not realizing she was hiding there.

Inching backward, Victoria's foot touched the bottom stair of the servants' staircase.

If Lucretia Noire wasn't in the library, she was probably upstairs resting in her room. She would have been given one of the bedrooms in the front of the house, for they were the biggest and most luxuriously appointed—probably the Southeast Room, where Jefferson Davis and Robert E. Lee had slept.

Leaning against the wall, Victoria slipped out of her shoes. She began to silently climb the stairs in her stocking feet.

The last bit of light ebbed away when Victoria turned the first landing.

She had a tiny flashlight in her bag, but she did not take it out. Victoria knew Arlington well enough to find her way through its rooms with her eyes closed. Except for the library, which she knew Booth had modernized, tastelessly in Victoria's opinion, Arlington Plantation's new owner had not seen fit to rearrange the furnishings.

At the top of the stairs, Victoria noticed a weird red glow coming from beneath the chapel doors.

Lydia Chase had told Victoria that Becker Thorne planned to convert the chapel into some kind of disco. Victoria could not believe he would do anything so vulgar, even though there was historical precedent for removing the chapel. Some members of the Jerusalem Historical Preservation Society had proposed doing so when they believed the organization was about to assume ownership of the plantation. Isaiah Buchanan had built a ballroom on the second floor of the "new" addition, which the sisters had converted into a chapel when they bought the plantation. Victoria had opposed the chapel remodeling plan. She'd seen photographs of the room as a ballroom, but she had always known it as a chapel, and it was difficult for her to imagine it otherwise. Besides, she'd argued with other preservationists, hadn't the sisters, during their long stewardship of Arlington, also become a part of its history?

Victoria paused outside the chapel door and slipped back into her shoes. She wondered what Booth—no, *Thorne*—had done to the chapel.

She told herself to quit foolishly worrying about Arlington Plantation and find Lucretia Noire.

Victoria started to turn away but stopped.

She had to know. She had to see what the beast had done to the chapel.

Biting her bottom lip, Victoria reached for the latch. Just a quick look.

The peculiar sensation of simultaneously not knowing and knowing, of not understanding and understanding, hit Victoria with an almost physical force when she pushed open the door.

Nightingale had left the neon sign plugged in, bathing the

room in the weird red electric glow. The air was filled with the singed ozone smell of faulty wiring and overheated insulators.

It was impossible even for someone as perceptive as Victoria to understand the obscene delusions that led Booth to have the neon Pegasus suspended from the cross above the altar. Still, it was obvious that the Pegasus altar represented some kind of twisted idolatry.

Idolatry.

Victoria turned the word over in her stunned and frightened mind. Victoria had thought of it as a primitive sort of sin, something from a time when pagans were still ignorant enough to bow down before a meaningless image like a golden winged calf.

Or a tin winged horse . . .

The door latch slipped out of Victoria's hand as she stared at Pegasus and tried to divine its meaning. She had already come to accept as fact several seemingly impossible things: that vampires were not mythical creatures but real; that John Wilkes Booth had cheated death by becoming a vampire. Was she now to believe that Booth—no, *Thorne*!—worshiped a neon sign salvaged from an old gas station?

Gravity began to pull the door open, swinging it back in a slow arc to reveal a part of the chapel that had been blocked from Victoria's view.

Victoria sensed something terrible off to her left the moment the dim outlines began to appear in the corner of her eye. She felt herself begin to tremble. Victoria could not find the courage to look.

The eerie red light outlined the figures—there was more than one, Victoria realized, too petrified with fear to back out of the doorway and run—hung back in the corner of the chapel, moving slightly from side to side in a strangely rhythmic fashion. With the detached awareness of a person on the verge of going into shock, Victoria realized that she'd bitten her bottom lip so hard that it was bleeding.

Without moving any other part of her body, Victoria slowly rolled her eyes to the left.

She strangled her scream almost before it escaped her throat.

The others in the chapel were no threat to Victoria, but that did nothing to lessen her horror.

Victoria's knees began to shake, and she knew she was about to faint. *No!* she commanded herself, reaching deep down inside to find a reserve of strength. No matter how terrible the scene in the chapel, Victoria told herself, she had to pull herself together and keep thinking. That was the only way she could hope to avoid becoming the fifth corpse in the chapel.

Stifling the urge to vomit, Victoria made herself look directly at the bodies swinging from the meat hooks suspended from the ceiling. One at a time, she noted the faces, praying that being almost mechanically logical would keep her from falling apart emotionally.

The first dead body was Nathan Bedford Forrest Nightingale. His head had been bashed in. It looked like someone had hit him with a baseball bat. Victoria was unable to believe either Marcus Cuttler or Dr. Chesterfield could have had anything to do with Nightingale's death, or his removal to the desecrated chapel. Booth—*Thorne*—must have turned on his accomplice.

The second body was Lysander Chase. He was wearing a tuxedo, but the trousers and shorts were hanging around his feet.

Victoria put her hand to her mouth.

Chase had been savagely mutilated. Someone had cut off his penis and testicles.

The third body was Lydia Chase, Victoria saw, and felt a chill sweat break out all over her trembling body.

Victoria and Lydia had been at odds all their lives, but neither Victoria nor any other sane person could have wished on their worst enemy what had been done to Lydia Chase. Her belly had been torn open, and her intestines were pulled out and wrapped around . . .

Victoria stumbled to the nearest pew and bent over it, unable to control the violent retching that failed to bring up anything out of her empty stomach.

Victoria fumbled with her clutch bag for a handkerchief, forcing herself to look at the fourth body. It was the furthest away, swinging in the shadows in the corner, barely visible in the red neon glow. The corpse looked almost like a mummy, with shriveled, shrunken skin that looked as if it had been sucked of its last drops of moisture. Victoria thought it was some long-dead corpse Thorne or Nightingale had dug up and dragged back to the chapel for some unholy ritual before the pagan altar.

Then the sense of recognition flooded into Victoria's mind.

"Oh, my God, no," Victoria said, her voice a low moan.

It was Amanda Hornsby Foster. First runner-up in the Miss Mississippi pageant. Victoria had seen her on the street only a day or two before. Amanda used to baby-sit Victoria's daughter, Michelle.

"What in the name of God did they do to you, Amanda?" Victoria asked out loud in a hoarse whisper, as if the corpse might answer.

The powerful enzymes in a vampire's saliva will heal discreet wounds, even if the host dies during feeding. However, the damage to either side of Amanda Hornsby Foster's neck was too severe for restorative action. She'd been sucked dry in a manner seen only in the most sadistic and unbridled expression of *Vampiri* hunger. Her ring finger on her left hand had been severed, Victoria saw—the killer's murderous signature, Inspector Toland had told them.

If they didn't find a way to stop Booth, her own daughter could end up like this, Victoria thought, her feeling of dread becoming so unbearably strong that she was about to start screaming when she heard something that made her heart skip a beat.

Victoria turned toward the door, her eyes wide. She forced herself to keep perfectly still. She did not even breathe as she stood, like a deer who senses a predator's approach through the darkened forest, listening.

She wasn't certain she'd heard a sound—distant, muffled, but unmistakable.

Was that a footstep?

Straining to listen over the sound of her heart pounding in her ears, she heard it again. There was no mistaking it this time. Someone was making his way slowly down the darkened hall toward the chapel.

Victoria threw herself toward the stairs. There was an unmistakable presence in the dark hallway, but Victoria did not take time to look as she flew past it. Her feet stumbled on the first stair. Clutching madly at the banister, she nearly fell but somehow managed to keep her balance. Half running, half stumbling, she made it down the first flight.

Victoria could hear the footsteps behind her.

She raced down the second flight two and three steps at a time. The sound of the party and the relative safety of the crowd were close at hand when she reached the main floor and ran around the corner.

Victoria's feet slid on the hardwood floor as she tried to stop without falling.

Blocking the hall was a large rolling metal cart loaded with plates and glasses, nearly as wide as the doorway and turned at an angle. Victoria knew in an instant that she would never get past it before her pursuer caught up to her.

She opened the library door and went through it as quickly as she could, closing it just as the footsteps behind her reached the bottom of the stairs.

This will never work, Victoria told herself, panting. She pressed her ear against the door to listen, hoping her pursuer would think she went into the kitchen instead.

"Good evening."

Victoria jumped at the sound of the voice. She looked over her shoulder, realizing for the first time that the light had been turned on in the library—not candles, but real electric lights.

The face in the hooded cape looked familiar. It was the woman from the Salvation Army—Captain Vittorini, she remembered. How odd it was, she thought in a flash, to find her at the Vampire Convention, dressed in a hooded velvet cape.

Victoria turned back to the door, her fingers frantically moving over the latch.

"What's wrong?" the woman asked with her musical Italian accent.

"Someone's taken the damned key!" Victoria said in despair.

The latch began to turn from the other side of the door.

Victoria backed away from the door and ran to the other woman, as if they might together be somehow able to fight off the monster.

The door opened.

The vampire Booth stood in the door frame, his body outlined in the darkness outside the room. He looked at Victoria and smiled. His teeth were exceptionally white.

"Victoria," Booth said warmly, as if there were no one in the world he would rather see. He stepped into the room, closing the door behind him.

Victoria began to tremble again. The other woman put a comforting arm around her shoulder, and Victoria felt inexplicably calm and protected.

"I was just chatting with David Parker. He and his friend from Austria decided to drop in and pay us a call tonight." Booth smiled again. "But then you know that."

"If you would be so kind as to excuse us," Captain Vittorini said. "I would like a few minutes alone with Victoria."

A dangerous look came over Booth's face as Captain Vittorini stepped forward and put her hand on Booth's arm as if to turn him toward the door.

Victoria began to shake again, certain the vampire was about to savagely kill Captain Vittorini while she watched. He didn't. With a dark scowl, Booth turned on his heel and left, slamming the door when he went out.

Victoria, still shaking, threw her arms around the other woman when she came toward her to offer her comfort. Victoria didn't know whether to laugh or cry and so she did a little of both, thinking that she had looked Death in the face and lived.

"You don't know how glad I am to see you," Victoria said, thinking that she was, at least for the moment, safe.

VIII

Return of the Prodigal

11 P.M. Friday—"Hello-o-o?"

The fluorescent grow lights above the withered flats of dead plants cast a weird purplish light in the greenhouse. Delores Chase Weller, Lydia Chase's daughter, raised her wrist and turned it to read the Rolex's dial in the dim purple light.

She was early.

"Anybody there?"

She began to tap her foot.

"Fucking great," she said to herself, and sniffed.

Delores began to mentally catalog the many perfectly good reasons she had to be in a foul mood. To begin with, Becker hadn't invited her to his big party. He'd said her mother might get suspicious if she saw them together. Then there was the phone call earlier that night from Zaharim, which had thoroughly irritated her. He'd summoned her to Arlington as if she were one of Becker's servants, telling her what time to arrive. "You are to meet Mr. Thorne at precisely 11:05. And do be punctual," the geek had ordered. She was supposed to avoid the guests, slip around through the gardens, and rendezvous with Becker in the greenhouse. And then, as if all of that weren't bad enough, Delores discovered that her mother had taken the convertible, ignoring the fact that *she* had expressly asked to have the Corvette for the night. Since the Jeep was in the shop, Delores had no choice but to drive the dowdy Jaguar sedan to the plantation.

Delores sniffed again—allergies, she told people—and looked past the outlines of the ferns and giant orchids. She could see the party-goers outlined against Arlington's windows. She loved parties, and the idea of a Vampire Convention certainly sounded like fun. The guests seemed to be enjoying themselves, Delores noted unhappily: laughing, sipping champagne, striking poses in the candlelight.

She was so angry that she wanted to break something—the brown clay pots and the greenhouse windows were tempting targets—but she held herself in check. She wasn't sure how far Becker Thorne could be pushed, and for some reason she was reluctant to find out.

She dug a Marlboro out of her purse, stabbed it into her mouth, and lit it with her gold Dunhill lighter, expelling a plume of tobacco smoke that temporarily masked the almost cloying sweetness of the moist hothouse air.

Delores heard a woman's laughter and looked over her shoulder. A man and woman were walking along the edge of the pool, holding hands. They stopped and embraced. The man's hand slipped down the woman's back until it rested on her derrière. Delores half expected them to peel off their clothes and dive into the water, but they finished their kiss and wandered back toward the house.

Delores had been skinny-dipping in the pool at Arlington a half-dozen times. She wondered if her mother could say the same. Probably not, Delores decided. Her mother was too paranoid about her age to take her clothing off anywhere but in the dark. She'd be afraid Becker would see her stretch marks.

"What!" Delores yelped and jumped, the cigarette flipping out of her hand to land harmlessly somewhere in the damp foliage.

She spun around and saw the killer standing with his hand suspended in the air where it had been a moment earlier when he'd brushed his cool fingertips against the nape of her neck.

"A little jumpy tonight, my darling?"

"Jesus Christ, Becker, don't sneak up on me like that."

"I apologize," he said without trying to sound sincere. And then, opening his arms, "Come."

Delores folded her arms across her chest and thrust out her lower lip.

"You are lovely when you pout. Come to me." His eyes looked deeply into hers. "Come," he commanded.

Delores found herself moving forward in spite of herself. That was the thing about Becker Thorne—no matter what he did to make her angry, Delores found it impossible to resist him.

His strong arms wrapped around her, and she experienced a delicious melting sensation. She moistened her lips with her tongue and tilted her face upward toward his, eyes closed. He kissed her then, and his kiss unleashed a stream of torrid fantasies in Delores's mind.

"God, but you turn me on, Becker," she whispered.

Delores knew he would have to get back to his guests, but she wondered if he'd have time to take her quickly first. She imagined them making love on the cutting table in the dull purple glow of the grow light. She'd never done it in a greenhouse before.

"I wish I could have come to the party."

"Your mother specifically asked me not to invite you."

"That bitch. Why would she do something mean like that?"

"She's jealous of you. And for good reason," he added, smiling as his eyes fell to her breasts, which were, he had told her many times, perfect.

"I think she might also be suspicious about us."

"Then we must be discreet," he said, taking her in his arms again and kissing her, his hands running all over her body. She tried to pull him down on top of her, but she was disappointed to feel his body stiffen and begin to resist.

"I'm afraid there isn't time for that now, my darling. Did you bring it?"

"Of course."

"May I have it, please? I've got to get back inside."

"Do you really have to?" Delores sounded like a child when she pleaded.

He nodded and held out his hand.

She lifted her purse on the cutting table and took out a plastic bag filled with white powder, which she handed over to him.

"It's the good rock, just like you wanted."

"Excellent," he said, holding the cocaine up and admiring it in the purple light. He took some money from his pocket and gave it to Delores, who dropped it into her purse without counting it.

"You are going to share that with your guests, aren't you?"

"That is why I needed it tonight—the party."

"I hope you're spreading it around a lot. I mean, jeeze, Becker, that's the third ounce you've bought this week."

"It's not me. You know I hardly touch it."

"You're not still carrying that basketball player, are you? The guy's an addict. You better cut him off."

"Eugene's passion for cocaine seems without limit. He'll stay up around the clock for days at a time, taking it until the supply is exhausted."

"Be careful that you don't end up making trouble for yourself. He'll kill himself with the stuff if you let him."

"It is a rather amazing thing to observe. He's the most insatiable coke pig I've ever known. Bigger even than you."

"Hey!" Delores took a mock swing at the killer's face. He caught her hand reflexively, easily, moving so fast that she didn't even see his hand fly out and catch hers. There was a dangerous glint in his eyes.

"I assure you, Miss Weller, that I did not mean to imply you were a pig, but rather that you are insatiable when it comes to cocaine and"—he gave her his most charming smile—"certain other things. Most deliciously insatiable."

He dipped a cocaine spoon into the baggie and pulled up a heaping mound of white powder.

"Care for a sample?"

Delores leaned closer. She'd already sampled plenty, but her brittle high was wearing off, leaving her nerves jagged. Otherwise, she thought, leaning over the spoon, she'd have never tried to slap Becker Thorne.

"Why don't you come inside a minute? I have something I'd like to show you."

"What about my mother? And my grandfather is here tonight, too, isn't he?"

"They're both probably hanging around somewhere." He

took a black opera mask from his jacket pocket. "Wear this. You'll be in disguise."

Delores pulled the mask down over the top of her head and adjusted the way it fit against the bridge of her nose. "This won't fool anybody," she said with a laugh.

"But of course it will. Besides, it looks very sexy."

"Give me a break," she said, and sniffed.

"I mean it." He moved closer and put his hands on her shoulders. "I'd like you to wear that mask the next time we make love."

"I knew you'd get around to the kinky stuff sooner or later," Delores said with a wicked laugh. She made as if to pull away, but Thorne grabbed her arm and brought her back hard against him.

"Oh, but I am, my darling young lady. I am into the extremely kinky stuff."

"You're hurting me," Delores said sharply.

"It's time I taught you that a small measure of pain can bring a large measure of pleasure."

He grabbed her by the hair, jerked her head back, and kissed her savagely.

"This isn't funny," she said angrily, turning her face to escape his lips.

"I think I'll do you right here," he said, pushing her back against the cutting table.

"Let me go!" The mask had slipped far enough on Delores's forehead that she couldn't see, and her anger was giving way to fear.

"How can I make love to you if you continue to struggle? It is most unladylike."

"Becker!"

Delores clawed at his face as she felt herself lifted into the air. Her body seemed to hang suspended for a moment or two, then slammed hard onto the cutting table. The mask came off when her head hit the table. Stunned, she looked up and saw the person she knew as Becker Thorne leering down at her. She began to fight the moment her head cleared, but Delores Chase Weller's strength was no match for his. The vampire effortlessly held her pinned to the table. She flailed her arms and legs. There was a muffled breaking sound as clay pots filled with dirt were knocked to the floor and smashed.

The vampire used his free hand to reach for a pair of rusty kitchen shears that had been used to prune plants. He put the scissors' tips against her belly and began to cut her Ralph Lauren polo shirt.

"Let me go!" Delores demanded, again trying to rake his face with her fingernails.

Thorne did let her go, but only long enough to slap her with the back of his hand. Then he pinned her down with his left hand and went back to cutting with his right. The scissors were dull and it took concentration to cut and tear his way through the material until both halves of the struggling young woman's shirt fell apart, exposing her naked upper torso. An angry red welt ran from Delores's belly to her neck, tracing where the tip of the scissors had scraped against her skin.

"You'll go to jail for this if you don't stop," Delores said coldly, suppressing her rage and fear long enough to try to reason with her assailant.

"Whore."

Delores tried to scream, but her attacker clamped his hand around her throat.

"Jezebel."

"Help! Please help!" Delores rasped.

"The Fury of the Lord is abroad in the land," Booth said, tilting his face upward toward the starry sky visible through the greenhouse's glass ceiling. He looked back down at the girl. "I am going to take you before Neon, Jezebel, and scourge you for your sins, and for the sins of your ancestors."

He held the scissors a few inches in front of her face and snipped them three times.

"First, I'm going to strip you of your clothes."

The scissors opened and closed in the air in front of her nose.

"Then I'm going to strip you of your skin."

The scissors clicked open and shut again. Delores felt a warmth spreading out beneath her and realized that she had wet her pants.

"After I've skinned you alive, daughter of Jezebel, I will allow you to die, if you do a good enough job of begging."

"Let the girl go."

Delores began to sob at the sound of the man's voice.

Booth had been paying so much attention to the girl that he hadn't seen someone slip into the greenhouse behind him. The interloper was a thin, haggard, middle-aged man in a cheap, out-of-fashion suit that looked like it had come off the rack at Goodwill. He was holding a .38-caliber revolver in his hand lightly, like a man who was used to guns and comfortable using them.

"Who are you to interrupt the Lord's work?" Booth snarled.

"Harlin Plummer."

"You'd better get the fuck out of here while you can."

"Let go of the girl and I'll consider it."

Booth flipped the scissors around in his hands and pressed the point against the skin over Delores's heart.

"Don't let him kill me!" Delores said desperately. "Don't let him kill me!"

Booth's eyes narrowed as he looked at the man with the gun. "I know you. You're that worthless drunkard."

"He's a policeman," Delores said desperately. "You better do as he says."

"He used to a be a policeman, Kewpie Doll. You know that as well as I do. And you should be glad for it. Otherwise, Harlin here would have to arrest you for cocaine trafficking."

"I'm not a cop anymore. I can't arrest her for the dope or you for assaulting the girl. But why don't you let her go? You know I can't let you hurt her."

"Are you threatening me?" Booth asked with a crooked grin.

Plummer cocked the revolver. "I'll do more than threaten."

"You're mean when you're drunk."

"I'm as sober as a judge," Plummer said. For a moment something like anger came into Plummer's eyes, but it quickly passed.

"Being a mean drunk was what got you fired, wasn't it?"

"I'm surprised you know about that," Plummer said, in command of his temper again. "It was a long time ago."

"I've made it my business to learn this town's dirty little secrets. For example, I know that you were arrested after Gregory Culpepper's murder."

"I am impressed. Most people don't know Greg was murdered. Henry Culpepper did his usual good job of covering that up."

"I know things about this poisonous little town that you wouldn't believe."

"I know a secret or two myself. Take Greg Culpepper's murder, for instance."

"What of it?" Booth asked in a taunting voice.

"Culpepper's death wasn't the sort of murder we see very often around here. We have our share of homicides. Not every day, mind you, but a couple every year. Usually it's nothing too complicated. Somebody shoots his wife, or gets shot by his wife, or shoots or stabs somebody over their wife or a girlfriend. Simple murder. A woman and liquor is part of it more often than not. It usually doesn't take much brain power to figure out who did what and why."

"You're hurting me," Delores sobbed. The tip of the scissors had broken her skin. A thin trickle of blood ran across her breast and down her side.

"Easy," Plummer said. "Why don't you let her go? Or at least put down those shears."

"Were you perchance getting around to making a point about Gregory Culpepper?"

The muscles flexed in Harlin Plummer's narrow face when he clamped his jaw.

"What happened to Greg Culpepper is pretty unusual in this part of Mississippi. So the cop in me, or what's left of the cop in me, got to thinking: maybe whoever did Greg wasn't someone from these parts. Maybe someone passing through killed him. Or maybe a new arrival. Say, someone from New York City."

"Becker," Delores whimpered. "The scissors . . ."

Plummer took a step forward, raising the gun barrel slightly so that it was aimed at Booth's head.

"I hope your aim is true, Harlin, because if you miss I'll bury these scissors in her chest up to the handle."

The gun in Plummer's hand trembled slightly—not much, but enough for Booth to notice and smile. Plummer relaxed his hand a little so that the gun seemed again to be aimed at nothing in particular. "Your suspicions are rather thin, even by the usual sorry standards of police work."

"But then you established a pattern."

"Indeed?"

Plummer nodded. "After I sobered up, I went to the library in New Orleans and read the back issues of the Jerusalem paper. Katharine Culpepper Simonette was the second murder. That established the pattern. Two murders, each displaying the same . . ."

Plummer's jaw muscles tensed and relaxed.

". . . each displaying the same tendency for violence."

"Why don't you just say that they were both tortured and slowly, sadistically killed with an almost-unheard-of savagery?"

Delores had started to cry silently, but she no longer resisted Booth.

"I was somewhat surprised that the police saw no connection between the two murders."

"I guess I'm just lucky," Booth said, and grinned.

"It's a small city and a small police force. They're not as good as I was." Plummer blinked slowly and looked at the man he knew as Becker Thorne as if for the first time. "I know everything I need to know about you, Thorne. The way you kill demonstrates that you like killing, that you'll kill again, and that you'll keep on killing until someone stops you." He made a dismissive gesture with the .38. "And so here we are."

"Yes," Booth said, twisting the scissors a bit to increase Delores's suffering, "here we are."

"My bet would be that you're responsible for the serial killings in New York City that stopped about the time you came to Mississippi."

"*Detective,*" Booth said with emphasis, "*now* you are beginning to impress me."

"I read up on that, too. Of course, somebody with as much money as you have could leave this state, or even the country, with a good chance that I would never turn up enough hard evidence to nail you. You got away with it in New York, so why can't you get away with it here, right? We both know that no prosecutor worth his party's endorsement is going to risk his career by hauling a billionaire into court without an airtight case. I'd lay odds that you're going to get away with it all."

"As you can see, I'm hardly quaking with fear that I'm about to be arrested."

"But it will be different if you hurt the girl. If that happens, there will be a witness, Thorne, and evidence, and all your past cleverness won't be worth a tinker's damn. Besides," Plummer added with a shrug, "if you hurt the girl, I'll be forced to shoot you where you stand. Of course, I'm a practical man. If you let the girl go and walk away from here a free man, you're just going to go on killing. The poker player in me says that maybe I ought to go ahead and put a slug in your head. Even if you did manage to put those scissors through the girl's heart, she'd be the last person you ever killed."

"No-o-o-o-o-o," Delores wailed.

"You do like to gamble," Booth said without giving any indication that he thought the man with the gun had the upper hand.

"I would say we have a Mexican standoff, Thorne, so let's work out a deal."

"What do you have in mind?"

"You put the shears down and let the girl go, and I won't blow your fucking head off."

"What kind of deal is that?"

"The only one I'm going to offer. You can take your chances after that. It'll be your money and your lawyers against whatever we can dig up on you to tie you to the other killings."

"I'll never say a thing about tonight if you let me go!" Delores promised in a pathetic voice. "I swear it!"

"You're not as stupid as you appear," Booth told Plummer, and chuckled. "You're right. We have played this little game to stalemate. Now, am I to understand that we will both behave like rational men if I let Kewpie Doll up off the table?"

"You have my word," Plummer said, his unblinking eyes on Booth.

"All right then."

The hand holding the scissors dropped to Booth's side.

Plummer lowered the revolver.

Delores dragged herself over the edge of the table and stood on shaky legs. She pulled the halves of her polo shirt together. The superficial but bloody wound instantly soaked the white cotton material.

Plummer nodded at Delores, motioning her forward with his left hand. She took a tentative step. Then, convinced that her assailant was really going to let her go, she began to run toward Plummer.

Booth's hand shot out and caught Delores, snapping her backward.

"Stop!" Plummer shouted, lifting the gun.

But Booth was not going to stop. He took the girl's head in both his hands and with one quick movement snapped her neck. Delores's eyes rolled up in her head, and her right arm and leg began to twitch spasmodically as her shattered spinal cord exploded with a flurry of random, meaningless nerve impulses.

Staring at Plummer with a look of triumph, Booth let the body slip slowly from his hands and crumple onto the greenhouse floor.

The crescendo of organ music from the party penetrated the

greenhouse as Plummer leveled the gun at Booth's chest and pulled the trigger three times.

Booth flinched three times, once for every slug that penetrated his chest.

Plummer stood looking at the killer, waiting for him to collapse, dead. Booth's right arm suddenly snapped upward. Plummer felt a peculiar tightness in his chest. He took a step backward, then all at once began to reel, his balance suddenly gone. He realized he was falling and grabbed a handful of palm leaves on his way down. He landed on the floor in a sitting position, the revolver clattering away on the cement.

Plummer looked down with disbelief at the scissors buried in his chest. He began to cough and tasted blood. He knew his right lung was punctured. Plummer looked up and saw Booth still standing in the same spot, looking down on him, a derisive grin plastered across his face.

Plummer knew he'd made a fatal error. The killer was wearing a bullet-proof vest under his jacket. Plummer silently cursed himself for taking the easy torso shot instead of the more difficult head shot. It had been a long time since he'd been to the target range, and he hadn't trusted his aim.

But still, Plummer thought, it didn't make sense. He could see arterial blood soaking the killer's jacket. It was leaching up his shirt as Plummer watched. The slugs he'd fired had hit at least one major artery. The killer was losing massive amounts of blood with each beat of his heart.

He's dead on his feet, Plummer thought, amazed the killer continued to stand.

Booth began to smile, revealing two oversized fangs hanging from his upper jaw.

Booth bent and grabbed the dead girl's arm, lifting her as if she weighed no more than a child's doll. Delores's head lolled back and forth unnaturally as the killer cradled her in his arms.

Booth winked rakishly at Plummer, then buried his teeth in the dead woman's neck.

I'm in shock, Harlin Plummer thought. I'm in shock and I'm hallucinating. . . .

He looked dumbly down at the scissors in his chest and realized he would bleed to death if he didn't get medical attention. His mind was already playing outrageous tricks on him. The mere thought of the blood leaking into his right lung seemed to cue another coughing fit. The pain was so intense that Plummer thought he would faint.

Plummer opened his eyes and blinked. Everything except the pain was hazy and indistinct. He'd been unconscious, he knew, but he didn't think he'd been out very long. The killer was still holding the dead girl, his face still buried in the crick of her neck. The skin on her arms had become very white and seemed puckered and wrinkled.

Booth, sensing Plummer's attention, lifted his blood-smeared face from the neck wound where he had been feasting on the dead girl's blood.

"This isn't real!" Plummer said out loud through clenched teeth.

"Don't waste what little time you have left trying to convince yourself your eyes are deceiving you. What you see is dead-on real."

Booth dropped Delores's body and wiped his mouth on the back of his jacket sleeve, managing only to smear the blood across his face. Even from where he sat, Plummer could see that the killer's eyes were clear, and his complexion, still pale, had taken on a healthier color. His cheeks were flushed, even rosy. He did not look like a man who should have already been dead from shock and blood loss. There was no more sign of frank bleeding from the three holes in his chest. It was as if the bleeding had miraculously stopped.

"My God," Plummer gasped. "You're a . . ."

Another coughing fit racked his body, cutting off his words.

"Yes," Booth said triumphantly, "I *am*! And just so you don't have to go to your grave not knowing for certain," he added brightly, coming toward Plummer, "I did kill Gregory, and Katharine, and so many others that I won't have time to tell you about them all in the little time you have left alive. The only thing you really need to know is that I am the Fury, who has come to Jerusalem to punish its wicked children."

Booth reached down and, gathering the lapels of Plummer's suit jacket in his right hand, effortlessly hoisted him up until their faces were inches apart.

"And," Booth added defiantly, the sneer lifting his right lip enough to fully expose the scimitar-shaped blood fang, "I am just getting started."

IX

The Buchanan Secret

11:05 P.M. Friday—The small woman in the hooded cape crossed quickly to Victoria Buchanan, reaching out her hands with their crimson-painted fingernails.

"You're trembling," she said, reaching up to put a protective arm around Victoria's shoulders.

"I'm . . . We're . . ."

Victoria could not speak. There had been no ambiguity in John Wilkes Booth's eyes. He had intended to kill her and gut her like a rabbit, she knew, and she'd only escaped through the inexplicable intervention of this tiny woman.

"It is quite all right, Miss Buchanan. Take as much time as you need to compose yourself. You're with a friend and safe from whatever it is that has so terrified you. Can I get you something to drink?" the woman asked kindly.

"A glass of water would be lovely."

She moved toward the door.

"No! Please don't leave me."

"Very well, child." The woman's eyes were filled with concern, yet she required no further explanation. "There is champagne."

"That would be fine, if there's nothing else."

The diminutive Italian filled a fluted crystal glass from the bottle in the silver bucket and handed it to Victoria.

"You had the most horrified look on your face when Becker came into the room. Does this have something to do with him? It is none of my business, but I hope he did not make some unwelcome advance. He is usually such a gentleman."

"Oh, no, Captain Vittorini. He is no gentleman. He's a, he's a . . ."

Her voice broke before the momentous accusation.

"He is what, Miss Buchanan?"

"A killer."

The woman looked at Victoria with a mixture of shock and disbelief.

"Tonight. In this house. Upstairs. I've seen the bodies."

The woman stared at Victoria.

"You've got to believe me. The man you know as Becker Thorne is extremely dangerous. You *must* help me."

The other woman looked at Victoria for a long moment, seemingly comparing what Victoria had just told her with what she knew, and sensed, about their host.

"What do you want me to do?"

"Help me find Lucretia Noire. She'll be able to help us convince the others to leave. We'll make something up. We can say there's a gas leak—anything to get them away from Arlington."

Victoria's eyes locked onto the other woman's. They were the most amazing shade of Tyrrhenian blue. For a few seconds Victoria almost forgot what she was about to say.

"If they stay, he will kill them all."

"Consider it done," the woman said with a Mona Lisa smile. "I know exactly where Miss Noire is at this moment."

"Oh, my God, suddenly it all makes sense to me. I couldn't figure out why you were wearing that robe, but now I understand everything."

"I beg your pardon, Miss Buchanan?"

"I came here to ensure that Miss Noire was able to escape unharmed, but you're one step ahead of me. You got here before I did and exchanged clothes with Miss Noire so that she could leave unnoticed. She put on your Salvation Army uniform and escaped, while you—as we both can see—put on her costume and remained behind."

The Italian woman's laughter was musical.

"You have the most wonderfully vivid imagination, Miss Buchanan. Lucretia Noire did not run away from Arlington Plantation in a Salvation Army costume. She is still here."

"Where?"

"Here." The woman swept her hand down across the front of her body to indicate herself.

Victoria still didn't understand.

"I am an extremely private person, Miss Buchanan. I never allow myself to be photographed. I travel incognito. It is rather fun to masquerade as someone new for a few days. It helps give me insight into the characters I create in my books. I visited Becker earlier this summer in the guise of Captain Vittorini. Do not look so shocked. It is only a harmless bit of misdirection to spare me the attention of my overly attentive fans."

"*You* are Lucretia Noire?"

"I confess I am. But Lucretia Noire is no more my real name than is Captain Vittorini. You will forgive me if I do not divulge my given name. I am, as I said, an extremely private person."

Victoria stared a moment and then began to nod. This was an incredible bit of information to assimilate, but not nearly so incredible as some of the other truths that had made themselves known to her in the past twenty-four hours.

"Miss Noire, you must believe me when I tell you what a great danger Booth—excuse me, *Thorne*—poses to us all tonight."

"By all means do let us call him Booth, Miss Buchanan. I know who he really is."

Victoria's jaw fell.

"And I know what he is."

Victoria's heart began to pound again.

"Do not misunderstand me, Miss Buchanan. I heartily agree that we must protect the others. But do not worry. I know exactly how to deal with John. He has episodes when his delusions overcome him. I won't equivocate with you, Miss Buchanan. During these periods he is indeed a threat to ordinary mortals—and to himself, of course. But you must not hold it against him. He's not entirely well mentally. But I can control him."

"The bodies I found in the chapel are hardly an indication that he's under anybody's control," Victoria said, her voice shaking.

"I am sorry that I cannot bring those unfortunate souls back to life. But you must not be so quick to condemn John. John is a special creature, wondrous and brilliant in many ways. As you've surely guessed, he belongs to a rare and precious species. He is not human—I do not mean this in a critical sense—and therefore is not bound by mortal values and mortal laws."

"*Mortal* laws?" Victoria echoed in disbelief.

"John Wilkes Booth is a vampire. I can see that you know as much, so I won't insult your considerable intelligence by denying it. However, you must not think of John as a monster, but rather as a member of a wonderful but secretive race of beings, with unique needs and desires. It is true that John requires fresh human blood to survive. I can see that, as a mortal, you find this frightening and repulsive, Miss Buchanan. It is not repulsive to John. His need to drink blood is something that is neither good nor bad. For the vampire, the Hunger is simply something that *is*.

"There is a side to John I daresay you have never imagined. He has the strength of twenty men. He can read a book in ten minutes and recite it back to you word for word. He knows more about Shakespeare than all the English professors in the world combined. The depth of his poetic sensitivity would astound you. I understand that you are an expert on Romantic and Victorian poetry, Miss Buchanan. Have you ever talked about poetry with John? You must hear him recite *The Rime of the Ancient Mariner*. Only a vampire with John's sensitivity understands what it means to be rejected by all of mankind, to have the cross of brotherhood and friendship exchanged for a stinking necklace of carrion."

"That hardly excuses the horrible crimes he has committed," Victoria said, her body trembling.

"We each have a beast living inside our souls, Miss Buchanan. Even you, I daresay, although perhaps you have never met it. Mortals are fortunate enough to be surrounded by family and friends; the ebb and flow of daily living serves to keep the beast in the background. But what of the vampire? He must live forever, and forever he must walk alone, always secretive, always on his guard against the jealous, prying eyes of the humans who would kill him without so much as a thought. Tell me, Miss Buchanan: Given the power to make it happen, would you not wish John Wilkes Booth dead in the blink of an eye?

"No—stop. Do not try to protest. I daresay I know the subject better than you, Miss Buchanan. The vampire has always been feared and hated by mortal society. When the mere fact of a vampire's existence becomes known, he is invariably hunted down and killed by mortals too insecure about their own powers to suffer such a creature to live.

"Is it any wonder that the sensitive souls of rare beings such as John turn inward on themselves with time and become twisted? The beast has an eternity to gain the upper hand in the vampire's soul. But it is not the beast as much as mortal society that drives vampires like John beyond the pale. If you starve a man, is it a crime that he steals food to live? If you persecute a man, is it a crime that he fights back? If you drive a man from society and treat him as an object of fear, is it a crime or a subject of wonder that he becomes an outcast and adopts a means of living that makes him fearsome?"

The woman smiled at Victoria, displaying her perfect white teeth.

"So you see, my dear Miss Buchanan, the question is infinitely more complex than you first imagined. I do not deny that I have tried to be a friend to John. It has not been easy. Not with the *Illuminati* out to destroy him. Do you know who they are?"

Victoria shook her head, wondering if the *Illuminati* was the organization of "watchers" Wolf Toland had said he belonged to.

"The Inquisition did not end with the Dark Ages, dear lady, but continues down to today in the guise of the *Illuminati*. The *Illuminati* is a secretive, elitist worldwide organization. Its purpose, as the self-appointed and self-righteous guardian of society, is to wipe out everybody and everything that threatens its myopic view of the world. *Illuminati* pogroms have driven the *Vampiri* race to the brink of extinction. Some of its few surviving members have, like John, been driven half-mad by the persecution."

The woman smiled sadly.

"Wolf Toland is an *Illuminati* agent. I know what that look on your face means, Miss Buchanan. Do not blame yourself for falling prey to his lies. Toland—that is not his real name, of course—is an extremely persuasive liar. Unfortunately, he has been able to delude David Parker into subscribing to his mindless, racist prejudice. The two of them came from New York for the express purpose of killing John."

Victoria had always known there was something peculiar about David, something that did not quite meet the eye. As attracted as she was to David, she had never been able to completely trust him. What the Italian woman told her merely confirmed what she had known, and suspected, all along.

"I am telling you more than I should, Miss Buchanan, but the *Illuminati* have given me no small measure of trouble. They are the real reason I pretended to be Captain Vittorini when I traveled to Jerusalem. They are the reason why no one, not even my publisher, knows my real name, and why I have never allowed 'Lucretia Noire' to be photographed."

The woman's eyes became sad.

"I've been trying to help John. You must believe me when I tell you that I've made remarkable progress. Yet I do not know if I can bring him back. Can I depend on you for help? You cannot imagine how great an effect it would have on him to meet another human being who does not loathe him with every breath she takes."

The idea shocked Victoria. Booth terrified her. She could not imagine abetting the maniac in any way that would allow him to remain free so that he might kill again.

"I don't think you understand what Booth is capable of doing, Miss Noire. I do. Maybe you should see the chapel for yourself before you think about helping him further."

"I know all about his excesses," she said, and sighed.

"I'm not sure you do," Victoria countered. "If John Wilkes Booth's life as a mortal was filled with mental instability and murder, how can his life as a vampire be any different?"

The woman looked sharply at Victoria.

"I would think that a Buchanan would be reluctant to condemn John Wilkes Booth."

Victoria's face became pale. "What do you know about John Wilkes Booth and my family?"

"Surely someone as haunted by the past as you knows that. Do you mean to tell me you don't know the Buchanan Secret?"

Victoria shook her head slowly.

"That is what your ancestor Isaiah Buchanan called it: The Buchanan Secret. Echoes of it are everywhere. Take, for instance, the words engraved on the Buchanan family tomb: 'Speak hands for me.' Do you know the quotation? It's from Shakespeare's *Julius Caesar*. It's what one of the assassins says as he stabs Caesar."

"But the Buchanan Secret . . ."

"The Buchanan Secret is simply that the Buchanans and the other Founding Families were in league with John Wilkes Booth in the conspiracy to kill Abraham Lincoln."

"That's a lie," Victoria said, unwilling to accept the full truth.

"No, dear lady, it is not. There is no one more unimpeachable than my source. John Wilkes Booth was, after all, a witness to history."

"He's mad."

"He is indeed mad, but that does not discount the Buchanan Secret. I know the entire story. Would you like to hear it?"

The part of Victoria that did was so at war with the part of her that didn't that Victoria found it impossible to answer. It hardly mattered, as Nicoletta was determined to tell the tale whether Victoria wanted to hear it or not.

"Your family met John for the first time when his Shakespearean troupe was touring the South. He was a radical secessionist, meaning he shared the same political sentiments as the Buchanans and the other wealthy planters in the Deep South. He became romantically involved with Anna Lee Buchanan. They were very much in love. Or so John thought.

"He became a spy during the war. It was a perfect job for him. He was an actor, a master of disguise, and traveled freely throughout the North. When it became clear that the South was going to lose the war, a cabal of wealthy men decided that desperate times called for desperate measures. The leader of this group of gentrified reactionaries was General Noah Buchanan."

"Please, stop," Victoria said, pressing her fingertips against her temples.

"His father, Ezekial, the former United States senator, was involved," the woman went on in a relentless tone. "Following the almighty Buchanan lead, all of Jerusalem's Founding Families became involved in the conspiracy. They donated the gold John Wilkes Booth needed to hire a cadre of special agents to go to Washington City. At first, the plan was for them to make mischief of one sort or another.

"In the beginning, they planned to kidnap key members of Lincoln's cabinet. None of their missions were successful. But as Lee and the other generals in the field succumbed to the obvious and surrendered, the conspirators decided to take one last desperate try at an action that would stun the Union so completely that the South might somehow be saved in the eleventh hour. It was Noah Buchanan who came up with the idea. And he gave Booth the order. He instructed Booth to murder Lincoln."

Tears began to stream down Victoria's cheeks. Everything she believed about her family was dissolving into a morass of treachery and treason.

"You know the story of the president's assassination, but there's more that the conspirators were careful to conceal. John employed a petty criminal who looked remarkably like him. It was this thief's body that the Federals recovered. John was already halfway to Arlington by the time the Yankees were gloating over the corpse of the man they mistakenly believed killed Lincoln.

"Anna Lee had promised to go to South America with John and become his wife. The first hint that his supposed brothers-in-arms had turned against him came when he returned to Arlington and discovered that he no longer had a place in Anna Lee's heart. It seems that Anna Lee would sooner betray her lover than disobey her family. Unlike his so-called friends, John truly was a Southern gentleman, and he freed Anna Lee of her obligation to him. That same night he rode alone to Arlington Landing to bid farewell forever to the men he thought were his allies. His duplicitous compatriots had promised him enough gold to start life anew in South America, although he hoped the Confederacy would rise after Lincoln's death, allowing him to return."

The woman went to the champagne and poured herself a glass before returning to the couch. Instead of speaking, she sat looking into the wine as if she had suddenly forgotten the rest of her story.

"Go on," Victoria said finally in a small voice.

"No, this is clearly too painful for you."

"I must hear it!"

"Very well." She took a small drink. "The Federals reacted aggressively to Lincoln's death. Anyone suspected of even knowing Booth and his agents was thrown into jail. Noah and the others didn't like the idea that they might soon find themselves being fitted for a hangman's noose. The bravado that had led them to plan such a daring blow against their Northern enemy left them once Lincoln's body lay dying in a bed across the street from Ford's Theater. Fortunately, they could take comfort in the knowledge that they had been exceedingly cautious. There was only one man who could connect them to the assassination—John Wilkes Booth.

"Desperate men do desperate things, Miss Buchanan. They might conspire to kill a president. Or they might plot to kill a friend. They were all gathered at Arlington Landing when John arrived. He made a brief speech about loving the South so well that he was willing to sacrifice his life for it. He went to shake hands with Noah Buchanan, but Noah raised a pistol instead and shot him in the chest. John fell backward into the Mississippi. The dark, swirling waters carried him away.

"Betrayed by the woman he loved. Betrayed by the friends he admired as the finest examples of Southern honor. Forget what they did to his physical body—can you begin to imagine the damage they did to John's soul?

"Can you still find it within your heart to condemn John when the Buchanans and their friends made him into what he is today? Your family helped shape Booth into the man who killed Lincoln, but they also helped turn him into the vampire who killed Amanda Hornsby and the others. Little wonder that he has come back to Jerusalem after all these years to revenge himself on the place."

"Is that why he's here?" Victoria asked, suddenly grasping the larger picture. "Booth came back for revenge?"

"John Wilkes Booth came back to Jerusalem for justice."

"What does the blood on his hands now have to do with justice?" Victoria asked desperately. "The men who wronged him have been dead for a century."

"John is interested in justice of a biblical kind. But I can appreciate the trouble you have understanding. When you look at Amanda Hornsby's body upstairs, the only thing you see with your limited understanding is the product of senseless savagery. John looks at the same body and sees an expression of eternal justice. More than a century later, the Founding Families are being made to pay for their sins. It says in the Bible that the sins of the fathers are visited upon the children."

Victoria shook her head in violent disagreement. "The Bible does not condone psychopathic violence. You are as insane as he is if you believe that."

"He thinks that he's a Fury, Miss Buchanan," Nicoletta went on lightly. "You know about the Furies from Greek mythology. But in his mind the Furies have become confused with avenging angels. He believes he's a combination of the two entities. And you saw the Pegasus sign in the chapel. He worships it. He thinks it's God, or that neon is, or that they both are. It's a terrible muddle, I'm afraid, although I suppose it makes sense to John."

Victoria looked at the woman with the profoundest kind of disgust.

"You're no better than an accomplice to his crimes."

"Yes," Nicoletta replied without remorse, "and in more ways than you understand. I made John what he is, you see. I gave him immortality."

Victoria pushed herself backward until her spine touched the arm of the couch and she could go no further.

Princess Nicoletta Vittorini di Medusa smiled at Victoria, revealing her distending blood teeth.

"My servants pulled John from the river that night," she said, a faraway look coming into her eyes. "From the moment I saw him I loved his sensitive, handsome face, which has an unmistakably tragic quality to it. He had become, quite unwittingly, the equivalent to one of the protagonists in a Shakespearean tragedy—surrounded by treachery and lies and betrayal. He would have died, but I transformed him. I gave him the gift of the blood. And then I took him to Europe. We were very happy there for a long time, although that's all over now, I'm afraid."

She finished her champagne and put down the glass, frowning at it.

"You will forgive me if I refresh myself with a drink that better suits my body's requirements."

Victoria raised her hands, but the vampire only laughed.

"Not you, darling," she said, amused by Victoria's terror. "John would never forgive me if I kept you all for myself. Kurt!" She clapped her hands twice. "Come to me, sweetness!"

A clumsy thrashing came from the other side of the door to the adjoining room. Many years before, the room had served as the Buchanan men's gun room; it was used as a storage area by the sisters, and for God knew what by Booth. The futile fumbling with the door handle filled Victoria with nameless dread.

The door swung open and a strangely dressed, attractive young man in an old-fashioned double-breasted business suit emerged. Kurt Teameyer stood looking straight ahead, his fedora lost and forgotten, his blond hair askew.

"Come to me, my lover," the vampire said, her voice low and caressing.

He walked forward with jerky, artificial movements, his feet lifting straight up and coming straight down noisily, arms hanging limp at his sides, his eyes fixed on nothing and apparently seeing nothing in his trance. His face had a pale, unhealthy pallor. Victoria could see ugly purple bruises on his neck, although there was no sign of any open wound.

"You can't—"

The words caught in Victoria's throat. She felt as if a powerful pair of invisible hands had taken her by the neck.

"Sit quietly," the vampire hissed, "or I will not bother saving you for John."

The stranglehold eased. Victoria sat gasping for breath, trying to bring her hands to her throat and finding her body inexplicably paralyzed. Her lack of command over her muscles did not, unfortunately, keep her eyes from following the macabre scene unfolding in the library.

Kurt Teameyer moved stiffly to the vampire and stood there at attention, as motionless as a Buckingham Palace guard while the vampire reached up to caress his face.

"Amore mio," she said lovingly.

The young man got clumsily down on one knee, then shifted heavily on the other knee, bowing his head. Even on his knees he was nearly as tall as the diminutive Nicoletta.

"My delicious young man," she said, combing her fingers through his tousled hair. "I am so sorry that our previous moment together was interrupted by this insipid woman. But now, my dear, we shall consummate our love for all eternity."

Victoria Buchanan was helpless to do anything but watch.

X

Temptation

11:45 P.M. Friday—"I say, old chap. William Champion's the name, *Sir* William Champion. This is Lady Champion."

David looked blankly at the man, his mind barely registering the fatuous grin beneath the waxed mustache.

"Simply smashing party, what? Jolly good fun."

The bogus Sir William was decked out in a faux-Victorian frock coat rented from a costume shop. He wore his hair combed straight down in front to conceal his receding hairline. His consort, a younger woman with uncertain balance on her spike heels, was inexplicably dressed as a flapper from the Roaring Twenties, an outfit that placed her character at least twenty years later in history than her companion.

"You must be one of the lucky chaps playing a character Miss Noire created especially for the Vampire Convention. I rather envy you, old boy."

Who was this fool?

Drunken laughter erupted nearby around a man pretending to bite a middle-aged brunette in the neck.

David cast a disparaging look around the room.

Who were any of these fools?

Couldn't they guess what was coming?

There was no hope for them—almost no hope. Everything depended on David now that Mozart was gone.

"What's so funny?"

The sardonic smile disappeared from David's face as he returned his attention to the phony Englishman.

"I beg your pardon?"

"I introduced myself," the man said, slurring his words, "and you ignored me, and then started to grin, as if I'd said something terribly damned funny."

"Excuse me, Sir William," David said as if placating a child. "I was smiling at a private thought that amused me."

David could read the man without even trying. His name was Peter McCormick. He was an insurance executive from Wisconsin. He'd brought his mistress to the Vampire Convention, leaving his wife at home with their five children.

"No problem then, old chap. It's just that for a moment I thought you'd cut me." David could see the belligerence win back possession of McCormick's drunken eyes. "I don't much like being cut at a party," he added. "In fact, I don't like it one damned bit."

McCormick was intoxicated—like almost everybody else at the party. David had never seen champagne served so fast. He guessed that Booth had ordered his hirelings to intentionally get his guests drunk as a way to blunt their ability to react when the violence began.

David matched McCormick's icy stare. "Leave me alone," he said.

McCormick's breath caught in his throat at the merest hint of David's inner strength.

"Come on, Valerie," McCormick said, taking his mistress's

arm as he backed away, using her to help keep his balance when he stumbled slightly. "I need another drink."

"May I please have your attention, ladies and lords of the vampire realm."

David looked sharply up to the first staircase landing. The speaker was a beautiful young woman with auburn hair dressed as a Roman noblewoman. She wore a long, sleeveless cotton dress with golden armbands and a necklace of ancient-looking coins.

"Draw near, my brothers and sisters in blood, for midnight is almost upon us. When witching hour tolls, our hostess, Lucretia Noire, will introduce you to a surprise guest: the prince of vampires."

The crowd broke into raucous applause, several of the men whistling as if they were at a sporting event. They'd had enough to drink to be ready for something exciting—and, hopefully, frightening. David heard a woman behind him mutter that there was no "prince of vampires" in Noire's books, but if that was true, it seemed to matter little to the other guests.

"I have been asked to warn you," the auburn-haired woman began again, then paused for dramatic effect.

The woman was a representative of Miss Noire's publisher. David *sensed* that the woman—her name was Mona Thompson—had deep misgivings about the evening. He gently probed her mind to learn why.

This party is a sham.

Mona Thompson was right, or course, yet she had only surmised a small fraction of the truth. Though she had never met Lucretia Noire before that night, Mona was certain that the woman claiming to be the author was an impostor. The alleged Lucretia had been evasive when Mona asked several specific questions about Noire's bestselling vampire novels. Mona was sure the woman hadn't written the books; she doubted the impostor had even read them.

Mona knew of Lucretia Noire's famous aversion to publicity. Perhaps the real Lucretia Noire had intended to attend the Vampire Convention, but found herself at the last minute unable to overcome her reclusiveness. Or maybe she never intended to come at all. Whichever, Mona Thompson found herself in the unenviable role of accomplice. She had been sent to the Vampire Convention to represent the publisher—and apparently also to represent the real Lucretia Noire. Though she found the situation extremely distasteful, she did not believe it was her place to expose the fraud.

"I have been asked to warn you," she said, picking up where she had left off, "that the remainder of this evening's entertainment is not for the faint of heart. Miss Noire's publishers are somewhat nervous about the likelihood that they may incur liability should one of you have a heart attack—although that hardly seems likely, since most of you are already dead."

The crowd laughed, but David didn't. Without Mozart to help him, they *were* already as good as dead.

David!

It was Victoria Buchanan. She was in danger.

David Parker had never been comfortable with the telepathic powers he gained when he became a vampire, but he was glad for them now as he pushed his way through the crowd, using his mind to order people to move out of the way.

David sensed Victoria was somewhere in the back of the house, somewhere down the roped-off hall.

"Sorry sir, but you can't go past here."

The gigantic man had positioned himself in front of the rope. When he spoke, the whiskey voice rumbling from deep inside his barrel chest managed to convey politeness and menace at the same time.

"Open the gate."

The man's pupils went out of focus.

"Yes, sir," he said, unhooking the rope.

David!

Victoria was in the library, David knew, even though he had never been inside Arlington and had not known, until that moment, that the mansion had such a room. He hurried down the hall, past a door discolored with the unmistakable aura of death. David knew Victoria didn't have much time left, so he did not waste time trying to help someone already beyond help—Gianni Rourke, though David was in such a panic over Victoria that he failed to realize that the body in the butler's pantry belonged to his old nemesis.

David stopped cold outside the library door.

The vibrations emanating from the room beyond the door were the strongest—and darkest—David had ever perceived. There was a vampire in the room with Victoria—an extremely powerful vampire who even in repose radiated twice as much power as David had ever witnessed in Mozart. Now David knew why even Mozart, the preeminent member of the *Illuminati*, doubted that he had the strength to match this vampire—not Booth, but the same ancient creature who had transformed Mozart on a cold spring night in Vienna centuries earlier.

Standing alone in the hall, David began to think the unthinkable. He knew he could not save the others from such a formidable evil, but he could save himself. He ran the familiar complaints through his mind. He hadn't volunteered for this job. He'd said from the first that he did not have the wherewithal to successfully bring the fiend from New York City to justice.

His situation at present devolved to a matter of simple logic. Opening the door to Arlington Plantation's library would be tantamount to suicide. The other vampire could destroy him with the lift of an eyebrow. David knew he was only being allowed to sense the presence because it suited the other vampire for him to do so.

Maybe the vampire had only revealed itself to David thinking it would frighten him away.

Or maybe it wanted to challenge him, to see if he was brave enough to come into the library and die trying to save Victoria Buchanan.

Or maybe in some strange and twisted way, David's was trying to entice him.

David!

Victoria's psychic cry for help jerked him back to reality.

David!

He could never abandon Victoria to an unspeakably savage death. He pictured her smile, her long golden hair, her lithe, lovely body. David still wanted to conquer the emotional wall she'd built around her heart, even though he knew there was no real chance for happiness between a mortal and one of the *Vampiri*.

David!

He looked at the door latch.

David!

Opening the door meant facing an ancient evil he could not hope to defeat, yet he was even more afraid of what would happen to Victoria Buchanan if he didn't.

Clenching his jaw, he reached down and threw open the door.

* * *

He'd sensed only two presences inside the library, but the moment David opened the door he realized there were in fact three individuals in the room—only two of them living.

Victoria lay back in a club chair, arms dangling over the armrests, her eyes shut, her head fallen as far back as the chair would permit. Her skin was pale, yet it lacked the marble pallor of lifeless flesh. David saw her breasts rise and fall with an almost imperceptibly shallow respiration.

The man on the floor at Victoria's feet, however, was quite dead. He'd been bled so severely that his skin was as shriveled as a ninety-year-old man's, but the corpse's thick blond hair and mustache revealed that the body actually belonged to a much younger man. The dead man's companions, if he'd brought any to Arlington Plantation, could probably identify him by his elegant double-breasted suit.

David's eyes carefully avoided the third individual in the library. After looking first at Victoria and then the corpse of Kurt Teameyer, David's gaze shifted to the middle ground, where it focused on nothing in particular.

The vampire stood over against the bookcases, her hands folded in front of her, quietly watching David with an expression that might have been mistaken for sympathy.

A curious lassitude took possession of David now that he and the evil one were in the same room. The fear and anger he'd felt outside the library drained out of him, leaving only a depressed emptiness at the center of his soul. He was suddenly very tired. The *Illuminati* had forced him to shoulder a heavy burden; now, all he wanted was to be free of it.

David!

He lifted his eyes to Victoria's insensate face. He looked into her mind and saw only the uniform gray horizon of unconsciousness. She had not called out to him from the library, David realized. It had been the vampire, mimicking Victoria's distressed thoughts to lure him into the room. David had not known it was possible to impersonate a mortal's psychic voice, but then the other vampire was very old and no doubt knew even more *Vampiri* secrets than Mozart.

Reluctantly, David raised his eyes.

Captain Vittorini smiled shyly, as if concerned that David was angry with her.

Except that this was not Captain Vittorini. Not really. That was only who she pretended to be when she came to Jerusalem to help her insane protégé, John Wilkes Booth, commit mass murder. Her name had been Princess Nicoletta Vittorini di Medusa in the dream he'd had in New York City. Maybe that was her real name. Maybe not.

The vampire raised her chin, her smile changing from apologetic to seductive. Her lips were the deep purple-red of wine, and her complexion was no longer a uniform, milky white but rose pink and flush with life—from gorging on the dead man's blood.

She was the one who gave Mozart eternal life. She was so tiny and beautiful. She was an unlikely repository for so much power—for so much evil.

Nicoletta blinked slowly, her smile deepening.

David was fascinated with Princess Nicoletta Vittorini di Medusa, even though he knew it was dangerous to think of her as anything other than a monster who must be destroyed. She was obviously capable of appreciating transcendental beauty, since she'd decided to preserve Mozart's genius for the world. Yet she'd given the same gift to John Wilkes Booth, a twisted killer who perverted his *Vampiri* powers to commit his horrific crimes.

"I know this is difficult for you."

David did not answer. It was a mistake to be drawn into conversation with an outcast. The *Illuminati* taught that the evil ones would use all their guile to confuse and defeat the good members of their race. Yet her voice—it was more like singing than speech, a bewitchingly lyrical sound that seeded David's mind with strangely familiar, dreamlike images of moonlit Roman ruins and warm, perfumed night breezes whispering through the olive groves on forgotten Mediterranean islands.

"I know you are extremely intelligent, David. It is plain to me that you have reached certain conclusions. Yet I beseech you, sir, do not be too hasty in your judgment of me."

David reminded himself that he must pay no attention whatsoever to what she said.

"The unfortunate young man." She indicated the body with an alabaster hand that moved in concert with her falling sigh. "I am afraid I have not been as successful as I would like when it comes to controlling John."

It required a conscious effort for David to keep from looking at the dead man. It had not occurred to him that anyone besides Nicoletta was responsible for his death.

"And things are also not what they seem with your beautiful

lady friend. It is easy to understand why you are half in love with her."

David directed his energy toward guarding his thoughts while desperately trying to think of his next move. His powers were no match for Nicoletta's, but maybe he could think of something that would at least make it possible for him to get Victoria safely out of the mansion.

"Miss Buchanan was quite outraged at the way John butchered this poor man. She was about to throw herself on John when I stopped her. I hardly need tell you what the consequences would have been if she'd angered him. I put her peacefully to sleep for her own protection."

David tilted his head slightly, looking at Nicoletta through narrowed eyes. Was it possible that there was some truth in what she said?

"I will awaken Miss Buchanan whenever you wish, but I do not think it is advisable to do so until certain matters are resolved. She is perfectly safe with her champion standing close by. A lady needs a champion. That is how it has always been—in my day and in yours, dear David."

David tried to shut it out, but it was impossible to block Nicoletta's aria from his mind.

"Pray do not close your mind to me, David. I already know more about you than you imagine. I know, for example, about your life in Chicago and your time with Tatiana. I know how you followed John here from New York City. You tried so valiantly to stop his brutal crimes in the city, but of course you couldn't."

Her sad smile told him that she understood everything—his failure to stop the "Dracula" serial killer, and the guilt he suffered for it.

"It is not a crime to be young and inexperienced. And you are so young, David, so very young. I remember what it was like to be young. It was a long time ago, but I remember everything."

Her eyes began to shimmer.

"We never forget, do we, David. That is the curse of our race: We never forget."

"No," he said softly, answering for the first time.

"But I feel as if I have an unfair advantage. I know so much about you, while you know next to nothing about me. I am not Captain Vittorini. My true name is Princess Nicoletta Vittorini di Medusa."

"I know."

"Mozart told you."

"No. Wolf has never spoken your name in my presence. I dreamed about you."

"I dreamed about you, too."

"We were in a garden."

"In *my* garden."

"Then did we both have the same dream?"

"It is rare, but it happens. Two souls call out to each other across the distance, across the ages. But for us to find one another . . ."

David had an almost irresistible urge to take Nicoletta in his arms. The women in his life—Tatiana, Victoria, and the others—had left him filled with yearning, yet his deepest and most infallible intuition told him that he might find in Nicoletta the sense of completion he'd hungered for all his life.

"I have dreamed of you many times, David, ever since you were given the blood. I know that you are young, that you have been one of us only briefly, but still I feel . . ."

Nicoletta shrank as if David had attempted to strike her.

"Surely you do not think the fact that I have tried to befriend a friendless and tortured creature like John Wilkes Booth means I condone this?" She gestured at Kurt Teameyer's body. "Do you honestly believe I am capable of such base self-indulgence?"

David wanted to say no, of course not, but something made him hold back.

"I promise you, David, I *swear* to you with all my heart and soul, that I could never participate in or approve of such sickening violence."

"If that's true, how could you have let Booth commit such crimes?"

"That is so unfair!" Nicoletta protested, her voice breaking so pitifully that David felt as if his own heart were being torn in two. "You must understand and believe that I did not 'let' Booth do anything. He is a power unto himself and controlled by his own demons."

Nicoletta sank onto the couch, her hands between her knees, her eyes on the floor.

"Beauty has always been my weakness, as women have been yours, *amore mio*. That is why I transformed Mozart. He had barely scratched the surface of his talent and he was dying.

There was only one thing to do, and I did it. I made him immortal."

Nicoletta compulsively twisted the emerald ring she wore on her left index finger.

"John was a tragic mistake. I know that now. But you had to know him when he was a mortal man to understand why I did what I did. He was such a beautiful mortal. So filled with passionate intensity. The first time I saw him on stage I cried. It was 1864. He was performing with his brother and father in New York City, playing the lead role in *Julius Caesar*. He had such strong, dramatic features. There never was born a man better suited for tragedy on the stage, or in life, than John Wilkes Booth. John's chief failing was that he was manipulated by the men he trusted most—by the Buchanans and their ilk."

"You would dismiss Lincoln's murder that easily?"

"Left to his own devices, John never would have contrived such an act. The decision to kill Lincoln was made by others." Nicoletta paused a beat. "Here, in Jerusalem, at Arlington Plantation, in this very room."

"That can't be true," David said without conviction.

"Sit down, my dear David, and I will tell you everything," Nicoletta said.

When she was finished with her story, David found himself even more adrift.

"Those Booth trusted and loved treated him in the most treacherous manner imaginable. Is it any wonder he devised his own plan to return to Jerusalem and repay it for what its citizens did to him?"

"But there's no justice in punishing the Founding Families' descendants," David said, unable to forgive Booth his deeds no matter what the circumstances. "It's insane to think it's right to come back here now and bleed this town."

"I quite agree," Nicoletta said solemnly, "but to John's unbalanced mind, it makes perfect sense."

David looked at Nicoletta with disbelief. "But why in the name of God haven't you stopped him?"

"Don't you think I've tried?" Nicoletta cried, clasping her hands together. "I've held him back for more years than you guess. You cannot know what a nightmare it has been for me. The malignancy in John's mind took many years to manifest itself, as it sometimes does with *Vampiri*. I did not expect it. I did not predict it."

"But New York," David said without elaboration, as if the

memory of so many torn and mutilated bodies was all the argument he required.

"I did everything I could," Nicoletta said, sounding deeply hurt. "But not because I think it is wrong to take a mortal's life. That's a conceit of the *Illuminati*."

"No," David insisted, "killing is wrong."

"It is not wrong to kill a mortal. It is self-indulgent. It serves no purpose. It invites the unwanted and uncomfortable attention of mortal authorities. But it is not wrong. What have vampires to do with mortals? They are hardly an innocent and harmless race. They kill us whenever they can."

"Now I understand why you are not one of the *Illuminati*."

"I do not need them to govern my life. I have always been the mistress of my own province, even when I was mortal. Life is not worth living unless one lives it independently, David. That is where I split with Wolfgang."

"You transformed him."

"Yes, but he disappointed me. Despite Wolfgang's unparalleled musical genius, he was born to the petit bourgeoisie. Has he talked to you about his Masonic activities? *The Magic Flute* is rife with Masonic symbolism. The *Illuminati* are essentially the *Vampiri* equivalent of the Freemasons. I apologize for the bitterness in my tone, David, but the years have not made me any less unhappy at having lost a promising protégé to the *Illuminati*. Wolfgang could not resist them. I suppose it was natural that his childish fascination with secret handshakes and mystical jargon led him to fall in with the *Illuminati*.

"I, however, remain a dedicated individualist. I insist on leading my own life, privately, quietly, peacefully, outside the strictures of any organization's petty rules and hierarchy.

"Mozart has dutifully fed you the propaganda that a vampire can lead a meaningful life only through the *Illuminati*, that good and evil and everything in between can only be properly measured against that organization's guiding laws. By the same token, some men teach their sons that only by becoming Masons—or Catholics, or Rotarians, or Skull and Bones initiates—can the moral center be found and maintained. The world is bigger than this kind of narrow thinking, David. There is no monopoly on truth and virtue. You don't have to be a disciple of the *Illuminati* to be a good vampire. The fact that you do not choose to include yourself among their self-righteous circle does not make you evil. That sort of intolerance—and make no mistake, it is nothing more than intolerance—is in and of itself evil. Use your mind, David. Think for yourself. You do not need the *Illuminati* to tell you how to live."

The room was very still when Nicoletta was finished. The sound of the party seemed faraway and unusually subdued. They were all waiting for Lucretia Noire to introduce them to the prince of vampires, David thought.

"Everything you say makes a certain amount of sense," David said, and paused. "But what about Booth?"

"He has gone mad," Nicoletta said with what seemed like genuine regret. "He has become a menace to all *Vampiri*, and to himself."

"Then help me stop him."

"I can't," she said in a small voice. "I simply can't. I gave him the gift of blood. I was his lover for many years, David, until he went mad. I am something between a lover and a mother to him. I cannot take his life."

"Then what can I do?" David asked helplessly.

"I hope and I pray that you will try to stop John. I can't do it for you, but I can help you, and my help might be enough to do the job."

The sound of applause came through the door.

"The killing is about to start, David."

"The killing has already started," David said curtly, nodding again toward the body of dead young man.

"I'm talking about the wholesale slaughter. John plans for it to start at midnight. You've got to stop him. You are the mortals' only hope. You are Victoria Buchanan's only hope."

He looked at Victoria and sighed deeply. He had hoped—but no, he'd known all along there could be no real happiness between him and a mortal woman. He shifted his gaze to Nicoletta. She was powerful and wise but vulnerable. He saw her smile at him, a smile filled with sadness, hope, and the promise of something even more eternal than the everlasting life of the *Vampiri* race.

"All right," he said at last. "I'll try."

Nicoletta came to David and took his hand.

"Dear David, I knew you wouldn't fail me. Come, my champion. I will take you to him."

"And Victoria?"

"We should leave her here. She'll be safe."

"I would feel better if we took her with us."

Nicoletta bowed her head.

"As you wish, *amore mio*."

XI
The Fury

Midnight—Victoria rose to Nicoletta's wordless command and went to stand beside the library door.

"One thing before we go, David," Nicoletta warned. "You must not underestimate John."

"If you need to worry about something, worry about how I'm going to keep him from slaughtering the rest of his guests like he did this poor fool."

David shuddered as he stepped around Kurt Teameyer's shriveled body. Such violence was not only sadistic—it was utterly without purpose. For a vampire like David, keeping the Hunger at bay required only as much blood as it took to fill a wine glass once every two weeks; an older vampire like Booth needed less blood, less often. But the Hunger was not easily controlled. Fresh human blood was like a powerful drug to the *Vampiri*, and even a tiny draft of it delivered a bone-numbing rush of euphoria and strength. All the more reason why a vampire had to be supremely self-disciplined to avoid becoming a savage killer who hunted mortals not out of biological need but for the high that gorging on blood brought.

"I am not worried, *amore mio*. You will find a way to stop John."

"I wish I had your faith."

"I wish I had your courage."

"I'm not brave," David said, meaning it.

"You could not possibly be more wrong. When I look into your soul, I see the sort of courage that makes all things possible. You have the courage a man needs to be master of a stag hunt. You have never been on a stag hunt, of course."

David shook his head.

"They are rare these days, it is sad to say. I will have to arrange for my friend the marquis to have you as his guest so that you can experience one. You will relish every moment of it. The hunt is the finest expression of courage outside of the bull ring, though the act the matador performs in the arena with his sword is a very crude business compared to the master of the hunt's *coup de grace* with the stag."

David stared at Nicoletta, wondering how she could talk of such things when he had to go out the library door and face John Wilkes Booth. But then it occurred to him that Nicoletta was obliquely telling him what he had to do to destroy Booth.

"Hunts begin early in the morning, before the dawn, when the grass is wet with dew and heavy with scent. The master of the hunt and his assistants take the best dogs from the kennel and begin searching for the trail of a grand stag. An ordinary hind will not suffice. What is required is a fully mature male, the seasoned buck that is strong and swift, experienced and full of guile. When the sun comes up, the hunters gather at the appointed place. The evidence the hounds have discovered is weighed and discussed, the best stag selected. The hounds lead, followed by the gentlemen on their hunters, through thickets and streams, over fences and logs, unstoppable in their pursuit of the stag. It is a little like an English fox hunt, except the stag hunt is many times more dangerous, and therefore more beautiful.

"The chase can last all day. A worthy stag will lead its pursuers up impossibly steep banks and down treacherous defiles, through seemingly impenetrable forests, across open fields, over stone walls, fording streams and rivers. A truly good stag knows a thousand ruses. He will get on the scent of a younger buck and push him ahead a mile or two, then double back and split off, trying to trick the dogs into following his proxy. He will flush does into clearings first before crossing to make sure the path is clear. It is not unusual for a truly good stag to get away. The quarry is only brought to bay if the hunters are as strong and determined and resourceful as the beast they hunt.

"The most beautiful part of the hunt comes at the end, when the stag has been brought to ground. The hounds are trained to surround the stag, but to hold back. Sometimes a younger dog will try to move in and take down the stag, only to be thrown or gored for its audacity. It is the duty of the master of the hunt to serve the stag, armed with nothing but his courage and a silver dagger. That is the term that is used: to serve the stag. I find that particularly beautiful, for it has two meanings: if the master is courageous and skillful, he serves the stag by releasing it from the torment of the hunt, and he serves the hunters by freeing them of the responsibility for dispatching the beast in a matter befitting the honor owed it.

"The master of the hunt waits for his opening with the dagger in his hand. When he gets his chance, he must move swiftly and plunge the dagger into the stag's heart."

"And if he misses?"

"If his aim is anything but true, or if his courage wavers, he may pay with his life. Then it is the responsibility of one of the other hunters to fulfill the duty."

David looked closely at Nicoletta. Any vampire—including John Wilkes Booth—could be killed by the most ordinary means, if one went about it the right way.

"Come, my love," Nicoletta said. "The hunt is joined."

Nicoletta closed the library door and followed David Parker and Victoria Buchanan into the darkened hall. Victoria walked behind David toward the stairs, the noise of the party behind them, her eyes unfocused in her trance. Her movements were slow and languorous, as if she were sleepwalking. The aroma of her blood was nearly overpowering—pure, fresh, healthy. In her trance she was as helpless as a child, too innocent to know guile or how to employ it.

A few ill-defined thoughts floated across the surface of Victoria's mind. David put aside his distaste for thought-reading and examined her mind long enough to make out the dim outlines of the memory of John Wilkes Booth draining Kurt Teameyer of his blood—a counterfeit memory Princess Nicoletta Vittorini di Medusa had implanted in Victoria to mislead David.

David turned on the landing and looked back down at Victoria, wondering if she was strong enough to bear this without losing her mind. Her face was an impassive mask with faraway eyes, but a single tear streaked down her cheek, a sign that she had some awareness of what was happening even from within her trance.

"I know you care for this mortal, David Parker, and for your sake I will do everything within my power to see that she and the others are unharmed. But surely you realize you are beyond being able to find happiness with a mortal woman."

David nodded. He started to speak but discovered it was impossible for him to find the words to express his feelings.

"When this business is finished, I will help you be happy," Nicoletta said, leaning on the silver-headed walking stick she'd brought with her from the library. "This I promise you."

David turned and climbed the rest of the way to the second floor. The closed chapel doors loomed ahead in the darkness, the ominous red neon glow from the Pegasus sign leaking through the space between the bottom of the door and the floor. The dark, purple vibration of death emanating from down the hallway—invisible to mortals but not to vampires—was so strong that it was almost as if the air were thick with acrid smoke.

Victoria whimpered. Her eyes were fixed on the chapel doors, the red glow reflected in her eyes. She was trembling.

"She was up here earlier," Nicoletta said. "She must be remembering."

The aura of death streamed more thickly now from beneath the double doors at the end of the hallway, billowing and curling like smoke, a thick wine-colored fog tinged about its edges with the psychic yellow residue of violence and terror.

Booth was in the chapel—David could *feel* him now. The killer made no attempt to conceal his presence. David took this as an expression of Booth's arrogance: showing himself plainly demonstrated disdain for David's power.

David swallowed dryly and commanded his body to relax. He looked back.

Nicoletta's eyes went from David to Victoria and back again.

"You know she will die if you fail. They all will die. I am not sure that even I will survive, now that I have betrayed John. But if you succeed . . ."

Nicoletta's smile contained confidence as well as encouragement.

". . . you will save this town. Your success will win life for Jerusalem, and the Buchanans, and the other Founding Families."

Nicoletta took David's hand and brought it to her lips, kissing it tenderly.

"The chase has been run from New York to Mississippi, but you have finally brought the stag to bay. Now, my champion, all that remains is for you to slay the beast."

David reached for the door latch but abruptly stopped, his hand suspended in midair at the shriek that erupted from within the chapel—the inhuman cry a mixture of exultation, anger, and madness.

The hardware rattled. The doors opened without being touched and swung inward.

Booth had been as busy in the past hour as a spider preparing its web. He'd completed the work his factotum Nightingale had begun, transforming the chapel into one of the inner circles of Hell. Cables wired to the roof beams crisscrossed the room without apparent logic or order, and from the cables dangled scores of meat hooks—nearly enough to supply one for each of Booth's guests, David realized.

The floor was littered with the miscellaneous tools the killer had planned to use to torment his victims. Scanning the floor, David saw a broken magnum champagne bottle; a coil of barbed wire; a chain saw; a garden hoe; a crowbar; an electric transformer, the copper ends showing at the ends of two sinister and gummy-looking black cables; an electric knife plugged into a long, orange drop cord that had been mended with black electrical tape; a car battery with grayed jumper cables; a rusty screwdriver-like device used for gouging dandelions and thistles out of the ground.

The victims Booth had already accumulated that night had been moved from the corner of the room and were now neatly arranged before the altar, purplish silhouettes outlined by the bizarre red neon of the crackling electric Pegasus. His murderous harvest of the Founding Families had already begun, David saw, suppressing the nausea rising up within him.

Nightingale's body was suspended with the other cadavers, David noted with surprise. The man's head had been bashed in, and the amount of blood that continued to ooze from the body, accumulating on the floor beneath his feet, indicated that he hadn't been bled. Fortunately, there was no sign of Marcus Cuttler or Dr. Chesterfield in the chapel. David hoped they'd both survived their encounter with the dead Klansman.

Booth was nowhere in sight—a trick, David knew, as there was no way out of the room except through the door he'd just come through.

Victoria whimpered behind him.

"Don't let her see this," David whispered.

"Sleep more deeply, my lovely," Nicoletta said softly.

Nightingale's body began to revolve slowly. All at once Booth was there, standing in a vacant spot between the bodies, grinning malevolently at David. His jacket was off, and the ruffled white shirt he'd put on in place of the one he was wearing when Harlin Plummer shot him three times was flecked with blood. His hands were sheathed in yellow rubber kitchen gloves.

Booth extended his hands above his head.

David braced himself for the coming psychic assault. It could come in dozens of ways. Booth could try to make David's brain swell until it exploded; he could make the blood boil in his veins; he could turn David's stomach inside out and pull it up through his throat; he could tie David's liver in a knot, or use his intestines to crush his kidneys. Or Booth could simply make David's body tear itself apart with a single, overwhelming burst of psychokinetic energy. In the past, David himself had, in self-defense, made several criminal *Vampiri* disintegrate in a similar fashion.

Yet Booth did not attack. As David directed all of his energy to maintaining a protective psychic shield around himself, the killer began to offer a prayer to his private god, Neon.

"Behold, Neon has delivered the infidels unto the Fury of the Lord. The time has come to punish the wicked and smite the sinners. Let the ears of the damned be filled with the screams of the dying. Let their tongues be torn from their mouths and hot irons plunged into their entrails. For so it has been written in the Book of Revelation, that *'men will seek death and will not find it; they will long to die, and death will fly from them.'* "

The killer's gaze lowered to settle on David.

" 'I know your works; you have the name of being alive, and are dead.' "

"It's over, Booth," David said, surprised at the quiet anger in his own voice.

" 'When the Lamb opened the seventh seal, there was silence in heaven.' "

"You're not going to hurt any more innocents."

" 'And the fifth angel blew his trumpet, and I saw a star fall from heaven to earth, and he was given the key of the shaft of the bottomless pit.' "

David's head began to throb the way it had that day in the restaurant with Gianni Rourke. The anger was growing in him, unfolding its lethal petals like a deadly flower. Bloody images of the people Booth had killed flashed through David's mind, releasing the accumulated revulsion and hatred he felt for the psychopath. David felt himself beginning to shake. He knew the veins in his forehead were bulging. His skull splitting with agonizing pain, he looked at Booth and focused squarely on the space between the killer's eyes.

An anguished cry—part pain, part relief—escaped David's mouth the instant the deadly psychic bolt shot out of him, a blinding blue-green shaft of light that seemed to spear directly into Booth's forehead.

The blinding light left David rapidly blinking his eyes to clear them.

He expected to see a pink haze of blood and flesh suspended in the air where Booth's body had been moments before, but as his sight returned, David saw Booth himself standing there, grinning, utterly untouched by his best attack.

Booth met his eyes and began to smile.

" *'He opened the shaft of the bottomless pit, and from the shaft rose smoke of a great furnace, and the sun and the air were darkened with the smoke from the shaft.'* "

Attacking Booth had used most of David's strength, and he suddenly felt so weak that he thought he might collapse. He took a step sideways and grabbed the smooth, polished wood of a pew to steady himself.

Booth raised one gloved hand and pointed at David. " *'Then from the smoke came locusts on the earth, and they were given power like the power of scorpions on the earth.'* "

"John, please don't!" Nicoletta begged quietly.

The pressure on David's head was external and hurt instantly. He felt something moist trickle down his upper lip. Another trickle moved slowly down the side of his face. He touched his fingers to it, then looked at his fingertips. It was blood. He concentrated on countering Booth's power with his own, but he knew he could only hold him off a few minutes longer before his skull would be crushed like an eggshell.

"We are the locusts of the Lord. Even *he*"—Booth indicated David—"is a divine locust."

The pressure mercifully abated.

"And are we not also the Lord's scorpions?"

Booth moved to Amanda Hornsby Foster's desiccated body and touched it lovingly.

"Do we not sting our foes and feed upon their moisture? I ask you most honestly and humbly, do any of these wretched sinners have the mark of God upon their forehead? And I say unto you, the answer is no. Neither is the lamb's blood smeared above the doorways of the homes in this Jerusalem to save the inhabitants from the wrath of the Fury. The angel of death has come to punish the wicked, and none shall be spared."

The neon Pegasus crackled and buzzed, its light increasing twofold so that the tortured faces of the dead were fully illuminated.

"Witness these sinners and the fruit of their damnation." Booth moved to the next swinging corpse. "Lydia Chase, the incarnate Jezebel. She was Nightingale's handiwork. Alas, poor Nathan, I knew him well. But now, as you can see, he swings beside her. I fear your compatriots, the negro and the elderly doctor—an unlikely team—dispatched him. But they have not gotten far. The Fury will soon commend them to this holy place."

Booth moved to the next body, his head tilted upward, an expression of bliss on his mad face. "Delores Chase Weller. Like mother, like daughter. I regret that I rather made a mess out of her neck."

David did not recognize the next corpse.

"And this is Delores's would-be protector, Harlin Plummer. He is an interesting specimen, a David come to judgment. He was a former Jerusalem policeman who was dismissed from his job for drunkenness, which proved fortunate for me, for Plummer could have caused me a certain measure of trouble had he still been a policeman. Aided by nothing but his intuition and some old newspaper clippings, Plummer sat in a drunk ward in a veterans' hospital in New Orleans and deduced that I was the one who killed Katharine Simonette and her sodomite uncle Gregory. A rare mind, *n'est-ce pas*?

"You know Lysander Chase, of course," Booth said as he took the next corpse by its feet and turned it around on its hook so that it faced the others. "He cheated me out of killing him properly. His heart was weak, and it gave out before I could begin my work in earnest."

David's strength was quickly returning as Booth made his deranged introductions. He continued to lean on the pew, however, and pretended to still be exhausted, waiting to be whole again, wondering what he might try next now that his *Vampiri* powers had proven woefully inadequate to overwhelm the killer.

"Here's Eugene Jones. This specimen is rather well preserved, excepting where he is hooked through the base of the skull. Drugs killed this young man, I'm afraid. I think there's a lesson in that for all young people today.

"Ah, yes, here's someone you'll be interested to meet, Mr. Parker," Booth said, glancing at David over his shoulder with a leer. "May I present Dr. Joan Oppenheim? Dr. Oppenheim has been conducting a highly technical analysis of original music manuscripts. I am, of course, grateful to her for the role she played in helping get Wolfgang out of my hair for the rest of the night."

David stood up straight in spite of himself and stared. There was a gaping hole in the breast of the woman's blouse where someone possessing superhuman strength and speed had thrust a hand into her chest cavity and snatched out her beating heart.

Booth touched his bony forefinger to his forehead.

"Mozart is powerful, but I am the crafty one," he said, and began to laugh.

"But you said she went . . ."

"Nothing more than a story, a clever ploy," Booth confirmed. "I hired a local whore to check Joan out of her motel, drive her car north, and abandon it before dawn. By the time your compatriot Mozart figures out that he's been sent to Coventry, my work in Jerusalem will be done."

"You bastard. You murderous bastard."

"I'll take that as a compliment. It takes more will than a weakling like you has to do the Lord's work."

"You mean Satan's work," David said.

Booth looked up at David with what appeared to be genuine surprise. "Why, what Lord did you think I meant?" he asked in a deadpan voice, and then began to laugh again in an insane cackle.

David lunged at Booth. The blow that hit him knocked David backward at an angle, slamming him into a pew, splitting the wooden backrest. It felt as if he'd been struck in the chest with a sledge hammer. At first David couldn't breathe, and he thought his ribs had been crushed. But after a moment his breathing resumed in deep, ragged gasps.

"Don't force me to kill you too quickly, Parker. I want you to see me do some of my finest work. But first . . ."

Booth bent over. There were more bodies hidden from view by the front pews. Booth hoisted another corpse into the air.

"Gianni . . ."

As much as David despised Gianni Rourke, he hated to see what had happened to him.

"This one stinks a bit, like Lydia," Booth said, kicking away Rourke's bluish distended intestines and effortlessly lifting the fat man's huge bulk into the air, maneuvering it against one of the steel hooks. David looked away so that he would not have to see what came next, but he could not stop his ears from hearing the wet tearing sound and the noise of the ceiling beam creaking against its new load.

"Tonight will be like a family reunion for some of the beloved Founding Families." Booth bent over again. "It's been a while since we've seen Katharine Culpepper Simonette. Ashley Prew the undertaker did his best with the body, but as you can see, even the best embalming techniques do not completely forestall the onset of decay after so many weeks in the family mausoleum during the sweltering Mississippi summer."

David tasted bile when he saw how the corpse's skin had turned waxy and taken on a distinctly green tinge. The eyes had sunken markedly in their orbits, and the cheeks were drawn inward in the unmistakable rictus of death that not even Prew's highest art could prevent.

"You're completely mad," David said with absolute disgust.

Booth just laughed and returned to the front row of pews, bending.

"And the party would be incomplete without dear cousin Gregory."

"Oh, Christ!"

Gregory Culpepper's body was little more than a putrefying sack of rotten flesh and bone held together in a disintegrating funeral suit. Booth made several attempts to skewer the corpse on the meat hook next to the one holding Katharine Culpepper Simonette, but it was useless. Booth had to content himself with hanging only the head, two arms, and part of the torso contained in the moldering suit coat, the rest of the cadaver breaking loose and falling toward the floor in a heap that remained connected to its upper portion by various blackened and reeking sinews and entrails.

"Now," Booth said, turning toward the others after admiring his handiwork a moment longer, "it's time for our guest of honor to join the party. I do apologize, Mr. Parker, but I am referring to Miss Buchanan, not you."

"Never," David said, ignoring the piercing pain in his left side as he struggled to his feet.

"Neon commands it," Booth said sternly to David. He

looked past David to Victoria. "It is time to awaken to your nightmare, Victoria Buchanan. Eternal justice commands it."

"Don't let him," David cried, looking back to Nicoletta who, like Victoria, had stood quietly behind David until now.

"I . . ." she began. The exertion was plain in her face. She was fighting Booth for control of Victoria's conscious mind, but it did not look as if she were winning. "I don't think that I . . ."

Victoria began to scream.

"Come, harlot!" Booth commanded as if he were ordering a dog.

Victoria's right leg jerked forward, then her left. Her body looked out of synch with itself. Victoria was resisting him with all her strength, but Booth was too powerful. It was obvious to David that the killer had left Victoria in command of her own mind; Booth wanted her to experience every moment of her death, and to suffer greatly.

"I won't let you do it, Booth," David cried, but the words sounded hollow even to him. He grabbed pitifully at Victoria as her spastic movements carried her past him, but he had to let go when he realized that making her the object of a tug of war between two *Vampiri* would only tear her in pieces.

Victoria was sobbing with as much defiance as fear as she reached Booth and was forced to kneel before him.

"Now, where has that device gotten to?" Booth asked himself, absently fumbling in his pockets. "Ah, yes, here we are."

The killer held a chrome corkscrew in his hands—the kind with two handles that are drawn down as the metal screw penetrates the cork, drawing it out when they are forced back.

"No vulgar gold geegaws are required to serve Neon," Booth said in a lecturing voice. "His sacred objects are ordinary things. The enlightened recognize that there is death in every living thing, that all things animate and inanimate are ultimately dead."

Booth unfastened Victoria's blond hair and brushed it back.

"A little pleasure," he said, dropping down on one knee, "and then a little pain."

Booth pressed his mouth against Victoria's, his eyes closed, hers open and filled with terror.

David rushed forward and threw himself on Booth. Booth, however, managed to deflect the assault, flipping David up and over. David felt himself flying upside down and backward through the air, then he crashed into the neon Pegasus, tubes shattering in a burst of sparks.

"You would continue to defy an angel of the Lord?" Booth roared, taking David by the lapels, swinging him around and slamming him again into the sign. David felt the metal stab into his shoulders and back and sharper pricks from the splintered glass tubing. An even greater shower of electric sparks cascaded away from Pegasus, along with dangerous crackling. Booth released David and jumped back. David looked down and noticed the appalling way in which his arms and legs were jerking, his head rolling back and forth on his neck so violently he thought it might snap free from his neck. The sign had short-circuited, routing two hundred and twenty volts of electricity directly through his body. He smelled flesh, his flesh, burning and the acrid stink of singed hair.

The chapel went suddenly black.

David's body flew away from the sign as if he had been hit by a speeding car, his face bouncing against the floor with a sickening thud.

"And now, my most sacred bitch," Booth said, dragging Victoria to the side of the altar as the sign flickered off and on several times before coming weakly back to life at a fraction of its former brightness. "I had thought to save you until last, but I guess I cannot help myself."

David, get up!

Nicoletta was speaking to David telepathically. Her voice was desperate. But it was no good. David realized that his heart had stopped. The next thing he knew, he was floating up toward the ceiling, looking down on himself. He could see Nicoletta, her hands clasped together in front of her face as if in fervent prayer. Booth was holding Victoria down on the desecrated altar with one hand. The killer held the corkscrew in his other hand, and he moved it slowly back and forth over the length of her body as if unable to decide where to begin his torture.

He's going to kill her if you don't stop him.

Thump-thump.

David's heart began to beat again. He was not dead. Electrocution could not stop his immortal heart.

He focused his eyes with difficulty and realized he was looking at the carpeted floor. He was no longer hovering at the top of the room. He was back in his body. What was it Booth had said? Oh, yes, he remembered: "Men will seek death and will not find it; they will long to die, and death will fly from them."

Quickly, David! Quickly!

Nicoletta had turned her silver-headed cane around backwards and was offering it to him as an aid, handle first. He reached for the silver lion's head—and felt it come free in his hand. David looked at the thing in his hand with bewilderment. Then, slowly, it occurred to him that it was a short sword that had been hidden in the handle of the cane until he pulled it free.

Pushing himself up on one elbow, he looked across at his adversary. Booth had discarded the corkscrew. He cradled Victoria in his arms. Her head was thrown back. Her eyes wide open, her expression of horror bordering on madness. Booth was lowering himself slowly, deliciously, toward her neck, his teeth gleaming in the hellish red light.

Courage, my love, Nicoletta urged. *Have courage.*

David willed himself to his feet in a flash and propelled himself the distance to his adversary without touching his feet to the ground. The power was in him now, though whether it was drawn from some deep reservoir within himself or supplied by Nicoletta, David did not know. But the courage—the courage was David's.

David stabbed the short silver sword into Booth's back.

Booth stood up abruptly, releasing Victoria, who fell back against the altar.

The look of amazement on Booth's face turned to savage anger, and he began to snarl and turn toward his attacker.

David grasped the sword with both hands and jerked the blade upward, bisecting Booth's heart.

Booth's head fell back against his shoulders. His anguished scream shattered the stained glass in several windows.

David jerked the sword to the left.

Booth began to thrash his body frantically, spastically, arching his back, reaching around behind in a futile attempt to get at the sword.

David jerked the sword to the right, completing the sign of the cross in the vampire's heart, rending it in quarters.

Booth's entire body began to shake. He weakly lifted his yellow-gloved hands upward toward the damaged neon Pegasus, shaking like an old man with palsy.

"Nicoletta—" he said in a beseeching voice, praying at the end for help not to the neon idol but to the vampire who had given him the gift of blood in 1865.

David staggered backwards and let go of the sword, leaving

it in Booth's back. The killer's legs buckled. He fell to his knees, then to his back, forcing the blade's silver tip further out of his chest.

David stood looking down on Booth, his breath coming in exhausted gasps.

John Wilkes Booth was dead.

"David!" Victoria screamed, trying to sit up.

"Poor child," Nicoletta said, stepping quickly to Victoria and putting her hand on the woman's brow. Victoria's head dropped away from Nicoletta's touch as she collapsed unconscious back on to the altar.

"The shock of tonight has been too much for her," Nicoletta said, looking back toward David.

"It's better that . . ."

David's voice died as he realized that the brightening red glow in the room came not from the neon sign but from the flames flickering along its top. As he watched in stunned disbelief, the flames turned into long tongues of crimson that licked upward, touched the beamed ceiling, and began to crawl toward the center of the room.

"Come," Nicoletta shouted over the fire's building roar. "This room is a tinderbox."

"We've got to get everybody out of Arlington," David yelled, picking up Victoria and holding her in his arms, turning his face away from the heat.

"Quickly, my love, or we won't even save ourselves."

By the time they reached the door a few moments later, the Arlington Plantation chapel was almost completely engulfed in flames.

PART X

✧

After the Ball

I

Auf Wiedersehen

4 A.M. Saturday—The red glow crowning the tree line could have been the dawn, except for the sky, which had not yet started to lighten; and the smoke, which made an ominous smudge against the darkness; and the sparks, which rose into the air at irregular intervals like flocks of incandescent birds, chasing each other upward in widening loops until they vanished into the black void.

A police car blocked the lane to Arlington, which was crowded with pedestrians milling back and forth, some wearing robes and nightclothes.

"Mein Gott," Mozart said, getting out of the rental car and wading into the pandemonium.

From a distance, the outline of Arlington Plantation smoked and steamed beneath the streams of water from the firefighters' hoses. The circular drive in front of the mansion was crowded with fire engines, police cars, and ambulances. More emergency vehicles were pulled up on the lawn on the sides and back.

A horn sounded behind Mozart, startling him. He moved to the side of the road to let a pumper truck carrying a fresh supply of water pass. As he got nearer, Mozart saw the bizarre collection of furniture scattered across the lawn in complete disarray—tables, chairs, oil paintings of Victoria Buchanan's ancestors, antique lamps, a tall stack of old books piled precariously high on the wet grass.

And what of the guests at the party? There was no sign of them—they had fled or been carried away in ambulances or hearses.

Mozart was immune to cold, but the sight made him shiver.

It was always chilly in August before dawn, and the dew was so heavy that it had quickly soaked through Mozart's shoes.

A knot of firefighters swarmed around the front door, then turned and made their way down the steps in a group. They were carrying one of their fellow firefighters. They put him on the ground on his back. A fireman in a white slicker, either a medic or an officer, clamped an oxygen mask over the man's face. The stricken man didn't move at first, but suddenly he slapped the ground with his arms and sat up, vomiting as he leaned forward and tried to hack out of his lungs the smoke he'd inhaled.

This was how it always ended with the princess, Mozart thought.

Princess Nicoletta Vittorini di Medusa did not come out of hiding often, but when she did, she left only destruction and death in her wake. She professed to be a patron of art and artists of every variety, but destroying beauty and talent was what really interested her. Mozart was keenly aware that Princess Nicoletta had only given him the gift of the blood so that she could pervert his genius and destroy him. Fortunately, he had escaped her, with the *Illuminati*'s help. John Wilkes Booth had not been so fortunate—although perhaps he got what he deserved, Mozart thought. But David . . .

The vampire sighed deeply.

David had so much raw talent. That was no doubt what had attracted Nicoletta to him—that, and the fact that Mozart loved the young composer almost like a son. She would delight in turning him into a monster and seeing him squander his God-given talent—if she hadn't quickly killed him to be done with it.

Mozart scanned the crowd, reaching out to see with more than just his eyes. There was no evidence of David amid the chaos, yet he doubted Nicoletta had killed him. That would be merciful, compared to the living damnation she would deliver to him. And mercy was not her métier.

"Look out!"

The fireman who had shouted was running backward, pointing at the mansion. As a dozen firefighters swelled the warning chorus, Arlington's "new" half began to lean as if the walls and floors were held together by hinges.

The night became curiously still as the onlookers stared, fascinated as well as horrified by the destruction of Jerusalem's most important landmark.

A timber snapped. The roar of splintering lumber erupted all at once, accompanied by the shrieking sound of nails being ripped from boards where they'd been lodged for years. The wing collapsed on itself, sending up in its place a choking cloud of smoke, ash, and sparks that billowed outward and upward, sending the more timid and weak-lunged onlookers running.

A sheet of flame shot out of the roof toward the back of the central structure, the fire there getting a supply of fresh oxygen now that the wing had collapsed. Two teams of firefighters turned their hoses on the new blaze, drowning it instantly.

It was impossible to tell how much damage had been done to the original part of the house from where Mozart stood. The rear part of the roof was burned away, exposing the eaves, which were charred black. Smoke had left black stains along the exterior walls where it had poured from broken windows on the second story.

Later that day or maybe the next, firefighters would begin to probe through the ashes and find bones. Mozart would have wagered Booth was among the dead, for otherwise the destruction would have been more complete. Maybe David's bones would be found, too, though Mozart tended to doubt it. But Nicoletta would not be among the dead—Mozart was certain of that. She was far too clever to allow herself to get caught in the conflagration. Mozart was sure she was off somewhere, laughing at them all. The *Illuminati* had never been able to stop her. Mozart doubted they ever would.

Mozart was turning to leave when a figure wrapped in a blanket sitting on the chrome running board of a fire truck caught his attention.

"Victoria?"

She seemed not to recognize Mozart at first when she looked up at him. Her face was streaked with soot, and her hair and clothing were drenched from carrying furnishings out of the mansion until Rick Hoskins, the fire chief, threatened to have her arrested if she didn't stay clear.

"Victoria?" Mozart said again.

Victoria Buchanan was in a mild state of shock, but she shook it off after a few more seconds and smiled weakly.

"You're still alive," she said.

"I was about to say the same thing to you." Mozart sat beside her on the running board.

"When I didn't see you again after we got Zaharim out of the way, I thought Booth must have killed you."

"David did not tell you I was called away?"

The name touched a wound. She shook her head.

"I am embarrassed to admit what happened. Booth contrived to send me on a wild-goose chase so that I would not be here to help the rest of you. He convinced me something extremely bad would befall the organization David and I serve if I failed to catch up with a certain young woman who was fleeing town."

Victoria stared at Mozart for a moment, as if too dazed to easily assimilate the new information. "Did you find her?" she asked finally, obliquely connecting his comment with the body of Dr. Joan Oppenheim in the chapel.

There was no point in explaining to Victoria how he'd verified that Dr. Joan Oppenheim had checked out of her motel and was seen driving north out of town in her Volvo. He'd caught up with the car, and the woman Booth had paid to impersonate Oppenheim, three hours later.

"No, *Fräulein*, I did not. I know now that she never left Jerusalem. I think it is likely Booth murdered her, although I have no proof at present."

Victoria nodded as if Mozart were making a commonplace observation, but her bottom lip quivered. She began to cry.

"You have been through much tonight, *Fräulein*." Mozart put his hand gently on her shoulder.

Mozart reached out again into the night, directing all his psychic power to detecting some faint sign of David Parker. There was nothing. David's life essence had departed from Arlington Plantation, one way or the other.

"I do not intend to cause you undue distress, *Fräulein*, but there is something I must ask. My friend David Parker—he does not seem to be anywhere about."

Victoria's eyes began to shimmer again.

"Tell me: did Booth manage to . . . ?"

Victoria shook her head.

"No. It was the other way around," she said. It was difficult for her to string more than a few words together at once. "It happened upstairs in the chapel. They fought. David stabbed him. There was a cane with a sword hidden in the handle; that's what he used."

"And the fire? Do you know how it started?"

"There was an old neon sign in the chapel. Booth had it hanging over the altar. Booth threw David into it when they were fighting. Sparks came out of the top of the sign, then flames. David killed him—Booth—and carried me out. The chapel was in flames. We barely escaped. Everyone panicked when they learned there was a fire. Some were trampled trying to get out, but I don't think anyone was seriously injured."

Mozart used his silk handkerchief to wipe away her tears, which also served to clean some of the soot from her pale cheeks.

"Booth is dead, isn't he?" Victoria asked, suddenly filled with doubt and dread.

"What did you see?"

She blinked and looked past Mozart. "I saw the blade go all the way through him. It pierced his heart." Victoria paused and swallowed dryly. The recollection made her shudder, even though it had been Booth. "He was still lying there amid the flames, with the blade still in him, when we escaped. It was an inferno, and Booth was in the middle of it. I watched as he disappeared in the flames. I remember that he was on fire—his body was on fire."

"Booth is dead."

"Except," Victoria interjected. Her voice dropped to a whisper. "Except that he was a *vampire*. Do you think that he is *really* dead? Could he be killed that easily? Can you be certain of it?"

Mozart looked around to ensure himself they were out of earshot of a policeman who loitered nearby, staring at Arlington with a stricken look on his face.

"A severe-enough trauma will kill even a vampire. And, of course, fire will consume anything."

Mozart fixed Victoria with a penetrating stare that made her feel like he was looking straight into her mind.

"My only question is whether you are absolutely certain that what you just told me is what you saw with your eyes. The *Vampiri* are very clever. They can make you 'remember' things that never happened."

"I would swear to it. I saw and heard everything." Victoria held her hand over her mouth as if afraid she were about the retch. "Bodies hanging from meat hooks. He must have gone out to the graveyard and dug up Katharine and . . ."

That was as far as Victoria could go. She buried her face in her hands for a full minute. Mozart finally sent her an autohypnotic suggestion that helped her regain her composure.

"But most of the people got out all right. Thank God for that. And thank God for David. If it hadn't been for him,

Booth would have killed us all. I have no doubt about that whatsoever."

Mozart permitted himself a small smile. So, it seemed that David had not been completely unsuccessful at his assignment after all.

"But what of David?" Mozart asked gently.

"Alive when I last saw him, but he is in the worst kind of danger."

"Ja?"

"He was with Captain Vittorini. Only she's not Captain Vittorini. She was only pretending to be in the Salvation Army. And for the Vampire Convention, she pretended she was Lucretia Noire. It's all very confusing, I'm afraid. I think that she murdered the real Lucretia and stole the author's identity so that she could help Booth plan his elaborate revenge. Her real name is . . ."

"What's wrong, *Fräulein*?"

"That's strange. The name is on the tip of my tongue, but I can't seem to recall it."

"Do not unduly strain yourself, *Fräulein*. You do not remember the vampire's name because she does not want you to remember. She has made you forget."

"Do you know her name?"

"Yes, *Fräulein*, but do not ask me to reveal it. It is far better that you do not know. It would make you a threat to her, and she would have to kill you if she found out."

"She nearly did kill me, but thank God David showed up."

"Victoria?" A uniformed policeman had come to stand in front of them. "They're ready to take you to the station."

"Just a minute, please," she told the policeman. He nodded and walked a discreet distance away.

"She's a monster."

"Ja."

"But it's strange: I didn't get the sense that she intended to harm David, although I don't know what else she could have in mind."

"There is more than one way to inflict hurt, *Fräulein*. Perhaps she does not mean to pose an immediate threat to his life."

Victoria considered that for a moment. "It was all very peculiar. She was Booth's ally, but she betrayed him. Booth begged her for help. She could have stopped David, but she didn't do a thing."

Victoria looked closely at Mozart and abruptly changed gears. "There's something I've been wondering about. I always thought that vampires could not come out in the sun."

"That is the generally accepted idea."

"But I saw Captain Vittorini, or whatever her name is, in broad daylight. I know she is a vampire—I know it only too well. And yet I saw her walk out into the sun just as you or I might."

At first Mozart did not answer, but it became apparent after an increasingly uncomfortable silence that Victoria would not be satisfied unless he supplied some sort of response.

"The laws of my order forbid me to discuss such things, *Fräulein*, but I will not lie to you. Perhaps there are some vampires who are strong enough to withstand the sun's ultraviolet radiation. I am speaking hypothetically, of course."

The look of triumph that crossed Victoria's face was not completely surprising to Mozart.

"Then perhaps there are other vampires besides Booth and his female counterpart in Jerusalem—other vampires who walk around during the day, completely indistinguishable from ordinary human beings. After all, how would one know?"

"How, indeed," Mozart replied dryly.

"You may laugh, Mr. Toland, but it has occurred to me that you and David could be vampires, too."

"How very amusing, *Fräulein*," Mozart said with a thin smile.

"Not like Booth and *her*, of course, but a different sort of vampire—benevolent vampires."

"Victoria?" The policeman pointed to his wristwatch.

"I'm coming," she said.

"What are you going to tell them?" Mozart inquired, the slightest hint of urgency in his low voice.

"That's what I was thinking about when you showed up. I don't think that I can tell them much of anything. They'd never believe it."

"No, they wouldn't. But the bodies."

"There won't be much left of them after the fire. The police will think they died in the flames. And even if they don't, what can they prove? Booth and Nightingale are dead, and the vampiress has fled, taking David with her. I don't imagine she will go anyplace the police are likely to be able to find her and David for questioning."

"I think you have made a proper assessment of the situation."

Mozart helped Victoria to her feet.

"And what of Marcus Cuttler and Dr. Chesterfield?"

"Doc is in intensive care at the hospital. He's not expected to last the night. Marcus is with him. He was mistakenly drugged, but he's fine now."

"I regret that our brief friendship was marred by so much unpleasantness, *Fräulein* Buchanan."

"Then we won't be seeing one another again?" Victoria asked, feeling regretful without knowing exactly why.

"I pray, *Fräulein*, that you never again have occasion to consort with vampires and the individuals charged with hunting them when they become criminals. Might I offer a bit of advice?"

"Please do."

"Forget what happened, and forget David. It will be for the best."

"I am a Southerner, sir. We never forget."

"Then remember everything—but pursue nothing."

"I shall leave the pursuing to you," she said with a crooked smile.

Mozart took Victoria's hand and kissed it.

A light mist was beginning to appear, hanging close to the ground in the wooded areas beyond Arlington's lawn. By the time the sun came up, the fire-ravaged estate would be shrouded in dense fog, as if Nature itself were ashamed of what had occurred at Arlington Plantation. One way or the other, everything would be concealed, for that is how it must be in the *Vampiri* world.

"Just tell me the truth about one thing, Mr. Toland, if that's your name. Is David a vampire?" She locked her eyes onto Mozart's. "Are you?"

Mozart broke into a broad smile.

"Auf Wiedersehen, Fräulein."

The Austrian turned and walked into the crowd, vanishing immediately. A few moments later, Victoria was almost ready to wonder if he'd ever really been there.

II

Deliverance

10 P.M. Tuesday—It was the kind of sweltering summer night that comes late in August, when the sun goes down but the heat continues to hang on, making tempers short and sleep impossible without air conditioning. There was no hint of breeze; the air was as still as it is before a thunderstorm, except that there were no clouds in the starry sky. Only the insects seemed to relish the heat, squatting beneath rocks and in damp crannies, buzzing and humming, singing to one another in the darkness.

Arlington Plantation was dark except for a single kerosene lantern burning in the front parlor. Three nights after fire destroyed the rear wing, the electrical service to the entire estate remained turned off at the transformer on the highway.

Behind the plantation great house, the charred skeleton of the ruined wing loomed ominously in the darkness. Windows broken by firefighters or shattered in the heat of the fire were shuttered or boarded with plywood. Inside, the smoke smell was nearly as strong as it had been immediately after the fire. Ceilings were discolored with soot, especially over the doorways, where the smoke left black fan-shaped stains. The heat and steam had weakened the glue in the wallpaper, making it droop in long, dogeared peels.

The first-floor rooms were crowded with a chaotic array of furniture. Pieces that had been carried outside in a rush when it had seemed likely that the blaze would swallow the entire structure were scattered pell-mell throughout the downstairs parlors. Many of the antiques had escaped damage, but some of the best pieces were deeply gouged, broken, or water damaged. A few tables and chairs from the second-floor hall were charred where flames had touched them.

General Noah Buchanan's portrait leaned unceremoniously against the newel post at the base of the staircase. A long L-shaped tear disfigured the upper left corner of the canvas, leaving it hanging slack in its gilded frame. Some of the oil paint, deeply age-checked before the fire, had been lost when the painting was inadvertently sprayed with a pressurized firehose. The picture was possibly beyond restoration.

The silhouette of a woman appeared at the front door, a black outline against the golden lamplight.

Victoria Buchanan opened the screen and came out onto the veranda, her chin upturned, searching vainly for some movement in the night air. She wore a sleeveless cotton T-shirt, cutoff blue jeans, and sandals. Her face and arms glistened with a light sheen of perspiration that made the T-shirt cling to her.

She went to the railing and leaned against it. She'd expected to see a visitor's car approaching, but there was none. That struck her as peculiar, since the feeling that she was no longer alone was so strong that it was more of a certainty than an intuition.

Victoria glanced back over her shoulder.

The shadows in the house were nearly impenetrable, the lantern doing little more than dimly illuminating the highlights of nearby objects.

There were too many valuables in the mansion to leave it unoccupied, and Victoria wouldn't be able to install a caretaker until the power was turned back on. She wasn't afraid to sleep alone at Arlington, but there were times when the ruined plantation played tricks on her mind. She would have stayed in the caretaker's cottage, but it had been destroyed, burned to its foundations after a flaming spark from the great house ignited its wood-shingled roof the night of the big fire.

She watched the fireflies flicker across the lawn and listened to the back-and-forth sound of cicadas singing to one another.

An owl screeched.

The cicadas fell silent.

The silence grew broad and deep; it seemed to crouch in the night, alive and waiting.

Victoria's eyes searched the darkness. The sensation that she was not alone crept back into her.

"Do you believe in ghosts?"

Victoria started at the voice, but she did not turn to face her visitor.

"Yes," she said. "I always have."

She continued looking across the lawn as long as she could, then turned to face David. He looked different. The hardness in his smile bordered on bitterness. He was dressed in black, and he had several day's growth of beard that made him look ruggedly handsome, but a little like an outlaw.

"There are ghosts everywhere," Victoria added, and nodded toward the house. "I have lived with them all of my life. I'm glad to see that you, at least, haven't become a ghost."

"But I have," David said, his smile disappearing.

Victoria reached out and touched him lightly as if to reassure herself that he still possessed corporeal substance. His chest was firm and warm to her fingertips.

"No," she said gently. "Not yet."

"I knew I would find you here. Are you staying at Arlington alone?"

Victoria nodded. "Michelle is with friends. I'm keeping the thieves and vandals away. Why are you smiling?"

"I'm surprised that you will still have anything to do with this place. If I were you, I'd never want to see Arlington again."

"I can't walk away from something just because it's caused me pain," she said, and gave David a significant look. "Not ever."

"What's going to become of this place now? I suppose the lawyers will have a heyday haggling over who owns it. I don't imagine 'Becker Thorne' had any relatives to leave it to."

"Actually, it's amazingly cut-and-dried. A will was found. Part of a will, anyway, but enough to stand up in court. He left Arlington to me, along with more than enough money to restore and maintain it. The property will go to the state of Mississippi after I'm gone, with an endowment to keep it open as a historic site."

David looked at Victoria as if she were putting him on.

"You find it difficult to believe that Booth would sign legal documents leaving property to a person he planned to murder?"

"Not to put too fine a point on it, yes."

"You're absolutely right. The papers deeding Arlington to me are forgeries, but they're very good forgeries. If I were a betting woman, I'd wager that they'd withstand any kind of challenge that might turn up."

"I never thought you, of all people, were capable of fraud."

"We do what we have to do. I think of it as serving the

greater good. In the wrong hands, this house would be bulldozed within the week. I've already been contacted by a group of people who think the grounds would make a lovely golf course. I'm doing what I'm doing to save what's left of Arlington."

"It's still fraud."

"I'm sure that everything Booth had was gotten by fraud. If Arlington was part of his ill-gotten gains, then it's as much mine now as anybody's—and probably more so. I am, after all, a Buchanan, for what little that means these days."

"Even when you know that everything this plantation stands for is corrupt?"

"Yes," Victoria said, ignoring the cruelty in his voice. "Arlington represents more than corruption and treachery. There is some good in the worst of us, David. And if I don't save Arlington for what was good in the Buchanan family and the Old South, then I will save it for the architecture and craftsmanship. If that is all it means, it will still be worth saving. The past is the only thing we really own, David. The future may never come."

"You're an amazing woman." His smile was genuine. This was the old David—the David Victoria loved.

"I thought you might have had something to do with my reversal in fortune. The organization you and Mr. Toland belong to is no doubt responsible. There's no other possible explanation. I certainly didn't forge the documents or Thorne's signature. I don't even know anybody capable of such work."

"I'm afraid I don't know a thing about it."

"You haven't spoken with your friend?"

"Not since the night of the fire."

Victoria didn't have to think about it to know the source of the problem. She looked at him boldly. There was no getting around the issue.

"Not since the night you went off with *her*."

David's eyes narrowed.

"I'm not avoiding using her name to be rude. The truth is that I don't remember it. She made me forget."

"I know."

"She's evil, David."

"No."

"She forced me to watch while she killed a man."

"You have no way of knowing what you really saw that night," David said hotly. "An *Illuminati* master could have easily put that into your mind. They're capable of such things, when it suits their purposes."

"I refuse to believe that Mr. Toland—if that's his real name—would play tricks with my mind. I know what I saw. I watched her commit cold-blooded murder."

David seemed to suddenly lose interest. He shrugged as if to indicate that whether Princess Nicoletta Vittorini di Medusa had killed Kurt Teameyer was of no real importance.

"She may have killed the man. I don't know. It doesn't matter."

"How can it not matter?"

David looked away.

"I asked you, David, How can it not matter? Does she have you so bewitched that you would dismiss the fact that she's a murderess?"

A dangerous light flashed in David's eyes. "You cannot judge her."

"I can't believe you're saying this."

"Do you feel remorse when you step on a bug? When you pull a weed out of the garden?"

"We're not talking about insects or plants. Besides, it's not necessary for her to kill, is it, David? Mr. Toland said that the amount of blood a vampire requires is far less than what it would take to kill a person. Especially for a vampire as ancient as she is."

Victoria interpreted David's silence as confirmation of his vampire lover's crimes.

"She kills because she likes to kill," Victoria said finally, driving home the point.

"That's not true," David almost shouted.

"She delights in it."

"Stop!"

"It's not her I care about, David. It's you. I'm afraid you've made a terrible mistake. Your real friends are here, and in the *Illuminati*."

"You don't know what you're talking about. You wouldn't defend them if you knew the things they demanded of me. In New York City . . ."

David broke off, momentarily overwhelmed with depression and failure over how he had stood by impotently while Booth terrorized New York City as the "Dracula" serial killer.

"They've kept secrets from me," David resumed more quietly. "In three short nights, I've learned more than the *Illumi-*

nati shared with me in my two years with them. I've learned . . ." His voice trailed off as he searched for the right words, "The most incredible things."

David looked harshly at Victoria, transferring his hostility to her. "So do not presume to tell me who my friends are. I know."

"You're heading in a bad direction," Victoria said gently.

"I came here tonight to give you a similar warning."

The menace that had crept into David's voice was startling.

"You know far more than you should, Victoria. Knowledge is dangerous. There are those who feel threatened by what you know. I'm surprised that my former associate left you in full possession of your memories."

David lowered his head and looked at Victoria through his eyelashes.

"No!" she cried, bringing her hands to her temples. "Get out of my mind!"

"I'm sorry, Victoria. It must be done."

"No," she pleaded. "Please."

"Your mind is strong, but it is useless to fight me. You only risk hurting yourself by resisting me."

As if to confirm his words, Victoria's knees buckled. She fell forward, and David caught her in his arms.

"I know what you are, David," Victoria said, looking up into his eyes. "I think I've known all along. But it doesn't matter. Nothing matters, except the fact that I love you."

"There is no chance that we could be happy together," David said hoarsely.

"Because of what you are."

"Because of what I am, and because of the things I must do to live."

"But you don't have to hurt people. I know in my soul that you don't have to kill."

"It's more complicated than that. Certainly you know that I will never age. I would have been happy to grow old with you, Victoria, but that is impossible for me now. Even if we could make our love last a few years, you would continue to grow older, and you would begin to hate yourself—and me—for it. Time would become a slow-acting poison for you."

"What do you think it is now?" she asked weakly.

"You understand that I could never make you one of us. You might think of the *Vampiri* as magical beings, but this life is a horror. We are tortured souls. We are the damned."

"I would never ask for that." Victoria looked into David's eyes and decided to risk everything. "I'm not asking for eternity, David. I'm only asking for tonight," she said, offering herself to the vampire.

David lowered his face but stopped just short of their lips touching. There was a feverish look in his eyes, a yearning that was more than passion. Victoria had never seen it before, yet she knew instinctively what it was: the Hunger.

"We could give each other what we need," she whispered. "I want to give you—everything."

David swept Victoria up into his arms, kissing her passionately.

Victoria knew that what she was about to do was supposed to be a sin—yet she knew that at the same time it wasn't. Love was its own ethic. Even if it lasted only one night, even if it was unhallowed and unconsecrated, love could be only good. And maybe, she thought, the love she would give him in the hours between then and the dawn would empower David with the strength required to resist the counterfeit love the vampiress had used to enslave him.

David carried Victoria into the house and to the staircase. His feet seemed to glide up the stairs. When Victoria looked down, she saw that he was not walking but floating.

The door to the bedroom nearest the stairs opened seemingly of its own accord. The window went up, the shutters flew back, and a cool breeze blew into the room, billowing through the curtains. This was no natural breeze, but one that David had commanded to comfort them, a soothing zephyr perfumed with magnolia.

The kerosene lamps on either side of the bed ignited. The soot-covered comforter slid off the bed and onto the floor. As Victoria watched, almost unable to believe her eyes, the room began to rejuvenate itself: the soot stains disappeared; the wallpaper reattached itself to the plaster; the burned smell disappeared.

The cicadas and owls were singing to Victoria. This was miraculous, too. She had never noticed that there was both a melody and a harmony to nature's song, but David had provided her with the power to hear it—either that, or he was using the force of his own preternatural mind to command nature's performance.

David put Victoria gently down on the bed and kissed her forehead.

Victoria pulled off her T-shirt. She kicked off her shoes and impatiently shed the rest of her clothes, hungrily pulling David down on top of herself, urging him to make love to her with the animal passion she sensed within his soul. But David forced her to go slowly. He gradually built her pleasure to the point of climax, then backed it down, only to rebuild it again and again until at last she knew it would be impossible for her to hold herself back a moment longer.

"Now, David!" she gasped, locking her legs around his back and turning her head to the side. "Do it now!"

Victoria wanted him to have her completely—her love, her body, her blood.

The predatory look that flashed in David's eyes was frightening, but she did not shrink from him. She saw but a glimpse of teeth as he lowered his face to her neck.

There was a brief moment of pain—more pinprick than stab—as David sank his razor-pointed blood teeth into her jugular.

Victoria exploded with a bliss so powerful that she screamed as it consumed her. It was as if a powerful electric current were pulsing through her body, but one that inflicted not pain but a pleasure unlike any she'd ever known.

Victoria felt herself floating away on wave after wave of warm, shuddering ecstasy, until the physical joy exhausted her so entirely that the light inside her tightly closed eyes faded from crimson to blue to purple and finally to black.

It was nearly nine in the morning when Victoria awoke.

She slid her feet out of bed. Her legs were shaky when she stood, and she wasn't sure about her balance. She carefully bent to pick up a sheet, gathering it around her like a towel, tucking a fold between her breasts to secure it.

This morning she felt—different.

Victoria wasn't usually aware of her body, but now she was strangely conscious of its every sensation. She lifted her hand in front of her face and turned it, enjoying the curious pleasure of observing herself in motion. She took a few tentative steps. Her skin tingled as the sheet moved against it. She felt a pleasant soreness that reminded her of an urge that she'd worked very hard to learn to ignore.

Victoria stood in front of the looking glass.

Her hair was her best feature, she thought, but maybe it was time to cut it short. She was tired of wearing it in a bun, and it only got in the way when she let it hang loose. She admitted to herself that she had a nice face, although she'd always thought she had a rather narrow head. She knew men said she was beautiful. Maybe she was.

It was time for some changes, Victoria thought, smiling at herself in the mirror. If something as damaged as Arlington Plantation could be brought back into the land of the living, there was hope for her, too.

Victoria heard voices in the yard below.

She went to the open window and looked down at the crew from the power company. One of the workers noticed Victoria. He elbowed his buddy, who looked up at her and whistled.

Victoria smiled, then turned and went to shower.

It was the start of a new day.

Postlude:
A True Patriot

Chronicle Notes: John Wilkes Booth searched in vain for his unpublished manuscript, *A True Patriot*, at Arlington Plantation and among the Founding Families' former homes in Jerusalem's dilapidated Gold Coast neighborhood. The manuscript was recovered from the wreckage of Arlington's "new" wing after the fire. The document was severely damaged. Only a few pages can be read.

—Editor

O war! thou son of hell!

This fight so gloriously joined now enters a new and desperate phase.

Four years we have fought to make a second Revolution, to free the Southern states from Federal tyranny. This pen need hardly recount our brilliant early victories. And yet our glories are now washed away in the blood of our fallen brothers. The winter wind blows through our hearts, bringing more chill news of defeat. Petersburg has fallen. The Government meets tonight to decide whether Richmond can be held. If not, the President and his Cabinet must withdraw toward . . .[1]

. . . disaster and defeat. We now know what Carthage felt when the last of its battered legions withdrew inside the city's ramparts for the final desperate battle. I do not think our brave soldiers can long hold back the immigrant legions the butcher Grant throws against our lines, each day dawning to reveal new . . .[2]

[1]Break in narrative. Manuscript damaged.
[2]Break in narrative. Manuscript damaged.

. . . gore and horror that surpasses anything that can be described in words. I know, for I have witnessed these great bloodlettings. One cannot experience such levels of carnage without becoming forever inured to the sight of men dying with their bowels cradled in their hands; of dismembered limbs stacked outside field hospitals like great cords of firewood; of the awful, futile screams of the injured in the no-man's land between the lines, crying out in the night for Death to take them and relieve them of their misery.[3]

. . . But the Confederacy will never surrender to the tyrant Lincoln—not so long as a single Southern man survives with the strength to raise a pistol. Let no man speak of dishonorable peace. Let the fire of this conflict rage unabated forever.

Your breath first kindled the dead coal of wards . . .
And brought in matter that should feed this fire;
And now 'tis far too huge to be blown out
With that same weak wind which enkindled it.[4]

. . . We draw our sustaining strength not just from Almighty God and the blessed land that has raised us up, but from the brave and honorable friends who fight beside us, and the women who love us, for without these most precious of boons, a man would not be a man at all but the lowest form of brute. It is above all else friendship and love that make defeats and heartaches . . .[5]

[3]Break in narrative. Manuscript damaged.
[4]Break in narrative. Manuscript damaged.
[5]Break in narrative. Nothing further is readable.